RICHARD LAYMON

DARKNESS, TELL US

LEISURE BOOKS NEW YORK CITY

A LEISURE BOOK®

March 2003

Published by

Dorchester Publishing Co., Inc.
276 Fifth Avenue
New York, NY 10001

ISBN 0-8439-5047-1

Visit us on the web at www.dorchesterpub.com.

To our great friends Chris & Dick Boyanski,
adventurers in mixology and the supernatural

To Kara and Kyle

And, of course, to Timmy
wherever you are
whatever you are

But 'tis strange:
And oftentimes, to win us to our harm,
The instruments of darkness tell us truths,
Win us with honest trifles, to betray 's
In deepest consequence.

—*Macbeth*, Act I, scene iii

Chapter One

"I don't think that's such a good idea," Dr. Dalton said.

"Oh, come on. It'll be kicks." Lana, standing on tiptoes, continued to pull the flat box of the Ouija off the bookshelf. The games stacked on top of it teetered. Monopoly and Careers, high above her, started sliding.

"Look out!" Keith warned.

She flung up a hand and blocked the boxes. But a leather dice cup, out of sight until now, slid down the tilted ramp of the Monopoly box and fell. It bounced off her forehead. She flinched, muttered, "Shit!" and plucked out the Ouija. The rest of the games dropped, jolting the shelf.

Howard grinned. Served Lana right for going against the professor's wishes. Some of the other students were laughing.

Dr. Dalton neither grinned nor laughed, but Howard saw a glimmer of amusement in her eyes. "I *told* you it wasn't a good idea."

"I didn't know you had booby-traps," Lana said.

"Every so often I get lucky and trap a booby."

1

"Funny," Lana muttered. Bending down with the Ouija box under one arm, she picked up the dice cup and set it on a shelf. She turned around and met the professor's eyes. "You don't really mind if we give this thing a try, do you? I've never seen a Ouija board in action."

"You're better off that way."

Keith went, "Oooooo, ominous."

Lana gave him a quick look as if she didn't appreciate his interference. To Dr. Dalton, with a smile and a shrug of her shoulders, she said, "It's just a game, Corie."

"So is Russian Roulette."

"Woooo," said Keith.

What a scrote, Howard thought. But he kept the opinion to himself. He was no dummy. Keith, who looked and acted like a jock in spite of being an English major, could probably demolish him with a single blow.

From a padded chair in a corner of the den, Doris said, "The analogy seems somewhat inflated, if you ask me."

"Nobody asked," Keith pointed out.

Lana, on tiptoes, studied the stack of games. "Have you got a revolver up there, Corie?"

"Of course not."

"Then why a Ouija board, if it's just as dangerous?"

"It's sort of a keepsake. Obviously, I *should've* gotten rid of it."

"What's the big deal?" Keith asked.

"One must beware of tampering with the unknown," Doris said, her voice full of menace. She widened her eyes at Keith, though he wasn't even looking in her direction. Then she swung her thick legs off the foot rest, bounded up and pranced toward the group.

Here she comes, Howard thought. Our fat Puck. Our spritely, pedantic gnome.

She raised a warning finger. "There are forces lurking in the shadowy corners of the universe that . . ."

"Stuff it," Keith suggested.

"That's enough," Dr. Dalton told him. She said to Lana, "Hey, we're here to have a good time. If your heart's set on

2

fooling around with that thing, be my guest. But just keep me out of it. A deal?"

"Sure! Great! OK, who's going to do it with me?"

"I'll do it with you any chance I get," Keith said.

He probably *does*, Howard thought.

Ignoring the remark, Lana asked Dr. Dalton, "How many can play at a time?"

"Up to four, I guess. More than that, it would get awfully crowded around the board."

"OK. We need two more hearty volunteers."

"Include me in," Doris said.

Keith looked as if he would rather "include in" a wad of used toilet paper, but he made no protest.

"That's three," Lana said. "One more. Any takers?"

Howard looked around. Professor Dalton was shaking her head. He saw Glen over in a corner, stuffing potato chips into his mouth. Angela was sitting at the far end of the sofa, hands folded on her lap, gazing into space.

I probably ought to go over and sit with her, he thought. He hadn't really spent much time with Angela tonight. She might think he was trying to ignore her.

But God, she was so weird. As if she were from a different planet or something, and longed for home.

Keith slapped Howard on the shoulder. Harder than necessary. "Join the fun, Howitzer. You can play kneesies with Doris."

He looked at Lana. "Is it OK with you?"

"Sure. Why wouldn't it be?"

He shrugged, feeling a little dumb for asking Lana's permission.

"So, Corie, how do we play?"

Before she could answer, Doris said, "I've done it before."

"Where'd you find a blind guy?" Keith asked.

"Oh, that's rich, Mr. Harris. It's wonderful that you've achieved the capability of amusing yourself with quips of such startling inanity."

"Oink," he said.

Lana swung her arm out. The back of her fist whapped

3

Keith's chest. It struck his left pectoral, a solid mound under his clinging shirt, with a sound like a mallet smacking raw beef. "Knock it off," she said.

Dr. Dalton raised her eyebrows. Her lips, pressed together tightly, were turned down at the corners. Howard had seen that expression before. She was delighted that Lana had given Keith a thump. Delighted, but determined to keep her grin in check.

"I have a card table in the kitchen," she said. "Why don't we bring it out here so the rest of us can keep an eye on you."

They went into the small, tidy kitchen. Dr. Dalton scooted chairs away from the table. She folded one of them. As she handed it to Howard, she gave him the special look. A look she never gave anyone but him. He returned his version of it. Not a wink, but it seemed to hold the meaning of a wink: they were secretly sharing a wry amusement at the antics of the others. *What are a couple of folks like us doing in the midst of all this?*

He felt himself blush. He supposed he always blushed when she looked at him that way.

She handed chairs to Doris and Lana, then squatted down and tugged at a metal cuff to release one of the table's folding legs.

Howard saw the way her white shorts were drawn taut against the smooth curves of her rump. Her blouse was stretched across her back. Through its fabric, he could see the pink hue of her skin and the bands of her bra.

His throat tightened. His heart pounded faster and he felt a tight pressure in his groin.

Turning away, he carried his chair toward the den.

He'd taken this special summer session class for only one reason: to be in Dr. Dalton's presence. He'd taken so many of her classes during his three years at Belmore University. But they were never enough. Ever since she'd stepped to the lectern on his first morning of freshman English, he'd been captivated by her. She was just so beautiful, so smart and funny, so caring.

4

She liked him a lot, too. He knew that.

But he also knew that she didn't think of him as a possible lover. Never would. A, he'd been born nine years too late. Not an overwhelming age difference, but still a barrier. B, he was only a rung or two up the ladder from being a nerd. C, Dr. Dalton was a loner who didn't seem interested in any men, much less wimpy twenty-one-year-olds.

Just be glad she's your friend, he told himself.

But an awful feeling of loss swept through him as he set the chair down in the den. Dr. Dalton's party tonight marked the end of the summer session. Howard would be packing tomorrow, flying home the day after. He wouldn't be seeing her again until the fall semester, nearly two months away.

As the others came in with chairs and the table, he found himself regretting that he'd agreed to join in. Dr. Dalton had no intention of messing with the Ouija. If he'd refused, he could be spending the time with her.

Keith held the table steady on its edge while Dr. Dalton snapped its legs into place. He flipped it upright, and she directed him to position it near the center of the living room.

Keith sat across from Lana, Howard across from Doris.

Lana was shaking open the box when Glen came over, a heap of potato chips cupped in his hand. The floor stopped shaking when he halted behind Doris. He gazed down at the Ouija and poked a chip into his mouth.

"Would you like to take my place?" Howard asked.

"When they're ice skating in hell, pal."

"Very sensible," Dr. Dalton said.

Does she think I'm *not* sensible? Howard wondered. No, she understands. She realizes I was pushed into this.

Maybe he could get Angela to take his place.

He looked toward the sofa. Angela was staring at him with those big, gloomy eyes.

"Angela?" he called. "Wouldn't you like to play?"

"Thank you, no."

"Quit trying to squirm out, Howitzer."

5

"I think you guys are nuts," Glen said. A wet fleck of chip flew from his mouth, sailed over Doris's head and landed on the Ouija. On the Y of the YES in its upper left-hand corner. Only Howard seemed to notice. "Didn't any of you read *The Exorcist*?"

"Get real," Keith said.

"That's how that little twerp got possessed, fuh . . . messing around with her Ouija board."

Doris said in her menacing voice, "No good can come of it." Then she chuckled.

Lana looked up from the back of the box. "It says here we put our fingers lightly on the message indicator and just start asking questions." She set the box on the floor, then placed the heart-shaped plastic pointer in the middle of the board and rested two fingers of her right hand on it.

"Atmosphere!" Keith said. "We oughta be doing this in the dark, don't you think?"

"How would we read the messages?" Lana asked.

"A flashlight. Have you got a flashlight, Prof?"

"I'll get one," she told him. "You'll probably want a pen and some paper, too."

Lana looked up at her. "Is this thing really going to *say* something?"

"I wouldn't be at all surprised," Dr. Dalton said, and walked off.

"I'll get the lights," Glen said.

As he started away, Angela reached up and turned off the lamp at her end of the sofa. She sat in the gloom for a few moments, gazing toward Howard and the others. Then she got up and came over. In her soft, hesitant voice, she said, "If it's all right with everyone, I'll record the messages."

"Thata girl," Keith said.

Howard suspected that she just didn't want to be left sitting alone in the dark.

"I like all this confidence," Lana said. "God, it'd be cool if the thing actually does come through."

"The spirits of the dead are always eager for human contact," Doris said, this time using her normal voice.

Could she be serious? "Spirits of the dead?" Howard asked.

"Who else?"

"Us? I mean, I've studied a little about this kind of thing. From what I've read, the consensus seems to be that the pointer's movements are probably controlled by the subconscious mind of one of the participants."

"Which, in itself, could be interesting," Lana said.

"A nice theory," Doris said. "Nice in its Elizabethan sense—meaning simple, naive, and ignorant."

Keith nodded, grinning. "Right. All the *smart* people know it's dead folks talking."

"You may mock me now, but . . ." Her head turned as Dr. Dalton came into the room. "Hey, Professor, do Ouija messages come from the subconscious of someone guiding the pointer? Or from discarnate entities?"

"I'm no expert," she said.

"But you've used this board, am I right?"

"I've used it. That's why I want nothing to do with all this. Who wants the light?"

"Me," Angela said. "I'll be taking the notes."

Dr. Dalton gave her the flashlight, a ballpoint and a pad of paper.

"OK?" Lana asked. "Let's give it a try."

As those at the table reached out and rested their fingers on the pointer, Dr. Dalton said, "Remember what I told you. Don't mention my name while you're fooling around with that thing."

"Mine either," Glen said, taking up his position behind Doris. "Can't be too careful when it comes to fooling around with spooks. Not that I believe in any of this."

"We won't mention anyone, OK? Let's get started."

"Just one of us should ask it questions," Doris whispered.

"I'll do it," Lana said. "OK. Here goes." Then she spoke in a clear, steady voice. "Oh, great spirit of the Ouija board, we your humble servants ask that you address us. Hello? Hello? Anyone out there? Yoo-hoo. Calling all ghosts, calling all ghosts . . ."

"Don't be frivolous," Doris muttered.

"Spirits of the netherworld, we beseech you to communicate with us. Denizens of the other side. Ghoulies, ghosties, long-leggity beasties . . ."

"Damn it, Lana."

"Speak to us. Oh great subconscious, oh great id, get this mysterious message indicator moving. Come on, we're losing patience."

The platform under their fingers suddenly began to slide.

"All right!" Keith whispered.

"Shhhh."

It made loops, jerked from side to side.

"Is somebody doing this?" Lana asked.

It stopped near Howard, at the end of the top row of the alphabet. Angela's hip brushed against his upper arm. She leaned over and turned on the flashlight. "M," she whispered, and kept the light on the pointer as it slid away and stopped. "E."

It remained motionless.

"Me," she said.

"Ooo, boy," Keith muttered.

"It made sense," Lana said. "Jesus. I asked who was . . ."

The plastic heart darted for a corner of the board. It stopped on NO.

"Not Jesus," Doris said.

"Thing's got a sense of humor," Keith said. He sounded nervous.

"You pushed it over there," Lana said.

"No way. I swear."

"Howard?"

"I didn't. Honest."

"Doris?"

The pointer moved. But not the way it had moved before. This time, it didn't glide lightly over the surface of the board. It felt weighted down, sluggish, *pushed*. "That," Doris said, "is how it feels if one of us steers it."

Lana pulled her hand back. She brought it up to her

chest. Fingering a button at the top of her blouse, she stared at the board.

"Problem?" Doris asked. Her voice reeked of sarcasm.

"Shut up," Lana said.

"We aren't feeling quite so frivolous now, are we?"

"Let's ask it something," Keith said.

Lana tapped the button with her fingernail. "I don't know about this."

"*This* is what a Ouija board is supposed to do," Doris informed her.

"Come on, Lana."

"OK, OK." She lowered her hand to the pointer. "Who are you?" she asked.

It moved slowly across the alphabet, stopping long enough at each letter for Angela to check with the flashlight, speak the letter, and copy it on her pad. "F-R-I-E-N-D."

"Friend," Lana said. "Glad to hear it. Where are you?"

"N-E-A-R."

"Ask if it's a ghost," Keith whispered.

"Are you a ghost?"

The pointer sped toward the crescent moon in a corner of the board near Howard.

"No," Angela said.

"Not a ghost. That's a relief. What are you?"

"S-E-R-V-A-N-T."

"Whose servant?"

"U."

Lana let out a quick laugh. "Well, terrific. What're you going to do for me, servant?"

"G-I-V."

"You're going to give me something? What?"

"U-G-I-V."

"Me? I'm supposed to give something?"

"K-I-S-S-K-H."

"Hey," Keith blurted, "that's me. It wants you to kiss me."

"Bull."

"I'm the only K.H. around here. Keith Harris."

"Am I supposed to kiss Keith?"

9

The pointer slid toward the sun in the upper corner and stopped on the YES.

"I'm starting to like this," Keith said.

"Who does the guy think he is, Cupid?"

"Just go ahead and do it," Doris said.

Keith took his hand off the pointer, stood up and leaned over the table. He pursed his lips.

Lana frowned at him.

Howard wondered why she was hesitating. He knew for a fact that she was going with Keith. They'd probably done a lot more than kiss.

"This is insane," she muttered.

"You don't have to do it," Dr. Dalton said. "If I were you, I wouldn't do *anything* it asked."

"Come on, honey."

Lana sighed, stood up, bent forward, and kissed Keith on the mouth. She dropped back onto her chair. Sounding a little miffed, she said, "OK, Ouija, I did it. Now what?"

When she and Keith returned their fingers to the pointer, it began moving rapidly.

"M-Y-T-U-R-N."

Chapter Two

"*His* turn?" Keith whispered.

"No way," Lana gasped. The beam of the flashlight glared on her face. A chill squirmed through Howard when he saw her lips squeeze together—as if they were being mashed by an invisible mouth.

She's doing that herself, he realized. *Afraid* it's going to kiss her.

She suddenly grimaced and turned away from the harsh beam of the flashlight. "Cut it out!"

"Sorry." Angela lowered the light.

"Are you OK?" Keith asked.

"Except for the fact that I've been blinded . . ."

"Did you feel anything?"

"No, of course not. Don't be ridiculous."

"I thought for a second . . ." Keith went silent as the pointer suddenly darted sideways. Howard caught his breath, startled by the sudden movement.

When it stopped, Angela leaned over the board. She aimed the flashlight at the indicator. "I," she said. The pointer kept moving, stopping, moving again.

"G-I-V."

"See?" Keith asked. "He didn't want a kiss, after all. 'My turn to give,' that's what he meant."

Lana let out a long breath. She seemed to slump forward a little. After a few moments, she said, "OK, Ouija. What are you going to give?"

"L-O-O-T."

"Loot? What do you mean? Money?"

The pointer slid toward the smiling face of the sun and came to a stop on YES.

"You're going to give money?"

The plastic heart under their fingertips remained motionless.

"Does that mean another yes?" Lana asked.

"I imagine so," Doris told her.

"I *really* like this game," Keith said. "We split the take, right?"

Lana didn't answer him. Staring down at the board, she asked, "Where is the money?"

The pointer darted over the curved rows of the alphabet, pausing while Angela read out each letter, then moving on. "C-U-S-H-U-N."

"Cushion? Under a cushion?"

"C-O-U-C-H."

"I'll check," Glen said. He rushed to the sofa, turned on the lamp at its far end, tossed aside the three seat cushions and started searching.

"Anything you find in there is mine," Dr. Dalton called to him.

"This guy's a real genius," Keith said. "Revealing the great secret of loot lost in the couch."

"They like to play games," Doris explained.

"Here we go." Glen held up a penny.

"Riches beyond our wildest dreams," Keith said.

"Maybe there's more." Glen got down on his knees and shoved a hand deep into the crevice at the rear of the seat springs. "Oh, yuck. Hang on. Hmmm. Anybody lose a comb?" He pulled it out, then resumed his search. "Some more coins," he announced. He fished them out, counted them in his palm. "Forty-six cents, so far."

"This is my lucky night," Dr. Dalton said.

Glen thrust his arm into the gap again. He swept it back and forth. "There's . . . some kind of . . . Got it." He drew out his arm and opened his hand. "Woops."

Nothing but a foil wrapper, Howard thought. Like the kind that Alka-Seltzer tablets come in, only red.

"Uh—oh. Sorry, Professor."

"Just throw it away," she said. She sounded embarrassed, defensive.

Keith and Lana both started laughing.

"I don't even know how it got there."

"Oh, sure," Keith said. "Right."

"It's nothing to be ashamed of, Corie."

A condom wrapper, Howard suddenly realized. Somebody'd done it to Dr. Dalton right there on the sofa. He saw her sprawled out naked, squirming and gasping as a strange man plunged into her. How could she *let* . . . ?

What'd you think, she's a virgin? She's thirty years old. She's probably done it with lots of guys.

No! She said she didn't know how it got there. She wouldn't lie.

"Quit digging around in there, Glen," she said.

"Just a . . ." He pulled his arm out of the crack, then lowered his head and inspected a new find. "What the hell?"

It looked like a chunk of paper.

"Another clue to Professor Dalton's secret, tempestuous life?" Doris asked.

"Give it a break," Dr. Dalton muttered.

Keith tittered.

Glen used both hands to pluck open the tightly wadded paper. It appeared to be green.

"A whole buck?" Keith asked.

Glen spread the bill apart, stretched it taut and held it up toward the lamp. "Holy smokin' Judas! A hundred-dollar bill!"

"You're shitting us."

He hurried toward the table. Stepping between Doris and Keith, he placed the crumpled bill on the Ouija board. Angela lit it with her flashlight.

"That's a hundred bucks, all right." Keith grinned up at Dr. Dalton. "I suppose you don't know how *that* got there, either."

She moved closer to the table. "I've never even *had* a hundred-dollar bill."

Lana gazed up at her. "How'd it get there?"

"It's a used sofa," Dr. Dalton said. "I bought it second-hand a couple of years ago. Some of this stuff might've been inside the thing when I got it."

"A likely story," Keith said.

"*How* the money got into the sofa is irrelevant," Doris said. "The fact is, he led us to it. He knew it was there, and . . ."

"Doesn't take any mental giant to figure out somebody might've lost some cash down the back of a sofa."

"But a hundred-dollar bill," Lana muttered. "This *has* to be some kind of a trick. I mean, it's weird enough that this Ouija thing is making any sense at all, but . . ." She looked at Glen. "The hundred bucks came out of your pocket, right? You figured you'd put one over on us, get us all worked up . . ."

"I found it where I found it."

"Swear to God?"

"I swear."

"Angela, you were sitting over there."

She took a quick step backward, retreating from the accusation. Howard twisted sideways and looked up at her. She was shaking her head. Her mouth opened, but she didn't speak.

I ought to say something, he thought. She's too timid to defend herself.

"I don't think . . ." he started.

Dr. Dalton interrupted. "Angela hasn't been anywhere near the sofa since you started this nonsense. So, unless she's psychic, she couldn't have known that the Ouija would suggest searching for lost treasures in the sofa. Speaking of which." She stepped up beside Lana, stretched out her arm, and retrieved the bill. "Thank you very much," she said. "My house, friends."

"Don't we even get a cut?"

"You got plenty of laughs at my expense, Keith. That should be reward enough."

"Are you going to let her keep it, Glen?" Lana asked.

"Like she says, it's her house."

"That's really not your bill?"

"I already told you. Hey, I wish it was, but it's not."

As Dr. Dalton backed away from the table, Keith put his fingers on the pointer. "Come on, let's see what else it has to say."

"Maybe this would be a good time to quit," the professor said.

"What about the rest of us? You struck it rich. We haven't gotten zip so far."

"I suppose I'd be willing to split the take with you folks. What the heck. It wasn't mine to begin with."

"Now you're talking."

"That wouldn't be fair," Howard said.

"I don't mind. If it'll keep everyone happy . . ."

Doris reached out and rested her fingers on the pointer. "Come on, people. We're in contact with a benevolent spirit here. Let's find out what else it has to tell us."

"I wouldn't be so sure it's benevolent," Dr. Dalton said.

"Seems mighty benevolent to me," Keith said. "Coughing up a hundred bucks."

He placed his fingers on the plastic heart. Lana hesitated for a moment, then did the same.

"Join the fun, Howitzer."

"If Dr. Dalton thinks we should stop . . ."

"That's OK," she told him. "Maybe this wouldn't be such a great time to quit, after all."

"Are you sure?"

"I'm sure if you quit now you'll all leave here thinking

15

the Ouija is some kind of terrific oracle. Keep at it for a while. I'm sure you'll decide otherwise in fairly short order."

Howard rested his fingers on the pointer.

"OK," Lana said. "Ouija, we found the loot in the couch. Is there more?"

"4-T-U-N-E."

"Huh? Four tunes? Songs? What are you . . . ?"

"He means a fortune," Angela explained.

"A fortune? Where?"

The pointer slid lightly over the board. Each time it stopped, Angela read the letter aloud. "A-W-A-Y."

"A way for us to get it?" Lana asked.

"That might be a single word," Doris said. "Away."

"As in 'away from here'? Far away?"

The indicator carried their fingers toward the smiling sun.

"Yes," Angela said.

"Where? Where's the fortune?"

"4-M-E-2-N-O."

"Huh?"

Angela finished copying the message. She frowned as she stared at what she had written.

"I don't get it," Keith said.

"For me to know," Angela explained.

"For me to know, and for you to find out. What is this guy, a bratty kid?"

"Games," Doris said. "He's playing more games with us."

Lana frowned at the board, "What do you want?"

"2-B-W-I-T-H-U."

"To be with you," Angela said.

"Oh, great," Keith muttered.

"Tell it no," Dr. Dalton said.

Ignoring the advice, Lana asked, "Where are you?"

"A-W-A-Y."

"Are you dead?"

The pointer drifted around, forming spirals.

"I don't think he's going to answer," Doris whispered.

It kept moving aimlessly.

"OK," Lana said. "Forget I asked. Who are you?"

"B-U-T-L-E-R."

"Your name is Butler?"

"YES."

"Nice to meet you, Butler."

"P-L-E-A-S-U."

"Please you?" Keith said as the pointer continued to move.

"R-E-I-S-M-I-N-E."

"Please you? Are e is mine?"

"That doesn't make sense," Lana said.

"Pleasure is mine," Angela read from her note pad.

"Ah. Butler's a polite fellow."

"Depends on how you look at it," Doris said.

"Is Butler your first name or last?" Lana asked.

"I-M-B-U-T-L-E-R."

"I am Butler."

"Maybe I.M. are his initials."

"Butler might be his profession," Keith suggested. "He already told us he's a servant."

"But he said it's his name. So. Butler, let's get back to this fortune you mentioned earlier."

"Y."

"Why?" Angela said.

"You're the one who brought it up in the first place, Butler. You must want to tell us more about it. What do you want to tell us?"

"M-I-N-E."

"It's in a mine?"

"Maybe he just means that it's his," Keith said.

"Is the fortune in a mine?"

"YES."

"Where's the mine?"

"4-M-E-2-N-O."

Lana sighed. "I don't enjoy being teased, Butler. I'm tired of your games. Maybe we should just let you go back to whatever you were doing when we interrupted. Is that what you want?"

The pointer darted to a corner of the board and stopped beside the crescent moon.

"No? Well, Butler, either you tell us where to find this fortune, or it's *adios*."

The pointer remained motionless over the NO.

"I don't think it's a good idea to threaten him," Doris said.

"Screw him," Lana muttered. She pulled back her hand. "Let's put this thing away."

Howard took his hand off the pointer. Keith and Doris did the same.

Lana folded her arms across her chest. A corner of her mouth turned up. "See what happens, Butler, when you don't cooperate? It's a two-way street, my friend."

The pointer began to move.

"Oh, my God," she murmured.

Angela flinched, her hip bumping Howard's arm.

He gasped for breath as he watched the heart slide. The beam of the flashlight followed its slow course over the board. When it stopped, Angela whispered, "U."

"This isn't happening," Keith said.

"Shhhh."

"G."

Howard looked up as Dr. Dalton took a step closer to the table and bent over it.

"I."

She clutched her thighs. She was frowning down at the board, gnawing her lower lip.

"V."

"You give," Angela said.

"Who?" Lana asked.

"A-L."

"Al?" Keith asked. "Who's Al?"

"Maybe it means 'all' of us," Lana said.

"Someone's initials?" Doris suggested.

"Angela Logan," Angela whispered. "Me. He means me."

"Butler, do you want Angela to give?"

The pointer swooped up the board and settled on YES.

"What do you want her to give?"

"B-L."

"Who's B.L.?" Keith asked. But the indicator continued to move.

"O-U."

"Oh you?"

"Shut up, Keith."

"S-E-2-H-C."

The pointer stopped, and Angela finished copying the message.

"What does it say?" Lana asked her.

"I'm not sure. Maybe 'below use to H.C.' "

"H.C. might be me," Howard said. "Howard Clark."

"It still doesn't make any sense."

"I don't know," Angela's voice trembled. "This is silly, anyway. He's not going to tell us where to find his treasure."

"He might," Lana said. "If we do what he asks. Let Howard take a look at what you wrote."

Howard turned. Angela stared down at him. Her mouth opened slightly, then closed. She handed the pad to him, and shone her light on it.

The message made immediate, perfect sense to Howard. It wrenched his breath away and started his heart thudding. "Well . . ."

"Cough it up, Howitzer."

"It says, 'blouse to H.C.' "

"All right! Shuck it off, babe!"

"Keith!" Lana snapped.

"Let's put this thing away right now," Dr. Dalton said. "I knew it'd start pulling some kind of crap."

As she reached for the pointer, Lana grabbed her hand. "Just hold it a second, Corie. Hold it! We might be talking about a fortune here."

"Bullshit. There's no fortune. This Butler—whoever the hell he is—is just messing with your heads. He's using you for his own cheap amusement."

"Maybe, maybe not. But let's give him a chance. Let's just

play this thing out, OK? All he asked was for Angela to give her blouse to Howard. It's no big deal."

"I'm sure it's a big deal to Angela."

"She's not a child, Corie. Why don't we let her make up her own mind. OK?" Lana released Dr. Dalton's hand.

The professor stared at the board for a moment, then thrust her hands into the pockets of her shorts. "It's just toying with you all," she said. "If you think this thing is going to make you rich, you're out of your gourds."

Lana raised her eyes to the girl. "You're wearing a bra, aren't you?"

Angela nodded.

"OK, so what's the big deal? It's not as if he's asking you to strip naked. You probably wear less when you go to the beach."

"But he's . . . a spook or something."

"A rich spook," Keith said. "Come on, Angie. Part of the treasure'll be yours, you know. We'll split it up equally."

"Why *me*?"

"Maybe he knows you're the most likely to refuse," Doris suggested. "He made the demand of you because he thinks you won't do it, and then he won't have to give his information."

"It'll be on your head," Keith said.

"Don't do it, Angela," Dr. Dalton told her. "Don't ever let anyone talk you into doing anything against your better judgment."

"But they'll all blame me . . ."

"Right."

"Keith," Dr. Dalton snapped. "Shut your damn mouth."

"Maybe this will help." Lana unbuttoned her own blouse and pulled it off. "See? It's no big deal." She dropped her blouse to the floor and sat up straight, her torso dusky except for the white of her strapless bra.

It covers as much as a bikini would, Howard told himself. But the sight of her breasts, bare along their tops, seemed to suck his breath away. He gazed at the smooth slopes, the valley between them, and felt an erection begin to push against his pants.

"You too, Doris," Lana said.

"Hey, Butler isn't interested in . . ."

"Just go ahead and do it."

Doris sighed, crossed her arms against her bulging belly, grabbed the bottom of her sweatshirt, and lifted. She peeled the shirt up over breasts encased in a mammoth bra. She folded it, and placed it on her lap.

"They did it," Keith said. "You can do it."

"All right," Angela murmured.

"For godsake."

"It's all right, Professor."

"Nothing about this is all right."

Angela switched off the flashlight. She reached down and set it on the card table close to Howard's arm. Glancing sideways, he saw her tug the ends of her blouse out of her skirt.

He fixed his eyes on Lana, wanting to spare Angela the embarrassment of being watched by him. If he looked at her, it would be so obvious. She was standing right next to him. He would have to twist around on his chair and . . .

Besides, Lana was so much more beautiful than Angela. He found himself gazing at her breasts. The bra curled over their fronts just enough to hide the nipples. A little pull, and the clasp would come undone.

"Quit staring, Howitzer."

Keith's words made him suddenly feel dirty. He murmured, "Sorry," and turned his head away.

Turned it toward Angela.

She had started with the lowest button. Her blouse hung open from the chest down. As Howard watched, she unfastened the button between her breasts. Then the one just below her throat, the last. She spread her blouse. She was gazing into space, not looking at Howard, so he studied her as she slipped it off her shoulders and down her arms.

She was skinny and her breasts were small. But heat pulsed through Howard's groin. Even though the single lamp was behind Angela, it gave off enough light for him to see right through her bra. Its cups were flimsy transparent pouches, stretched tight over breasts shaped like cones. Her nipples were dark and erect. They looked huge. They looked like fingertips trying to poke through the wispy bra.

She turned toward Howard. The lamplight found her left breast. So close above his face.

Howard had never been this close to a breast.

She had a tiny freckle beneath her nipple.

If he stood up just a little bit, he would be able to feel the fabric against his cheek, as smooth and soft as a breeze. Hardly there at all. The skin beneath it silken, warm. He could press his face into it, feeling the springy softness. The nipple would push against his eyelid.

"Here," she whispered.

Her voice startled him.

He lowered his eyes. Angela offered the blouse to him. He set the note pad and pen on the table, accepted the blouse from her and folded it slowly, wondering at the strange magic that made the garment feel electric. It seemed to send warm vibrations through his fingertips, up his arms.

It's just Angela's blouse, he thought.

But it had been next to her skin. It had caressed her breasts through the bra. It had been tucked deep into her skirt, down against her panties.

He freed his hands from the garment, and felt its gentle weight against his lap. A heaviness there, pushing down on his erection.

Cut it out, he told himself. Angela's not so hot. I don't even like her.

Not much, anyway.

"Come on, Howitzer."

"Huh?"

He saw that Keith, Lana and Doris had already placed their fingers on the pointer. He reached out. As his fingertips met the warm plastic, he looked sideways at Angela.

She had taken a few steps back from the table. She was standing rigid. She seemed to be trembling. Her arms were crossed, hands cupping her breasts. When she saw him looking, a corner of her mouth twitched as if she were trying to smile.

"OK, Butler," Lana said. "We kept our part of the bargain. Your turn to give."

The pointer slid, stopped on YES.

"Terrific," Keith whispered.

"Tell us where the fortune is."

The heart carried their fingers to the top row of the alphabet. Keith leaned over the dark board. He shook his head. "Need the flashlight."

Howard picked it up with his left hand. He turned it on and aimed its beam at the pointer.

"I," Keith read.

Howard tracked the gliding pointer with the flashlight as Keith spoke the letters.

"M-E-E-T-U."

"I meet you," Doris said.

"Where?" Lana asked.

The doorbell rang. Howard's heart kicked. Lana's hand jerked away from the pointer.

"Jumpin' Judas!" Glen gasped.

It rang again.

"Just calm down, everyone," Dr. Dalton said. "I'll see who's there."

"I got a feeling," Keith said, "it ain't Jehovah's Witnesses."

Chapter Three

"I'll go with you," Glen said as the doorbell rang again.

"Thanks. I appreciate it." Oh, how *much* I appreciate it, Corie thought.

"Whatever they're selling, we don't want any," Keith said as she stepped around the table.

"Knock it off," Lana told him.

Angela hurried toward Howard, holding out her hand. He gave the blouse to her.

The poor thing, Corie thought. Wearing that nothing of a bra. Why didn't I put my foot down?

At least no one made any cracks about it.

But God, she must've been mortified.

The bell rang again, and a fresh surge of dread pushed away her concerns about Angela. It was close to midnight. Who could be showing up at this hour?

Butler.

If it's Butler, I'm going to drop dead on the spot.

In the foyer, she flicked on a light. She halted and gazed at the door.

24

Glen put a hand on her arm. She jumped.

"It can't be *him*," Glen whispered. "No way. You know what I mean? Relax. Just relax."

She nodded. She took a deep breath and called out, "Who's there?"

"Coreen?"

She gasped.

"What's wrong?" Glen blurted.

She lurched forward, pulling away from Glen's hold. Her strength seemed to fall away. She slumped against the door, unlocked it and staggered backward, pulling it open.

"Chad!" The name was out of her mouth before she realized the man on the stoop wasn't him.

A wild, bearded stranger stared in at her.

Some kind of derelict in a shabby hat, a filthy shirt and jeans. He wore a backpack, and carried a wooden staff.

But he had Chad's voice!

"What do you want?" she blurted.

He grimaced, lips and mustache twisting away from his teeth. "I guess I'm not so sure anymore," he said. "I just wanted to see you, Coreen. I know it's awfully late and you weren't expecting me, but . . ."

"Chad? It *is* you?"

"Well, sure."

"Oh, my God."

"So I guess you know him, huh?" Glen murmured.

She squeezed Glen's arm, nodding as tears made her eyes sting. "Go on in with the others." He started away. "Get in here, Chad."

"Are you sure it's OK?"

"What do you think?" She sniffed and wiped her eyes as he entered the house.

He shut the door and locked it. He propped his walking stick against the wall, lowered his pack to the floor and put down his hat. When he straightened up, Corie wrapped her arms around him. He hugged her. His beard was scratchy against her face. He smelled of sweat and wood smoke.

25

"You look like the Wild Man of Borneo," she said, stepping back from him.

"Been in the mountains a while. Playing Thoreau."

"My God, it's good to see you."

"You look great, Coreen."

"You, too. You lost a lot of weight. I honestly didn't recognize you."

"Well, it's been a long time."

"A very long time," she said, feeling a stir of the old, familiar anger. "You could've at least kept in touch."

"I know. I . . ." He shook his head. The look of sorrow in his eyes made Corie's throat go tight.

"But hey," she said, "you're here now. That's the important thing. You're going to stay, aren't you?"

"Well . . . You've got guests."

"Just a few of my summer-session kids. I threw a little party to celebrate the last day of class. I'll send them packing pretty soon. They've had enough fun for one night."

Chad grinned. "A rowdy bunch?"

"I wouldn't say rowdy." She took his hand. "They've been monkeying around with the Ouija board, and it hasn't exactly been a picnic."

"Jake's old board?"

She squeezed his hand as memories started to come. "The very same."

He sighed. "We used to have some good times with that thing."

"Yeah. And some bad times."

She led him into the den. It was brightly lighted. She saw that the girls had put their clothes back on. Even better, Lana was fitting the lid onto the Ouija board's box. They were done with the damn thing.

Lana looked up and grinned. "Who's the hunk?"

"I'd like you all to meet my old friend, Chad Dalton."

"Dalton?" Lana asked.

"He's my brother-in-law, actually." Seeing the looks of confusion and surprise on their faces, she realized that none of them knew she'd been married. "Chad's brother was my

26

husband," she explained. A hollow feeling spread through her. "He passed away a few years ago." She quickly added, "Anyway, Chad and I are old buddies. Chad, this is my motley crew of students."

She introduced them, and Chad gave each a cheerful greeting.

When she finished, he nodded toward the closed box. "So, did the Ouija board keep you properly mystified?"

Angela's face went red.

"It was pretty strange," Lana said. "I can't believe the thing actually communicated with us."

"That's what it's for."

"Did it tell?" Corie asked.

She saw Lana glance at Keith. "You mean about the treasure?"

"A treasure?" Chad asked.

"It hinted around about a hidden fortune," Corie explained.

"No fooling?"

"You showed up just as they were trying to find out where to lay their hands on it. So, did Butler come through with his end of the deal? What did he have to say after I left?"

Lana grinned. "For us to know."

"Hey, whose Ouija board is it, anyway?"

"I thought you didn't want to get involved."

"Calamity Peak," Howard said.

"I was *going* to tell her."

"Sorry," he muttered.

"So was that all? Calamity Peak?"

"Right after it said that, the pointer went off the board. Do you have a map?" Lana asked. "Might be interesting just to see if there is such a place."

"Oh, there is," Chad said. "Calamity Peak's in the Shadow Canyon Wild Area. About eighty, ninety miles east of Red Bluff."

"Red Bluff?"

"Down in California."

"You've *been* there?" Lana asked.

"Close by. I've seen Calamity Peak from across a valley."

"Man, this is weird," Glen said.

"Weird?" Lana's eyebrows climbed her forehead. "What's weird? Butler tells us the fortune's at Calamity Peak just as who should walk in but a guy who's *been* there. What's weird about that?"

"Coincidence?" Doris asked in an ominous tone. "Or fate?"

Keith turned to Chad. "How long would it take us to get there?"

"You can't be serious," Corie said.

"Just curious."

"It's probably over four hundred miles," Chad said. "But I have to warn you, the area isn't very accessible. The base of the mountain's at least a day's hike from the nearest road-head."

"So it would take what—two days at most?"

"About."

"Keith, no," Corie said. "I can tell you right now that you won't find any fortune at Calamity Peak. You won't find anything but trouble. I don't know what the deal is with Ouija boards—what makes them work or who or what Butler might be. But I do know that you can't trust the things. Butler is screwing around with you. He's playing with you. He's jerking you around. For godsake, look what he made you do."

Keith glanced toward Angela, then met Corie's eyes. "He didn't *make* us do anything. Nobody forced Angela to . . ."

"That's right," Lana said. "She did it of her own free will."

"Oh, come off it. You people forced her into it, and you know it. Butler said 'Jump' and you said 'How high?' "

"I don't know what went on here," Chad said, "but Coreen's right about the Ouija board. It's a sly thing. It'll trick you. You'd be wasting your time if you went searching for that treasure."

Lana nodded. "I'm not real keen on the idea, myself. The way Chad talks, we'd have to hike all day and maybe even camp out."

"No maybe about it," Chad said.

"You can count me out."

"Me, too," Doris said.

Keith raised his eyes to Glen. "How about it, my man? Up for an adventure?"

"Butler gives me the creeps."

"Wuss."

"That's me."

Keith glanced from Howard to Angela. "I don't suppose either of *you'd* be interested."

"No thanks," Howard said.

Angela shook her head.

"Professor? Chad?"

"I've had enough of the wilds to last me a while," Chad told him.

"I guess you're on your own," Corie said. "And if you have any sense at all, you'll give up the idea."

"Don't worry," Lana said. "I know Keith. He's not about to do something like that all by his lonesome." She scooted her chair back and stood up. "Anyway, it's getting awfully late. About time we hit the road."

As she carried the Ouija board's box to the bookshelf and shoved it into place beneath the stack of games, the others got up from their seats.

She returned to the table. "Let's put this stuff back where we got it."

"Oh, that's OK," Corie said.

"No, we'll take care of it."

She folded her chair. Keith flipped the card table onto its side to collapse its legs.

"Somebody want to get my chair?" he asked, glancing at Corie.

She folded it and picked it up.

Starting toward the kitchen, Lana looked over her shoulder at Chad. "You spooked us all pretty good when you showed up like that. Butler had just said, 'I meet you,' and suddenly, whammo, there goes the doorbell."

"Lousy timing," he said, and walked along with the group.

"It was great timing," Corie said. "Four o'clock in the morning would've been fine, as far as I'm concerned. I'm just glad you're here."

They entered the kitchen. In the breakfast nook, Keith set down the table. He snapped one of its legs into place, then grimaced at Howard. "You want to take care of this? I've gotta hit the john."

"Sure."

Keith hurried away. Howard set up his chair, then crouched to open the rest of the table's legs.

"So, Chad," Lana said, "were you on a camping trip?"

"You might say that. I've been pretty much living in the mountains since the spring thaw."

"All alone?"

"Just me and mother nature."

"What a drag." She grinned. "Are you some kind of a hermit?"

"That's me."

"Sounds neat," Glen said.

Howard set the table upright. As Lana slid her chair under it, she frowned at Corie. "Do you think I could have a cup of coffee before we go?"

The request surprised her. Lana had seemed ready to leave. But she wouldn't mind having some coffee, herself. "I'll make a fresh pot," she said.

"Oh, you don't need to go to all that trouble. A cup of instant would be . . ."

"No trouble. It'll just take a few minutes, and then there'll be plenty for everyone. Chad and I might be up half the night, anyway. Right?"

He smiled. "More than likely."

It'll be like old times, she thought. Sitting around the card table late into the night with Chad, drinking coffee and talking for hours the way they used to do while they waited for Jake to return from the job.

She started to remember the night of the telephone call. The night of Jake's death.

Quit it!

She hurried past Chad, opened a cupboard and took out a coffee filter. With a can of Yuban from the refrigerator, she went to the counter. "I won't make it especially strong," she said, scooping grounds into the filter. "Don't want to keep everyone awake till dawn or anything. Three scoops. Enough for plenty of flavor, but you won't be able to stand a spoon up in it. Chad, you know where I keep the mugs. Why don't you take a head count and see who's interested?"

I'm babbling, she thought.

But Chad showing up like this. Though she was so happy to see him, his presence would be a constant reminder of Jake. All the great times they'd had, the three of them. And how he'd stayed on, looking after her, during the period following Jake's death. And how he'd left her, finally. Abandoned her. Disappeared from her life for five years until turning up tonight.

Corie watched coffee dribble into the pot, and felt her anger rising.

He'd better have a damn good explanation, she thought.

Hey, don't spoil it. He's back. That's what counts.

How could he *do* that to me?

Why did he suddenly come back now, after all this time?

She looked at him standing over by the table, chatting casually with Lana and Glen about the pleasures of solitude. Howard was staring at him, scowling a little as if he didn't care much for what he saw. Angela's head was down. She seemed to be gazing at the floor.

They sure put that girl through it tonight, Corie thought.

I never should've let them drag out that damn Ouija board in the first place.

Keith came in. "The pause that refreshes," he said.

"We're going to have some coffee," Lana told him.

"I thought we were leaving."

"Pretty soon."

31

*   *   *

When they were finally done with their coffee, Corie realized she wasn't eager to see them go. But nobody wanted a refill.

"It's getting awfully late," Lana said. "And I bet you have a lot of catching up to do with Chad."

Corie gave each student a quick hug at the door, then she and Chad followed them outside to Lana's car.

"Are you all going to fit in there?" she asked.

"We'll manage," Lana said. "We made it out here OK."

"Well, have a great summer, everyone. See you in September."

They waved and called out farewells through the car's open windows.

Corie stood by the curb. She watched until the car swung out of sight at the end of the block. Then she took hold of Chad's hand and smiled up at him.

It's just us, now.

"Nice bunch of kids," Chad said.

"Yeah. They're not bad. Ready to go in and polish off the coffee?"

"Could it wait a while?" he asked as they started back toward the house. "I'm filthy as a dog. I'd sure like to take a quick shower, if that'd be all right."

"Oh, fine. It'll give me a chance to put some fresh sheets on your bed."

"A bed? Fresh sheets? I don't know if I'll be able to stand it."

"If you'd rather throw down your sleeping bag in the back yard . . ."

"Trying to get rid of me already?"

"Don't even say that joking, Chad."

Chapter Four

"Did you get it?" Lana asked after turning the corner.

"Of course," Keith said. "But you'd better pull over."

She stopped at the curb. "Where is it?"

"Back at the Prof's."

"You *left* it there?"

"You didn't give me the car keys. What was I supposed to do, stick it on the hood? I hid it in the bushes near her front door."

"OK. Well, let's wait a minute. Give them time to get back inside." She shut off the headlights and engine.

"If you want my opinion," Angela said, "I think what we're doing is lousy."

That's for sure, Howard thought. He was glad Angela felt the same way.

"Nobody asked," Keith said.

Howard felt her flinch a little against his side.

Say something, he told himself. Don't let Angela take all the heat.

But he'd gone along with it this far, and so had she. Nei-

33

ther of them had made any protest at the house when it might've made a real difference.

The moment the Ouija board had spelled out Calamity Peak, Lana had shoved back her chair, snatched up the board and pointer, and rushed across the living room to hide them under the sofa. Returning to her seat just as Glen came back, she'd said, "I'll distract Corie, get her into the kitchen. Keith, you get out here quick and take the Ouija board out to my car. We're going after that treasure. The six of us. Play dumb when Corie comes in."

By the time Dr. Dalton had entered with Chad, Lana was in the process of putting the lid onto the Ouija board's empty box.

That's when one of us should've blown the whistle, Howard thought. Before it went this far.

I almost did, he reminded himself.

Damn it.

He'd really expected someone else to speak up, though, and save him from being the traitor.

"OK, Keith. Go get it. We'll wait here."

Glen opened the passenger door. His side of the car rocked upward when he climbed out. He waited on the curb until Keith was out, then climbed back in. The car sank again under his weight. He banged the door shut.

"It's theft, you know," Angela said. "The Ouija board doesn't belong to us."

Lana twisted around in her seat. "We're just borrowing it. We'll return it to her when we're done with it."

"It's still wrong," Howard said. Immediately, he felt better. He wished he'd protested a long time ago.

"Corie would've flipped her lid if she thought we were planning to go for the treasure. You heard her. She thinks the whole idea's insane."

"Maybe she's right," Howard said. Angela's hand slipped onto his thigh, squeezed him gently, and stayed there.

"What've you got against money?" Glen asked him.

"Who says we'll find any money?"

"Butler does."

"A spook," Angela muttered.

"Dr. Dalton thinks we shouldn't believe him."

"He was right about the hundred dollars in the sofa," Doris said, leaning forward and putting her hands on her knees. She spread her legs until her left knee pushed against Howard. She didn't seem to notice. "As far as I can see, there's only one way to find out whether he's telling the truth about the fortune. *I'm* certainly willing to devote a few days to the project. If we fail, at least we'll have the satisfaction of knowing we tried."

"Besides," Glen said, "it'll be a blast."

"I thought you didn't want anything to do with the Ouija board," Howard said, easing his leg away from Doris.

"That was before it started coming up with money, pal. Anybody starts telling me where I can lay my hands on a pile, I'm all for it. A guy can always use dough. I can, anyway. Maybe you're so rich you don't care, but . . ."

"I'm not." He felt a rush of guilt, and told himself there was no reason for it. Why should he be ashamed of the fact that his parents could afford to pay for his education? It's not a sin, no matter what people like Glen might think. "I just think letting ourselves be pushed around by the Ouija board isn't all that smart."

"If Howard and Angela are so against the project," Lana said, "maybe they should bow out."

"Yeah," Glen said. "More for the rest of us."

"Do you two want out?" she asked.

"I don't know," Howard muttered, and looked at Angela. "What do you think?"

She shrugged one shoulder just slightly.

"We're not going to force you into it," Lana said.

"Hell, no," Glen said. "Better for us."

"That's not necessarily true," Doris pointed out. "While I don't think they should come if they prefer not to, it's conceivable that their absence would put the project in jeopardy. Item, Howard was among the four of us in contact with the message indicator. Item, Butler appears to have a special interest in Angela; i.e., he requested that she remove her blouse as a precondition to giving us the actual location of the fortune."

"Knew she was the one wearing a see-through bra," Glen said. "Poor bastard's probably horny out there on the 'other side.'"

Angela's fingers tightened on Howard's thigh.

"Be that as it may, they've both been significant participants. If they aren't among us when we reach Calamity Peak, we might not be able to re-establish our contact with Butler."

"That makes sense," Lana said.

"Of course."

"If either of you decides not to come, and Doris turns out to be right, it could screw things up for the rest of us."

"They're coming," Glen said.

Howard let out a soft laugh.

"What's so funny, Howie?"

"Nothing," he muttered. No point in making the guy mad. But Glen, like Keith, had always seemed to delight in sneering at Doris's pedantry. Now, Glen was latching onto her theory as if it were gospel.

All of a sudden, she's *not* full of shit?

"We aren't going to force anyone," Lana said.

"If there's a chance we'll find money . . ." Angela muttered.

"Thata girl," Glen said. "How about you, Howie?"

"Are you sure?" he asked her.

"The whole idea scares me," she said, speaking softly and looking into his eyes. "But . . . my scholarship only covers tuition. Even with the jobs, I never have nearly enough for . . . to buy the things I'd like to. I know there's probably not much chance of really finding the money Butler told us about, but I guess I'd better . . . you know, go along with the thing. You'll go, too, won't you?"

He sighed.

"What's it gonna be?" Glen asked.

"Don't rush him," Lana said.

He didn't know what to do.

Going along with the group would be a betrayal of Dr. Dalton. They were not only stealing her Ouija board, but they'd lied to her, pretended they had no interest in making the trip. Obviously, they had no intention of giving her a share of the money—if they found it.

He didn't trust Butler. Whatever else Butler might be, he was nasty. He'd made them *do* things.

On the other hand, he felt sorry for Angela. She was scared, only going along with the others because she needed money so badly. She'd already suffered at the hands of Butler. Instead of sticking up for her, the rest of them had goaded her on, pushed her into taking off her blouse.

A lot of help I was to her then.

If I'd told her I didn't think she should . . .

He suddenly found himself thinking about the way her breasts had looked, how he'd ached to feel them. The memories aroused him now, and her hand was still on his leg and he realized he would be with her for days if he agreed to go along. No telling what might happen.

He wouldn't exactly mind being around Lana, either. She was hard to take, sometimes, but she was sure beautiful. She'd been awfully quick to take off her blouse. Hiking and camping with her for a few days, he was bound to see plenty more of her.

The thoughts excited him, but also made him feel guilty.

Angela needs me, he told himself. I'm the only one who gives a damn about her. That's what matters.

He met her eyes and said, "I'll stick with you."

"You're not going along just because of me, are you?"

"What's wrong with that?"

She didn't answer. Instead, she turned and kissed him softly on the cheek. Though her upper arm pressed against him, her breast didn't. If she'd turned a little more . . .

"Should've given him one on the mouth," Glen said as she eased away.

"Why don't you butt out?" Howard said.

Glen laughed.

"So," Lana said. "We're all in. What we'll do, I'll drive

us around to everyone's place, and . . ." She looked to the side as a quick scuff of footfalls approached the car.

Keith rushed up to the passenger door and flapped the Ouija board at the open window. The chest of his tight, knit shirt bulged over the heart-shaped pointer. He pulled open the door. "Out of my way, big guy."

Glen climbed out, and Keith got in.

"Any trouble?" Lana asked.

"Right where I left it. What'd you think, it wandered away by itself?"

"Nothing about that thing would surprise me at this point."

"Only trouble I had was the message indicator. Stuck it down inside my shirt here, and it kept sliding around. I think it was trying to tell me something."

"You're kidding, right?"

He laughed.

Glen slid in beside him and slammed the door. "Probably Butler checking out your tits."

"You're the one with tits, man."

"And proud of them. Here, want a feelie?"

"Fag."

"Knock it off, guys," Lana said. She started the car, out on its headlights, and swung away from the curb. We've gotta figure things out. I don't think we should wait for morning."

"You want to drive there *now*?" Keith asked.

"As soon as everybody's got their stuff. From what Chad told us, we can expect to be in the mountains three or four days. So we'll need packs, sleeping bags, clothes, mess kits."

"Food," Glen said.

"We'll stop in a town along the way and pick up food and whatever else we're missing. Who doesn't have camping gear?"

"*Moi,*" Doris said.

"I don't, either," Angela said. "All I have is a sleeping bag."

"What about you, Howard?"

"I've got stuff."

"I can get my hands on another sleeping bag," Lana said. "Doris, you can use that. We'll pick up a couple of extra packs when we stop to buy the food."

"Who's gonna pay for all this?" Glen asked.

"I'll bankroll the whole operation," Lana said.

"All *right*! I knew there was something I liked about you."

"I get paid back when we find Butler's stash. OK? I'll drop all of you off, and pick you up later. But make it quick. Just throw together some clothes and whatever gear you have. It'll probably be cold at night, so don't forget to bring coats. Once we're on our way, we'll figure out what we're missing and make up a shopping list."

"Maybe we should take two cars," Keith said. "I mean, we've got an eight- or ten-hour drive ahead of us, and it's kind of tight in here. Howitzer's got a car. He could take Angela and Doris, and we'd have a little room to spread out."

"Then we'd have to keep track of each other," Lana said.

"Besides," Howard said, "my car overheats." It was a lie, but they had no way of knowing.

"Let's just take my car," Lana said. "I think it's best if we all stay together."

"Let us all hang together," Doris said, "or we shall most assuredly each hang separately."

"Spare us the shit," Keith said.

Chapter Five

"Hang on a second," Coreen said. "I'll get you something to put on when you're done." She stepped across the corridor and disappeared into her bedroom. When she came out, she had Jake's old plaid bathrobe.

"You kept his clothes?" Chad asked.

"A few things. This," she said, handing the robe to him, "some shirts and things that I can wear around the house."

"They must be huge on you."

She nodded, smiling a little. "Huge and loose and comfy. That's why I kept them, not . . . you know, because I couldn't bear to part with them. I got rid of the stuff I couldn't use. Which means I've got no pants, underwear, anything like that for you to wear. If you'd like me to throw your clothes in the washer while you shower . . ."

"Oh, don't go to the trouble. Tomorrow will be plenty soon enough. I should probably hose everything down first."

She smiled. "That bad, huh?" She opened the door of the linen closet, reached up, and pulled out a neatly folded blue towel and washcloth. She carried them into the bathroom, set them on a counter beside the sink. "Anything else?"

"That should do it. Thanks."

"See you later, then." She stepped out and shut the door.

As Chad draped the robe over the doorknob, he thought about thumbing in the lock button.

Afraid she'll come barging in?

She never did, she won't tonight.

He went ahead and locked the door. Better to eliminate the possibility than to start dwelling on it the way he used to.

He lowered the toilet lid. He sat down and removed his scuffed, dusty boots, and sighed. Always such a pleasure to get them off. He felt as if his feet had been trapped inside them, cramped and suffocating. At last, they could breathe. He peeled off his damp, filthy socks and tucked them into the necks of the boots. The tops of his feet looked shriveled from the moisture.

He stood up, took off the rest of his clothes, and piled them in the far corner. Backing away, he saw his reflection in the full-length mirror.

The Wild Man of Borneo, she'd called him.

Not so far from the truth.

Almost three months in the mountains, and it had been longer than that since his last haircut or shave. Not much of his face was even visible through the thick tangles of hair. He rubbed his beard. An old pine needle fell out.

He stepped into the tub, drew the curtain shut, and turned on the shower. The spray splattered against him. Not as cold as he was used to. It didn't give him goosebumps, didn't squeeze his genitals like a handful of ice. But he supposed he would get accustomed to it.

Back in the old days, in this same bathroom, he used to take such hot showers that the mirrors would be all steamed over when he stepped out.

It seemed like a different person who'd done that.

A confused and tormented kid, shy and overweight, obsessed with Coreen.

He squirted a syrupy puddle of shampoo into his palm, and sniffed it. Coreen's shampoo. The same aroma he remembered so well. He started to picture her sitting in the tub, lathering her hair. He shoved the image from his mind.

OK, he thought. I haven't changed all that much.

But it'll be different this time.

He slipped into Jake's robe and knotted its cloth belt. The fabric clung to his lower back where the towel had missed a few drops of water. Its sleeves, turned up, reached only partway down his forearms.

Because Coreen has been wearing it.

I won't think about that.

Crouching, he found his comb in a front pocket of his jeans. He went to the mirror. He tugged the comb through the tangles of his hair and beard. Then he rolled his clothing into a bundle, tucked it under his arm, picked up his boots, and carried them through the house. He opened the sliding glass door and took them outside. He left them on the patio next to his pack.

The night was warm. A soft breeze stirred the robe against his legs. Turning, he saw a glow of light from the kitchen window. A squirmy sensation crawled through his bowels.

Coreen's probably sitting at the card table, waiting for me.

Maybe I shouldn't have come back.

A little late for second thoughts.

Up in the mountains when he'd made his decision to return, he'd felt sure he was ready. He had grown strong mentally and physically. He was no longer the self-conscious fat guy who saw himself as a loser. He could stand in front of Coreen as a new man.

A new man, all right. She didn't recognize me. Hell, she actually looked scared.

But that went away once she realized who I was. She seemed awfully glad to see me.

Nervous, though.

OK, we're both nervous. It's only natural.

"Listening to the call of the wild?"

Heart thumping, he turned around. Coreen stood in the doorway. Her feet were bare. She wore a red jersey night-shirt. It reached down nearly to her knees, but Chad could see her thighs through the fabric. The way the light behind her . . .

I don't need *this*.

Why hadn't she left on the clothes she was wearing ear-lier? Because I'm only wearing a robe. She probably thought I'd be less self-conscious if she was dressed for bed.

"We could have our coffee on the patio, if you'd like."

"The kitchen will be fine."

He started toward her. When she turned away from the doorway, he got a side view. She wore a bra under the night-shirt.

Thank God.

Following her into the kitchen, he glimpsed the outline of a band just above her buttocks. So she was wearing pan-ties, too.

He felt some of his tension subside.

He sat at the card table. Coreen brought over the coffee pot. "I had to make some more," she said, starting to fill his mug. Her hand trembled. She poured coffee for herself, re-turned the pot to the counter, and sat down across from him.

She took a sip. "So. How does it feel, being back?"

"A little strange, I guess. Have you been OK?"

She stared into his eyes. A corner of her mouth turned up. "Lonely."

"I thought you might be married and have kids by now."

"Why did you go away like that, Chad?"

So sudden. It struck him like a punch. He'd known the question would come. But he wasn't ready for it, in spite of the countless times he had rehearsed answers in his mind.

"I had to," he said.

"That's what you said in your note. It's no explanation. Did *I* do something?"

"No, it wasn't your fault."

"Are you sure? I know I . . . tied one on the night before you left. It seemed like we were having a good time, though. We didn't have an argument, did we? God knows, I've tried to remember everything about that night. Some of it's a little fuzzy, but . . . did I say something to upset you?"

He gazed at her, stunned. "No! Of course not."

"Then *why*?"

"I fell in love with you."

Coreen's face went red. Her mouth hung open. She gazed at him, then looked down at her mug.

"I'm sorry," Chad murmured.

Staring into her coffee, she said in a low voice, "That's not something that usually requires an apology."

"You were my brother's wife."

"His widow."

"Yeah. When I left. But I loved you for a long time before that. Almost from the first time we met. It kept getting worse and worse until I couldn't even think straight anymore."

"Oh, man." She looked up at him. "I never realized."

"You weren't supposed to. Hell, I couldn't have shown my face around here if you or Jake had known. You certainly wouldn't have let me *live* with you guys after Mom died."

"Might've been a little awkward."

"And it wouldn't have accomplished anything if I'd told you. I didn't want your pity, which is about the most I could've hoped for. It was better just keeping the problem to myself."

She shook her head, frowning. She looked troubled, bewildered. "You were *in love* with me? You sure never did or said anything to make me suspect . . . When I think of all the times we spent together, just the two of us, and you never . . . My God, *you're* the one who convinced me not to leave Jake."

"I wanted to break his head in. It just tore me up, the hell he was putting you through." Thinking about it, Chad felt his throat go tight. "I hated him then for what he was doing.

He had you. He *had* you. How the hell could he even think about messing around with other women? How could he do that to you?"

Coreen reached across the table. Her hand covered his, closed around it. She looked blurry. He realized he was seeing her through tears.

"Oh, shit," he muttered. Turning away, he rubbed his eyes dry with his other hand.

"It's all right."

He sniffed. He tried to smile. "Maybe we ought to knock off this kind of talk before I make even a bigger fool out of myself."

She squeezed his hand. "I've got a better idea. Let's forget about the coffee—it's just getting cold, anyway. I'll haul out a bottle of Scotch and we'll have a little nightcap to calm us down."

"OK."

Her hand went away. She scooted back her chair and stood up. "Why don't we move into the den? It'll be more comfortable. And there're some munchies out there. You go on out. I'll be along in a minute."

She was crouching down, reaching into a cupboard when Chad walked past her and went into the den. He felt strange, a little dazed. He was ashamed that he'd wept. But he had actually gone through with his confession. Most of it, anyway. He'd admitted that he loved her. That was the main thing, and maybe that was all she really needed to know.

The sofa's seat cushions were on the floor. He was pushing the last of them into place when Coreen came in.

"Glen tore the thing apart looking for money," she said.

"Any luck?"

"He came up with a hundred-dollar bill."

"Are you serious?"

"I've got no clue as to how it got there, but it sure convinced those kids that the Ouija board was on the level."

"I'm surprised you let them fool around with that thing."

"Big mistake." She sat on the sofa, leaned over the coffee

table, and poured Scotch into the two glasses she'd brought from the kitchen. She lifted a glass.

Accepting it from her, Chad turned toward a nearby armchair.

"Just sit right here. I don't bite."

"Are you sure you can trust me?"

Her fingers hooked his side pocket. The robe started to pull open as she tugged him down. He grabbed its front and dropped onto the sofa. A tongue of Scotch slopped over the brim of his glass. It splashed his robe and seeped through to his thigh.

"I'm sorry. I didn't mean to make you spill. Do you want a paper towel?"

"It'll dry."

She turned toward him. Looking into his eyes, she took a sip. She lowered her glass. Her tongue slid across her lips. "I wish I'd known."

"Known what?"

"What do you mean, what? My God, Chad."

"It would've screwed up everything."

"Nothing. It would've screwed up nothing. You were all I had. Even before Jake was killed. Even before I found out about his other women. It was always the job, the job. I was a widow long before he walked into that 7-Eleven. From the day he pinned on his shield. Then you moved into the house, and I wasn't alone anymore. You meant so much to me."

"As a friend," he said, and took a drink. The Scotch went down, spreading heat. "If you'd known what was going on in my head . . . I was such an imposter."

"Because you *loved* me?"

"Because I loved you and because I *wanted* you. I felt sick from wanting you so much. And it got a lot worse after Jake was shot. I couldn't get it out of my mind that you were free. And we spent so much time comforting each other, holding each other. Every time I had you in my arms, I was tempted to . . . try something. I hated myself. And it kept getting worse and worse. So I left."

"Oh, Chad."

"Sooner or later . . ."

"What?"

"I might've tried to rape you."

Her eyes, deep blue and solemn, stayed fixed on him as she sipped her drink. "Maybe you should've given it a whirl."

"I'm not kidding."

"Neither am I."

"What're you saying?"

"It wouldn't have been any rape, Chad. Not the way I felt about you. I don't think it's technically possible to rape a willing partner."

"You *wanted* me?"

"I'm pretty sure I wouldn't have tried to stop you." A wry, sad smile formed on her mouth. "Now, aren't you sorry you left?"

"I was always sorry I left."

"Not as sorry as me, I'll bet."

"Don't count on it."

"At least *you* knew why. All I knew was that my only friend in the world had pulled a disappearing act. A day never went by that I didn't wonder what made you do it."

"Well. Now you know."

"Now I know. Jesus H. Christ." She gulped down the last of her drink, turned away and lowered her glass toward the table. Suddenly, she slammed it down. She twisted sideways and faced him, glaring. "I could just kill you! You think Jake put me through hell screwing around with those gals? Well just take a look in the mirror sometime!" Her voice cracked. Tears filled her eyes and streamed down her cheeks. "Damn you! Selfish son-of-a-bitch! How could you do that to a *friend*, much less someone you thought you were in *love* with?"

She shoved his chest, then turned away and curled down, hugging her head with both hands.

Chad, stunned, set his glass on the table. He put a hand on Coreen's quaking back.

"Don't touch me! Just get out of here!"

"OK."

He hurried from the living room. In the hallway, he could still hear her sobs. They felt like knife blades pounding into his chest. He shut himself into the guest room and sat down on the bed.

Dear God, what had happened?

She'd seemed to be accepting everything so well. A lot better than he'd expected. All of a sudden, WHAM! Totally bonkers. It didn't make sense.

What am I gonna do? I can't leave.

I can't stay. She told me to go.

Chad slumped forward and rubbed his face.

She couldn't have meant it.

Want to bet?

You knew it might turn out this way.

Just get dressed and get out of here. Never should've come back.

He raised his head and looked around the room for a moment before realizing that his clothes and pack were outside on the patio.

Now what?

How could he get to them without going past Coreen?

There isn't any way.

Wait a while. Maybe she'll go to bed.

He heard the faint, distant sound of running water. Probably from the bathroom.

He rushed to the door, opened it a bit, and eased his head through the gap. The bathroom door was shut.

He kept his eyes on it while he made his way through the hallway. He grimaced when the water shut off. Slowing down, he crept past the door. Three strides later, he heard it open. He kept walking. He felt sick. He ached to look back.

Don't. She told you to leave. You can't leave without your stuff.

"Chad."

Her voice seemed to grab his heart.

He stopped and turned around.

She was puffy and red around her eyes, and the crying had given her nose a ruddy, raw look. Some strands of wet hair clung to her forehead. The way the nightshirt draped the smooth mounds of her breasts and jutted over her nipples, he realized she no longer wore her bra.

"I was just going . . . to get my pack and things."

"No. Don't."

"You told me to leave."

"Do you *want* to leave?"

"No."

She walked slowly toward him. "I didn't mean those awful things I said."

"I deserved them."

"It's just that I missed you. You hurt me so much."

Chad opened his arms. She stepped between them and pressed herself against him. "I'll never hurt you again," he whispered.

"You won't leave?" she asked, her warm breath tickling the side of his neck.

"Not unless you throw me out."

She hugged him hard, then relaxed her hold and tilted back her head. He kissed her soft, open lips. Her breath went into him. She moaned and squirmed.

Chad's penis began to stiffen, lifting against her belly. He stepped away quickly and turned around. "Why don't I help you clean up the mess from your party?"

She was suddenly warm against his back. "It can wait till morning." Her hands moved slowly down the front of his robe, rubbing the soft fabric against his chest, his belly, his thighs. He felt her kissing the nape of his neck through his thick hair. He felt her breasts mashed to his back. He could feel her gasping for air. He could feel the throb of her heartbeat.

"Coreen," he gasped.

"Huh?"

"You . . . don't have to do this."

She made no answer. Her hands continued to caress him

49

through the robe. They came close to his groin, only to slide away. Their motions loosened his cloth belt. The robe opened a little. Wider when she slipped her hands inside and they roamed over his belly.

"You don't have to . . ."

"Do you still love me?"

"I'll always . . ."

"Then hush." She swept the robe off his shoulders. Only the pressure of her body kept it from falling as she rubbed his chest. Her hands glided lower. Trembling, Chad reached back. He felt the hanging tail of her nightshirt. He lifted it and caressed the smooth, warm skin of her rump. He clutched the firm mounds as her fingers curled around him, slid down the length of his shaft and gently squeezed his scrotum.

Then her hand was gone and she was stepping back. The robe fell to the floor and he turned around.

Coreen pulled the nightshirt up over her head. She dropped it and stood there, staring at him. Her eyes looked frenzied. Her mouth hung open. Her breasts rose and fell as she gasped for air. Reaching out, she took hold of his wrists.

She lifted both hands to her breasts. He could feel her trembling as he caressed them. When he stroked the nipples with his thumbs, she shuddered and caught her breath and jerked his hands away. She stretched his arms out wide to either side and eased forward, stopping when her belly met the head of his penis and her nipples touched his chest. Then she swayed slowly from side to side, gazing up into his eyes as she slid herself against him.

"Is this . . . how you imagined it?" she whispered, her voice breathless and husky.

"Nothing quite like this. Whatever it is you're doing."

She continued to sway. Chad felt himself leaving a wet, slick path across her belly.

Keeping his arms outstretched, she raised them overhead. She pressed downward and remained standing while he sank to his knees. He kissed her belly. She released his wrists, and he caressed the backs of her thighs.

Holding onto his shoulders, she spread her legs far apart and slowly squatted down. The inner sides of her thighs rubbed his chest. So did the tuft of hair between them. The hair felt wet. She slid lower, her belly tight against him. He clutched her buttocks as she descended. Then his face was between her breasts. He turned his head and kissed the side of one. It slid away from his lips.

She eased lower, taking Chad into her. She was tight and slick and deep. She kept easing down. She seemed to be sucking him into her core. Then her face was level with his. She kissed him on the mouth.

"Welcome home," she whispered.

Chapter Six

When Howard finished packing, he went to the window of his second-floor apartment and looked down. A few cars were parked along the curb. Lana's Ford Granada wasn't among them.

The road stretched away, empty and desolate, a bleak gray under the streetlights, black in shadows cast by the trees.

He didn't want to go out there.

He didn't want to leave the safety of his room and venture into the night, not with those people, not on such a bizarre quest.

He'd given his word, though.

Angela was counting on him. He couldn't let her down.

But he had no intention of betraying Dr. Dalton, either.

He should've phoned her the minute he got into his apartment. Instead, he'd only *thought* about it. Thought about it while he changed his clothes, while he packed.

Procrastinating.

You're such a chicken. Scared to blow the whistle on them.

Wait long enough, and maybe you wait too long. Lana shows up, and then you've got an excuse not to make the call at all.

Already, it was probably too late for Dr. Dalton to intervene. If he'd called earlier, she might've driven over in time to intercept the group, stop the whole thing.

There still might be time.

He stepped around to the other side of his bed, picked up the photocopied invitation to the professor's party, and sat down beside his nightstand. His hands shook as he unfolded the paper. At the bottom, beneath directions to her house, was her telephone number.

Should I?

She *has* to be told.

Maybe she'll ask me to stall them. Shouldn't take her more than ten minutes to get here. I could figure out a way to slow them down. Maybe tell them I've gotta use the john. Then just stay in there and wait for her.

He checked his wristwatch. 1:35. More than an hour had passed since they'd left her house. She might be asleep by now.

So wake her.

Maybe she hasn't gone to bed yet, anyway. She'd said something about staying up to all hours, talking with that guy who'd dropped in.

Her brother-in-law.

God, she'd actually been married to someone. A widow. Maybe that explained why she seemed to be such a loner. Maybe she's still in mourning, or something.

Howard realized his mind was wandering. He'd better make the call before it was too late. Lana could show up any minute.

He lifted the phone off the nightstand, set it on his lap, and picked up the handset. The dial tone buzzed in his ear.

He stared at the number on the invitation. His heart thundered.

Do it!

He took a deep breath, trying to calm himself. Then he

punched in her number, listening to the strange, brief tune.

What'll I tell her?

Just the truth.

He heard the first ring.

I'm probably scaring the hell out of her. A call this time of night, she'll think someone died.

He pictured her at the kitchen table, flinching, maybe spilling her coffee. Now she's scooting back her chair. Getting up. Saying *Who could be calling at this hour?* to that Chad guy. Hurrying toward the telephone. Was there an extension in her kitchen? He didn't know.

How many times had it rung?

Six or seven, at least.

Eight. Nine.

Where *are* you?

Even if she was already asleep, the first couple of rings should've awakened her. She could have easily gotten to a phone by this time.

Twelve.

And what about that Chad guy? Can't *he* pick up the phone?

Maybe they went out somewhere.

Maybe I've got the wrong number.

Maybe Butler isn't letting the call get through.

Don't be stupid, he told himself. I've probably got a wrong number and the phone's ringing its head off in an empty house—the owners on vacation or something.

Hang up and try again?

By now, it must've rung nineteen or twenty times.

He lowered the handset onto the cradle. He stared at the invitation. He was certain he hadn't punched in any wrong numbers: he'd watched his finger peck every key. Maybe, somehow, an incorrect number had ended up on the invitation.

But he knew she was listed in the directory. He'd called her a couple of times.

He set the telephone on the floor, got to his knees in front of the nightstand, lifted the magazines stacked on its bottom shelf, and started to pull out the directory.

The beep of a car horn stopped him.

They're here!

Shoving the phone book into place, he rushed to the window. A car was stopped on the street. But it didn't look like Lana's Granada. Hers didn't have a luggage rack.

It does now, he realized. Must be one of those clamp-on, removeable things.

The rack was empty except for a single backpack and a small suitcase. A suitcase?

The horn honked again.

Great going, Lana. Wake up the whole neighborhood, why don't you?

He hurried to the bed, hefted his pack and shoved his arms into its straps. On his way to the door, he patted the pockets of his jeans. Keys. Wallet. Knife. Checkbook, just in case.

Forgetting anything?

Address book?

He remembered sliding it into his pack. Sometime tomorrow, maybe when they stopped for supplies, he needed to phone home so his parents wouldn't end up waiting for him at the airport.

He'd once considered writing Dr. Dalton's number in his address book. But he'd decided against it on the grounds that someone might see it there and wonder.

Feeble. Big deal if someone saw it.

He gave the telephone a final glance, then opened his door, switched off the light, and stepped into the corridor.

As he strode toward the car, its passenger door opened. Glen climbed out and came around to the near side. "Let me have it, pal." He took the pack and hefted it onto the luggage rack. While he was strapping it into place, Howard ducked and looked into the car.

Lana was behind the wheel, Keith sitting beside her. Doris sat alone in the backseat.

Glen slapped the pack. "All set." He hurried around to the other side.

Howard opened the rear door, got in, and swung it shut.

"OK," Lana said. "We pick up Angela, then we're off."

"Off to see the Wizard," Keith said.

The car shook as Glen dropped onto the front seat. His door slammed.

"Don't break it," Lana muttered. Then she stepped on the gas.

Howard felt cold and tight in his stomach as he watched his apartment house slip out of sight. He doubted that he would've felt much worse if he were being abducted by strangers. Four other people in the car, but not a real friend or ally among them.

It'll be better once Angela's here.

Not that she was much more than an acquaintance, really. He'd rarely seen her outside classes. Their only bond, at least until tonight, seemed to be that neither of them quite fit in. They both slinked about, cloaked in shyness. Like fugitives fearing discovery. Similar that way, recognizing it, and being drawn together—though never close enough to become real friends.

Doris was an outsider, too. But of a different kind. She considered herself superior to everyone else, and made no secret of it. Howard could barely stand her. To be trapped in the backseat beside her all night . . .

Maybe Angela will back out.

If she does, I'm not going either.

He looked out the window. They were passing the university. The sight of the old, familiar buildings, lawns and walkways should've been comforting. But tonight the campus seemed forbidding. Howard imagined figures hiding near the walkways, shadowy forms lurching through empty classrooms. He turned his gaze to the back of Lana's head.

He wished someone would talk. The silence didn't seem natural.

As the car turned onto Tenth Street and entered the

town's deserted business district, he decided to break the silence himself. "Where does Angela live?"

"You know that thrift shop over on Cherry?" Lana asked.

"Huh-uh."

"Across from the secondhand book store," Doris explained. "Gabby's."

"Oh." He'd been to Gabby's just once. During his freshman year. And avoided that neighborhood, ever since. "She *lives* there?"

"Up above the thrift shop," Lana said.

"Jesus." How could she live in an area like that? And without a car. What about those nights she worked late at the campus library? Walking home alone . . . How does she stand it?

"You should've seen the weirdos hanging around when we dropped her off," Keith said.

"They're not weirdos," Doris protested. "They're merely indigents who haven't had the good fortune to . . ."

"So adopt one, why don't you? There's one now. Take him home with you."

Howard spotted the man—a shabby, bearded specter tipping a bag-wrapped bottle to his mouth. In spite of the balmy night, he wore an overcoat. His pants looked too big. Their cuffs dragged on the sidewalk as he shambled along.

Lana turned the corner. Onto Cherry Street.

Howard saw a dark figure curled in the recessed entryway of a pawn shop.

Lana drove slowly past the sleeping derelict. She swung to the curb in front of a thrift shop. She stopped. She beeped the horn.

"Neat play," Glen said.

"Do you want to go up and get her?"

"Thanks but no thanks." He started cranking up his window.

The window beside Doris was already shut. She reached forward and punched down her lock button.

Keith glanced back at her. "What'd you do that for? You aren't *scared* of these poor unfortunates, are you?"

She didn't answer.

Howard cringed as Lana honked the horn again.

"She probably heard you the first time," Keith said.

"Along with every wino on the block," Glen added.

"So what? They're drunks, not cannibals."

"You hope," Glen said.

"Just give her a few minutes," Keith said.

They waited. Only Lana's window remained down. Howard wished she would roll it up and lock her door. Wasn't she nervous at all about being here?

She'll probably roll it up in record time if a bum comes along.

One was across the street, standing in front of the closed liquor store next to Gabby's. He seemed to be watching them. He stood motionless except for his right hand. Every few seconds, he rapped on the side of his head.

Howard twisted around and glanced out the rear window. The area behind the car looked clear. The horn had probably awakened the wino in the doorway back there, but he wasn't coming.

"One of us had better go up and see what's keeping her," Lana finally said.

"How about it, Howitzer?"

Lana turned and looked back at him. "Would you mind? You know her better than we do."

"Well . . ." He didn't want to look like a coward in front of Lana.

"Please?"

"Sure. Why not?"

"Good man," Glen said.

Lana stretched an arm across the seatback, pointing at the thrift shop. "There's an outside stairway over on the right. She went in the door at the top."

"All right."

Howard pushed open his door, glanced back to be sure no one was coming, then stepped into the street and swung the door shut.

The thrift shop was dark, its entrance and display windows caged for the night behind a folding metal gate. The second story windows glowed with murky light that seeped through stained, yellow shades.

Howard moved around the rear of the car. The stairway, just ahead, was in a narrow, dark space between the thrift shop and the pawn shop.

He crossed the sidewalk and stopped at the foot of the stairs. He peered up them. Too dark. He couldn't be sure they were clear. But he couldn't turn back.

Taking a deep breath, he started to climb. The boards creaked under his weight. His legs trembled. He dug a hand into the pocket of his jeans, and felt a little better as he gripped the smooth plastic handle of his Swiss Army knife.

Not that he would have time to pull it and get a blade out . . .

With each step, he expected to collide with a foul, dark shape.

How can Angela climb these stairs at night?

At last, he reached the small balcony at the top. He knocked on the screen door and called out softly, "Angela, it's me. Howard."

Nothing.

He knocked again.

What if they sent me to the wrong place? Somebody's idea of a big joke. Take the wimp for a ride to the worst part of town, make him get out and knock on a stranger's door. A laugh a minute.

No, they're too serious about going after Butler's treasure to waste time fooling around.

A latch clacked. The inner door swung open. Just a crack. A strip of light spilled out.

"Go away." The voice was high, raspy. He couldn't tell whether it belonged to a man or a woman. It sure didn't sound like Angela.

He ached to whirl away and run down the stairs.

"Is this where Angela Logan lives?" he asked.

"No. Get the fuck outa here."

"OK. But I thought . . ."

From somewhere beyond the opening came a rough thud. Like a wall or door being kicked.

"*Angela!*" he called.

And heard the faint cry of his name.

"Hey, what do you mean, she's not here!"

"Fuck off."

Who is this? Her mother? Her father?

The door started to shut.

"What is she, locked up or something? I'm gonna call the cops."

The door stopped, still open an inch.

Another thud.

"Howard?" Distant, muffled.

What the hell's going on?

Should he rush down to the car, bring back Keith and Glen? They'd tease him. *What's the trouble, Howitzer?* Besides, this might be some kind of a family thing. He didn't want to give them ammunition to use for taunting Angela.

"I just want to talk to her for a minute. If you won't let me, I swear I'll call the cops."

"She's busy."

"The cops, then." Howard took a step toward the stairs.

Light flooded out as the door swung wide. The screen door was pushed open by a skinny, hunchbacked old man wearing only boxer shorts. Except for his bald head, he was furry with gray hair. His face looked greasy with sweat. His eyes were huge behind thick glasses. "Comin' around fuckin' with me this time a night. Get in here, you slimy little bastard."

"Why don't you . . . just have her come to the door?"

"Y'want her, come in 'n see her."

"All right." Howard held open the screen door, waiting while the man turned and began to hobble away. He tried not to look at the hump. It was knobby and bristling with hair.

He stepped inside. Stuffy, hot air wrapped around him. It reeked of cigar smoke.

The screen door banged shut at his back. From the appcarance of the old man, he'd expected the room to be a filthy ruin. The furniture was old, but there was no mess. The place looked tidy and clean. If not for the awful heat and the stinky haze of cigar smoke, it might have been reasonably pleasant in here.

Why didn't the old creep open some windows?

"Just gonna stand there?" With a gesture of his hairy arm, he signaled Howard to follow.

Another thump. From the hallway at the other end of the room.

"Hold yer water. I'm comin."

They entered the hallway and stopped at a closed door. From behind it came a soft hum. Maybe from a fan. An electrical cord ran under the door and was stretched along the hallway baseboard, joining an extension that led into the front room.

"Angela?"

"Howard?" Her voice came through the door. "You'd better . . . just go away."

"Why?" If she didn't want help, why had she called out his name? "What's going on?"

"Nothing. Just go. Please."

"This the slimy bastard ya was out with tonight?"

"I told you, it was a school party."

"Did he fuck ya?"

"No!"

"Slut."

"Nobody did anything wrong," Howard said, his mind reeling with confusion and anger. And shame. If this guy knew what had really happened . . .

"Howard. Please. You're just making things worse. Just go. Tell the others I'm sick."

"Have a look 'n see what y'done to her."

"Skerrit, no! Please!"

Chuckling, the old man knocked back the bolt and pulled the door open.

Chapter Seven

Heat gushed out. So did odors of sweat and menthol.

The closet glowed red.

Not a fan, but a space heater hummed on the floor at Angela's feet.

Howard stared at Angela.

This can't be.

She was standing near the back of the small enclosure, her outstretched arms bound at the wrists to the clothes bar. She was dressed in a sweatsuit. Maybe more than one; the garments made her thick and bulky. The gray outer layer appeared wet. Her stringy hair looked glued to her head. Her ruddy face dripped.

She turned her head aside as if embarrassed.

"Tell him to fuck off," Skerrit said.

"Go away, Howard," she murmured. "Please."

"What *is* this!"

"You heard her, get outa here."

"I'm just being punished. It's all right."

"All *right*?" Howard lurched forward, crouched into the

62

awful heat and twisted the knob at the top of the heater.

"Hey!" Skerrit grabbed his shoulder.

Howard sprang up, whirled around, and rammed both hands against the man's sweaty chest. Skerrit gasped and stumbled away.

"No!" Angela blurted.

His back—his *hump*—pounded the wall. His glasses fell off. His knees folded, and he slipped down the wall until his rump met the floor.

Howard watched, shocked by what he'd done to the man. Skerrit glared up at him.

"Stay down! Stay down, damn it!" He dug into his pocket. He pulled his knife and pried out a blade.

"Don't hurt him!"

"Y'slimy bastard, I'll . . ."

"Shut up! Don't move!" He turned away, ducking, and hurled the space heater into the hallway. Then he stepped deeper into the closet. So damned hot. "Was he trying to kill you, or something?"

"Oh, Howard."

The menthol in the stifling air made his nostrils sting as he started cutting through the ropes. "What's that smell?"

"Ben-Gay."

"Huh?"

"You know, the heating rub. An ointment. He uses it for his arthritis."

The locker room odor. He suddenly remembered. High school. Track. Rubbing Ben-Gay on his sore legs. And how it felt like fire.

"You've got some *on* you?"

"All over." Her voice trembled.

He finished cutting her loose. "On your *skin*? Under those sweats?"

She sagged against him and wrapped her arms around him.

"*Skerrit* did that to you?"

She nodded.

"My God." He turned sideways and walked her out of the

closet. The fabric under his hands was wet. And thick. How many sweatshirts was she wearing?

He eased her against a wall. She sagged, but stayed up.

Skerrit was still sitting on the floor. He'd put his glasses back on. His magnified eyes looked enormous and scornful.

"Get up," Howard said. He waved his knife toward the closet. "Get in there."

"Y'gonna let him, Angel?"

"Howard. Don't. Please."

"How can you stick up for this guy?"

"I *live* with him. He lets me stay here free."

"So he can *torture* you?"

"You don't understand."

"I sure don't. Skerrit, get into that closet."

The old man struggled to his feet. He turned his bulgy eyes toward Angela. "Yer gonna be real sorry."

Howard grabbed his slippery arm and swung him into the closet. He threw the door shut. He bolted it.

"I'll let him out when we leave."

"I can't go anywhere."

"You can't stay. He's a madman."

"Not really. He's just . . . strict."

"Strict?"

"Yeah." Leaning forward a little, she clutched the bottom of her sweatshirt and peeled it up. It dragged a red sweatshirt and a second gray one along with it. She struggled with all three, tugged them over her head, and tossed them to the floor. She was left wearing a faded blue sweatshirt that looked as if she'd taken a shower in it.

"He's only done that to me a few times," she said.

"Only a few times? How thoughtful of him."

She stepped away from the wall, drew several layers of sweatpants away from her waist, and pulled down all but the blue pair. Stepping on them, she freed her bare feet.

"He's OK usually. It was just because I snuck out for the party."

"He's a madman. You can't live with someone like him."

"I've got nowhere else."

"Fuckin' right, Angel."

She grimaced. She looked at Howard with bleak, desolate eyes.

"You shut up in there."

"He's right," Angela whispered. "I just can't afford to stay anywhere . . ."

"Don't worry about that. I'll help you find a place."

She shook her head. "Just go and tell the others I'm sick. I can't go."

"You'll go if I have to drag you. But I'd better tell them something. They're waiting down on the street. Why don't you take a shower and I'll be back in a couple of minutes."

She glanced at the closet door.

"Don't even think about letting him out." Howard took her by the arm. The sleeve was drenched. "Where's the john?"

She nodded to an open door just up the hall. He led her toward it. The sleeve slid a little on her skin. Sweat and Ben-Gay.

"Take a real good shower. I'll be sitting next to you in the car. I don't want to be smelling that stuff all the way to Calamity Peak."

She gave him a forlorn smile that tore his heart.

He guided her into the bathroom, turned on the light, and stepped out. "You'd better lock the door, just in case he gets out. But I'll be right back. Don't worry about anything."

"You won't tell them about Skerrit, will you?"

"No. No way."

He pulled the door shut. He waited for the clack of the lock, then hurried away. As he walked past the closet door, he gave it a hard punch. A gasp came from the other side. He kept on walking.

He made his way down the outside stairway, remembering how nervous he'd been on the way up. Worried about running into a wino. Ridiculous. Scared of winos, and Angela's living with a sadistic lunatic.

A man. Old and deformed, but a man. Who let her stay

without paying. Just so he could punish her whenever he got the urge? What else did he use her for?

Free room or not, how could she live with someone like that? Unless she's just as weird as he is. Or so poor and desperate that she'll accept any situation just in order to finish college.

Howard stepped off the final stair, strode past the corner of the thrift shop, and halted on the sidewalk.

Lana's car was gone.

"Oh, great," he muttered.

He glanced up and down the street. Her car was nowhere in sight.

He saw no derelicts, though he supposed some might be lurking about, out of sight.

Where had Lana gone?

I wasn't up there all that long. Maybe ten minutes?

Did they leave without us?

The possibility seemed remote.

But if they'd really left, he was freed from having to accompany them on their crazy search for Butler's fortune. He could go back to the safety of his apartment and forget about it.

But what about Angela? Would she come with him? Spend the night with him?

The chance of that excited him, but the disappearance of Lana and the others left him feeling abandoned, tricked, humiliated—like a kid ditched by his playmates.

Maybe they never intended to take us along.

A bigger split for the rest of them.

But what about Doris's theory that Butler might *want* him and Angela . . . ?

A car turned the corner at the end of the block. Squinting against the glare of its headlights, Howard made out the luggage rack.

They changed their minds?

He muttered, "Shit."

But in ways he felt relieved.

The car swung toward the curb and stopped in front of him.

"Where's Angie?" Glen asked.

Howard stepped up close to his open window. "She isn't ready yet."

"Figures," Keith said. "Women."

"Well, she's a little sick. She's in the bathroom."

"A case of the trots?" Glen asked.

"Yeah. Where'd you guys go?"

"Some asshole came across the street to visit with us. Figured it'd be less hassle if we kept moving."

"We've been circling the block," Lana said from the far side of the seat.

"I thought you might've left without us."

"Wishful thinking, Howitzer."

"Will Angela be much longer?" Lana asked.

"Maybe another ten minutes. I'm not sure. I told her I'd go back up and help her pack."

"What a Boy Scout," Glen said.

"OK," Lana said. "We'll keep circling. Try to hurry her up. We've got a lot of miles ahead of us."

"All right. See you later."

The car pulled away. Howard rushed back up the stairs and entered the living room. He heard water running as he went to the hallway. He checked the closet door. Still bolted shut. He supposed Skerrit was capable of bashing it open. But maybe the creep was afraid of him, preferred to stay locked up rather than risk being attacked again.

Howard felt guilty, remembering how he'd shoved the old man.

What if I'd really hurt him? Jeez, he's gotta be close to seventy.

He stepped close to the door. "Skerrit, are you all right in there?"

"Le' me alone, y' cocksucker."

"I'll let you out when we're ready to leave."

"Y' take her away, I'll kill y' both."

"You'll have to find us first, you miserable old shit." Stupid remark, Howard thought, hurrying up the hall. Arrogant and childish. Like giving the finger to a bully who's threatened to clean your clock.

He stepped to the bathroom door. The water was still going. As long as she's in the shower, he thought, it's safe.

Feeling like a sneak, he went to the doorway across the hall and looked in. A lamp was on beside the bed. A single bed, neatly made. A bureau, a rocking chair. Everything tidy except for a pair of old loafers on the floor, trousers and a shirt tossed across the bed. Must be Skerrit's room.

Heart pounding, he hurried on. The only remaining doorway was on the left. He went to it, reached into the darkness and flicked a switch. After pausing for a moment to make sure he could still hear the shower, he entered the room.

A minty aroma of Ben-Gay lingered in the hot air.

This must be where Skerrit had put the stuff on her.

The scene of the crime. Angela's bedroom.

A mattress on the floor beneath the window. A plaid sleeping bag spread out on the mattress. On the sleeping bag, a gray stuffed kitten with a missing ear. Along one wall, a couple of cardboard boxes, clothes neatly stacked inside. In one corner, a folding chair, a card table with a portable typewriter among stacked books and binders. A doorless closet. Inside it, a few garments on hangers, a pair of shoes and a suitcase on the floor.

More a cell than a bedroom.

God, the poor girl. To be living like this.

Howard's throat tightened.

He lowered his gaze to the clothing she'd worn to the party. The garments were strewn about the floor as if they'd been flung from her: the pleated skirt, the blue blouse, the white socks and sneakers; red, bikini-style panties; the flimsy little see-through bra.

Had Skerrit stripped her naked, throwing the clothes every which way?

When he saw the kind of undergarments she wore, the old creep must've really gotten mad.

Or turned on.

Maybe he *forced* her to wear such things. Maybe he even bought them for her. No telling what might've gone on between the two of them.

Crouching, Howard picked up the bra. He stared at his fingers through the wispy fabric and remembered how her breasts had looked. Small and smooth, with such large nipples.

Had Skerrit actually rubbed them with the heating ointment?

He'd put the stuff all over. That's what Angela had said. *All* over?

That dirty bastard!

The faint hissing sound of the shower went silent. Howard gasped and dropped the bra. A wave of guilt swept through him, as if he'd already been caught. He stood up fast.

She still has to dry off, he told himself as he hurried for the door.

What door?

Hinges on the frame, but there was no door at her bedroom entrance.

That fucking bastard!

Once in the hallway, he slowed down. He walked as quietly as possible past the bathroom, past the closet, and on into the living room. He sat in an armchair just as he heard a door open. Then came soft footfalls.

Angela stopped under the hallway entrance. A white towel was wrapped around her waist. She held another towel to her chest. Her black hair clung to her head, draped her shoulders. She gave him a timid smile. "Oh, OK. I just wanted to make sure you were back."

"Feeling any better?"

"A lot. Thanks."

"I talked to the others. They want us to hurry."

She looked worried. "You didn't tell them anything, did you?"

"They think you've got the runs."

"Oh, wonderful," she said, and a real smile spread over her face. "Thanks a lot."

"Would you like some help getting your stuff together?"

"No, it's fine. You just stay there. I'll be quick." She turned away. Howard glimpsed her bare back, the curves of her buttocks through the towel. Then she vanished up the hallway.

He took a deep, shaky breath as he pictured her walking toward her bedroom. He began to imagine himself following her, spying on her. No door.

Cut it out!

That's the kind of shit Skerrit must pull.

Howard scanned the living room, trying to distract his mind from dwelling on Angela.

And saw a telephone on a stand near the kitchen entrance.

Try Dr. Dalton again? Maybe this time she'll answer.

He would have to look up her number or call directory assistance, but . . .

Are you nuts?

Thank God his last attempt to phone Dr. Dalton had failed. What if he'd told her about the plan and she'd put a halt to it?

We've *got* to go after Butler's treasure, he realized. Angela can't come back and live with this maniac. Hell, I won't let her. And money's her only way out. Even if we're wasting our time on a wild-goose chase, we've got to try for it.

Finding that money is her only chance.

Not her only chance, he thought. There's me.

He heard Angela's voice. She was talking softly, and he couldn't make out the words.

He pushed himself out of the chair, took a couple of steps toward the hallway, then stopped.

It's none of my business.

"Y'can't go!" Skerrit whined. "What'm I gonna do?"

Angela spoke some more.

"Maybe I'll just throw yer stuff out, how'd you like that? Burn it all."

What if she lets him out?

Howard walked to the hallway entrance. Angela was leaning forward, both hands against the closet door, her head down. She wore the clothes that had been scattered around her bedroom floor. Her hair was pulled back in a ponytail. Her suitcase and the rolled bundle of her sleeping bag rested on the floor beside her. She glanced at Howard, then turned her eyes to the door. "It'll just be a few days," she said. "Please. You can get along without me for a few days, can't you? It's important."

"Y' go 'n yul be sorry! Sorry ya was ever born!"

Her open hand slapped the door. "Skerrit!"

"All I done for ya!"

She glanced again at Howard. Her eyes were red and shiny. "I've got to go."

"Then go, cunt! Rot in Hell!"

She pushed herself away from the door. Bending over, she picked up her suitcase and sleeping bag. She came toward Howard, her lips pressed hard together, chin trembling.

"Are you all right?" he whispered.

She shook her head.

"It'll be better once we're on our way."

"I never should've gone out tonight. None of this . . . He was supposed to be drunk. He's *always* drunk by ten or eleven. I figured he'd be passed out, you know? He wasn't supposed to *catch* me. I'd just sneak in and out, and . . ."

"DON'T GO!"

Angela flinched.

"Come on." Howard lifted the suitcase from her hand. He took her gently by the elbow and led her toward the front door. "Go on down to the street. I'll be along in a minute."

"You're going to let him out?"

"Yes."

"Don't hurt him."

71

"I won't."

He stepped outside with her and set down the suitcase. "If the car isn't there, don't worry. It'll be along pretty soon."

"Oh God, Howard. I shouldn't be doing this."

"Everything'll work out fine. I promise."

She looked into his eyes for a moment, then started down the stairs.

He went back inside. At the hallway entrance, he paused and pulled off his shoes. He crept silently to the closet door.

From its other side came wrenching sobs.

The old creep was blubbering.

Howard carefully slid back the bolt. Turning away, he tiptoed back to where he'd left his shoes. He pushed his feet into them, then hurried to the front door. On the balcony, he picked up the suitcase. He eased the door shut and rushed down the stairs.

Chapter Eight

When Corie woke up in the morning, she turned her head and saw Chad beside her on the bed. He lay on his side, facing the other way, the sheet covering him to the hips.

He's really here. He finally came back to me.

She felt as if her heart were swelling with joy. She resisted a sudden urge to slide over and curl herself against the smoothness of his back and hold him.

Let him sleep. He had a rough night.

Smiling, she turned her gaze to the ceiling and folded her hands behind her head. She took a deep, lazy breath. She had no sheet at all, but that was fine. The breeze from the open window rolled over her skin like soft, caressing waves. It carried aromas of grass and pines.

Maybe I'll just lie here all day. Or at least until he wakes up. We'll make love, and then we'll make breakfast.

She stretched, savoring the mild stiffness of her muscles and her knowledge of how they had gotten that way.

You really took a beating, kid. Inside and out. You'll probably spend the day walking bow-legged.

73

She laughed softly, but it didn't seem to disturb Chad's slumber.

Why don't I go ahead and wake him up?

Brush my teeth first.

She got up slowly, careful not to jostle the bed, and moved toward the door.

Not so bad, she thought.

In the hallway, she smiled down at her nightshirt, Chad's robe. She stared at them, and it was last night again. Chad on his knees as she sank onto him. The feel of him pushing into her. How neither of them had moved for a long time, as if stilled by astonishment that finally, finally, they were joined and they wanted it to last forever.

Then the telephone had started ringing.

"Aren't you going to get it?" Chad had murmured.

"Are you out of your mind?"

Then she had lifted herself, pushing at his shoulders and feeling him leave a long empty space in her depths, an aching hollowness that she savored for a few moments while the telephone continued to ring, that she filled by dropping down, plunging him all the way up.

The telephone.

Who the hell *had* called at that hour?

And let it ring forever?

The thing was still clamoring when she lost her footing and went down on her back and Chad thrust so hard that he scooted her over the carpet and that thrust was one too many for both of them.

When she could breathe again, she'd said, "I don't know how it was for you, but I heard bells."

He'd laughed, his flat belly jiggling against her, his penis twitching a little deep inside her. "I finished fast so you could answer it," he said.

"Very considerate, but you were a tad too late."

"Sorry. I tried."

"Probably just a wrong number or a crank, anyway. If it's important, they'll call back."

Nobody had called back.

It couldn't have been anything too urgent, she told herself now as she crouched and picked up the nightshirt. If there was a real problem . . . if something had happened to Mom or Dad . . . Not likely. Somebody would've called again.

That's what she had told herself last night when worries had intruded a few times. At one point, after Chad had left her to use the bathroom, she'd considered getting out of bed and calling home. By then, however, it was after two in the morning. She didn't relish the idea of waking them up. Hell, *they'd* think some tragedy had struck.

So call them now. Just to make sure.

She slipped into her nightshirt, carried the robe into her bedroom and draped it over the end of the bed, then crept out of the room and went to the kitchen phone. She glanced at the clock. Five after nine. They were probably up by now.

She tapped in their number.

It rang only twice. "Hello?"

"Hi, Mom. How're things?"

"Oh, dear. I'm afraid your father's already left for golf. He'll be disappointed he missed you."

They're fine. I *knew* they would be, she thought, but she felt a tightness in her throat.

"Is everything OK?" Mom asked.

"Sure. I finished my summer-school classes yesterday, and just thought I'd call."

"Will you be coming down?"

"Maybe in a couple of weeks. I'm not sure just when, yet."

"Well, just let us know. We're seeing our Tiburon group the last week in August, but other than that, we're pretty much free."

"Great. I'll give you a call in a few days." Should I tell? "Hey, guess who showed up last night. Chad."

"Chad?"

"Yeah. He just popped in. I was throwing a party for the kids in one of my classes, the doorbell rang about midnight, and there he was."

Silence. Shouldn't have told her.

"I hope he came equipped with a good excuse."

75

"Mom."

"I suppose you've forgotten all about the hell he put you through. Leaving you all alone at a time like that. Just when you were starting to get better, and he walks out without so much as a goodbye. I sure hope you gave that young man a piece of your mind."

"I did," Coreen admitted, blushing now as she remembered how she'd raved at him.

"And what did he have to say for himself?"

"He was sorry he left."

"I'll just bet he was. Did he tell you why he did it?"

"It was just that he didn't feel right, staying any longer. With Jake gone . . . he thought he didn't belong in the house anymore. You know, like he was intruding. It was just a misunderstanding, really. He didn't realize how I felt about him."

"That's still no excuse."

"Maybe not. Anyway, it all happened a long time ago, and he's back now."

"Exactly why is he back?"

The question surprised her. "I don't know," she said. I really don't. "He got in pretty late and I never got around to asking him that."

"Well, I should think you might want to know."

"I do. I'll ask him. He's not up yet, but . . ."

"Well, I suggest that when he *gets* up, you make certain to find out exactly why a young man all of a sudden drops in unexpectedly in the middle of the night after all these years. For all you know, he might be in some kind of trouble. I think you should most definitely question him on that topic. That would've been the first thing out of my mouth even before I so much as let him into the house. He's been gone a long time, and he always was a little peculiar. No telling what he might've gotten himself into."

"I'm sure he's not in any trouble, Mom. Anyway, I'd better go now. I left the bacon on the skillet. Say 'hi' to Dad for me, OK?"

"I will. And you watch yourself with Chad. You just can't be too . . ."

"I know. I've really got to go, Mom."

"All right. I'll tell your father that you called. Goodbye now, honey."

"Bye-bye, Mom. Talk to you soon." She hung up and slumped against the kitchen wall.

Lord! When will I learn to keep my mouth shut? Probably never. But at least I didn't blab everything.

She went into the living room, noticed the mess from the party, and began to collect empty snack bowls, used glasses and napkins. Her buoyant mood was gone. Leave it to Mom to put a damper on things.

It's only because she worries about me. And she's right, I do need to find out why Chad decided to return.

Does it matter?

It might.

Until now, Coreen realized, she'd simply assumed that he had returned because he could no longer stand to be away from her. But maybe there was a different reason.

Suppose he'd had a woman? Maybe they'd broken up, and that was why he finally came back. On the rebound. Hoping to get lucky.

He got lucky, all right.

Coreen suddenly felt used and humiliated—and worried. The way he'd talked about his passion for her, she hadn't even considered the possibility that he might've been with other women. Stupid!

Good God, let's not jump to conclusions. And so what if there *was* someone else?

Plenty of what.

I never would've thrown myself at him like that.

We didn't even use condoms. Shit!

Protection had been the furthest thing from her mind. But if he'd been with one woman, maybe he'd been with dozens. Who knows? Maybe he picked up AIDS . . .

Don't think about it! You're letting your imagination run

wild. For all you know, he never touched anyone. Just calm down. Finish cleaning up.

She returned to the living room once again and looked around. No more mess. All taken care of.

Seeing the couch, she wondered what Glen had done with the condom wrapper. Probably kept it as a souvenir.

Jeez, they all thought it was mine.

That damn Ouija board led them right to it.

Butler. Almost as if he knew the wrapper was there, and lured Glen to the sofa with a promise of money just so it would be found. A typical Ouija-board brand of mischief. Toy around with people. Humiliate them.

I sure don't want that wrapper popping up again.

Coreen got down on her knees and crawled the length of the sofa, running her hand along the gap at its bottom. She found a potato chip, but not the wrapper. She tossed the broken chip onto the table, then headed for the shelves.

If *I* was embarrassed, poor Angela probably wanted to curl up and die.

Never should've let it go that far.

Never should've let it start.

Stretching upward on tiptoes, she reached high and grabbed the Ouija board's box. She slid it forward, along with the games stacked on top of it. When the box was halfway out, she strained higher and shoved the other games back.

"Good morning."

She flinched a little, startled, then looked over her shoulder at Chad. "Morning."

"Could you use a hand?"

"I'm gonna throw this damn thing away before it causes more trouble," she said. She pulled it out some more.

"I'll get it for you." He started toward her.

"That's OK." She pushed back the upper games. She almost had the Ouija box clear when he wrapped his arms around her and kissed the side of her neck. The kiss sent pleasant shivers through her. Squirming, she lost her grip on the box. It fell. Its edge bumped the tops of her toes, but didn't hurt.

She nudged it out of the way, turned around and embraced Chad. When he tried to kiss her mouth, she murmured, "No, just a second." Her heart was pounding, but not with excitement. She felt a little sick. And the shocked, crushed look in Chad's eyes didn't help. Not at all.

"What's wrong?"

"We . . . need to talk."

He actually winced. "Sure. OK."

"Hey, it's no big thing."

"Yes, it is. When someone says 'we need to talk,' it's always a big thing." He lowered his arms as if he thought she might find his touch offensive.

Coreen kept her arms around him. He felt hot through the robe. "It's just that . . . I'm wondering why you finally came back."

"That's all?" Such relief in his voice.

"Pretty much."

"I came back for you."

"But why? After all that time . . ."

"It took me that long to grow up. I was just a kid when I left here."

"You weren't a kid. You're only two years younger than me."

"But I wasn't ready for you. I wasn't good enough. I was fat, immature, an emotional wreck. You deserved a lot better."

"That's silly. I loved you."

"Maybe so, but I was a loser. I had to stay away until I was good enough for you. Until *I* felt I was good enough for you."

She smiled. "So now you think you are?"

"I came back, didn't I?"

"That you did." She squeezed him hard, then looked again into his eyes. "Came back all strong and hairy."

His hands returned to her, big and warm through the nightshirt, sliding down until they curled over her bottom.

"Were there . . . very many others?" she whispered.

"Other what?"

"Women."

He didn't answer. Coreen's heart felt as if it were trying to punch its way out of her chest.

"Chad? Were there?"

"None like you."

"But you had lovers?"

"Does it matter?"

"Yes!"

"Good." He sounded amused.

"Did you?"

"This really bugs you, doesn't it?"

"I just want to know."

"How about you?"

"I asked you first."

"It's an awfully personal question, you know."

"Your hands on my butt are awfully personal, you know." They gave her a firm squeeze. "Chad? Tell me."

"There were a few women," he said. "Some became very good friends. But I never went to bed with any of them."

Relieved, she asked, "Did you go to the hallway floor with any of them?"

He laughed for a moment, then moved his hands up her back and pulled her more closely against him. "There's been nobody else. Not since I met you."

"Nobody? Not since we met? Not even in college? You're kidding, right?"

"I know it might seem a little crazy."

"It sounds downright insane."

"Well, you asked. Would you be happier if I admitted to sleeping with a dozen other women? I don't think you wanted to hear that, did you?"

"Not really. But it's the truth? You didn't sleep with any-one?"

"It's the truth."

"Jeez. It makes me feel so . . . really special, in a way.

But . . . I don't know. Being to blame for something like that . . ."

"I fell in love with sunsets, too. But that's not the sun's fault."

"But still . . ."

"Last night made it worth all the waiting."

She covered his mouth with a kiss, squeezed him tight to her body, felt his breath inside her, his hands caressing her through the nightshirt. After a while, she eased her mouth away. "You're so grown-up and strong and manly now, let's see if you can carry me into the bedroom."

He did.

Chad's stomach growled.

"I suppose that means you're hungry now. Men. All you want to do is screw and eat."

"Got me a powerful hunger, woman. But don't you stir yourself. I'll throw together some vittles for us."

She smiled up at him. "You'll make breakfast? Seriously?"

"Hey, I'm a whiz-bang with a skillet."

"That'd be great. I'll take a bath while you're getting it ready."

"Good idea. You're a terrible mess."

She slapped his rump. "Anyway, everything's where it always was. What'll you make?"

"What do you want?"

"How about sausage and eggs?"

"Coming right up." He kissed her gently on the mouth. Then he eased backward, sliding out of her. He kissed her breasts and belly as he crawled to the end of the bed. Getting to his feet, he said, "Do you still like your eggs over easy?"

"That would be just fine."

After he was gone, she began to gather clean clothes. She held them away from her body. She *was* a terrible mess. Chad had been teasing about that, but not wrong. Her skin was slick with sweat, in many places sticky.

As she pushed a bureau drawer shut, Chad came back into the room.

"What do you suppose *this* means?" he asked. He held the Ouija board's box, its bottom in one hand, its lid in the other.

Coreen frowned. "Where're the board and pointer?"

"Good question. I just stopped to pick up the box. It fell open when you dropped it. Nothing inside."

"Oh, man."

"Guess you've been ripped off."

"Oh, man," she muttered again as the implications rushed through her mind. "Those damn idiots."

"Looks to me as if they might be planning on a treasure hunt."

"I know, I know. *Damn* it! Well, that's their problem, isn't it? If they're such damn fools . . . I've got a bath to take."

Chad followed her into the hallway. "It might not be too late to stop them," he said. "Do you know where they live?"

"The hell with them. They made their choice." At the bathroom entrance, she turned to Chad. She shook her head. She was having a hard time catching her breath. "How *could* they?"

"They're kids. The Ouija board promised them a fortune."

"Those idiots!"

"I'll go on and make breakfast," Chad said. He gave her shoulder a brief, gentle squeeze, then walked away.

Coreen could think of nothing but her students as she bathed.

Lana must be the culprit; she had the brains and spirit for this kind of thing. If she was involved, then so was Keith. Maybe the two of them had made off with the board and the others knew nothing about it. Keith might've swiped it. He'd gone off, supposedly to use the bathroom, while everyone else was in the kitchen. That's probably when he snatched the board.

If it's just those two, she thought, it's not so bad.

And she realized that her only real concerns were about Howard and Angela.

She ought to be worried about all of them. They were all her students, all her responsibility.

It's my Ouija board. It's my fault if something happens to them. Any of them.

But she cared more about Howard and Angela. She couldn't deny that. They were special to her. More sensitive than the rest of them. Loners, and probably lonely. Maybe a little less mature than the others, certainly more vulnerable. The idea of those two going along . . .

They're too smart.

But easily controlled.

Look at Howard. He hadn't wanted to mess with the board at all last night. But they'd easily talked him into it.

And poor Angela had actually been pushed into taking off her blouse.

If Lana wanted them to join in on her damn treasure hunt they probably wouldn't have offered much resistance.

It doesn't matter who's in on it, she finally decided, just Lana and Keith, or the whole bunch of them—they've got to be stopped. I can't have my kids rushing off into the mountains. Not with my Ouija board. Not with that damn Butler pulling the strings. Not after the way they'd *all* gone along with his whims last night.

Coreen finished her bath quickly. She climbed from the tub, dried off, brushed her hair, and hurried into her clothes.

Aromas of coffee and sausage greeted her as she entered the kitchen. Chad, standing at the stove, smiled over his shoulder at her. "You look terrific."

"I've got to find out what those kids are up to."

"Anything I can do to help?"

"Not at the moment. Just finish with breakfast. I'm starving." She lifted the handset of the wall phone, called directory assistance, and asked the operator if she had a listing for Lana Tate.

This was a girl who *must* have a telephone.

And she did.

Coreen punched in the numbers, listened to the ringing. Chad watched her, frowning a little.

Someone picked up. "Hello?" A female voice, but it didn't sound like Lana.

"Hello. Is Lana there?"

"Afraid not. Could I take a message?"

"This is Coreen Dalton. I'm one of Lana's . . ."

"Oh, Dr. Dalton! Hi. This is Sue Hughes."

She knew the girl, an honors student majoring in psych, who'd been in her advanced composition class last spring. "How are you, Sue?"

"Oh, just fine. Is there something I can do for you?"

"I really need to talk with Lana. Do you know when she might be back?"

"Not for a few days, maybe longer."

Corie felt herself sinking inside.

"I hope it's nothing too urgent."

"No. She . . . wasn't feeling too well when she left here last night. I just wanted to find out if she's any better."

"She seemed perfectly fine. She must be OK. I mean, I don't think anybody'd go on a camping trip if they—she?—didn't feel all right."

"She went camping?"

"Right. She left last night. Well, this morning, to be more accurate."

"What time did she go?"

"I'm not certain. Sometime after midnight, though. She only popped in long enough to get her gear together. Then she took off to pick up the others."

"In the middle of the night?"

"That's Lana. You live with her a while, nothing surprises you."

"Do you know who else was going along?"

"I'm sure Keith was. Oh, and Doris Whitney. She asked to borrow my sleeping bag for Doris, but I didn't want . . . Anyway, I let Lana take it for herself with the understanding that Doris could use *her* bag. It's not that I have anything *against* Doris, but I just thought I'd feel better if it was Lana who . . ."

"Did she mention anyone else going along?"

"Is something wrong, Professor?"

"I'm not sure. I don't know. Look, I didn't really call to find out about Lana's health. The kids had talked about a trip to the mountains. I thought I'd talked them out of it. Some of them haven't had any experience at all in wilderness living. It just didn't seem like a good idea. And the last I'd heard, they'd decided to call it off."

"Well, they went, all right. But you shouldn't be too concerned. I've been backpacking with Lana. She's no tenderfoot, and I know for a fact that Keith has spent a lot of time camping around. So they know what they're doing. I'm sure they can take care of anyone else who might've gone along with them."

"I hope so. And you say they started out last night?"

"Right. Maybe around one o'clock, but I'm not sure about that."

"Well, thanks a lot, Sue. You've been a lot of help."

"No problem. And really, you shouldn't worry about them. They'll be fine."

"Probably so. Have a good summer, Sue."

"You, too. What's left of it. So long, Professor."

"Bye." She hung up. She frowned at Chad. "They left last night."

"So I heard."

"At least three of them. Probably Glen, too. Maybe the whole bunch." She checked with directory assistance again, got Howard's number, and called. His phone rang twelve times before she hung up. "God, I think they all went."

"What do you want to do about it?"

"I don't know."

"Yeah, you know."

"Shit!"

"I'm sure you could use the services of a guide."

"We can't go after them."

"I don't think we have a choice."

Chapter Nine

Howard left the others at the entrance to a sporting goods store and walked down the block, heading for a pay phone he'd noticed when they drove by.

It felt good to be out of the car. The sun was hot, but he didn't mind.

This isn't so bad, he thought.

Last night had been pretty awful.

Not that anyone caused trouble. Once Lana had filled her tank at the twenty-four-hour Mobil and they got onto the highway, most of the talking stopped. Howard sat close to Angela, leaving nearly half the backseat to Doris. Angela snuggled against him. He put his arm around her as soon as Doris fell asleep.

He remained awake for a long time, his mind in a turmoil.

He thought about Dr. Dalton, how they had tricked and betrayed her. He wondered why she hadn't answered the phone. For a while, he even sickened himself with worries that she hadn't picked up the phone because she couldn't.

Suppose Chad had murdered her? The guy looked like a tough character, and the way he'd shown up unannounced late at night . . . but they seemed to be awfully good friends. Besides, everyone at the party could testify that he'd been there. Howard finally managed to convince himself that the notion of Dr. Dalton's murder was farfetched. No point in getting himself worked up over such a remote possibility. She was probably fine.

During the long hours while sleep evaded Howard, he also thought about the Ouija board, the strangeness that it made any sense at all, much less slid around that time all by itself. He thought about Butler. A spirit? A ghost? A force projected by someone in the room? Whatever Butler might be, he had a mean streak. But he'd been right about the "loot" in the sofa. Maybe he'd told the truth about the fortune. What would he ask them to do in return for leading them to its exact location? Something weird, probably.

Most of all, Howard thought about Angela. Over and over again, he relived the minutes he'd spent in the rooms she shared with Skerrit. Often, he found himself imagining what must've happened there when Angela returned from the party. He dwelled on Angela at the party, too. How the others had forced her to take off her blouse. How he'd just let it happen. And the way she'd looked standing beside him, her breasts showing through the bra.

In the backseat with his arm around her, she fell asleep. But Howard remained awake, remembering and wondering and worrying about Dr. Dalton, the Ouija board, and Angela. Feverish with the storm in his mind. And constantly aware of Angela's body curled against him. He was very tempted to touch her. Nobody would ever know, not even Angela—unless his touch woke her up. He imagined himself feeling her breasts through the blouse. He might even unfasten a button and slip his hand inside. He could probably get away with it. Maybe he could even sneak a hand under her skirt.

Though he ached to try such things, he struggled against his urges. To feel her while she slept would be perverted.

And she'd already been violated in God knows how many ways by that bastard Skerrit.

All she needs is to wake up and find *me* pawing her.

When Howard's arm finally fell asleep, he managed to lift it over her head and bring it down in front of him. He waited for the numbness and tingling to subside, then eased Angela aside so that she slumped against the door.

Her leg still pressed against him. He stared at it, at the way the skirt draped her thigh. Closing his eyes, he continued to see it. He folded his hands on his lap. He saw his hand disappear under the skirt, felt the smooth warmth of her leg, and then it wasn't Angela beside him. It was Dr. Dalton, and he touched the silken fabric of her panties and she lifted his hand away and whispered, *Howard, I'm ashamed of you. I thought you were above this kind of thing.*

I thought you were Angela.

That's no excuse. Honestly, Howard.

A sudden swerve of the car threw him against Angela. Coming out of a restless sleep, he saw that the sky was gray. He was vaguely aware of the car stopping at the side of the highway, Angela asking in a groggy voice "What's going on?" and Lana saying, "Just changing drivers. No problem." Doors had opened, letting chilly air into the car. Then, with Keith behind the wheel, the car started moving again and Howard drifted back into a world of bizarre, vivid dreams.

He jerked awake gasping for breath, his heart slamming.

Daylight. They were stopped at a gas station. Angela was frowning at him. "That must've been an awful nightmare," she whispered.

"Yeah."

He settled back against the seat and shut his eyes, trying to calm down.

Skerrit, he remembered. It was Skerrit. He'd found the old man at the end of a long, black tunnel where Angela and Dr. Dalton were hanging next to each other by their wrists. Their sweaty, naked bodies gleamed in the fire of Skerrit's torch. They writhed and screamed as Skerrit, giggling, pranced from one to the other, jabbing his torch against them. Howard ran and ran, shouting "Stop it!" and digging the Swiss Army knife out of his pocket. He pulled at the main blade, but it wouldn't come out. His thumbnail tore off. Skerrit seemed unaware of his approach, kept on giggling and burning the women. But they had seen him. Between shrieks of agony, they cried out for him to hurry, to save them. He tried to pry out the blade with his front teeth. His teeth crumbled and he spit them out. Then he remembered that the knife was a switchblade. He pushed its button. The blade sprang up and locked into place and he hurled himself at Skerrit. The man screamed as Howard pounded the knife into his back. Into his hump. Soft, not bony. As the blade tore it open, gore slopped out. And then a pair of small hands reached out of the flabby, deflating sack, grabbed Howard's cheeks and tried to pull him in. Small hands, but so terribly strong. Tugging him closer and closer to the gaping split. In the darkness of the hump, eyes opened. A mouth spread wide, and he woke with a jolt of panic.

"Are you OK?" Angela asked.

He opened his eyes again. "Yeah. No big deal. It was just a nightmare."

"I had some bad ones, too. I'm sure glad it's morning."

"Yeah." For the first time, he looked around. Doris was still sleeping. The front seat was empty. Turning around, he saw Keith behind the car, pumping gas. "Where are the others?"

"The bathroom."

When Lana and Glen returned to the car, Howard followed Angela to the side of the service station and entered the men's restroom. He used the toilet. He washed his hands and face with cold water. He came out into the fresh morning sunlight.

The night was over.

The long hours of torment had finally come to an end.

He waited for Angela. When she stepped out of the women's restroom, she looked younger and prettier than ever before. And carefree. As if she didn't have a worry in the world. Smiling, she took hold of his hand.

"Isn't it just wonderful here?" she said as they walked toward the car.

"It's awfully nice."

"I may just decide never to go back at all."

"Here come the lovebirds," Glen called out his window.

Howard found that he didn't mind. Angela glanced at him, blushing, and squeezed his hand.

They climbed into the backseat. Keith started the car. Glen, on the other side of Lana, grinned over his shoulder at them. "I saw what you two were doing last night when you thought we were asleep."

"Oh, sure," Howard said, surprised that the teasing didn't bother him.

"You jealous, Glenny?" Angela asked.

Howard laughed, amazed to hear such a cheerful, bold retort from the girl. Especially considering that they'd done nothing. He would've expected Angela to deny they had fooled around, or simply to remain silent and lower her eyes.

What's going on with her?

Whatever it might be, he liked it.

He felt himself liking everything that morning: the ride along the quiet highway, the smell of the air, the deep green of the wooded hills all around, Angela sitting beside him seeming almost reborn, even the banter and arguments and speculations in which they both participated.

Somehow, he no longer felt like such an outsider. From the way Angela behaved, he supposed she must be feeling the same way.

It's almost as if we're suddenly a family, he realized. He didn't know how it had happened. He could remember his impression of being trapped among virtual strangers when they'd started out. Somehow, a kind of intimacy had developed overnight.

His deeper feelings about Angela were easy to understand. But why the others? Just because they'd shared the misery of spending a night cramped in the car? Or because they were all together in unknown territory, joined in this crazy hunt?

Whatever the reason, he liked the new feeling of closeness. He liked being here.

They stopped at a cafe in Redding for breakfast. He drank coffee, ate bacon and fried eggs and hash browns, and thought that a meal had never tasted so fine. Lana, checking her map, explained that Red Bluff was only an hour's drive. She suggested that they stop there to pick up the equipment and supplies. "After that," she said, "it's the boondocks."

At the pay phone, Howard called home. His father answered. His mother joined in on the other line.

He'd already decided to tell them the truth. Part of the truth, anyway.

"I'm going to be a few days late getting home," he said. "If it's OK."

"What's up?" Dad asked.

"A couple of the guys invited me to go camping with them."

"How nice," Mom said. She was always pleading with him to make new friends.

"We're planning to leave today and go up into the mountains for four or five days. Is it all right?"

"Fine by me," Dad said. "Should be fun. Are your friends familiar with the area you'll be going into?"

"Yeah. They've been there before."

"Well, sounds good to me."

"These are boys you know fairly well?" Mom asked.

"Sure. They've been in a few of my classes."

"Well, that was very nice of them to invite you along."

"Yeah. They're good guys."

"You'll call us when you get back?" Mom asked.

"Sure."

"What about your airline ticket?" Dad asked.

"Well, I haven't bought it yet. I was going to make my reservation today, but I guess I'll wait till I get back."

"Fine. Let us know when you'll be arriving."

"I will. See you soon."

"Be careful, honey."

"I will."

"Have fun," Dad said.

After hanging up, Howard grinned. He'd half expected trouble about the abrupt change of plans, but they'd both seemed happy to hear about his little adventure. It would've been a different story, he knew, if he'd told them everything. Especially about the girls. But he hadn't needed to lie very much.

Feeling good, he walked back down the block and entered the sporting goods store.

He found Keith and Glen tossing food into a shopping cart.

"How'd it go with your folks, Howitzer?"

"No problem."

"If they didn't hassle you," Glen said, "you must've lied through your teeth."

"What they don't know won't hurt them."

"Which is why I don't tell mine anything," Glen said, and went back to gathering food. In the cart were packets of freeze-dried meals and fruit, bacon bars, pudding desserts, trail mix, punch and cocoa and instant coffee, "Tropical" chocolate bars and cookies. Howard wondered where the girls were, but he decided to stay with Glen and Keith for a while.

Glen did most of the picking. He seemed to know just what he wanted, but gasped "Far out!" or "All right!" when he discovered surprising items on the shelves. Keith went along with the choices, sometimes laughing at Glen's enthusiasm. He told Howard to go ahead and grab anything that looked especially good.

"Oh, I think Glen's doing great," he said, then wandered away to look for the girls.

He found them in a far corner of the store. Angela smiled as he approached. She had a red pack in each hand. Lana passed a couple of fuel bottles to Doris, who set them inside a shopping cart.

"Did it go OK?" Lana asked him.

"Fine."

In the cart were ground cloths, plastic water bottles, mess kits and packets of eating utensils. Two of each.

Lana checked the list that they had composed during the drive from Red Bluff.

"That pretty much covers it," she said. "We've got everything but the t.p., soap and insect repellant."

They started walking toward another area of the store.

"What did you decide about a tent?" Howard asked.

"The hell with it. We aren't going to be out all that long, anyway. If we run into a storm, we'll pile into mine and Glen's."

"Let us pray for fair weather," Doris said.

"Two should be plenty. And they're heavy suckers to lug around."

"All the food Glen's grabbing," Howard said, "we probably won't have room in our packs for an extra tent, anyway."

Lana laughed.

He'd *caused* her to laugh. It made him feel good. He tried to think of a witty remark that might make her laugh again, but decided not to press his luck.

Dropping back, he joined Angela behind the shopping cart. "Carry those for you?"

"Sure. Thanks."

He took the two packs. "Have you got everything you need?" he asked.

"Well, I think so. I've never gone camping before."

"I guess the list covers most of the necessities. Do you have something warm to wear at night?"

"My sweats."

Her sweats. The closet. Howard's heart started hammering.

"I wonder if they're dry yet," she said, and gave him a strange look. It seemed to be a mixture of embarrassment and regret and fondness and hope. It made Howard very glad he'd resisted his temptation to sneak feels last night in the car. He felt like hugging her.

"Did you bring a coat?"

She shook her head. "It was too big and heavy."

"Why don't we get you a windbreaker?"

"No, that's not really . . ."

"You might freeze in just a sweatshirt. I'll buy it for you, OK?"

"No, you don't have to do that."

"I want to."

She hesitated.

"If you'd feel better about it," he said, "you can pay me back when we find Butler's loot."

"Well. OK."

They wandered away from Lana and Doris. In the store's clothing section, they picked out a lightweight red windbreaker. Angela tried it on. She looked wonderful in it.

Nearby was a female mannequin wearing a pink, long-billed cap, a purple tank top and shorts. The shorts matched the top, but were made of a shiny fabric so thin that the barely moving air inside the store was enough to stir it.

"How about shorts?" Howard asked. "Did you bring shorts?"

"Yes, I did. Howard, you don't have to buy me anything else. Really."

"A pair like these would be great. It gets awfully hot in the mountains."

Angela stepped up to the mannequin. She stared at the shorts. She rubbed the material between her thumb and forefinger, then looked over her shoulder at Howard. She studied his eyes for a moment. "OK. If you're sure you want me to have them."

She knows I just want to see her in them, he realized. And she's going along with it!

"They'll be comfortable," he said. Could he get her to go for the tank top? Don't push it.

He waited while she searched through stacks of shorts

beside the mannequin. "Do you like the purple?" she asked.

"Whatever color you want."

She chose white.

"You'll need a hat," Howard said. "Did you bring a hat?"

"No."

"That one's neat."

"Yeah."

They stepped over to a rack of caps similar to the one worn by the mannequin. Angela picked a white one, put it on and faced Howard. "Like it?"

He shifted a pack to free one of his hands, reached out and turned up the bill.

She grinned.

God, she looked happy! And so cute.

"Great. Let's get it. Do you see anything else you'd like?"

"This is plenty. We'd better go and find the others."

"I'll go ahead and buy these." He gave Angela the packs, took the windbreaker, cap and shorts, and hurried toward the counter while she went looking for the rest of the group.

Chapter Ten

"That might've been it," Lana said.

"That *was* it," Doris said.

Howard glanced out the rear window. He couldn't spot the sign, but he noted that the highway was clear behind them. "Nobody on our tail."

As Keith backed up the car, the sign came into view on the right. Carved in its redwood was SHADOW CANYON LAKE—22 MI and an arrow pointing toward a dirt track that twisted into the forest.

"Twenty-two miles on *that*?" Glen said.

"Worse," Lana said. "My map shows it stopping a few miles short of the lake. We'll have to do some hiking before we make camp."

"Terrific," Keith muttered. He swung the steering wheel and started forward. They left the two-lane highway behind, the car jolting and rocking as it started along the rough road. Howard looked at Angela. She grinned as she bounced and bumped against him. She took hold of his leg. He covered her hand, then glanced at Doris. The girl's heavy cheeks were vibrating. Looking out the back window, he saw a cloud of yellow dust behind them.

"This is gonna take a while," Keith said.

Howard checked his wristwatch. Eleven-fifteen. It was ten after one when they reached a clearing at the end of the road.

They climbed out. Howard felt unsteady on his feet as if he'd just stepped onto land after a boat ride across choppy waters. He held onto the side of the car and looked around. The clearing, large enough to allow parking for several vehicles, was deserted except for their car. The shadows of surrounding trees blocked out most of the sunlight. Only a few rays got through, slanting down and making bright patches on the carpet of pine needles, cones and twigs.

"Isn't this wonderful?" Angela said.

"Nice."

"My ass," Glen said, reaching up to unfasten the straps on the luggage rack. "Bloody fucking hot."

"But wonderful," Angela said. She stretched, took a deep breath, and sighed.

After the car was unloaded, Keith and Glen began dividing the food and other supplies into six piles on the hood of the car. While they did that, Doris and Angela emptied their suitcases into their new packs. Howard saw that Angela had brought her stuffed, one-eared kitten along. Fortunately, nobody else seemed to notice.

He opened his own pack, added his share from the hood, closed it and strapped his sleeping bag into place. Then he helped Angela get ready. When he was about to pull down the top flap of her pack, she stopped him. "Just a second."

Crouching, she opened the bag from the sporting goods store. She took out her windbreaker, cap and shorts, wadded the bag and tossed it into the trunk. She folded the coat and put it into her pack. She put on the cap. Then she stepped into the shorts, pulled them up beneath her skirt, took off the skirt and stuffed it into the pack. "Now you can shut it," she said.

Howard finished closing the pack. He strapped her sleeping bag onto the frame at the top.

"Can I borrow your knife?" she asked.

He dug it out of his pocket. A sudden memory of the nightmare intruded as he pried open the main blade. But the memory was swept away when Angela took the knife and lifted her blouse. The skin of her belly, though fair, looked almost dusky next to the stark white of the shorts.

She knotted the front of her blouse so its tails wouldn't fall and get in her way. The tags hung from her waistband by a tough plastic thread at her hip. Twisting sideways, she pulled at the tags and cut them loose.

"Thank you," she said, and handed the knife back to Howard. In a whisper, she added, "Thanks for the shorts, too. They're fabulous. They're so light and cool." She tugged at the knot, and the lower part of her blouse fell, draping the shorts.

As Howard put the knife away, he saw Lana tucking the Ouija board's plastic pointer into a side pocket of her pack. He felt a quick flutter in his stomach. He wished he hadn't seen the thing.

It's only because of the Ouija that we're here, he told himself. I should be grateful to the thing, not scared of it.

But sooner or later, probably after dark, they would gather near their campfire and place their fingers on the pointer and try to contact Butler. The six of them. Alone in all this wilderness. Surrounded by the night.

Thoughts of that made something cold squirm through Howard's bowels.

Maybe the pointer won't move. Maybe we lost Butler, left him behind at Dr. Dalton's house.

The squirmy feelings faded a little.

Just don't think about the Ouija board or Butler. Maybe nothing bad will happen. Shouldn't worry about what *might* happen, anyway. It's a waste of time and it'll spoil the good stuff. This could be like a great vacation or adventure or something if you just don't screw it up worrying. It might end up being the best few days you've ever spent.

Crouching, he opened a side pocket of his pack. He pulled out his battered old gray felt hat and put it on.

Angela laughed.

"Dashing, huh?" he asked.

"You look like a moonshiner."

Lana glanced over her shoulder at him. "Jed Clampet."

Doris snickered. She was tying a red bandana around her head, her armpits showing. Though her sleeves were cut off at the shoulders, she had to be awfully hot in that sweatshirt. She always wore sweatshirts, regardless of the weather. Maybe she thought she looked good in them. Howard couldn't imagine her looking good in anything.

Lana slammed the trunk lid, swung her pack onto it, and leaned back to put her arms through the straps. "Are we all set?" she asked.

"Looks like the trail starts over there," Keith said.

"Let's hit it," Glen said.

Howard held Angela's pack for her. When she had it on, he saw Doris struggling. He took a step toward her. "Could you use some help?"

"I'm perfectly capable of managing my own affairs," she said, swinging the pack up behind her.

"You've got affairs?" Glen called. "Where'd you find guys that hard up?"

"The Braille Institute," Keith said.

"Such wit," Doris said. "I'm doubled over with hilarity."

"Come on, children." Lana took a few steps backward, studying her car as if wondering if she'd forgotten anything. Then she turned around and strode to the trail sign. She waited there for the others.

They gathered in front of the sign. Its two short planks both pointed at the same path. The upper board read SHADOW CANYON LAKE—4 MI. The lower, CALAMITY PEAK—9 MI.

"Oh, brother," Keith muttered.

"Not so bad," Lana said. "Only five miles from the lake to the peak."

"But does that mean to the peak of the peak," Glen asked, "or to the foot of the peak?"

"I guess we'll find out," Lana said. "Right now, let's just worry about making it to the lake."

She led the way. Keith followed. After a few steps, he apparently decided that the path was wide enough for both of them. He hurried forward and joined her. Glen went next.

"Be my guests," Doris said, gesturing for Howard and Angela to go ahead.

"Are you sure you want to take up the rear?" Howard asked.

"And why wouldn't I?"

"Stragglers get picked off."

Angela laughed.

Doris sneered. "For godsake, Howard. Have you started taking quip lessons from Tweedle-Dee and Dumb-Dumb?"

"No, I just . . ."

"You're not a bad fellow. Why don't you try to keep it that way?"

"We'll go next," Angela said. "It's no big deal." She pulled Howard by the arm.

They hurried up the trail, leaving Doris behind. When they rounded a bend, Glen came into sight. They slowed their pace. Angela took a few sidesteps and looked back, then turned to the front again.

"I think she likes you."

"Yuck."

"What's wrong with that?"

"She's miserable and sarcastic, for starters."

"I think she's just lonely."

"Of course she's lonely. Everybody hates her. She seems to thrive on it. It wouldn't have killed her to let us take up the rear."

"Then *we'd* get picked off."

Howard laughed. "Better her than us."

"Right. But we really should try to be nice to her. You know? I mean, we're all in this together, and she's here without any friends at all, and it's terrible the way Keith and Glen pick on her."

"They pick on us, too."

"Yeah, but it's not the same. I mean, we have each other."

The words gave him a strange, warm feeling in his chest. If she had spoken them yesterday, Howard realized, he probably would've been appalled. Though he'd always felt a certain bond with Angela, he'd never been attracted to her. In fact, he'd often gone out of his way to avoid her company. He'd thought of her as "weird Angela," the "space cadet" and the "Melancholy Dame."

Last night had sure changed him.

Starting when she took off her blouse. That was the moment when he really began to want her. And later, when he found her in Skerrit's closet, he really began to care about her. From that time on, his feelings for Angela had grown until now, hearing her say "We have each other," he wondered if he might actually be falling in love with her.

That's crazy, he told himself. If I'm in love with anyone, it's Dr. Dalton.

If I had to pick between the two of them, it wouldn't be any contest.

That's sure likely to come up.

Looking into Angela's eyes, he suddenly realized that such a fantasy choice might not be made quite so easily. Yesterday, there would've been no contest. At this moment, however . . .

"Are you all right?" she asked.

"Yeah."

"Is something wrong?"

"No. Huh-uh."

"When I said that . . . you know, about how we have each other . . ." Her face blushed furiously. "I only meant that . . . I don't know . . . just that we're sort of friends. And Doris doesn't have any friends."

"I'll try to be nice to her," Howard said. He glanced back at Doris. She was slogging along, far behind them. "Should I ask her to come up and join us?"

Richard Laymon

Angela laughed. "You don't have to overdo it."

They walked for a while in silence. Then he said, "I'm really glad we're here."

"So am I."

Soon, the trees thinned out and the trail led upward along a rocky, glaring slope. Howard's legs began to feel heavy. The heat pushed down on him. The straps of his pack made his shoulders ache. Sweat dripped down his face. His shirt and underpants were sodden and clinging. The legs of his corduroys seemed to scorch his thighs with each step, and the heavy fabric trapped the heat inside.

He wished he had changed into shorts before starting the hike. But he wasn't about to stop now and do it. Maybe if Doris weren't back there.

At least I don't have to worry about my legs getting sunburned.

"How are you doing?" he asked Angela. Her face was dripping. She was gasping for breath. Her blouse was unbuttoned partway down, and the skin of her chest gleamed. Much of her pale blue blouse was dark with moisture. But the shorts floated around her as if they were filled with breezes, and her legs looked cool.

"Butler's . . . sure making us work for that treasure."

"I think his whole plan is to torment us."

"Probably." She huffed along for a while. "Do people do this for *fun*?"

"It feels so good when you stop."

"If we ever do."

At the end of a long, dusty switchback, they came upon Lana, Keith and Glen resting among the rocks with their packs off. Glen's eyes were squeezed shut as he chugged water from his plastic canteen. Keith sat cross-legged in a patch of shade cast by an outcropping. Lana sat atop a boulder, spreading suntan lotion on her arms.

"You'd better put some of this on when I'm done," she told Angela. "At this altitude, the sun'll really cook you."

They took their packs off. Without the weight dragging

him down, Howard felt buoyant. The breeze chilled the sweat on the back of his shirt.

"I don't think we're far from the top," Lana said, rubbing her legs with lotion.

"Maybe someone would like to carry me the rest of the way," Glen said.

"In your dreams," Keith told him.

"This'll make football practice look like a picnic."

"Just think of the great shape you'll be in," Lana said.

"If I don't drop dead up here."

Doris showed up, red and gasping. She flopped backward against a slab of rock.

"How are you doing?" Howard asked her.

She gave him a scowl, and said nothing.

So much for being nice to her.

Angela sat down on a small, flat rock with Lana's suntan lotion. When she leaned forward to squirt it on her legs, her left breast showed inside the shadowed opening of her blouse. She wore a bra, maybe the same one she'd had on at the party. The side that Howard could see looked like a small, transparent bag clinging to her breast. He supposed it must be wet and cool against her skin. He imagined it gone, imagined his hand there instead.

Feeling guilty, he looked away and watched her spread the lotion up and down her long, slim legs. He wished he could be the one rubbing it onto her. Then he pictured Skerrit crouching in front of her, leering as he slathered hot ointment onto her legs and up between them.

Dirty, rotten bastard!

She's got me, now. She'll never have to let that old pervert touch her again.

Maybe she *liked* being rubbed all over with the stuff. Maybe she'll want me to do it to her.

She didn't like it. Are you nuts?

But the thought excited Howard.

Get off it! That's Skerrit's shit. I would never do anything like that to her.

He turned away quickly, sat down in front of his pack,

103

and fixed his eyes on the wooded valley below the trail.

Skerrit stayed in his mind long after they resumed their hike. He hated the man for abusing Angela. But he knew that his hatred was mixed with envy. Angela had lived with the guy. His victim. His slave.

She could've been living with me, Howard kept reminding himself. I was all alone. I wouldn't have done anything to hurt her.

Maybe after we're done up here, she *will* live with me. She can't go back to Skerrit. I'll get her a ticket and we can fly home together and she can stay in the guest room until it's time for the fall semester.

Would Mom and Dad go along with that?

I'll explain how she hasn't got anyplace else to live. Won't tell them about Skerrit, of course.

As they trudged up the mountain trail, he ached to ask Angela about Skerrit. How had she ended up living with that horrible old man? How long had they been together? What other abuses had he inflicted on her? Did he beat her? Did he spy on her when she undressed?

Did he fuck her?

That was the real question.

Howard wasn't sure he really wanted to know the answer. But he couldn't ask Angela. He found that he couldn't ask her anything at all about her relationship with Skerrit. He could only dwell on it and let it torment him during the long hike up the mountain.

Finally, the switchbacks ended. The top of the mountain still loomed above them, but the trail curved along its side and led them through a pass, then angled downward into a wooded valley.

"Can't be far, now," Howard said.

Angela looked exhausted, but she smiled at him. "This isn't too bad."

"At least there's shade."

"I just hope we don't have to climb another mountain."

"We'll probably have to go up Calamity Peak."

"Not today. Lana said we'd camp by the lake. I can't

imagine there's actually a lake way up here."

Soon, however, Howard spotted a glimmer beyond the trees. "Look there," he said.

"Fabulous!" Angela quickened her pace.

More of the lake came into view as they hurried forward. Rounding a bend, they came upon Lana, Keith and Glen waiting at a fork in the trail.

"Thar she blows," Glen said, pointing at the lake.

Its shore was straight ahead, just beyond a clearing that looked like a regular stopping place for campers. There was a campfire area—a circle of rocks surrounded by makeshift benches of split logs. Someone had left a grille behind, and even a small pile of kindling. Patches of sunlight dappled the ground. The surface of the lake gleamed.

"Decent," Keith said.

"Let's check around before we set up camp," Lana said. "We might find a better place."

"We might find a troop of Girl Scouts," Glen said.

Angela gave Howard an uneasy glance.

"What?" he asked.

"We might find Butler."

They all looked at her.

"He said, 'I meet you.' Remember?"

"At the mine," Keith pointed out. "The mine's supposed to be at Calamity Peak and we're . . . what? Five miles away."

"Yeah," Glen said. "Geez, don't be such a downer."

Chapter Eleven

Coreen leaned forward and rested her forearms on the steering wheel. The wind from the open window was tossing her hair, flicking the collar and short sleeves of her blouse. The back of the blouse didn't stir; its checkered fabric looked glued to her skin.

"Getting tired?" Chad asked.

"No, I'm fine. Just cooling off."

"I'll take over, if you'd like."

"I'll hang in a little longer. What's it been, three hours?" She glanced at her wristwatch. "Yug. Only three-thirty. We got away at what, one?"

"Maybe a little earlier."

"Sure seems like longer than two and a half hours."

"Time flies when you're having fun."

Coreen settled back against the seat. She reached over and gave Chad's leg a gentle squeeze. "I guess I haven't been very good company. I'm sorry."

"You're great company."

"I'm pissed off, is what I am. Here you are, you've finally

come back, and we've gotta go chasing after a bunch of damn kids. I could just kill those jerks."

"It'll be great once we're out in the mountains. There's nothing like it."

"Then why did you leave them?" She glanced at him, a teasing look in her eyes.

"You're better."

"You may change your tune after you've been around me for a while."

"Probably."

She laughed and pounded his thigh. "So tell me, aside from pining away for me all the time, what did you do with yourself out there in the wilds? Just wander around yodeling and communing with chipmunks?"

"That's about it."

"No, really."

"Well, I worked at ski lodges during the winter. I waited tables the first year, then spent a winter bartending, and finally I got into ski instructing. Each spring, I'd load up with supplies and take off on my own. I usually made it into early September before heading back for civilization."

"And you liked living that way?"

"Most of the time. You know what Thoreau said."

" 'Simplify, simplify, simplify'"?"

"That. And 'I never met a companion so companionable as solitude.' "

"Present company excluded, right?"

"Right."

"I think it'd drive me crazy, being alone that much."

"I got a pretty good fill of society during the winters. And occasionally I'd run into hikers. I tried to stay clear of the main trails, but people popped up anyway, once in a while."

"Then you'd set a spell and palaver?"

He laughed. "Yeah, sometimes. Mostly, I did my best to avoid them. You'd think I was the boogey-man, the way some of those people got spooked when they bumped into me."

"I can imagine. You spooked *me* last night. Mostly the beard, I guess."

"Do I look harmless enough now?"

"It's nice to be able to see your face."

That morning, after their decision to pursue the kids, Coreen had driven off to buy supplies. Chad had stayed at the house and thrown his clothes in the washer. While they were being cleaned, he had taken a razor to his beard and mustache. He'd been a little worried about Coreen's reaction, but when she came back her delight was obvious. "Hey," she'd said, grinning. "I know you." And she'd caressed his cheeks, and kissed him, and rubbed her face against his. "Gee, I let myself get screwed by some wild old mountain man last night. If I'd known you'd be showing up today, I might've been able to curb my lust."

"I saw him on his way out," Chad had told her. "He said you were just too hot for him to handle, and he wished me luck."

"He was sweet in his rough and rustic way, but I prefer you."

Then Coreen had shown him what she'd bought. In addition to food and supplies for the trip, she'd purchased clothes for him: crew socks; skimpy briefs in a variety of colors; two pairs of tan hiking shorts with deep pockets and button-down flaps; three short-sleeved shirts with epaulettes; and a hat that looked like something Indiana Jones might wear. "No bullwhip?"

"They didn't come in your size," she'd said, slipping the robe off his shoulders. "Come on, let's see how you look in this stuff."

"I thought we were in a hurry."

"We can't leave till you're dressed, can we?"

The memories brought a smile to Chad's face.

"What?" Coreen asked.

"Just feeling good. About everything."

"I'd feel better if the air conditioner worked."

"Don't you like the fresh air?"

"Fresh air's fine. Hot air I can do without."

"You'll look back on it fondly tonight when you're freezing your tail off."

"I'm counting on you to keep me warm."

"Well, I'll sure . . ."

Thunkthunkthunkthunk . . .

"What the hell!"

Coreen slowed down. The car no longer shook quite so much and the pounding slacked off. *Thunk thunk thunk.*

Chad felt his alarm beginning to subside. "Must be a flat," he said, speaking loudly, almost shouting to be heard over the pounding noise.

"Shit!"

"Just pull over and I'll change it."

"Who's got a spare?" she asked, riding the highway's breakdown lane.

"You haven't got a spare tire?"

"Not at the moment. I meant to get it fixed but . . . I'll try for that off-ramp."

The ramp was no more than fifty yards ahead. Chad spotted a Mobil station at the top. But the thunking went on. It sounded like a hammer whacking the front of the car. "Maybe you'd better not try. I'll walk up there and get help."

"I can make it."

"God knows what you're doing to the tire."

"I've got a sneaky suspicion it's a goner, anyway."

"Your rim . . ."

She started up the off-ramp. "I don't know. Feels like the tire's working. Sort of."

"Well, you're almost there now."

"Come on, baby," she whispered.

At the end of the ramp, she turned right, clumped along the road for a short distance, then swung into the station. She stopped in front of the service bay. There was only one. A Toyota was up on the rack. The mechanic beneath it spotted them, nodded, and went back to work.

"This might be a while," Chad said.

Coreen didn't answer. She was slumped back against the seat, hands on her thighs. Her cheeks puffed out as she slowly blew air through her pursed lips. She looked haggard and relieved. As she turned her head toward Chad, a corner of her mouth lifted. "Boy, did we luck out."

"If we had to have a flat," he said, "I guess it couldn't have happened at a much better time."

She tipped her eyes upward. "Somebody up there likes us."

"If he likes us so much, how come he blew our tire?"

"Don't get technical," she said, and shoved open her door.

Chad climbed out. It felt good to be standing again, but his legs were a little shaky. Scares always seemed to leave them that way, and he'd been damn scared for just a second there with the clamor pounding his ears and the car shuddering—before he'd had a chance to figure out what was going on.

Must've given Coreen some bad moments, too.

"Good God," she said, bending down and gazing at the left front tire.

Chad joined her.

The tire wasn't flat, but it looked as if it had been scalped. Most of its tread was gone. A remaining section was still attached but hanging loose, and Chad realized that it had been responsible for the pounding noise. With each revolution of the wheel, the flopping panel of tread had hammered against the car. It had dented the chrome trim at the rear of the wheel well.

"Looks like you've got a problem there," the mechanic said. He came sauntering toward them, rubbing his hands with a dirty red rag while his mouth played with a toothpick. He was a stocky, dark man. He looked Mexican, but had no trace of a Spanish accent. "Yep," he said, and squatted beside the tire. "You aren't going much farther on this one. Lucky she didn't explode on you."

"I thought this only happened to retreads," Coreen said.

"Nope. Happens all the time with your steel-belted radials. You gotcha a little too much wear, maybe a structural flaw, you run 'em too long in this heat, it's slam, bam, *ad-*

ios." He looked up at Coreen. Opening his mouth wide, he turned his toothpick end over end with his tongue. "Interested in buying a new tire?"

"I don't suppose I have much choice."

"I could put your spare on for you, but then you'll be in mighty deep waters if another tire goes south on you."

"I don't have a spare, anyway."

"Well, now." The man pushed at his knees, grunted and stood up straight. "If you wanta go for two, I can fix you up with a couple of fine new radials every bit as good as what you've got on there. They'll run you about eighty bucks each." He grinned. "In fact, I'll give you a deal on 'em—two for the price of two."

Coreen shook her head and laughed. She met Chad's eyes.

He found himself smiling. "I don't know how we can beat an offer like that."

"Sounds good to me."

"What I'll do for you, I'll put both the new babies on the front, balance 'em up real fine for you, give your junk tire a toss, and throw your other tire into the trunk for your spare. That way, you'll be riding with a brand fresh pair up front where it counts."

Coreen looked at Chad. He nodded.

"Great," she told the mechanic. "How long'll it take?"

"Give me an hour. Now hang on a second, we'll write this up and I'll get started." He swaggered away, tucking the rag into a seat pocket of his coveralls.

As he entered the office, Coreen said, "This isn't too bad. We'll only lose an hour or so."

"It sure could have been a lot worse."

She nodded toward a coffee shop across the road. "Why don't we go over there? We can eat while he's putting the tires on, then we won't have to stop later for dinner. That'll save us some time."

"We might as well not worry about the time," Chad said. "We got such a late start, and now this. I don't see much chance of catching up with your kids today."

111

She fixed her eyes on him, a grimace baring her upper teeth. "We have to try," she said.

"We'll try. But it's going to be dark before we even make it off the main roads."

The mechanic came back carrying a clipboard. "Checked the prices for you while I was in there. The tires'll run you just sixty-nine ninety-nine each, plus ten apiece for installation and balancing."

"Fine," Coreen muttered. She sounded as if her spirits had taken a nosedive. Chad wondered whether she was disturbed by the cost, or brooding over what he'd told her about their chances of finding the kids today.

Probably worried about the kids, he decided.

The mechanic handed the clipboard to her. A work order was clamped to it. "Need your name, address and phone number."

A ballpoint dangled at the end of a dirty string which was knotted to the eye of the metal clamp. She caught the pen and began filling out the work order.

"You folks oughta head on over to Rusty's," he said, jabbing a thumb in the direction of the coffee shop. "Sit down, relax, have a drink, have a bite. I'll come over and let you know when she's ready to roll."

"Thanks," she said, and gave him the board.

"Keys in the ignition?"

She nodded. She glanced at Chad, then took his hand. They started walking. "I don't like this."

"I can tell."

"It's what you said."

"Figured it might be. I'm sorry."

She squeezed his hand. "It's not your fault. You're right. It'll be dark before we're anywhere close to the kids."

They waited on the curb for a Jeep Wrangler to speed by, then stepped down and hurried across the road.

"I'm just afraid for them," she said.

"They'll be all right."

"God, I hope so. But . . . This is gonna sound stupid, but

what if we're not *supposed* to reach them? At least not in time, you know?"

Chad was tempted to tease her. *Yeah, sounds stupid, all right.* But she was blushing. Though obviously embarrassed by her idea, she'd trusted Chad enough to share it with him. "It was just a bad tire," he said. "People have car trouble all the time."

She tried to force a smile. "So you don't think it was Butler's way of trying to slow us down?"

"If it was, he's not much of a manipulator. Why didn't he rip the tread off the tire when we were twenty miles from the nearest station? For that matter, why didn't he knock out the steering so we'd crash? Or just forget subtlety and blow us to smithereens?"

"I guess you're right," Coreen said.

He opened the door of Rusty's, and they stepped into the restaurant. It was air-conditioned. Chad felt his damp clothes turn cold.

"Just take a seat anywhere, folks," a woman called from behind the serving counter.

They walked to a front booth, and Chad sat down across from Coreen.

"I know you're right," she said, leaning forward and resting her elbows on the table. "We had a little car trouble. There's no reason to read anything supernatural into it."

"No reason at all."

"But I just can't help feeling that Butler might've been behind it. If he has the power to guide a pointer around a Ouija board, maybe he has enough power to do other stuff. And maybe he doesn't want us to interfere with his plans."

Chapter Twelve

"Come on, you chickens," Glen called, looking over his shoulder at Howard and Angela. He had stripped down to his boxer shorts and was knee deep in the lake.

"I'm fine right here," Howard said.

Angela, sitting beside him on the rock slab with her bare feet dangling in the water, said, "Me, too. Besides, I didn't bring a suit."

"Big deal. So come in in your undies, nobody's gonna tell on you."

"You're going to freeze," Howard told him.

"It's not so bad." As if to prove his point, he waded farther out from shore. The water climbed his legs, and when it reached his groin he jerked rigid and cried out, "Yeeeeah! My balls!"

Angela laughed. "It's not so bad," she told Howard.

"I'm sure it's very refreshing."

Glen shuddered and gasped for breath. He was bent over slightly at the waist, arms away from his sides, fists clenched.

"You look like you stepped in a bear trap," Howard called.

"I'm OK. I'm OK. I'll be OK in a minute."

"I'm glad that's him and not us," Angela said.

"Same here."

It was the truth. He didn't want to get into that frigid water. But going for a swim would've given him— and Angela—an excuse for stripping down to their underwear. If she'd been willing, he would've done it, too.

As soon as the subject of swimming had come up, however, she'd said, "Not me." Nobody had tried very hard to talk her into it. So Howard, partly relieved but mostly disappointed, had said, "I'm not going in, either. The rest of you can freeze if you want."

Then he and Angela had wandered down to the shore and found the boulder. It was flat and fairly smooth, and slanted downward at a mild angle toward the water. Once they were sitting down, Angela had pulled off her shoes and socks and lowered her feet into the lake.

"How is it?" Howard had asked.

"Ice cold. But kind of nice."

"Are you sure you don't want to go in?"

"I didn't bring a suit."

"Neither did I. I'm not sure anybody did."

She had grinned and raised her eyebrows. "Think they'll go skinny-dipping?"

"Maybe."

"I wouldn't do that. Not around Keith and Glen."

But she would *around me*? "I wouldn't either. Not around Doris."

She'd laughed.

About that time, Glen had trotted down to the shore in his shorts. Howard wouldn't have been surprised to see him shuck them off at the last moment and charge into the lake bare-assed, but they were still on, and now they were wet.

"Here goes!" Glen bounced up and down a few times, apparently trying to gather his courage. Then he raised his arms and flung himself forward. His big body dropped, shoving the water aside. An instant later, the water rushed back and shut over him.

"He did it," Angela said.

"He must be crazy."

Glen's head popped to the surface. He bellowed, "Oh, my God!"

"How is it?" Keith called.

Glen swiveled around and answered, "Takes a little getting used to." His voice had a higher than usual pitch.

"If you can take it, we can." Lana's voice.

Howard felt a quick tug of excitement. "I guess they're going in, too," he said. Sounded inane, he thought, but he had to say something. He forced his gaze to stay on Angela. What would Lana be wearing? A bra and panties? Nothing at all?

"Must be masochists," Angela said. She leaned back slightly to see past him. So Howard looked.

Keith, slim and muscular and tanned, wore cut-off jeans.

Lana wasn't naked. She wasn't in her underwear. She wore a swimsuit. It wasn't even a bikini, but a one-piece tank suit with a high neckline.

Oh, well, Howard thought. That's the way it goes.

But he quickly noticed that the suit wasn't all bad. Its glossy fabric hugged her body, showing every detail. The sides were cut so high that they left her hipbones bare. When she waded in, he saw that the suit was backless—and almost bottomless. Its tight, gleaming seat was a slim triangle that covered very little of her buttocks.

Lana waded forward until the water reached her thighs, and then without breaking stride she bounded forward, curved, and slipped beneath the surface.

"Whatcha waiting for, Keithie?"

Keith acted as if he didn't hear Glen. He stood motionless in water up to his ankles, staring at the place where Lana had vanished. He bared his teeth. He rubbed his hands together. He muttered, "Oh, shit." Then he charged, yelling, smashing through the water as if it were a defensive line.

"Go for it!" Glen shouted.

Keith let out a battle cry and hurled himself down.

Laughing, Glen pumped his fist in the air. "All right!"

Lana surfaced and stood up. She was no more than six feet from Howard. He supposed she had circled around after diving, and headed back toward shore. The water where she stood was only waist deep.

She paid no attention to him as she wiped her face with both hands.

Her hair, the color of hay after a rainstorm, was slicked down against her head. Her shoulders and arms gleamed. When she lowered her arms, Howard saw how the suit was sticking to her body like a thin sheath of skin. If it were flesh-colored instead of royal blue, she would've appeared— at least without close inspection—to be naked.

He could feel himself getting hard as he gazed at her.

The clinging fabric bulged over her breasts. It looked perfectly smooth until the very front. There, it was pushed outward by small, pointed nipples.

Howard met her eyes, hoping she hadn't caught him staring. "How is it?" he asked.

She blew out some air, puffing a fine spray from her lips. Her chin was trembling just a bit. "If it was any colder, you could skate on it. But I figured it'd be like this. You get used to it. You two really ought to come in."

"I think I'll just sit here," Angela said, "and watch you three turn blue."

"You know, if it's just because you don't have a suit . . ."

"Well, that's one thing."

"There's no law that says you've got to strip down. You could jump in wearing what you've got on. Whatever."

"Well, I'll think about it."

"What about you, Howard?"

He shrugged. "It's pretty nice right here."

"Suit yourselves. You wouldn't believe how great it feels, though, once you're in." With that, she sank down, pushed herself off the bottom, and floated on her back. Arms by her sides, she began to kick. Howard watched her glide slowly away. Her long legs gleamed in the sunlight. Her breasts were out of the water, shaking a bit from side to side with the rhythm of her swishing legs.

"She looks great, doesn't she?" Angela said.

"Not bad."

"Do you want to go in? If you do, go ahead. I mean, you shouldn't stay out just on my account."

"I'm not crazy about the idea. I'll go in if you want to, though."

She wrinkled her nose. "Let's not, and say we did." Twisting around, she squinted toward the clearing where they'd left their gear.

"What is it?"

"I don't see Doris."

Howard turned and looked back. "Maybe she ducked into the trees to change, or something."

"I hardly think she's planning to take a dip."

"Could be answering a call of nature. Or maybe she's gone off to sulk."

Angela grinned. "You're mean."

"I just hope, wherever she went, she doesn't come back for a while. Things are a lot nicer when she's not around. It's like she's on her toes every second, just waiting for a chance to unload on somebody."

"I hope she's all right. That's the only thing."

"Why wouldn't she be?"

"I don't know. But doesn't it seem funny? I mean, when was the last time you saw her?"

"It probably wasn't more than ten or fifteen minutes ago," Howard said. Doris, he remembered, had been sitting in the shade with her back against a tree while the others had discussed whether they should pitch camp before or after taking a swim. She had still been sitting there, the debate continuing, when he and Angela had wandered down to the lake. "She was right under that tree," he said.

"Yeah."

"Wherever she went, she didn't take her pack."

Angela smiled at him. "What does that mean?"

"It means we're not in luck. She didn't bug out on us.

She's not hurrying down the mountain, burning up the trail on her way back to civilization."

"Maybe we should go and look for her."

"I guess we could," Howard said. "Why don't we wait a while, though? She'll probably show up."

"I'm in no hurry."

They both turned to the front. Lana, Keith and Glen were out near the middle of the lake, splashing and laughing. Glen seemed to be swimming after Lana, chasing her while Keith fled in a different direction.

"Think they're playing tag?" Angela asked.

"Looks like it."

We could be in the water doing that, Howard thought.

He pictured himself pursuing Lana, reaching out to tag her, his hand finding a bare cheek of her rump. The skin would feel chilly. Maybe rough with goosebumps. But warm underneath.

And he wondered why he was daydreaming about Lana when he had Angela sitting right here beside him.

Maybe because it's safe. You know Lana's out of reach.

Far out on the water, Glen caught up to her. He grabbed her ankle. They both went under. They came up together in a burst of froth. Lana, laughing, broke away from him and back-pedaled. "Hey, you!" she gasped. "Watch it!"

"You're it."

"You're a lech!"

"What'd you do to her?" Keith called. He sounded amused.

"Tagged her, that's all."

"Yeah? Where?"

"Never you mind," Lana said. "Here I come, ready or not." She went for Glen, who bolted. After a few strokes, she broke off her pursuit and headed for Keith.

"Thought she might," Angela said, scooting backward a bit before lifting her feet out of the water. She brought up her knees, and braced herself up with stiff arms. Her wet calves were shiny. Water trickled down them and made dark spots on the granite. "I guess I'll take a walk around," she said. "Want to come along?"

"Sure." Howard's heart quickened.

Maybe it's not just to look for Doris, he thought. Maybe she wants to get me alone.

The others were certain to stay in the lake for a while longer. Once he and Angela were away from the shore, they would have complete privacy.

Except for Doris.

Some of his nervous excitement faded. Angela probably had nothing more in mind than searching.

But if we go looking for her, we *will* be alone. As long as we don't find her.

Angela leaned forward, reached around her bent legs, and used her crew socks to wipe her feet dry. Instead of putting them on, she spread them out on the rock. Then she stretched out her legs, crossed one, and worked her bare foot into a sneaker.

Howard had taken off his own boots and socks. He'd considered soaking his feet, but given up on the idea because he didn't want his pants to get wet and he'd thought he would look like a turkey if he rolled up his cuffs.

As Angela put on her other sneaker, he plucked his wadded socks out of his boots. They were filthy and damp. He dropped them onto the rock. Without socks, he wasn't eager to shove his feet into his boots. He knew they would feel awful: not only tight on his tender feet, but dank and slimy. He had a pair of Nikes in his pack. He wondered if he should go for them barefoot. Not a good idea. He might step on something sharp. Getting a foot injury way out here in the middle of nowhere . . .

"Oh, there's Doris. Over there." Angela pointed toward the far side of the lake.

Howard spotted her at once. She was in plain sight, making her way across the sloping jumble of rock above the lake's eastern shore.

"What the hell's she doing?" he muttered.

"Exploring?"

"Didn't she get enough exercise for one day?"

"Apparently not."

Howard shook his head and followed Doris's progress. She walked across the face of a tilted block the size of a car. At its end, she used her hands to climb a boulder. When she reached its top, she leaped across a gap and landed on a block of granite that looked like an overturned refrigerator.

"Maybe the heat drove her buggy," Howard said.

"She's pretty agile."

"Wait'll she gets back, she'll probably fill us all in on expertise as a mountaineer. She probably assaulted Everest last year."

Angela cast a glance at Howard. "Hope she didn't hurt him."

He laughed. Then, mimicking Doris, he said, "You been taking wise-guy lessons from Tweedle-Dee and Dumb-Dumb?"

Her head bobbed. She was mugging like a dope, her eyes fixed on Howard, and he felt a sudden rush of affection for her so strong it seemed to blot out everything else. It was a very odd sensation. Even as it swept through him, he realized it was nothing like sexual arousal. It was like tenderness or sorrow. It made him feel almost like weeping. He reached out and curled a hand behind her head and leaned toward her until his mouth found her lips.

They were soft and warm and moist.

God! he thought. What am I doing?

Before he could pull back, Angela's hand went to his face. She caressed his cheek. Then her mouth eased away. Looking into his eyes, she whispered, "Do you want to take that walk now?"

"Yeah."

She turned forward. She tied one of her shoes. As she tugged at the bow, she raised her eyes. They suddenly went wide. She sucked in a quick breath. Her back stiffened.

Howard shot his gaze out across the water. He spotted Lana, Keith and Glen. Swimming, laughing. He searched the slope for Doris. There she was, striding along a granite slab.

"Angela?"

She still stared into the distance. The alarm on her face spooked him.

"What's wrong?" he blurted. "What is it?"

"In front of Doris," she said. Her voice was hushed, little more than a whisper. "Just above her. See?"

Howard found Doris again. She was almost straight across the lake, now. He moved his eyes ahead of her, and upward. And heard himself gasp. His stomach seemed to drop. He went weak and shaky. "My God," he murmured.

The man stood motionless on an outcropping. He was hunched over slightly. His head was down, and cocked toward Doris. He seemed to be watching her. Waiting for her.

He looked like a man who might've just stepped off the stage at the Mr. Universe contest. His bronze skin, bulging with knots of muscle, had an oily sheen. He seemed to have no hair at all. The top of his head gleamed in the sun. He wore sunglasses. He wore a G-string with a shiny black pouch. In his right hand was a machete.

And Doris was scurrying over the boulders, moving closer to him, unaware of his presence.

Angela leaped to her feet, cupped her hands to the sides of her mouth, and yelled, "DORIS!"

Doris halted and turned her head toward them.

"LOOK OUT!" Howard yelled, springing up. "A MAN!"

"What's going on?" Keith called to them.

"A *guy's* up there!" Howard answered. "He's got a machete! Up ahead of Doris!"

Angela flapped her hand, waving Doris back and shouting, "GET OUT OF THERE! RUN!"

Doris shook her head as if she didn't understand.

The man began to leap from rock to rock.

"HE'S COMING FOR YOU!" Angela yelled.

"BEHIND YOU!" Lana cried out.

Howard glimpsed Keith and Glen in motion—swimming toward the far side of the lake.

Not all that far.

But they wouldn't make it in time. They wouldn't come close.

Doris, apparently getting the message at last, began to turn around. The man was above her. Rushing at her straight down a steep rock slab.

He was gleaming skin and bouncing heaps of muscle. He was a stud in his black shades. He was a gayboy in his itsy-bitsy G-string. He was a skinhead. He was a madman with a machete.

Doris didn't scream. She made no sound at all that Howard could hear when she turned around and saw what was coming down for her. She jerked and flung out her arms and scampered backward.

To the edge of the boulder she'd been crossing.

Where she tried to stop.

She teetered on the brink, windmilling her arms.

"God!" Angela gasped. She grabbed Howard's hand.

Her fingernails dug into him when Doris sprawled out into the air.

The man reached for Doris.

He didn't swing his machete at her. He stretched out his left arm and tried to grab the front of her sweatshirt.

But missed.

She flapped her arms. She kicked. She had only six or eight feet to fall, but it seemed to go on forever. Howard knew he was about to see her die. In slow motion. Her head would be first to hit the granite. It would blast open . . .

But her rump hit first.

Then her legs and back slammed the tilted plate of rock. Her head snapped down, but it was beyond the edge and struck only air.

Howard thought he saw her bounce a little. She looked limp.

On her back, head first, she began skidding down the face of the rock.

She didn't fly off as if shooting down a slide. Her descent was too slow for that.

Her head drooped lower. Her shoulders followed. Her arms flopped off the edge and dangled toward the lake. Her back bent as if the weight of her upper body were trying to snap it. Suddenly, her legs were flung upward and she somersaulted off the slab. Accidents of gravity spread-eagled her. She looked like an obese skydiver, the slipstream flapping her sweatshirt and baggy shorts, lifting her hair.

She smacked the surface of the lake. Water exploded up.

And rained down on Keith and Glen. Lana had almost caught up to them. They all dove and disappeared.

The man with the machete gazed down from the rocks.

What if he goes in after them?

"No," Angela whispered. "Don't. Don't."

Dives in with that machete and hacks them all to pieces. Nobody's left but me and Angela . . . and him.

But he didn't dive in. He turned aside. He strode along the top of the boulder, leaped a gap and landed on a tilted block. His back to the lake, he let the machete dangle from his shoulder by a strap and began to climb the wall of an outcropping.

Chapter Thirteen

Howard, trembling, lowered his gaze to the lake.

Lana was boosting herself out, climbing onto a shelf of rock that jutted into the water not far from the place where Doris had fallen in. Glen was towing Doris by her hair. She floated along on her back, neither struggling nor helping. Keith swam near her feet, his head up. He seemed to be watching for the assailant.

"Is she all right?" Angela asked, her voice little more than a whisper.

"I can't tell. Doesn't look like she's moving."

"God."

Howard wished they would bring her to this side of the lake, but he could see that Glen was taking her toward the place where Lana had climbed out. It made sense to get her to the nearest shore. It would've been safer to come this way, though. The guy was over there.

"I don't see him anymore," Angela said.

Howard raced his eyes up the slope, found the cluster of rock where he'd last seen the man, and scanned the area above it. Except for a few stunted trees, he saw only pale, glaring granite and shadows where odd formations blocked the sunlight.

"Must be hiding up there."

At the shore, Lana was crouched over the water holding onto one of Doris's arms while Glen climbed out.

"We'd better go over there," Angela said. She glanced from side to side, apparently judging the distances. "It'd probably take us ten or fifteen minutes if we walk."

"Should we swim across?"

"It'd be a lot quicker. Can you swim that far?"

"Sure. You?"

"Yeah." She held onto his arm while she shifted her weight from one foot to the other and yanked off her shoes. When she let go, Howard started taking off his shirt.

"Guess we're going in, after all," he said.

"Suits or no suits."

"We'll freeze, you know."

"Just for a few minutes."

"Jeez, I hope she's all right."

He tugged down his corduroys and stepped out of them. Angela kept her blouse and shorts on.

Side by side, they jumped into the lake. Howard let out a cry of pain as he met the water. It was so cold it seemed to sear his legs. He felt as if his genitals had been grabbed and crushed by a frigid hand.

Angela, waist deep beside him, gave him a stunned glance. Her lips were peeled back, her teeth gritted. But she didn't hesitate. She took a wading step or two, then plunged beneath the surface.

Howard snatched a breath into lungs that felt shriveled and tight. Then he keeled forward, leaving his feet, submerging himself. A vice clamped his temples. A scream gathered in his throat. But he stayed under and kicked. The water slid over him. It seemed to search out hidden places on his body—pockets and creases of warmth—and pry into them like a frozen blade.

We should've walked, he thought.

126

Too late now.

He wondered how Angela was doing.

He wondered how Doris was doing.

What'll we do if she's dead?

She isn't. She's OK.

Who the hell was that lunatic?

Howard kicked to the surface. He dragged air into his tight lungs and saw Angela just ahead of him. She was gliding along, low and sleek against the water. The way she swam looked effortless. Her strokes and kicks sped her along, but caused hardly a splash.

He glimpsed Lana and Glen huddled over Doris's body. Keith was just climbing out of the lake.

When his teeth started to chatter, Howard hurled himself forward and resumed swimming. He kicked as hard as he could. He shot his arms out and dragged them back. He held his breath until his chest ached, then blew it out, rolled, filled his lungs and kept on swimming.

As he began to tire, he took breaths more often.

He realized he wasn't freezing anymore. The water felt cold but good.

He switched from the crawl to the breaststroke. Keeping his head up, he was able to breathe steadily and see. Angela had increased her lead. She was about thirty feet in front of him. A few more strokes took her to the shelf where the others were crouching around Doris. She boosted herself up.

Howard liked the way her blouse was pasted to her back and the straps of her bra showed through. He knew he would've been able to see through her shorts, but their seat was draped by the hanging tail of her blouse.

As she climbed out, water streamed down the gleaming backs of her legs. She took a couple of steps, then sank to her knees beside Doris. The bottoms of her feet looked ruddy, as if she had been running barefoot across a field of snow.

She swung her head around and called, "Doris is all right."

Thank God, he thought.

But it almost seemed like bad news. Along with his relief, he felt a little cheated, disappointed.

Get off it, he told himself. I didn't want her to die. No way!

It would've gotten us out of here, though. Loot or no loot, nobody'd be ready to stick around if Doris had been killed.

Howard grabbed the gritty rock edge. He jumped and swung himself up. He started to rise. His briefs felt heavy and clinging. But nobody was looking at him, anyway. He hurried forward and knelt beside Angela.

Doris was stretched out, forehead resting on her crossed arms, her nose almost touching the granite.

"Are you OK?" Howard asked.

"Ha ha, very funny."

"Guess you are."

"She's just resting," Lana said. "She had her wind knocked out, but we don't think she's hurt."

"Nothing broken?"

"Just her butt," Keith said.

"Knock it off," Glen told him.

Glen sticking up for Doris. That was a new one.

Howard ducked low. Her eye was open. It didn't look at him. It stared at the wet surface of rock under her face. A drop of water fell off the tip of her nose. "Are you really OK?" he asked.

"Fine and dandy."

He pushed himself up and glanced at Angela. She shrugged. He looked at the others. They were all kneeling or crouching around Doris, watching her. Glen reached down and rubbed her back.

"Hands off," she said.

"Don't be such a jerk," he said, and kept his hand where it was. "You damn near got killed."

"Tell me about it," she muttered.

"What'll we do now?" Howard asked.

"Just give her a few minutes," Lana said. "She's pretty shaken up."

"We shouldn't stick around too long," Keith said. "That crazy bastard might come back." Straining his head around, he scanned the slope.

"He won't come back," Lana said.

"Don't count on it."

"If he had the guts to go up against all of us, he wouldn't have run off like that."

"What's he up to, anyway?" Glen muttered, massaging the nape of Doris's neck.

"A fuckin' maniac," Keith said.

"Yeah, but he had a chance to chop her. Looked like he tried to catch her, instead."

"He did," Angela said. "I saw that, too."

Keith quit searching. He scowled down at Doris. "The guy's some kind of a pervert. So, he didn't whack her head off when he had the chance. What do you think he would've done if he'd managed to grab her and pull her back? Shake her hand and say 'Charmed to make your acquaintance'?"

"Maybe he wanted to take her with him," Angela said.

"That's what I'm thinking," Glen said.

"Either that," Keith said, "or fuck her right there on the spot. And maybe *then* slice her up."

A hitch of breath came from Doris. It sounded like a sob.

"Let's watch what we're saying," Lana muttered.

"What do *you* think he had in mind?"

"I don't know."

"You saw him. Did you see what he was wearing? Nobody's gonna go running around the mountains like that unless he's lost his marbles."

"He might've just been coming down for a swim," Angela suggested.

"Get real."

"Well, it's possible."

"Come on. He's sneaking around with a machete, for godsake."

"I think Angela's got a point," Howard said. It felt good to be sticking up for her. And if she was right, maybe there was no actual reason to fear the man. "If he really was on his way down to go swimming, that would explain why he was dressed that way."

"Sure. I know I always like to swim in my G-string."

"We just got here," Lana said. "He might've thought the place was deserted. Hell, I've gone skinny-dipping in lakes like this when nobody else was around. At least he was wearing something."

Skinny-dipping, Howard thought. She does go skinny-dipping. He looked at her kneeling there. Her bare shoulders sparkled with water drops. Her nipples were hard, jutting against the filmy fabric of her suit. Lowering his gaze, he could see the indentation of her navel. He followed the sleek blue downward. Between her legs, it was very narrow. It bulged a little over twin lips, dipping in the center.

If she didn't have the suit on . . .

Howard realized his penis was rising, pushing into the wet front of his briefs.

No! They'll all see it!

That thought was enough to make his erection begin to subside. He stared down at Doris and tried to think about her fall. He was still shrinking.

Don't look at Lana again, he warned himself.

"Maybe when he saw we were here," Angela said, "he decided to just watch us for a while."

"I'll buy that part," Keith said. "A little wilderness voyeurism."

"But it could've been perfectly innocent. Maybe he thought he might come down and meet us . . ."

"Sure, and have a friendly chat."

"But then Doris came along, and we spotted him and started yelling like we thought he was a mad slasher or something and it all got out of hand."

"That might be how it happened," Howard said, daring to speak up now that his erection was gone.

"It's a possibility," Lana said. He didn't look at her.

"Bullshit," Keith said.

"Keith is an asshole," Doris muttered. "But he isn't a total idiot. This time, he's right." She pushed herself up. On her knees in the center of the group, she turned her head and looked at everyone.

Howard had heard the single sob a while ago, but he hadn't realized she'd actually been crying. He would've guessed that she didn't know how to cry. But she did. She was doing it now. Her eyes were red and flooded, and tears were trickling down her cheeks. Her nose was running. The tip of her tongue darted across the slick, and she sniffed.

"That man was no innocent, happy camper coming down for a dip," she said. "You people are just trying to make yourselves feel better. The functional term here is 'denial.' You're creating a comforting fiction because the truth terrifies you. The truth is, the man's a fucking maniac. He's demented. He's a pervert."

"We don't know that for sure," Lana told her.

"I do. He almost got me. I know. I could smell him. I could *hear* him."

"What'd he say?" Glen asked.

" 'Ohhh, yes-yes-yes-yes-yes.' Like that. Very quiet and breathy. I could hardly even make it out, but that's what he said when he came running down at me."

Doris lifted the wet front of her sweatshirt and wiped her face with it. The drooping mound of her belly looked as if it had never been touched by sunlight.

"You think he wanted to kill you?" Lana asked. Howard looked at her, this time. But he didn't let his eyes wander down from her face.

"I think he wanted to fuck me," Doris said. "Fuck me, split me open and climb in. I could *feel* it."

Some of the color went out of Lana's face. She glanced around at the others. "OK. Let's just say the guy *is* some kind of homicidal maniac. He might not be, but let's just say he is."

"He is," Doris said.

"What do we want to do about it?"

"What are the choices?" Glen said. "We either beat it out of here or we stay. Personally, I don't relish the idea of letting some Muscle Beach freako run us off."

"I'm with Glen," Keith said. "Shit, we came all this way. We came after a *treasure*."

"If there is a treasure," Howard said.

"Butler came through with the hundred bucks in the couch," Glen pointed out. "We believed him enough to drive all night and hike our butts off to get up here. The only new factor is the creep."

"And he might be gone," Angela said.

"Or he might sneak up on us after dark," Doris said, "and slaughter us all."

"If you're scared of him, just take off," Keith told her.

"I intend to."

"Not by yourself," Glen said.

"Just watch me." With that, Doris got to her feet. She grimaced as she straightened up. She stepped past Lana, limped across the shelf and started to climb the hump of a boulder.

"Hold on," Glen said, rising. His drooping boxer shorts left the tops of his buttocks bare. He reached back with one hand and pulled them up. "Where are you going?"

"Back to the campsite, for starters."

"You're planning to *walk*?"

"Indeed I am."

"It'd be easier to swim."

"I don't swim," she said.

Not, I *can't* swim. I *don't* swim. As if she were stating a preference.

"Well look," Glen said. "I'm not wearing any shoes."

"So what?"

"I don't want to kill my feet."

"So swim. Do you see me requesting an escort?"

Tough words, Howard thought. Typical Doris. But he thought he saw something a little frantic about her eyes.

He stood up. So did Angela. "I'll go with you," he said.

"Me too," Angela said.

"Don't do me any favors."

"You don't have to get snotty with us," Angela told her.

"I wasn't planning to swim back across, anyway. That water's *awful*."

"We'll all walk," Lana said.

Doris scowled. "You're just trying to make me feel like a shit."

"You are a shit," Keith said.

"Cut it out," Glen warned.

"Just go on and swim across. I don't want you people to ruin your feet and blame me."

"Let's see how it goes," Lana said. "We'll stay as close to the water as we can. If we run into a place that looks too rough for walking, we'll just jump in and swim around it."

"Do whatever you want," Doris said.

"Does that go for me?" Keith asked. " 'Cause I want to kick your fat ass."

That got him a sharp glance from Glen.

"What're you, suddenly her protector? Jesus, man."

"She's been hurt."

"Big fucking deal, it didn't improve her attitude."

"Let's all just cool it," Lana said. "We've got enough problems without bickering among ourselves."

Doris, sneering, turned away and trudged up the side of the boulder.

Glen followed her. Lana went next.

"I'll cover the rear, guys," Keith said in a quiet voice to Howard and Angela.

"She *is* a bitch," Angela whispered.

"You're telling me."

"But you should try being nicer to her."

"Who died and made you camp counselor?"

Angela blushed.

"Don't talk to her that way."

"Fuck you, Howitzer." Dropping to a crouch, he picked up a jagged rock.

Howard took a step backward.

"Don't flatter yourself. It's not for you."

Angela tugged on Howard's elbow. "Come on," she muttered.

"Keep your eyes open," Keith said as they started away from him.

Howard considered picking up a rock. But he didn't want to look as if he were copying Keith. Besides, he wasn't much good at throwing things. If the guy did show up, he would probably miss.

"If that nut comes back," he said to Angela, "we oughta hit the water."

"Good idea."

He wished he was in the water now. Its freezing cold might be better than walking along in nothing but his underpants. They were no longer so wet that they clung to him. Except for the elastic around his waist, they felt loose and saggy. He thought he could feel air coming up through the leg holes. His genitals were bouncing and swinging. He felt naked.

"I don't think he'll show up," Angela said. She glanced at Howard's face and quickly looked away. "Do you? I mean, he ran off. But Doris could be right about him sneaking back after dark. He might wait till we're asleep tonight."

"I know. Maybe we *should* head back down to the car."

"I guess that's what Doris is going to do."

"We can go with her, if you want."

Angela looked at him. "Is that what you want?"

"It might not be a bad idea."

"We really can't let her go by herself."

"I wouldn't mind getting out of here."

"What about the treasure?" she asked.

"It might not even exist. Or we might not be able to find it."

"We've got the Ouija board," she said. "I imagine that's why they took it last night—so we could ask more about how to get there."

"Yeah, but Butler's weird—whatever he is. What if he's just screwing around with us? Maybe he never intended to lead us to that loot of his. Maybe he just wanted to get us up here." An awful thought struck Howard. He muttered, "Oh, man."

"What?"

"Suppose Butler lured us here just so that weirdo could nail us?"

Angela wrinkled her nose. "That's a pretty yucky idea."

"I know, I know. It's probably crazy."

Angela frowned and turned away from him. They walked along in silence for a while. Howard realized that he was no longer bothered about being out here in nothing but his underwear. Probably because Angela seemed OK about it.

The hike wasn't as bad as he'd expected. When he had to jump across a gap or climb, he didn't like how the skin pulled on the bottoms of his feet. Other than that, it was all right. Walking was no problem at all when the surface was fairly level. The granite felt rough and gritty, but it had few sharp places. Though it was hot, it didn't burn him.

He and Angela were both taking care to avoid being scratched by the dry, withered branches that sometimes grew out of crevices. They stayed away from the loose rocks with jagged edges sometimes littering the way.

Could've been a lot worse, he thought.

Now, if I just don't get sunburned so bad my skin falls off . . .

"I've got an even crazier one for you," Angela said.

"A crazier what?" he asked, trying to remember what they'd been talking about.

"Idea. Than yours that Butler sent us here so the guy could get us."

"You have a crazier idea?"

"Maybe that guy *is* Butler."

"Wonderful."

She made a quiet, nervous laugh. "Just a thought. I mean, it's pretty far-fetched. When you mess around with a Ouija board, I guess it's supposed to be *spirits* who contact you."

"Yeah. Dead guys. Ghosts. That's the general belief, anyway."

"The fellow looked pretty alive to me," Angela said.

"He wasn't any ghost, that's for sure."

"On the other hand . . ."

"How many ghosts have I met?"

"He never did touch Doris. Maybe he couldn't."

"Because he's a spook?"

"How do we know he *isn't*?" Angela asked.

"You got me. But I sure couldn't see through him. And ghosts don't normally go running around in broad daylight, do they?"

"How should I know?"

Howard shook his head. "I don't think I can buy it. This guy was prancing around in a G-string and shades."

"Just because he doesn't fit our preconceptions . . ."

"I know. But still."

"Do you think we should mention it to the others?"

"Are you kidding? They'd think we're nuts."

"I'm not so sure of that. I mean, look at us. We're all here because of a Ouija board. They'd have a lot of nerve jumping on us about ghosts."

"They would dump all over us."

"If that guy *is* a ghost, you know, it wouldn't be such a bad deal. It's one thing to have a flesh-and-blood maniac running around with a machete. It's not the same at all if he's nothing but an apparition."

"If he's a ghost, in other words, he wouldn't actually be able to chop us up."

She grinned. "Exactly. Or at least I don't think he could. I mean, the machete would be an apparition, too, right?"

"I suppose."

"So we wouldn't have anything to fear."

"Except getting the crap scared out of us."

"But there wouldn't be any reason to leave and go running back to the car, you know?"

"That's true. *If* he's a spook."

"So, maybe we should talk to the others about it."

"Doris will just say it's wishful thinking or denial or something."

"Do *you* think that's what it is?"

"When it comes right down to it, I think the guy's real. Don't you?"

Angela wrinkled her nose. "I guess there's an awfully good chance of it." She took a few steps without speaking, then said, "So now we're back to him being some kind of a maniac."

"Yeah. And I think we should get out of here. It'd be stupid to spend the night with that guy around."

"We just forget about Butler's treasure?"

"Like I said . . ."

"I know, we might not get it anyway. But what if we can, Howard? What if it's a lot of money and we go running away because of this guy? I could use it, you know? I don't think I can go back to Skerrit after last night, and . . ."

"You *can't* go back to him."

"I don't *want* to. *God!*"

Lana heard her outburst and looked back.

"It's OK," Angela called to her.

Though Lana was frowning with concern, she nodded and turned away. She leaped off a rock, and Howard saw that she was clear of the boulder area. Doris and Glen, ahead of her, were on a path that curved around the end of the lake.

"I've got to stay," Angela said. "I've got to. No matter what Doris or any of the others decide, I have to stay and find Butler's treasure."

"If you stay, I stay."

"You don't have to."

"Sure I do."

She took his hand and squeezed it.

"Get it on!" Keith called from the rear.

They ignored him, and hopped down to the path. The earth felt cool after the heat of the granite. It was springy with brown, matted pine needles.

A few strides took them into the shade of nearby trees, and Howard could feel a mild breeze. He watched his step, being careful to avoid pebbles and twigs and cones on the path.

At the end of the lake, they waded across a rapid stream. Soon, they came to the clearing where they'd left their gear.

Doris, already wearing her pack, was standing over Glen while he pulled his pants on.

"You're going to leave for sure?" Howard asked her.

"Watch my dust."

"I'll be going with her," Glen said.

"We're planning to stay," Howard said.

"It's your skin," Doris told him.

He turned to Lana, who was squatting beside her open pack and digging into it.

"What about you?" he asked.

"I'm not leaving," she said. "Maybe no one is."

"Just try to stop me," Doris said.

Lana pulled a holster out of her pack, stood, turned around, and drew out a revolver. "Maybe this will change your mind."

Doris went pale. Her mouth dropped open.

"Hey," Glen said, gazing at the weapon.

"You two can run off if you want," Lana said. "But I didn't come all this way to get chased off by some damn lunatic. He shows up around here, he'll catch a few bullets."

"My kind of gal," Keith said, grinning. "Where'd that hummer come from, anyway?"

"I always bring it along when I go camping. You just never know."

"Well, all right!"

"Gosh," Glen said. He looked at Doris. "This does change things."

"Marvelous," Doris muttered. "Now I suppose you aren't coming with me."

"Hey, look," he said. "I know you're shook up. But we don't have to be afraid of the guy, now. It doesn't make any sense to leave. We've got a gun."

"Big deal. A firearm is not a panacea."

"It's all the panacea *I* need," Glen told her.

She stared at him, looking sad and betrayed. Then she glanced at each of the others. "So nobody will come with me?"

"We'll stay and watch your dust," Keith said.

"Shut the fuck up!" Glen snapped at him. To Doris, he said, "No, I'll go with you if you *have* to leave. But we won't have the gun, you realize, and that guy could be anywhere."

"That's right," Keith said. "He might jump you guys on the way down."

"And if we do get to the car OK, we'll just have to stay there. For a couple of days, probably."

"Maybe longer," Lana said. "I guess I could give you the keys so you can lock yourselves in at night."

"Hang on, now," Keith protested. "What if they drive off?"

"They won't."

"Yeah? Who says?"

"I say," Glen told him.

"Oh, yeah. Right."

"Never mind," Doris said.

They all looked at her. Head down, she tugged the straps off her shoulders and let the pack fall.

"Just forget it," she muttered. "I'll stay. You won. All right? You won. So fuck it." She turned away, kicked her pack, then stepped around it and walked toward the shore.

Glen, fastening his belt, hurried after her. He didn't say anything. He caught up to Doris and put a hand on her shoulder.

Whirling on him, she blurted, "Just leave me alone!" Then she threw herself against him, pushed her face against the side of his neck, wrapped her arms around his back, and hugged him hard.

"Let's get dressed," Lana said quietly to the others. "We've got to start setting up camp."

Chapter Fourteen

Corie wondered where the kids had gone. Just a minute ago, they'd been surrounding the table, all of them leaning over it with their fingers on the plastic heart-shaped pointer. But now they weren't there.

Must've gone home, she thought.

Good. I didn't want them playing with this thing, anyway.

She reached down for the pointer. It scurried away from her hand.

"Don't pull that crap with me," she said.

As it slowed down, she made another grab for it. The pointer darted. Her fingertips thudded against the board, shaking the table beneath it.

"Damn you! Knock it off!"

It glided in a slow circle, and stopped near the middle of the board.

It wants me to look, she thought. It has a message for me.

A message that starts with T.

"OK, T," she said. "Go on."

It didn't move.

"Do you want to tell me something, or don't you?"

When it still didn't move, Corie bent down for a closer look. She peered through the pointer's clear plastic window. The T shimmered, inflated, turned blue, and suddenly it was no longer a letter. It was Jake. Jake in his police uniform, legs together, arms outstretched, a bloody hole above his left eye. Jake as he must've looked after the shooting. Jake dead.

Corie gasped and swiped at the pointer. It leaped straight up. Her hand swept under it. She cried out as she struck Jake. The blow sent his miniature body tumbling across the Ouija board, arms and legs flopping.

The pointer came down on the back of her hand. It clutched her skin. How *can* it? She jerked her arm up close to her face. And saw. The felt pads at the bottom of its three plastic legs were gone, replaced by tiny human hands. Their fingers were hooked into her skin. Turning wet red.

With the back of her other hand, she swatted the pointer. Her blow sent it hurling away, streamers of shredded flesh trailing from its clenched hands.

She thought she was rid of the horrible thing.

But it landed on her knee.

That's impossible! she thought. I'm standing up.

She *had* been standing. Not anymore. She couldn't remember sitting down, but now she was seated on a chair and the pointer was clinging to the front of her knee.

She flinched with pain as its fingers dug in.

It began to climb.

"Damn you!" She tried to swing at it, and found that her hands were cuffed behind her back.

No!

How could she be handcuffed?

Jake? No. Impossible. He's dead.

The pointer began creeping along the top of her thigh. It took its time. With each step, it sank its needle-sharp fingertips into her skin.

141

It was inching slowly closer to the flap of red nightshirt that draped her lap.

I'm in my nightshirt!

No! This can't be happening!

Corie squirmed and bucked and pounded her legs together, but she couldn't dislodge the plastic heart.

Its blunt tip dipped down until it touched her skin, then nudged its way under the edge of her nightshirt. Corie froze. Her heart pounded. She gasped for breath.

The tiny hands groped and clawed. The rest of the pointer slipped out of sight. The thing crept sideways and down the inner slope of her thigh.

She slammed her legs shut on it.

And her knees bashed together, waking her up. For just an instant, she was disappointed; she wanted to know whether she'd crushed the thing or not.

Then she realized it didn't matter. She was awake. The pointer wouldn't get her.

She found that she was sitting upright in the passenger seat of her car. Her legs were wide apart, her hands gripping her thighs. Not exactly a lady-like pose, she thought. But she was wearing her red shorts, not a nightshirt. They had loose, baggy legs that reached halfway to her knees.

She felt a trickle of drool on her chin. On the right side, so maybe Chad hadn't seen it. She ducked her head a little and rubbed the spittle off against the shoulder of her blouse.

She lifted her hands off her thighs. She must've been squeezing hard. There were ruddy fingerprints on her skin, and her nails had made tiny, crescent-shaped impressions.

She looked at Chad.

He met her eyes. "Welcome back," he said.

"Glad to be back. Jeez." Lifting the front of her blouse, she wiped some moisture from under her eyes.

"Must've been some dream you were having."

"Yeah. Thanks for waking me up."

"I figured you could use your sleep. Besides, dreams are a good release."

"Is that so," she muttered.

142

" 'Dreams, that knit the tattered sleeve of care.' "

"That one unraveled mine."

"Sorry. Maybe I should've woken you up."

"Would've appreciated it."

"Next time."

"Thanks. Hope there isn't one." She rubbed the heels of her hands against the fingernail marks. "How long was I out?"

"A couple of hours."

She nodded. Though she felt as if she'd only been asleep for a few minutes, the look of the sun was enough to tell her that she had slept into early evening. It hung low over the hills to the west, bathing the woods in a dusty, golden hue. Slopes and valleys were masked by patches of darkness. A car in front of them cast a shadow that stretched across the entire lane beside it.

She checked her wristwatch. "Quarter after seven," she mumbled. "Man, I *was* out of it."

"What were you dreaming?"

She shook her head. "I don't know, something about a Ouija board." The memory made her feel squirmy. She eased her legs together, trying not to be conspicuous about it, and crossed her ankles. "Its pointer was attacking me. It had little hands. It was *crawling* on me."

"Hard to imagine why you might come up with something like that."

"Isn't it, though?"

"Under attack by your Ouija board."

"If I ever get it back from those rats, I'll burn it. I should've burnt the damn thing years ago. They sell them as *parlor games*, do you believe it? People *play* with them. As if they're toys."

"It's our culture," Chad said. "We're basically pretty frivolous about the supernatural. Thomas Edison's fault."

"Huh?"

"Oh, there was a gal I met at a ski lodge a couple of years ago. A refugee from Vietnam. She used to tell me stuff. She was just full of creepy stories. According to her, we tend to ignore the supernatural over here in the States because we have so many lights."

"It's a clean, well-lighted place."

"That's right, Papa. And spooks don't like the light. But over in Nam, there's plenty of darkness. If you go into dark places, they get you. Those people take it seriously. Parents over there actually warn their kids not to play hide-and-seek, because the good hiding places are where the evil things might be lurking."

"Like the V.C.?"

"I don't think it was the V.C. they were worried about. Anne—that was her name—told me about a girl she knew who went ahead and played hide-and-seek one night. Her friends looked and looked for her, and finally gave up. She was found a few days later. She'd apparently hidden in a ditch or gully or something. Anyway, she was dead. She'd died of suffocation. Her mouth was packed with dirt. When they opened her up—I guess they autopsied her—they found that she was completely stuffed with dirt. She was full of it. Her esophagus, her stomach . . ."

"God, how weird."

"That's what happens when you hide in dark places."

"I guess hide-and-seek's another game to stay away from."

"Anyway, Anne also told me that they've got a Vietnamese equivalent of the Ouija board. They don't call it that. And it didn't sound like it was put out by Parker Brothers. What they do is dig up the coffin of a virgin and use its lid. She didn't tell me what they use for a pointer . . ."

"Maybe a bone . . ."

He smiled. "Whatever. A severed finger."

"Oh, gross."

"But I guess they write the alphabet or something on the coffin lid, then gather around it and start popping questions. It's a fortune-telling device, just like the Ouija."

Corie realized she was shivering. "God, I've got goosebumps," she said, and rubbed her arms. "I don't know whether it was the hide-and-seek or the coffin lid, but . . ."

"That stuff kind of gives me the creeps, too. Just talking about it. But you ought to hear Anne tell it. That'd really shake you up. Because she believes every word of it. The way she talks, you know it scares her. But she just loves it here in this country. 'Too much light for ghosts,' she says. 'No ghosts in United States.' " Chad laughed softly. "Sounds like so much bull, I suppose. But I think she's got a point. It's easy to be a skeptic when you don't have to confront the dark. Pretty soon, you stop believing there might be something out there—monsters or ghosts or demons. You lose those things, the next thing you lose is God."

Corie glanced at him. "I hope you're not gonna start quoting scriptures."

"Are you washed in the blood of the lamb?"

"Oh, Jesus."

"Blasphemer."

"You and the horse you rode in on."

He held up a hand as if signaling a halt. "I've spent a lot of time away from the lights, that's all. And it changes you. You find out very fast that there's a lot more to life than meets the eye. It's something, I think, that a lot of people tend to forget when they live in a city."

"Unless they fool around with a Ouija board."

"True, true."

"It'll remind you real quick that something's out there. It might not be something you want to *know* about, but it's there. Just waiting for your call."

" 'Reach out and touch someone.' "

"Yeah." Corie grinned. "Maybe we should write promotional slogans for the things. 'Bring a Ouija board into your home, and add a taste of darkness.' " Her grin fell away. She stared at Chad. "They really *ought* to be made out of coffin lids."

When the house went dark, *Monday Night Football* vanished from the television screen and Jake muttered, "Oh, shit, wouldn't you know it!"

145

Corie, making notes for tomorrow's lesson on *Othello*, said, " 'Put out the light, and then put out the light.' "

"But for godsake," Chad said, "don't put out the boob tube."

"Hilarious," Jake said.

Because of the rainstorm and heavy winds outside, Corie doubted that the loss of power was due to a blown fuse. But she set her book and notepad aside, climbed out of the chair, and made her way carefully across the dark room. She opened the front door. A blast of chill wind spread her robe, billowed it out behind her, fluttered her nightshirt against her skin and scurried up beneath it.

The streetlights were out. The neighboring houses were dark.

She had seen what she came out to see, but she remained on the threshold savoring the feel of the wind. It gave her goosebumps. It made her shiver. It felt like secret hands exploring her body, caressing her everywhere.

She imagined herself running out onto the front yard. Naked. The wind sliding all over her, the rain streaming down her back. She saw Jake giving chase. Tackling her. She would go sprawling onto the cool wet grass, Jake hugging her legs then scurrying up her body, mounting her as she got to her hands and knees.

Right out of *Lady Chatterley's Lover*, she thought.

And where would Chad be while this was going on? Watching from the doorway?

No, he'd be too embarrassed for that.

The poor guy wouldn't know what to do with himself.

What if Jake were on duty? she wondered. And I went running out into the rain like that? Would Chad just ignore me, pretend it isn't happening, or would he . . . ?

"You nuts or something?" Jake called. "Close the damn door."

Reluctantly, Corie stepped backward and swung the door shut. The rushy noise of the storm faded. The still air in the house felt warm and safe. But the storm had left some of its wildness inside her.

146

"The whole neighborhood's dark," she said.

"I figured as much."

"Why don't we do something exciting?"

"What've you got in mind?" Jake asked. He still sounded miffed about missing the game, but there was a slight note of interest in his voice.

"Oh, I don't know. Let's run naked in the rain."

"Sure thing."

Chad, hidden somewhere in the dark, said nothing.

"We could sit around and tell ghost stories."

"That sounds cool," Chad said.

"Forget it," Jake said. "Why don't you make yourself useful and go get some candles?"

"Spoilsport."

"I'll go with you," Chad told her.

She heard a chair creak. Moments later, his broad shape loomed out of the darkness. "Right here," she said.

"I see you."

She looked down. Her robe was still hanging open. She knew she ought to close it, but she didn't want to.

No big deal. He's seen legs before.

She reached out and took his hand. He walked along beside her into the kitchen.

"Maybe we could play cards," he suggested.

"That's not very exciting," she said. Letting go of his hand, she crouched and opened a cupboard. She felt around inside. "We ought to do something . . . I don't know . . . appropriate for the darkness."

"Like hold a seance?"

"I think you need a real medium . . ."

"Lets me out. I'm an extra large."

She laughed, and her searching hand found the box where she kept her collection of used candles. "I know! The Ouija board."

"Jake's old Ouija board? You've still got it?"

"Sure. He never throws anything away."

As she lifted out the box and stood up, Chad said, "We

147

used to fool around with that thing all the time when we were kids. It can really spook you out."

"Perfect." She set the box on the counter. Gathering up a handful of candles, she stepped aside. She stuffed all but one into a pocket of her robe. "Go ahead and grab a few," she said, then went over to the stove.

She turned on a burner, ignited her wick, shut it off and faced Chad. "Want me to light your fire?"

In the fluttery glow, she saw him grimace. "Jeez, Coreen."

"Oh, don't get so embarrassed. I was just kidding."

"I know, I know." He tilted a candle toward her.

As she moved her flame up close to it, she saw how its tip was jittering. "My God," she whispered. "Look at you shake. What's wrong?"

"Nothing. Just a little nervous, maybe."

"The storm? The dark?"

He shrugged. "Maybe both. I don't know."

Corie held his hand steady while she lit his candle.

He's just a big kid, she thought. Like all men. They grow up, but there's always a kid hidden inside, scared of the dark and a million other things, scared most of letting it show.

She gave his hand a gentle squeeze. "You think you're nervous now, wait till we get going with that Ouija board."

Stepping past him, she led the way into the living room.

"We thought we'd get out the Ouija board and . . ."

Jake's easy chair in front of the television was empty.

She felt a quick little drop in her stomach.

Gone.

For just a moment, Corie imagined him truly gone. Gone from his chair, gone from the house, gone from her life forever.

That's crazy, she told herself fast to stop the rush of panic. He's fine. He probably went to the john. Or he's playing games.

A dark shape came scurrying out from beside the chair. Jake on his hands and knees. "Beware the beast of the storm! It comes for thee!" He charged her.

"Now, don't. I'm serious. I'm holding a candle."

Growling, he lunged at Corie. His arms wrapped around her calves. His head pushed against her legs.

"Jake!" she gasped as she teetered, about to fall.

His hands shot up the backs of her legs. They clutched her buttocks, holding her steady while his head ducked beneath the front of her nightshirt.

"Jake!"

"It's all right," Chad said. "I'll leave the room."

"It's *not* all right. Jake, stop it. I mean it." Through the bulging fabric of her nightshirt, she knuckled the top of his head.

"Ouch!"

"I said not now. Come on. Chad's watching."

He wasn't watching, she realized. He was standing right beside her, holding his candle up and gazing in the other direction. Averting his eyes. Probably embarrassed as hell.

"You watching, Chadwick?"

"She asked you to stop," he said. "I think you should stop."

"Party poopers." He gave her buttocks a hard squeeze that hurt, then crawled backward.

Corie yanked her robe shut and tied its belt. She knew she was blushing.

Jake shouldn't have done that. Not in front of his brother. And he had no right to hurt her.

"I'll find the game," she said.

Stopping in front of the shelves, she searched for the Ouija board. She moved her candle slowly, illuminating books and stacks of magazines, framed photos, trophies and various knick-knacks, and several games. She found the Ouija board's box on a low shelf near the corner of the room.

When she turned around, she saw Chad with two lighted candles, Jake with two more. They were bent over the coffee table, dripping wax onto plastic coasters.

"This table all right?" Jake asked her.

It was low and they would have to sit on the floor. But Corie didn't want to play in the kitchen, and hauling the

149

card table into the living room would be a bother. "This is OK," she said.

She gave some of her candles to the men. While they were busy lighting them and sticking them onto coasters, she removed the Ouija board and pointer from the box. She set the board near the end of the table.

"Why don't you grab a pen and paper before you sit down," Jake said. "And a flashlight."

She took her candle, and went to get them. By the time she returned, Jake and Chad were already sitting on the floor across the table from each other. Four candles stood just beyond the far side of the board. Others had been placed on the sofa's end tables. The room shimmered with soft, golden light. But much of it was dark.

"We've sure got the atmosphere for this," she said. The candlelit room might have seemed romantic, she thought. But instead the presence of the Ouija board made it seem eerie. She realized she had goosebumps crawling up her body.

She lowered herself onto the floor at the end of the table and crossed her legs.

"Haven't done this in years," Chad said.

"Remember Mona?" Jake asked.

"Oh God, yeah. Scared the hell out of me."

"You weren't scared, you were jealous 'cause she liked me better than you."

"Can't figure that," Corie said.

Jake lifted the pointer onto the board, and they each placed the fingers of one hand on its cool plastic. "Mona told us she'd been murdered by her boyfriend. She died without having any kids. That was her one big regret—she never had a child."

"And she wanted Jake to correct the situation for her."

"You're kidding," Corie muttered.

"He fell head over heels for her."

"Bullshit," Jake said.

"You did. You couldn't wait for her to show up in the flesh some night."

"Bullshit."

"It's true."

"If you want to know the *real* truth, Mona didn't even exist. I made her up. It was just me pushing the pointer around, making her say that stuff. And, boy, were you gullible! You ate up the whole thing. There never was any Mona."

"Uh-huh," Chad said. "Right. Then why did you pound the crap out of me when I hid the board?"

"I just enjoyed pounding the crap out of you." He grinned at Corie. His stretched lips and bare teeth looked sinister in the fluttery light. "Man, I really had Chad going. He was so scared he hid the board out in the garage attic, and we didn't find it again until . . ."

His voice stopped as the pointer began to slide.

"Hope this isn't Mona," Chad muttered.

"We lost her when we moved," Jake said in a hushed voice as the pointer glided in small circles.

"I thought you said she didn't exist," Corie reminded him.

"Yeah, that's right. She didn't."

"You didn't have to . . ."

The pointer halted.

". . . lie about it."

They all leaned forward. The row of candles at the other side of the board gave enough light to see the letter beneath the raised plastic heart. "I," Corie read. The pointer slid and stopped, drifting around the board, spelling out its message while Corie took notes with her right hand.

When it seemed to be done, she tilted her notepad to catch the light. "I-B-L-O-N-L-Y," she read. "I be lonely?" She felt a cold knot in her stomach.

Maybe Mona's back. Why did Jake lie about her? Come on, this is just a Ouija board. A game. Calm down.

Forcing herself to chuckle, she said, "Whoever it is won't win any English awards."

"Who are you?" Jake asked.

She read the letters out loud as the pointer roamed and stopped. "U-N-O-M-E. You know me."

151

"Who does?" Jake asked.

"U."

"Jeez," Chad murmured. "Maybe it *is* Mona."

The cold in Corie's stomach grew and spread. "Maybe this wasn't such a great idea," she said.

Ignoring her, Jake said, "Who are you?"

"W-A-N-T-U."

"Me? What for?"

"L-O-N-L-Y."

Voice trembling, Corie asked, "Is this Mona?"

"Hey, I told you she wasn't . . ."

The pointer carried their hands toward the top of the board. To the moon in its corner. To the NO.

Thank God, Corie thought.

Jake let out a single huff of laughter. "See? It's not Mona. There *isn't* any Mona. So who are you?" he asked.

The pointer began moving again. Each time it stopped, Corie spoke the letters. "J-E-S-S-E-W-A-S-H . . ." Then her voice failed. She felt as if she'd been kicked in the stomach. She gasped for breath. Her heart slammed. She jerked her hand away from the pointer. Under the fingers of Jake and Chad, it continued to drift and halt, moving to the letters she knew would follow.

A surf seemed to be crashing in her ears. Through the noise of it, she heard Jake whisper, "Jesse Washington."

"Oh, shit," Chad said. He pulled his hand back. He glanced at Corie, then at Jake. Let's put it away."

Jake shook his head sharply from side to side. "What do you want, Jesse?" he asked. Using his official voice. The one he used on the job, but rarely in front of Corie. Talking firm. As if Jesse were an actual suspect, not the spirit of an armed robber he'd shot down three months earlier.

Corie watched the pointer carry her husband's hand over the shadowy board. "Write it down," he told her.

"Jake."

"Do it."

She followed orders.

After the pointer stopped, she studied what she had written. "U-B-D-I-N-K-W-I-K-L-I-K-A-B-U-N-N-Y. I can't make any sense out of it."

"Let me see."

She handed the pad to Jake. He lifted it close to one of the candles. He peered at it for a long time, frowning. Then a corner of his mouth turned up. "I think I've got it," he said. " 'You be dyin' quick like a bunny.' " He smirked down at the board. "Wishful thinking, asshole."

He gave the pad back to Corie.

"Keep track," he said.

"Don't *do* it anymore!"

"I'm anxious to hear everything this scumbag has to say."

The pointer darted.

"C-U-N-H-E-L-L."

Eight days later, Jake walked into a holdup in progress at a 7-Eleven. During the exchange of gunfire, a 9 mm. slug caught him above the left eye, plowed a tunnel through his brain, and blew a chunk of skull out the back.

"If they were made out of coffin lids," Corie said, "people might figure out the damn things aren't toys."

"And you could use them for surfboards."

Chapter Fifteen

Keith hunched over and blew steam off the surface of his coffee. He took a sip. Then he looked over his shoulder into the darkness beyond the campfire's glow. "I wonder what our pal is doing right now."

"Changing into a fur-lined nutbag," Glen said.

"We're not amused," Doris muttered.

"If he's got any sense," Lana said, "he's all bundled up and sitting by a fire, same as us."

"Howitzer, why don't you go and see if you can spot his fire."

Howard started to rise.

"Don't pay him any attention," Lana said.

"That's OK. I sort of want to take a look around, anyway." He straddled his log seat and hopped clear of it. Away from the fire's heat. But also away from its smoke. As much as he liked the smell of woodsmoke, he'd had enough of it. Ever since they'd returned to the fire after washing their supper dishes, the smoke had been going for his face as if seeking him out, ignoring the others.

154

He took a deep breath, enjoying the clean night air.

"Want me to come with you?" Angela asked.

"Sure, if you want."

While she climbed over the log, Howard rubbed the seat of his corduroys. His rump felt cold and a little numb.

"Don't go far," Lana warned.

"If you two had any sense," Doris said, "you wouldn't go at all. Look around you for a second. He might be anywhere."

Howard didn't bother. He knew that Doris was right. The man could be lurking in any direction just beyond the reach of the firelight. Maybe he was watching them from among the trees. Or hidden beside one of the tents. Or crouched among the rocks near the shore.

Angela took his hand. "Where should we go?"

"Down to the lake?"

"Sure," she said. They started walking. "I'll feel better if we keep the rest of them in sight. It really gave me the creeps when we had to go looking for firewood."

"Me, too," he admitted. "But the guy's probably gone for good. I bet Lana's right. He's probably sitting by a fire somewhere, trying to keep warm."

"In his fur-lined *thing*."

Howard laughed. His chest felt tight and shivery. "I bet he's wearing more than that now."

"One would hope so. I sure am glad you bought me this jacket."

"Are you warm enough?"

"My top is, anyway. The wind feels like it's going right through my sweatpants."

"Do you want to put something else on?"

"No. Then I'd probably be too hot when we get back to the fire. Shall we go out onto our rock?"

"Our rock. That's just what I had in mind."

They stepped up onto the slab of granite and took a few short steps down its slope before Howard pulled Angela to a stop. "Let's not fall in."

"Can you imagine anything worse?"

155

"It wouldn't be much fun."

She let go of his hand. As she leaned against his side, he felt her arm press gently against his back. Her hand curled over his hip. He put his own arm around her.

"It's so beautiful out here," she said.

"Isn't it?" The night sky was sprinkled with stars. A few tufts of clouds floated along, glowing white in the light of the full moon. A silver path glinted on the surface of the water. Across the lake, the piled granite blocks looked as if they'd been dipped in milk.

It really is beautiful out here, Howard thought. But then he noticed the patches of black on the far slope. And he found himself searching for the figure of a lone man.

He turned his head slowly, scanning the valley, looking for firelight.

The only fire was the one behind him.

Amazing how distinctly he could see Lana, Keith, Glen and Doris sitting around it. Every detail was brightly lighted and clear.

Sitting ducks, he thought.

"I haven't been camping since I was a little girl," Angela said. "I don't remember it being like this."

"Where was it?"

"Gosh, I have no idea. Somewhere in the mountains like this. I was only four years old."

"That's really young. I'm surprised you can remember any of it."

"It's all pretty hazy. But my mother was alive, then. She carried me part of the way. It's about the last thing I remember about her. Carrying me piggy-back somewhere in the mountains. Except for that, all I remember about the trip is being scared and wanting to get home where it was safe."

"I imagine the wilderness would seem awfully strange and terrifying to a kid that age."

"Yeah."

He wondered if he should ask what happened to her mother. He didn't want to ask. It might upset her. On the other hand, Angela might think he was insensitive if he pretended to ignore the subject. "Your mother passed away?" he asked.

Angela nodded. "I guess it was a few days after we got back from that camping trip. She drove off to buy a carton of cigarettes and she was in a car accident."

"I'm awfully sorry."

"Thanks. So am I. The thing is, it happened when I was so young. I can hardly remember her at all. I wish I could've gotten to know her."

"It's terrible."

"That's the way the ball bounces, I guess."

Howard got a lump in his throat.

She patted his hip. "Anyway, that was my one and only wilderness experience till now. If I'd known it could be like this . . ."

"Madmen running around . . ."

"Yeah, but you can find them anywhere. I've been finding them all my life." She spoke as if stating a simple observation. Howard detected no anger or self-pity in her voice.

"Like Skerrit, you mean?"

"Skerrit. But he's not the only one. Or the worst." She turned to him. The moon dusted her face with white. Her smile looked lopsided. "I think I must attract them."

"Maybe I'm a madman, then. You sure attract me."

She leaned against him. As he wrapped his arms around her, she tilted back her head and closed her eyes. He pressed his mouth gently to her lips. They were soft and warm and open. Her arms tightened around him. He felt the push of her small breasts. He felt her chest rise and fall as she breathed. Her breath went into his mouth.

She was trembling. So was he.

"Cold?" he whispered against her lips.

"A little. You?"

"Yeah," he said. But he knew it wasn't just the cold making him shiver. "Should we go back to the fire?"

She answered by squeezing him hard and mashing her

mouth against his. There was something almost desperate about the fierce way she clung to him.

My God, he thought. This is incredible. Why's she acting this way?

Why me? I'm not all that special.

But she thinks I am.

I bet she'll let me do whatever I want. Tonight, when everyone's asleep . . .

She trusts me. That's the thing. I can't take advantage of her. I can't do anything to make her start wondering about me. If she's been running into madmen all her life . . .

What the *hell* did she mean by that?

Skerrit isn't the worst?

She loosened her embrace. Her lips eased away and she turned her head toward the campsite. "Do you think they can see us?" she whispered.

His heart slammed. His legs went weak. "Maybe. The moon's awfully bright."

"We could walk a little ways."

"I don't know." His voice came out sounding thick and shaky. "That guy might be around. Or they might worry about us and come looking."

"It was just an idea."

"Maybe we'd better get back."

"I suppose so."

I'm *nuts*, he thought as he led her up the face of the rock. She wanted to fool around and I talked her out of it! What's the matter with me?

I'm a chicken, that's what. I'm a chicken and I blew it. Shit!

They jumped down onto the shore. He glanced at Angela. She met his eyes, managed a quick smile, and turned her face away.

Oh God, she probably thinks I backed out because I didn't want to be with her.

"It just wouldn't be safe," he muttered.

"No, you're right. I know. It was kind of a dumb idea."

"If it weren't for that guy . . ."

"It's OK, Howard. Really."

It wasn't OK. Somehow, she suspected the truth.

That he was scared. But not of the stranger. Scared of her.

How *could* she know? She isn't a mind reader.

She squeezed his hand as if to comfort him. Without looking up at him, she said, "I don't bite, you know."

She *is* a mind reader.

Howard wanted to cringe and hide. At the same time, he had an urge to hug her.

"You must think I'm such a coward."

"I don't think any such thing."

"Well, I am."

"What do you think I'd do to you?"

A blush heated his face. "I don't know."

Hurrying ahead of him, she turned around. She walked backward. From the bounce in her step, Howard figured she must be feeling pretty cheerful. Probably grinning, but he couldn't see her face at all; the firelight behind her made it look black. "If you don't know," she asked, "what are you scared of?"

"I don't know."

"Do too."

"No I don't."

"Should I tell what I wanted to do?"

"OK."

She flung her hands up. "Gee, I don't remember. Too bad. Gosh, I knew a minute ago."

"Angela."

Laughing, she spun around. She stayed a few strides ahead of him, but kept glancing over her shoulder until she walked into the light of the campfire.

"See anything out there?" Lana asked.

"No." Angela stepped over the log and sat down on it.

"We did," Keith said. "Right, Glen?"

"Yeah yeah yeah."

"So cough it up."

Howard sat down beside Angela.

159

"My wallet's in my pack," Glen said. "I'll pay you later."

"You're just trying to worm out. Get it now."

Mumbling, he got to his feet and trudged around the campfire.

Keith grinned. "I'm five bucks ahead already, and we haven't even found the treasure yet."

"They wagered on whether you two would kiss," Doris said. "Charming fellows, eh?"

Howard felt heat rush to his face. The rims of his ears seemed to be burning. He looked at Angela. Her face was ruddy, but that might've been due to the firelight. She couldn't be blushing, not while she wore such a big smile.

"I warned Glen he was throwing his money away," Lana said. "I *knew* you'd do it."

"Great," Howard muttered. He was surprised to find that, mixed with his annoyance and embarrassment, he felt a certain pride. Maybe Angela felt the same way, and that's why she was smiling as if so enormously pleased with herself.

She leaned back and looked past him. Howard, turning his head, watched Glen crawl out of a tent and lumber toward the fire, a bill fluttering in his hand.

"You shouldn't have bet against us," Angela told him.

"Figured neither of you had the guts to make the first move."

"And I quote," Keith said. " 'They wouldn't know how to kiss if they tried.' "

"Thanks a lot, Glen," Howard said.

Angela suddenly pulled him by the nape of his neck, turned him, drew his head toward her. Searching his eyes.

Are you kidding?

Her smile went away and she pressed her open mouth against him, softly mashing his lips. He went breathless as her tongue pushed in.

Right in front of everyone.

What's gotten into her?

He was shocked, embarrassed—and dazed with the excitement of it.

"All *right*!" Keith blurted. "Go for it!"

"The call of the wild," Glen said.

"Go for some tit, Howitzer."

"Cut it out, Keith," Lana said.

"Double or nothing says he won't," Glen blurted.

Angela's body seemed to stiffen slightly. As if she were afraid Howard might try it. But she didn't pull away.

She's letting it be my decision, he thought.

"You guys are sick," Doris said.

"Come on, man. Are we on?"

"No way," Keith told him. "Howitzer hasn't got the guts. Not for that."

He felt Angela nod slightly. For a moment, he wondered if she was agreeing with Keith that he didn't have the guts to touch her breast. Then he realized she was telling him to go ahead. *Do it if you want to, Howard. It's OK with me. Go ahead and show them you aren't a chicken.*

Not this way, he thought. Not for a bet. Not to prove myself to these guys.

He shook his head enough for Angela to get the message. Her mouth went away. She kissed him again gently, a brief touch of her wet lips. Then her smile returned. She eased back, rubbing a sleeve of her red windbreaker across her mouth.

Keith reached sideways and plucked the bill from Glen's hand. "Thank you very much."

"Not so fast," Glen said. "It'll cost you five bucks for your share of this." He pulled down the zipper of his coat, reached inside the drooping pouch at the front of his sweatshirt, and pulled out a pint bottle of bourbon. "A little something to take the chill off."

"Oh, for godsake," Doris muttered, rolling her eyes upward.

"All right!" Keith, grinning and nodding, handed the five back to Glen.

"He's just paid for everyone," Glen said.

"I don't believe this," Doris muttered. "Lana, are you going to let them *drink*?"

"I'm not their mother." Putting on a heavy, Irish accent,

she said, "I wouldn't mind having a wee taste meself."

Howard laughed. "That's pretty good!"

"Ah, thank ye, dear boy."

Glen uncapped the bottle, took a swig, and reached it to his right. Toward Doris, sitting alone on a stump with her back to the lake. She sneered. "I don't care for any, thank you."

"More for the rest of us," Keith said.

"Just take it and pass it onto Angela."

Nodding, Doris accepted the bottle. She leaned toward Angela and stretched out her arm.

"Thanks," Angela said. She tilted it to her lips. A moment after swallowing, she made a face and shivered. She blew air from her pursed lips. Her eyes glimmered. They were watering. In a hoarse voice, she said, "Good stuff."

She handed the bottle to Howard. He took a small sip. The bourbon felt cool in his mouth, but it seemed to catch fire as it ran down his throat. He took a deep breath. His own eyes began to water.

Lana was too far away. Howard got up, stepped around the fire, and gave the bottle to her. "Thanks," she said, and took a sip.

By the time Howard returned to his seat, Keith was already raising the bottle.

"Very smart, drinking," Doris said. "God only knows where that horrible man might be. He's probably watching us right now."

"If he is," Keith said, "we oughta ask him over for a sip. Hey, fella!" he called. "Schwarzenegger, Rambo, whoever you are! Come on over and have a drink!"

For just a moment, everyone sat motionless and silent as if awaiting an answer from the darkness.

"Look at this," Doris said. "He's not even drunk yet, and he's already acting like an imbecile."

He grinned and passed the bottle to Glen. "So a little booze won't make any difference, right?"

After taking a drink, Glen frowned at her. "Do me a favor," he said. He sounded serious. "I know you think I'm crude and a moron and all that. But you've got to admit, I pulled you out of the lake today. So I think you owe me one."

"Depends."

"Just take a drink of this. As a favor to me. It won't kill you. You'll feel better."

"That I doubt."

"I firmly believe," Glen said, "that there's a nice young woman in you."

She smirked.

"I mean it. I've caught glimpses of her once in a while. Maybe if you have a couple of drinks, it'll help her get out."

"Trapped inside the snotrag," Keith said, "is a crumb of angel food trying to get out."

Lana elbowed him.

Doris stared at Glen. Howard remembered the way they'd embraced after her decision to stay. He suspected that Glen might be right about the nice person buried inside her.

"What you see is what you get," Doris said. "If you think your rosy little speech or a few drinks are going to change that, you're even a bigger fool than you appear. But you did pull me out. I grant you that." She reached out. He handed the bottle to her. She raised it to her mouth and took a big swallow. "There. Are you happy?"

"I'm just trying to be nice to you, for godsake."

"Who needs it." She passed the bottle to Angela.

"You do," Angela said.

"What?"

"You might have some friends if you'd stop being such a pain all the time."

"I liked you a whole lot better when you were a meek little whipped twit who kept her mouth shut."

"Let's just cut it out, everyone," Lana said. "Why don't we knock off all this crap and have a good time? OK?"

Angela nodded, took a gulp of bourbon that made her shudder, and gave the bottle to Howard. She had a hurt look in her eyes as if she'd been slapped. It made him want to smack Doris. He shifted the bottle to his other hand, and rubbed the back of her neck.

"Let's sing campfire songs," Keith suggested, smirking.

"How about telling some ghost stories?" Glen said.

Howard took a drink and carried the bottle to Lana. "I've got an idea," she said as he returned to his log. "We're all English majors. Why don't we make up a poem?"

"Get real," Keith said.

"Come on. We'll publish it in next year's *Orpheus*." She took a swig. "I'll start." She squeezed her eyes shut. "Around the campfire sat the six, a bold and fearless crew." She passed the bottle to Keith. "Your turn."

He was about to take a sip when Glen stopped his hand. "Verse first, Longfellow."

"Shit. OK. Around the campfire sat the six, a bold and fearless crew . . . while out in the dark the *fiend* kept watch, though his balls were turning blue." Laughing, he drank and handed the bourbon to Glen.

"Great! OK!" Glen scowled at the neck of the bottle. "He shivered and shook in the bitter cold, and he ached for the heat of the fire. But he ached even more for the flesh of the gals, burning with lust and desire."

"Lurid," Keith said.

Glen chuckled, drank, and gave the bottle to Doris.

She stared at it. She grinned as she spoke. "And Doris, the fat obnoxious bitch, full of righteous ire, took the bourbon from the turds and hurled it in the fire." With that, she flung the bottle. It shot through the flames, knocked aside a burning stick and smashed against the far side of the low rock wall. Glass exploded. Booze splashed back and flared.

Glen gaped at her.

Keith seemed stunned. Blinking, he muttered, "Did you see that? Did you see what she did? She broke the bottle. She broke the fucking bottle. Did you see that? I don't believe it."

While he rambled, Doris got up from her stump and walked around behind Angela and Howard.

"Doris, you don't have to go," Lana called.

"Why would I want to stay there with such a group of cretins?"

She hefted her pack off the ground and carried it to the front of the nearer tent. There, she crouched and began to lower the zipper of the tent's fly screen.

"Hey, man, that's your tent!"

"It's OK," Glen muttered.

"She'll stink it up for you."

"I know who it is. She's upset. If she wants to use my tent . . ." He shook his head. "I'd rather sleep out here by the fire, anyway."

Doris crawled in. Her pack followed.

"My stuff's in there," Glen said. He spoke softly as if talking to himself.

"Won't be for long."

They watched the tent.

Glen's sleeping bag and pack didn't come flying out.

"Looks as if you're not being evicted," Lana said.

"Wonderful," he muttered. "*Now* what'm I gonna do?"

Howard checked his wristwatch. "It's not even nine yet. She isn't going to stay in there all night, is she?"

"Hope she never comes out," Keith said.

"Thanks. What am I supposed to do without my sleeping bag?"

"It's your tent. Go in and get it. Or better yet, give her the boot."

"Maybe one of us should talk to her," Lana said. "We'll need her, anyway, when we try to contact Butler."

"Who says we want to contact Butler?" Keith asked.

"Well, hell, don't you? How do you think we'll find his treasure unless he gives us some directions?"

"I thought . . . you know, maybe we could wait till morning. We're not going after the thing tonight, are we?"

"I'm with you," Glen said. "We've got our freak to worry about. The last thing I feel like is having a chat with a spook."

"I think we *should* try to talk with Butler," Angela said. "I mean, he scares me, too. And we could go ahead and wait till tomorrow before asking him about the treasure. But maybe he knows something about that guy. He might. He sent us here. Maybe the weirdo's part of it. I think we should ask Butler about him."

"Let's not," Glen said.

"Butler might even *be* the freak," Angela added.

"Oh, that's a cheerful thought," Lana said.

"It's bull," Keith said.

"I know it's probably crazy. But he did say he would meet us up here."

"Quit it," Glen said. "You're giving me the creeps."

Lana leaned forward and tossed a small segment of branch onto the fire. "She's got a point. I hardly think Butler *is* that jerk, but there might be a connection. It wouldn't hurt to ask."

"Can we do it without the happy wanderer?" Keith asked.

"I don't know. She was on the Ouija last night."

"It was *her* theory that we might need all the same people," Glen said.

"You want to be the one to drag her out?" Keith asked.

"Why don't we give her a while to calm down," Lana suggested. "There's no big hurry. It's too early to turn in, anyway, and I'm not sure any of us will be sleeping very well tonight with that lunatic around."

"All right!" Keith blurted. "This must mean you plan to hit the sack eventually. You had me worried there. I thought you'd be up all night, standing guard."

"Glen can do that," she said. Leaning forward, she grinned at him. "You wouldn't mind, would you? You haven't got a sleeping bag, anyway."

"I was thinking maybe I can use yours. You won't need it. You'll be in Keith's."

"Which is why *you've* got to stand guard," Keith told him. "I don't want that bare-ass bastard sneaking up on me while I'm laying pipe."

Lana's mouth fell open. She gaped at him. "Laying pipe?"

"Just a figure of speech."

"Try this on for a figure of speech, pal: take your pipe and lay it where the sun don't shine."

"Hey, I'm no contortionist."

"I'm glad you're amused."

Glen smiled across the fire at Howard. "Five bucks says they get it on before morning."

"Take the bet," Lana said. "A fool and his money are soon parted."

"I don't know."

"Smart move, Howitzer."

Angela smiled at him. "Should I take the bet?" he asked. She shook her head.

"Thanks for the vote of confidence," Lana said. "You think I'm a pushover?"

"It's a long night," Angela told her. "It's cold. And we're all a little scared. When you're lying all alone in your sleeping bag, I think Keith might start looking pretty good to you."

"Sounds to me like you're the one who might need him."

"Keith? I don't think so."

"That's 'cause she's got Howitzer the cannon."

"Let's put some money on them," Glen suggested.

Angela stood up.

"Ooo, now we've driven *two* away."

"I'm just going over to see Doris. I'll get her to come out so we can get in touch with Butler." She walked over to the tent, sank to her knees, and crawled through the flaps.

Chapter Sixteen

"The next time we come to a passing lane," Chad said, "I'm going to pull over and take another look at the map. The turnoff's gotta be around here someplace. I'd hate to miss it."

"You don't trust your trusty navigator?" Coreen asked.

"I'd trust her more if she'd stay awake."

"Oh." She turned her head. Chad saw the white of her teeth, and knew she was smiling. "That goll-durned mountain man hardly let me get a wink of sleep last night."

"You've sure made up for it today."

Just ahead, a sign read SLOWER TRAFFIC USE PASSING LANE. Beyond the sign, the road widened. Chad checked his rearview mirror. The area behind them was dark except for the glow of moonlight. He eased to the right and stepped on the brakes. The car abruptly slowed.

When it was stopped, he turned the headlight knob. The dashboard got brighter. The courtesy light came on. Coreen leaned forward, spread her legs, searched between her thighs and under them. With a quiet "Oh," she doubled

Join the Leisure Horror Book Club and
GET 2 FREE BOOKS NOW—
An $11.98 value!

— Yes! I want to subscribe to — the Leisure Horror Book Club.

Please send me my **2 FREE BOOKS**. I have enclosed $2.00 for shipping/handling. Each month I'll receive the two newest Leisure Horror selections to preview for 10 days. If I decide to keep them, I will pay the Special Members Only discounted price of just $4.25 each, a total of $8.50, plus $2.00 shipping/handling. This is a **SAVINGS OF AT LEAST $3.48** off the bookstore price. There is no minimum number of books I must buy and I may cancel the program at any time. In any case, the **2 FREE BOOKS** are mine to keep.

— Not available in Canada. —

NAME: _____

ADDRESS: _____

CITY: _____ **STATE:** _____

COUNTRY: _____ **ZIP:** _____

TELEPHONE: _____

E-MAIL: _____

SIGNATURE: _____

If under 18, Parent or Guardian must sign. Terms, prices, and conditions subject to change. Subscription subject to acceptance. Dorchester Publishing reserves the right to reject any order or cancel any subscription.

over. Chad saw the way her breast pushed against the top of her leg. She reached behind her left heel, picked up the map and smiled.

"Some navigator," he said. "Lost the map."

"But did you catch how fast I found it again?"

"Looked like quite a hunt to me."

"But I did find it. That's what separates the men from the boys."

He laughed. Coreen slapped the map into his waiting hand.

"While you're busy locating us, I'll pay a visit to the trees." She took a small plastic flashlight and a pack of tissues from the glove compartment.

"Don't go far, OK?"

"Back in a minute." She opened her door, climbed out, threw it shut and strode into the darkness.

When she was out of sight, Chad checked the map. He found the thin, shaky line that angled to the northeast out of Red Bluff. Following it with a finger, he located its Y-shaped branch. They'd come to the branch only a few minutes ago, and taken the eastern arm.

The dotted line marking the unpaved road to Shadow Canyon Lake was about half an inch up. According to the scale, that should be about ten miles.

If we miss it, he thought, we'll know soon enough. Just another half an inch above the turnoff was the town named Purdy.

He didn't think he'd ever been there.

He wondered if it had a motel. He'd been wondering that a lot while driving the curvy road, fighting grogginess as Coreen dozed in the passenger seat. The town was bound to have at least one place. But would Coreen be willing to postpone the last leg of the trip until morning?

She climbed back into the car and pulled the door shut. "*God*, it's cold out there." She shivered and rubbed her arms. "So, did you find us?"

"I've got a pretty good idea where we are. We're not far from the turnoff." He watched her stuff the flashlight and pack of tissues into the glove compartment. She snapped it shut. "The thing is, we'll end up on a dirt road. I have my doubts about trying it in the dark."

"We can make it."

"I'm not sure we should take the chance. It's some fifteen, twenty miles long. In the dark. With one lane. I've been on roads like that. We'd be lucky to do ten miles an hour. So we're talking about two hours at the least. On rough terrain. It'd be tough enough even if we could see where we're going."

"You think we should wait for morning?"

"I know you'd rather get to the kids tonight."

"I really would."

"But there's a town just a little ways beyond the turnoff. We could go onto it, get a good night's sleep in a motel or something, and hit the dirt road at dawn. Then we'd be able to see what we're doing. We'd be less likely to bust up the car or get stuck."

She sighed. "I don't know, Chad."

"Even if we're lucky and don't run into any trouble, it'll be midnight before we reach the roadhead. I hope it's the *right* roadhead."

"Oh, it has to be."

"It probably is," Chad said. They'd already discussed the several different approaches to Shadow Canyon Lake and decided that, coming from the northwest down Highway Five, the kids would be mostly likely to settle on this one. *If* they found it on their map. *If* they didn't, for odd reasons, choose to take a less direct route that would lead them into the same general area from either the southern or the distant northeastern road.

"More than likely," he said, "we'll find their car—or cars—at the end of it. But I doubt that *they'll* be there."

"These aren't Marines, you know. We figured it's what, five miles to the lake? And uphill? I can't see them going for it. I really can't. Not after they've spent all night and most of today on the road. I bet they just said, 'The hell with it,' and pitched camp right where they parked."

"You know them better than I do," Chad admitted. "I'm just saying that, if it were me, I'd push on for the lake."

She smiled. "You and Jim Bridger."

"Me and John Muir."

That brought a chuckle.

"So what'll it be?" he asked, turning off the overhead light.

"I honestly find it surprising that you'd *want* to spend the night in a motel. Wouldn't you prefer sleeping in the great outdoors?"

"Probably," he admitted. He started the car. Accelerating, he checked the rearview mirror and swung over. "I guess I just want to avoid that stretch of road."

"I'll drive it."

"That's OK. I'll do it. But you'd better keep your eyes peeled for the turnoff."

Coreen was silent for a few moments as Chad steered around a bend. Then she said, "If you'd really rather go onto that town . . ."

"No, it's all right. You're worried about the kids. I understand."

"If they were just on a camping trip, you know . . . It's the fact that they're doing this because of the damn Ouija board. You should've seen them last night. The way they pushed Angela into taking off her blouse. Just because the thing told them to do it. They're good kids, basically. But they went ahead and made her do it. What'll it ask them to do next time? What if it won't tell them where to find the 'loot' unless they do something really awful?"

"If they're good kids," Chad said, "they won't do it. They'll draw the line."

"I don't know. I don't know them *that* well. They did that to Angela. They swiped the Ouija board. They drove all the way out here. They're really into it. I just don't know what it might take before they'd back off."

"Well, we'll go ahead and get to them tonight. If we can."

"Thanks." She made a soft laugh. "Say, aren't you glad you showed up when you did? Just in time for all the fun."

"I'm very glad," he said. "I've been thinking about that. My timing."

"Lousy timing, huh?"

"Not the way I see it. What if I'd come a day later?"

"You would've waited for me, wouldn't you?"

"Sure." He glanced at her. She was watching out the side window. "You would've done this on your own, I guess."

"Yeah."

"Well, thank God I showed up when I did. It's almost *too* lucky."

"That's occurred to me, too. It's as if you were meant to arrive when you did. 'There is a divinity that shapes our ends, rough-hew them how we will.' "

"Does make a person wonder," he said.

She looked at him and smiled. "God figured I could use the services of my own Natty Bumpo."

"Yup. Case we run into Injuns."

"Uh-oh."

He saw it, too. The road sign, briefly illuminated by his headlights, read PURDY—8 MILES.

"If we're that close to Purdy," he said, "we must've missed our road."

"Damn."

"No problem. It's probably tough to spot the thing even in daylight." He took his foot off the gas pedal. "I'll just wait until we're clear of this curve, then hang a U."

As he came out of the turn, his lights swept across a stopped car. Stopped with its left side hanging into the narrow lane. Coreen gasped. He swerved, missed it, and eased down on the brakes.

"Jesus," Coreen muttered. "That was a close one."

Chad was trembling. "The only car we've seen the past hour, and it's blocking the damn road."

"Somebody might hit it."

"Somebody almost did." He stopped. Twisting around, he peered out the rear window and started to back up.

"What are you going to do?"

"I don't know. Check it out." He steered toward the

shoulder. The passenger side dropped a bit as it left the pavement. The tires made soft crunching sounds. "A hell of a place to leave a car."

He stopped several yards in front of it. Coreen, also gazing out the rear window, said, "I don't see anyone inside."

Chad shook his head. He couldn't see anything through the dark windshield. But he'd seen nobody during the moment his headlights had flooded the car.

"Wait here." He shifted to park and set the emergency brake, but kept the headlights on, the engine running. "Back in a second."

"I'm coming with you."

"Coreen."

She opened her door and got out.

Chad flung his door wide. He called, "Just hold on and wait for me."

Coreen waited for him at the edge of the road. Hunched over slightly, arms hugging her chest.

"It's warm in the car," Chad said.

"I'm not gonna sit in there alone. In fact, I'm not so sure we should've even stopped. I don't like this."

Though the road was flecked with moonlight, none touched the car.

"Anybody there?" Chad called.

No answer came.

Side by side, they walked closer to the car.

"If this is Christine, I'm gonna shit."

Chad laughed. He realized he was shaking. "We ought to put on some warmer clothes before we take off again."

"Let's do it now and forget about the phantom Fury."

"This isn't a Fury," he said. "It's a Pontiac." He felt a sudden rush of relief when he noticed its lopsided position. "And it's got a flat."

"Must be an epidemic," Coreen said.

"Well, that explains what it's doing here."

She stayed behind him as he walked around the front bumper, paused for a moment to look at the flat, then stepped up to the driver's door. Its window was rolled up.

Bending over, he peered in. The interior was black. "Can't see a thing."

"God, if there's someone inside there . . ."

Chad stepped back and tried the door handle. It lifted. The door unlatched. He pulled it open. A loud buzz. He flinched. Coreen gasped. But the dome light was on, the car empty. Leaning in over the steering wheel, he saw that the key was in the ignition. He plucked it out and the noise stopped.

"Weird," Coreen muttered. "Why would anyone go away and leave the keys in the car?"

"I don't know. Unless they just went off to take a leak, or something. Hang on, I'm gonna honk the horn." He pressed the steering wheel's hub. The horn blared through the night like the blast of an angry bugler. He let it go on for a long time, paused to listen, then gave the horn three short toots and another long one.

Coreen tapped his back. "I think that's plenty."

He stopped. The silence seemed oppressive. As if the noise of the horn had deadened his ears in much the same way that a brief, brilliant flood of light would've left him blind in the returning darkness. He listened for sounds of footsteps in the woods beyond the car. But he heard nothing at all.

"I don't think anyone's around," he whispered.

"It just doesn't make sense to leave your keys in the car and go away."

"I know. But everybody isn't sensible." He sat down behind the steering wheel. As he leaned sideways, reaching for the glove compartment, he noticed a leather handbag on the floor. It was tucked in close to the front of the passenger seat. "A purse," he said.

"You're kidding."

He picked it up and showed it to Coreen. She shook her head.

"Should we see who it belongs to?"

"It'll be pretty embarrassing if we're caught at it."

"Well, the horn didn't bring anyone running."

"Go ahead," Coreen said. "I'll keep watch."

"Watch out for cars, too." He pulled the door toward him, leaving it ajar so the light would stay on, then opened the purse. He glimpsed a billfold, a checkbook, some tampons, a pack of chewing gum, a hair brush. He removed only the billfold. He unsnapped it and flipped it open.

The driver's license had a photo of an attractive brunette who appeared to be in her early twenties. "Mary Louise Brewer," he read. "From Stockton."

"You'd better put it away," Coreen said. She sounded nervous.

"Just a second." He spread the bill compartment. A couple of twenties, a ten, a few ones, and several credit cards. He pulled out a Visa card. It had been issued to Roger Brewer. He put it back, returned the billfold to the purse, and wedged the purse back into position where he'd found it. "OK, stand back. I'm going to pull off the road a bit."

"Oh, God."

"We can't just leave it sticking out like this."

"OK. But hurry."

He started the car and eased it forward, steering to the right. It moved sluggishly. The flat tire made whumping sounds. There was a slight bump as the tires on the left dropped off the pavement. He quickly shifted to park, set the emergency brake, and shut off the engine. Taking the ignition key with him, he climbed out. He threw the door shut and the car went dark.

Coreen followed him to the trunk.

He opened it. Darkness inside. Dim shapes. Bending over, he searched with his hands. He felt suitcases, some smaller luggage, and a spare tire. "They've got a spare," he said.

"Maybe it's no good."

"Or Roger doesn't know how to change tires."

"It can be tricky with these crappy jacks they give you." She paused a moment. "Who's Roger?"

"Mary's husband, probably. One of her credit cards is in his name." Chad shut the trunk and turned to Coreen.

"Can we go now?" she asked.

"I'm not sure. I need to think. Something's wrong here."

"I know. It's all pretty queer. But I'm freezing. You moved the car out of the way, which was a very good idea. What else can we do?"

"Get into something warm."

"Now that's a terrific idea." She followed him alongside the car and waited while he returned the key to the ignition. The buzzer sounded again, then went silent when he shut the door. She hurried ahead to her car. She came back to its rear with the keys and flashlight, and opened the trunk.

Chad held the flashlight while she searched through her backpack. She took out a windbreaker.

"They probably decided to walk to town for help," Chad said.

Coreen zipped the front of her windbreaker. She draped a pair of dark warm-up pants over the edge of the trunk. "No telling how long the car's been sitting there. They might *be* in town by now."

"Eight miles. That's a pretty good distance."

"Yeah. I suppose we ought to keep going and give them a lift if we can find them." She unfastened her shorts, pulled them down and stepped out of them. "Ohhhh, my God!"

"A little nippy?"

"Yes!" She tossed her shorts into the trunk and grabbed the warm-up pants. Chad braced her by the shoulder while she thrust one foot, then the other, into her pants. She pulled them up, and sighed.

"Better?"

"Much, much."

She held the flashlight for him. He dragged a denim jacket out of his pack, put it on, and dug out a pair of corduroy pants. When he took off his shorts, the cold seeped like cold water through the skimpy briefs Coreen had bought for him. He groaned and she laughed.

She held him steady while he thrust his feet into the cords. The heel of his left sneaker got caught inside the pants. He lost his balance. Coreen hugged him from behind, keeping him up, and they staggered around for a moment before he pushed his foot through.

"Thanks."

"My pleasure."

Laughing, he tried to button his waistband. But Coreen's wrist blocked the way. Her hand cupped the front of his briefs. "Warm you up a little," she said, her breath tickling the side of his neck. She squeezed him gently, and rubbed. Chad squirmed as her touch ignited a fire in his groin.

"It's working," he muttered.

"Warming me up, too." She squeezed him once more. Then her hand went away. She kissed his neck. "We'd better get while the gettin's good."

She stepped away and shut the trunk. Chad fastened his pants. They got back into the car. With a last look at the abandoned vehicle in the rearview mirror, Chad swung onto the road.

"Maybe Mary and Roger are off in the trees making whoopy," Coreen said.

"It's possible."

"That would explain everything, wouldn't it? They're driving along, Mary reaches over and does something like this." Coreen reached over and rubbed his groin. "Roger gets all worked up, pulls over, and they both run into the woods. He doesn't bother taking the keys, she leaves her purse. We come along and honk, but they're going at it too hot and heavy to care."

"What about the flat?"

"Forgot about that." Her hand moved to his thigh and patted it. "OK. They get the flat. He says, 'I'd better jack up the car and change it.' She says, 'Jack me up first.' "

Chad laughed. "If that's the way it went, why are we looking for them?"

"Beats me."

"Should I turn the buggy around?"

"How'll we give them a lift into town?"

After that, they went silent and watched the roadsides. They saw nobody. Once, headlights came at them from around a bend. A tow truck? As the vehicle sped by, Chad saw that it was a Jeep. No one inside but the driver.

A few minutes later, they passed a dirt road leading off into the dark trees on the left. Then they came upon a gravel driveway leading to a small house with lighted windows.

"Maybe our mysterious Roger and Mary went there," Coreen said.

"We're almost to the town."

A short distance farther, they passed another house. Then another dirt road winding into the forest. Then a dark cafe with boarded windows. More houses, more unpaved roads tunneling into the trees.

Chad slowed as his headlights found the city limits sign. WELCOME TO PURDY, GATEWAY TO THE HIGH COUNTRY, ELEV. 6,240 FT, POP. 310.

"A metropolis," Coreen said.

"Should we keep going?"

"I don't see much point in it. If they got this far, they're hardly in need of a lift."

"And you're still not interested in a motel?"

"I never said I wasn't interested. But . . ."

"I know. It's all right." Chad made a U-turn.

"I hope they're OK."

"The kids?"

"Them, too. But I meant Roger and Mary."

"They must've made it into town. If they couldn't get help for the car tonight, they probably checked into a motel or something."

"If you really *want* to stay in a motel . . ."

"Nope," he said. "We're gonna tackle that road."

"Thanks. You'll be handsomely rewarded for your sacrifice."

"In this life or the next?"

"In this life, for sure. Shortly after we reach the roadhead, I should think."

He punched the gas pedal to the floor, and Coreen laughed. Then he settled down to normal speed.

* * *

The abandoned car was where they had left it, a dark shape hunched in the shadows like a beast hiding from the moonlight. Looking at it, Chad felt the hairs on the back of his neck crawl.

"I wonder if we should've gone to the police," Coreen said.

"What?"

"In Purdy. Told them about it."

He glanced at her dim face. "They probably walked to town. They're probably in a service station or motel right now."

"I don't know."

"Neither do I."

"We're just *hoping* that's how it went, aren't we?"

"I guess so."

"Or pretending."

"You think something happened to them?"

"Don't you?" she asked.

"Are you watching for the turnoff?"

"Yeah. But what do you think?"

"They probably had a flat tire and walked to town. They were probably too careless or preoccupied or trusting to take the car keys and purse. Probably. Logically, that's more than likely what happened. On the other hand, I don't quite . . ."

"This might be it."

Chad slowed the car. Moments later, the headbeams met a wooden sign. SHADOW CANYON LAKE. An arrow pointed to the left. "Yep," he said.

Just ahead, across the road, was another sign. It faced the other way. Beyond it, Chad saw a patch of bare earth, an opening in the trees. He pulled forward and stopped adjacent to the dirt road.

"Shall we do it?" he asked.

"I don't know. What do you think?"

"The kids are your responsibility. I guess they should take priority over a couple of strangers who may or may not be in trouble."

He didn't wait for a response from Coreen.

He turned the steering wheel hard to the left, and stepped on the gas.

"You're right," Coreen said.

They dropped off the edge of the pavement. Even with the windows shut, Chad could hear the tires crunching over gravel and forest debris. The car shook, bounced, trembled. Out in front, the pale probes of their headlights traced the narrow way through the trees.

Chapter Seventeen

Howard put more wood on the fire. The pile of sticks and broken branches they'd gathered after supper was dwindling, but there should be enough to keep the fire blazing for a while longer. He hoped an expedition to gather more wouldn't be needed. If they wanted to keep the fire going all night, though . . .

"Tough luck, Glen," Keith said.

Howard looked over at the tent. The bundle of a sleeping bag, apparently shoved out, stopped rolling. The tent flap bulged, and Angela crawled out backward. She dragged a pack with her. Standing up, she lifted the pack and sleeping bag. She carried them toward the fire.

"Evicted after all," Lana said.

"That's OK," Glen said. "I wasn't about to sleep in the same tent with her."

Angela put down her load, came to the fire, and sat beside Howard. "I couldn't talk her into coming out. She's pretty angry."

"What else is new," Keith muttered.

"What was it?" Glen asked. "The poem?"

"Mostly. She thought it was pretty rotten of us, making up cutesy stuff about the guy who jumped her. She said it just goes to show how we don't have any regard for her. She also said we wouldn't be making jokes if it'd been Lana he attacked."

Keith, grinning, shook his head. "We're so cruel and heartless."

"She brings it on herself," Glen said.

"She has a point, though," Lana said. "It was pretty callous of us to be joking around about that guy. Especially in front of Doris. We shouldn't have done it."

"Ah, fuck her."

"Shut up," Glen said.

Lana turned to Angela. "Did you tell her we wanted to contact Butler?"

"Yeah, and she said that's another good reason to stay in the tent."

"I guess we can try it without her."

"Let's not bother."

Ignoring Keith's remark, Lana got up and walked toward the other tent. She brushed off the seat of her blue jeans. She rubbed her rump as if it was sore. Then she got down on her knees and crawled into her tent. Moments later, she came out with the Ouija board and pointer.

She stopped in front of Glen's tent. Crouching, she swept open one of the flaps. Howard heard her voice, but the sounds of the wind and the popping fire interfered so he couldn't make out the words. She didn't stay long.

As she approached the fire, Keith asked, "What'd you tell her?"

"I apologized. I think she's in there crying."

"Awwwww," Keith said.

"Don't be such a bastard," Lana told him.

"If I'm supposed to feel sorry for her, forget it."

"Anyway, Doris isn't coming." Lana sat down on the log. She placed the Ouija board on her lap and stared at it. "I'm not quite sure how we're going to do this."

"Good. Let's not."

"It might be a waste of time, anyway," Glen said. "We don't have Doris, so the four from last night . . ."

"Maybe the original four aren't needed."

"Last night," Howard said, "it moved that time when *no one* was touching it."

Lana nodded. "Yeah. Well, why don't we try it different ways? Maybe start with the three of us. If that doesn't work, we'll have Glen or Angela sit in for Doris. We can't do it here, though. Right there might be a good place." She nodded toward a clear area of ground beside the campfire, and got up.

While the others gathered around her, Glen went to his pack. He returned with a flashlight and tarp. They spread the tarp, one edge close to the campfire. Lana sat down facing the fire and placed the Ouija board in front of her crossed legs. Keith and Howard sat opposite each other, the board between them. Glen started to sit in the space near the fire, but Lana suggested that he move so he wouldn't block the light. He crawled to the other side of Keith, and knelt there. He shone his flashlight on the board. "All set?" he asked.

"Just a minute," Angela called. She was crouched over her pack, searching the pocket on its right side. When she stood up, she was holding a pen and a small spiral notebook. "You need somebody to keep track, don't you?"

"If we get lucky," Lana said.

Angela came back to the tarp. The plastic made crackling sounds as she crawled on it. She knelt behind Howard. He felt her body press against his back. The hand on his right shoulder held the pen and pad. The other hand held only his shoulder. He felt her chin against the top of his head. It moved slightly when she said, "Ready."

Howard leaned forward to reach for the pointer. Angela stayed with him, blocking the cold wind and sharing her warmth.

This is so great, he thought.

Maybe the Ouija board's not such a bad thing. It sure brought us together.

Lana, Keith and Howard rested their fingertips on the pointer.

"OK, Butler," Lana said. "We're waiting for you. Are you here?"

The pointer didn't move.

"We're here, Butler."

"Maybe we gotta attract his attention," Keith said.

"Like how?"

"Maybe if you gals strip down."

Angela's left hand tightened slightly on Howard's shoulder.

"There won't be any of that," Lana said.

"Too cold," Angela said, and made a soft laugh that sounded nervous.

"Just an idea."

"Why don't we try calling out his name?" Glen suggested. "All together. On the count of three. One . . ."

"No way," Keith said. "That's stupid. He isn't a deaf guy, he's a spook. Besides . . ." He went silent.

"Besides what?" Lana said.

"I just don't think we oughta be making a lot of noise, you know what I mean? It's not like we're *alone* out here."

"You really take the prize," Glen said. "You're the guy that called out and invited *el creepo* to come in and have a drink with us."

"That was different."

"Oh yeah? How?"

Before he could answer, the pointer slid half an inch.

"OK, who did that?" Keith asked.

Lana shook her head.

"Not me," Howard muttered.

Angela pressed herself more tightly against his back.

"Butler," Glen whispered.

"Butler," Lana said in a clear voice. "Are you here?"

The pointer began to move in slow circles. But it didn't

stop. The circles grew larger, carrying their hands around and around.

"What is he, confused?" Keith said.

"Butler, are you here?"

The pointer picked up speed. It made a series of figure-eights. And suddenly stopped.

"B," Glen said.

Howard felt Angela's hands leave his shoulders, and realized she must be copying the letters as the pointer moved and halted and Glen read from the board.

"W-A-R."

" 'Be war'?" Angela whispered.

"Maybe 'beware,' " Glen said.

"Oh, shit," Keith said.

"Beware of what?" Lana asked.

"M-A-N."

"What man?"

"As if we didn't know."

"N-E-A-R."

"The guy we saw this afternoon?"

The pointer sped to the smiling face of the sun.

"That's a yes," Glen said. "Jesus. And he's *near?*"

"What does he want?" Lana asked.

"F-U-K-N-S-P-L-I-T-N-C-L-I-M-N."

After reading off the letters, Glen shook his head. "What the hell was that all about?"

"Starts with 'fuck,' " Keith said. "Couldn't follow the rest."

Lana looked over at Angela.

"Just a . . ."

Howard heard the gasp from above his head, felt her belly push against his back.

"Oh, God," she murmured.

"What is it?"

"It looks like what Doris said."

"Come on!"

" 'Fuck and split and climb in.' "

Angela's warmth wasn't enough to keep an icy tide from flowing up Howard's back.

"It's what Doris thought the guy wanted to do to her."

"Butler's quoting Doris back at us?" Glen asked.

"Who does he wanta do it to?" Lana asked, gazing down at the pointer.

"A-N-Y-1."

"Anyone?" Lana asked. "Not just the women?"

"A-N-Y-1."

"I knew the guy looked like a fag," Keith muttered.

"He must go both ways," Lana said. She looked up at Angela. In the fluttering glow of the firelight, Howard watched a corner of her mouth turn up. "Better odds for us gals."

"Very funny," Keith said.

She returned her gaze to the board. "Is he going to attack us?"

The pointer darted to the sun.

Angela let out a low moan, but it stopped abruptly when the pointer sped to the moon.

"Yes, no," Glen said.

Back to the sun again.

"Must mean maybe," Lana said. "You don't know whether he'll attack us?"

"B-W-A-R."

Keith huffed out a breath. "Damn right we will."

"We'll be careful," Lana said in the tone of voice she used when speaking to Butler. "Do you know this man?"

"M-A-D."

"He's a madman? Or are *you* mad at him?"

The plastic heart slid to the sun.

"Ambiguous son-of-a-bitch," Keith said.

"Probably means yes to both questions," Glen told him.

"Butler, did you know he was here?"

The pointer remained on the sun.

"Either that's a yes," Glen said, "or he's not answering."

"Butler, did you bring us here because of him?"

Their fingers were carried from the sun to the moon.

"That's a no." Glen sounded relieved.

"What does he have to do with all this?" Lana asked.

"M-A-D."

"Can't we get any straight answers from this guy?" Keith said.

"P-R-O-T-E-C-T-A-L."

Angela flinched. "A.L.? That's me. Protect me?"

Cold spread through Howard's bowels.

"Protect Angela?" Lana asked.

The pointer rushed to the sun.

"Oh, God," Angela murmured, and pressed her chin against the top of Howard's head.

"Why Angela?" Lana asked.

"Butler's got the hots for her, that's why."

"Shut up, Keith."

"That look he got at her tits last night . . ."

"Keith!" Lana snapped. To the Ouija, she said, "Why Angela?"

For a long time, the pointer was motionless under Howard's trembling fingers. Then it sped around the board, stopping and darting.

"S-H-E-T-A-K-E-U-2-L-O-O-T."

"She take you to loot," Angela whispered. "Me? I don't know where it is."

"Does Angela know where the loot is?"

"W-I-L."

"She will? She doesn't know yet?"

"I-G-O."

"I go?" Glen said.

"No! Wait! Where should we go tomorrow?"

The pointer didn't move.

"Butler! Hold it! Where are we supposed to go?"

They stared down at the still, plastic heart.

"Guess he's gone," Glen said.

Keith took his hand away. "Thanks a heap, Butler. Shit."

"Let's give it a couple more . . ." The pointer glided, halted, slid and stopped.

"Up," Glen said.

"We go up?" Lana asked.

"2-M-A-R-K-N-G-O-W-I-T-H-E-A-R-T-I-G-O-N-O-W."

The pointer shot out from under Lana and Howard's fingers, flew off the end of the board and flipped over on the ground, its three plastic legs in the air.

Lana let out a short laugh. "Well, I guess that's that."

"What was that stuff at the end?" Glen asked.

"I don't know," Angela said. "I've got it all down, here." Howard felt her belly push against his back as she took a deep breath. "We go . . . let's see . . . to marking o with e art. I gone ow. I go now."

"What the hell is 'marking o with e art'?" Glen asked.

Angela moved over and sank to her haunches beside Howard. She held the pad in front of him. The paper shimmered with ruddy light from the fire. "What do you think?"

He studied the message. "To mark . . . Maybe the n and g aren't connected. N might mean 'and.' "

" 'To mark and go with . . . e art.' "

"If the h belongs to the next word, it would say heart."

"Go with heart?"

" 'To mark and go with heart. I go now.' "

"OK," Lana said. "So we're supposed to go up to the mark and go with heart. Whatever that means."

"The bastard likes his riddles," Keith complained. "Why can't he just come out and say what he means?"

"He was pretty clear about warning us," Glen said. "Man, I'm glad Doris wasn't in on this. Would've really freaked her out."

Lana twisted around and looked toward the tent. "We'd better not leave her alone. Nobody'd better do *anything* alone. If Butler's right about that guy . . ."

"And who should know better than a fuckin' *spook*?"

"I wonder if he's watching us," Angela said.

"Who? Butler or our friendly local psycho?"

"I guess we know Butler's watching us," Glen said. "Or listening, anyway. Who is this guy? Big Brother?"

"He seems to be looking out for us," Lana said.

"For Angela, at least," Keith said.

"It's not my fault," she told him.

"No, it's not," Howard said. "And there's something we're forgetting."

"Oh, yeah? Lay it on us, Howitzer."

"How do we know he's telling the truth? About anything? We don't know what he's up to. He might have us up here for some weird reason we know nothing about. That crazy guy might even be part of his plan. Maybe the guy doesn't mean us any harm, but Butler *wants* us to be afraid of him."

"More of that denial Doris was talking about," Glen said.

"Well," Lana said, "he has a point. We probably shouldn't be so quick to take Butler at face value."

"I think Howard's right, too," Angela said. "This whole Ouija board thing gives me the creeps, and I think Butler's playing some kind of a game with us. I mean, why should he bring us up here to give us his treasure?"

"He's got a generous spirit," Keith suggested.

"He's got some kind of ulterior motive," Angela said.

"Yeah," Howard said. "He wants something out of us. Either that, or he wants to *do* something to us."

"Well, we're here." Lana got to her knees and leaned over the board. Bracing herself with one hand, she picked up the pointer. Then she pushed herself back, lifted the board and stood. "It's a little late to call it quits, so I think our best course of action is to be careful but go for the loot." With that, she turned away and walked toward her tent.

"Hang on." Keith sprang up and hurried after her. "Nobody does anything alone, remember?"

Turning, Lana drew the revolver from her coat pocket. "I'm the gal packing the heat, remember?"

Together, they strolled to her tent. Keith reached it first, glanced inside, then held the flap out of the way for Lana. She crawled in. He followed, and the flap dropped shut behind them.

Chapter Eighteen

"They're coming back, aren't they?" Glen muttered.

"I imagine," Angela said.

" 'Cause we've gotta do something about Doris. We can't just leave her alone."

"Maybe you should go and have a talk with her," Howard said. "I mean, it is your tent."

Glen sighed.

The three of them crawled off his tarp. Howard helped him fold it. Glen carried it the few steps to the place where Angela had left his pack and sleeping bag. He dropped it to the ground. Then he turned toward Lana's tent. "You're not turning in yet, are you?" he called.

"Don't get your shorts in a knot!" Keith shouted.

Glen faced the other tent. "Doris?"

No answer.

He walked over to it, squatted, and swept aside the flap. He didn't go in, but he started to speak.

Howard stepped closer to the fire. He picked up a few sticks and added them to the blaze, then sat on the log.

Angela sat beside him. He put an arm across her back, and she snuggled against him.

"How are you doing?" he asked.

"I'm a little scared."

"Yeah, me too."

"Why does Butler keep *picking* on me?"

"I don't know."

"Maybe it's like Keith says."

"Keith is a jerk."

"But what if he's right? What if Butler . . . *wants* me?" She shuddered. "I mean, he's a ghost or something."

"I guess he doesn't mean you any harm. He told us to protect you."

"Protect me from the weird guy. Maybe that's only so Butler can have me for himself."

"It might not be that at all." He squeezed her hip. "Besides, what can he do about it even if he does want you? He's a spirit, right?"

"Who knows what he is? Did you ever see that movie *The Entity*?"

"I read the book."

"Do you remember what happened in it?"

"Yeah."

"That demon, or whatever, kept *raping* that woman."

"It was just fiction."

"But I heard it was based on a true story."

"I doubt if anything like that really went on."

"God," she muttered. "I couldn't take it. I'd rather have that *creep* get me, than . . ."

"Hey, you guys, come on! I've got Doris."

Howard, looking over his shoulder, saw Glen and Doris standing between the two tents. The flap of Lana's tent bulged, and she crawled out. Keith's head appeared in the opening. "Miracle of miracles."

"Let's get on with it," Doris said. Zipping the front of her jacket, she hurried toward the fire. The others followed. They all went to their former seats like theater-goers re-

191

turning after intermission. "OK," she said. "So what's the big urgent deal?"

"We can't have you staying alone in the tent," Lana told her. "We can't have *anyone* alone tonight. Not with that lunatic around."

Her lip curled. "I'm sure our armed guard will protect us."

"We'll have people on watch," Lana said. "But that's no guarantee. I think anyone who's alone is taking a risk. An unnecessary risk."

"You don't really want to be alone," Glen said.

"I'm not about to have you in the tent."

"It's his tent," Keith pointed out.

"Who is acceptable to you?" Lana asked.

Doris's tiny, porcine eyes roamed the group. "Anyone but Glen or Keith, I suppose."

"It should be a guy. That leaves you, Howard."

His mouth fell open. He suddenly felt sick, persecuted. "Ohhhh, no. No way."

"Thanks a lot," Doris muttered.

"It isn't fair," he said, not looking at her, looking at Lana instead. "It's Glen's tent. If he's gonna let her use it, that's his business. Just leave me out. It's not my fault she's got a problem with him."

"We have to pair up," Lana said.

"I *am* paired up. With Angela."

"Yeah. We're together. And we already have plans to sleep by the fire."

Howard knew of no such plan, but he nodded vigorously.

Lana sighed. Glancing from Glen to Doris, she said, "We can't have someone alone in a tent."

Those two stared at each other. Doris looked surly, Glen annoyed.

"I could put my sleeping bag right in front of the tent," he finally said. "That way, my presence wouldn't be an insult to Doris's sensibilities, but I'd be blocking the entrance and I'd be able to get inside fast if I hear anything."

"Chivalry ain't dead," Keith said.

"I guess that would be all right," Doris said.

"It means he'll be your partner during guard duty," Lana pointed out.

"OK."

"As far as guard duty goes," Lana said, "I think the first shift should keep at it till one-thirty. With two shifts after that, three hours each, we'll get to seven-thirty in the morning and everybody'll end up with six hours of sleep."

"You should've been a math major," Keith said.

"Does that sound all right to everyone?"

Nodding, Howard glanced at Angela. "Should we go first?" he whispered.

"Sure."

"We volunteer for the first shift," he said.

Nobody objected.

"Keith and I'll take it from one-thirty to four-thirty, so wake us up when it's time. Have either of you got a watch?"

"Yeah," Howard said.

"And we'll have the gun?" Angela asked.

"Right. The sentries get the gun."

"Know how to use it, Howitzer?"

"I think I'll be able to manage."

"But what are we supposed to do?" Angela asked.

"Keep your eyes open," Lana said.

"And keep the fire going," Keith added. "If I gotta get out of my nice warm sack in the dead pit of the night, I want a good hot fire waiting for me."

"OK," Howard said. He wondered if enough wood remained on the pile to last through their shift.

Maybe. If we're careful with it.

"The main thing," Lana said, "is to make sure that maniac doesn't sneak up on the camp. You've got a fairly good view of the tents from here. If he goes for one, shoot him."

"Just try to miss the tent," Keith suggested.

"Is class dismissed?" Doris asked.

"What about going to the bathroom?" Angela asked.

"Hang it out anywhere, but don't put out the fire."

"Let's take care of that now."

193

"Sounds good to me." Keith stood up, grinning.

Lana stood, clutched his shoulder, and pressed him down to his seat. "The guys can wait here."

"Aw, shucks."

Angela and Doris got up. They followed Lana to her tent. She ducked inside and came out with a flashlight and a roll of toilet paper.

"You sure you don't want us to stand guard?" Keith called. "You don't want to get caught with your pants down."

"We'll take our chances. And don't try sneaking around for any voyeur crap, or you might catch lead."

"Give a lady a gun and she thinks she's Dirty Harry."

Lana in the lead, the girls walked single-file into the trees beyond the tents. After they were out of sight, Howard still caught glimpses of the flashlight's beam.

"Why are they going so far?" Glen asked.

"They probably think we *might* sneak up on 'em."

Howard faced the fire. "I wouldn't dare."

"I know. You're a wuss."

"I'm just afraid I might catch a glimpse of Doris's ass."

Keith and Glen both laughed. Howard grinned.

"I don't want to get nightmares," he added.

"That's pretty good, Howitzer. There's hope for you."

"Lucky me," Glen said. "I get stuck with her for guard duty."

"Do us all a favor and fuck her lights out. It might improve her attitude."

"Yeah, sure."

"You could put a bag over her head," Howard suggested.

"You'd have to bag her whole body."

Glen didn't look amused. "Not that I would, but if I *did* try putting moves on her, she'd probably make some kind of fucking wisecracks. Who needs it, you . . ."

"NO!"

The distant, shrill outcry hit Howard like a kick. He leaped to his feet as Keith blurted "Holy shit!" and sprang up and Glen shoved him. All three were running when more shouts came from the woods.

"Help! It's him! It's him!"

That was Angela.

But the first panicked shriek hadn't been her. He didn't think so.

What's happening?

Why doesn't Lana shoot?

"Nnnooo!"

Lana?

They raced between the tents. Keith was first to reach the edge of the clearing. He sprinted into the trees, Howard close behind him, Glen at the rear.

Howard kept his eyes on the dark shape of Keith's back. He heard nothing except the wind shuffling through the night, their own huffing breaths, their shoes pounding the matted ground.

"Let her go!" Angela again.

A blast crashed in Howard's ears. Then another. He couldn't hear the wind or anyone panting for air. The footfalls sounded faint and far away through the ringing in his head.

In front of Keith and off to the right, a pale beam sliced sideways and down.

"We're here!" Keith yelled.

The light swung toward them. "Over here!"

Angela's voice.

She's all right.

But what about the others?

Seconds later, he found out. He glimpsed Lana on the ground, legs bare, jeans bunched around her ankles. Angela, kneeling by her head, shut off the flashlight.

"She's OK," Doris said. She sounded breathless. She was standing behind Angela.

"I'm OK," Lana gasped.

"Jesus, what happened?"

"He grabbed her," Angela said.

"He took off that way," Doris said. Raising an arm, she

pointed into the trees beyond Lana's feet. She had the revolver in her hand.

"You didn't get him?" Keith blurted.

"Huh-uh."

"Give me that!" He rushed to her and grabbed the gun.

"No," Lana said. "Don't go."

"Blow his fuckin' head off."

"Stay here!" Lana snapped.

Glen put a hand on Keith's shoulder. "We might not find him anyway. And we shouldn't leave the girls."

Keith whirled on Doris. "Why didn't you shoot him, you fat ox?"

Glen shook him. "Knock it off!"

"For godsake," Lana said, "she saved me. She couldn't shoot at him without hitting me. The bastard was running off with me."

"He dropped her when Doris fired," Angela said.

"Oh," Keith said.

"Yeah. Oh." Lana sat up. Leaning forward, she began pulling at one of her shoes. "Piss all over me," she muttered.

"Do you want the light on?" Angela asked her.

"No thanks." She yanked the shoe off and began tugging at the other. "He got me right in the middle of taking my leak," she said. "Comes up behind me and jerks me over backward." With the second shoe off, she struggled to free her feet from the pants. "Next thing I know, he's got me over his shoulder. God only knows where he was going with me. But I'd be finding out if it hadn't been for Doris."

"Where was the gun while all this was going on?" Glen asked.

"I had it in my jacket."

"It must've fallen out," Doris said, "when he picked her up."

"It did," Angela confirmed. "I heard it hit the ground."

Lana started putting her shoes back on.

"She went and tried to tackle the guy," Doris said. "Held on to him long enough for me to get the flashlight. I just happened to see the gun there next to it. I got hold of it just when he broke loose from Angela. He had Lana over his shoulder and I couldn't see where she left off and he started, so I didn't aim for him. I fired in the air, and he threw her down."

"That's when you should've nailed him," Keith said.

"You weren't there," Lana said, getting to her feet. She brushed off her rump and made a disgusted "Ugh" sound. Howard stared at her pale buttocks as she bent over and picked up her pants. "Let's get back to camp," she said. "I'm freezing."

Angela gave the flashlight to Keith, then stepped over to Howard and took his arm. Together, they led the way.

"I should've tried," he heard Doris say.

"You did great," Lana told her. "I really owe you."

"It was just so dark. I was afraid I might miss him, and then we'd only have three bullets left."

"If you'd hit him," Howard said, "we wouldn't need to worry about saving bullets."

"Would you please cut it out?" Lana said, a pleading tone in her voice. "She saved my life. She and Angela both did."

"Did the guy have his machete?" Glen asked.

"I don't think so," Lana told him. "He was holding onto me with both hands."

Angela looked over her shoulder. "It was on his belt," she said, keeping her head turned.

Howard wanted to look back, too. Maybe he'd be able to see Lana from the front. But the others might catch on that he was trying for a peek. Besides, there wouldn't be enough light to see much. He managed to keep his eyes forward.

Through the trunks and low branches ahead, he saw the faint, distant glow of the campfire.

"Was he wearing clothes this time?" Keith asked.

"Fur," Lana said. "I felt fur under me. It's wet fur now."

"And he had leather pants on," Angela added.

"Did he? I couldn't see."

"They felt like leather, anyway. They didn't smell too great."

As Howard stepped into the clearing, Lana said, "Why

197

don't you guys hurry on ahead and build up the fire? I'm going to be an ice cube. Keith, how about getting my towel and sweatpants? Clean socks and my boots, too."

"Sure."

Howard heard quick footfalls behind him. Then Lana ran by, holding her jeans out to the side. She rushed between the two tents. Her rump and legs were creamy in the moonlight, golden as she raced past the campfire, dim when she was beyond its glow.

"Here." Keith's voice. "Stay with her. I'll be along in a minute."

Doris jogged by with the revolver.

In the distance, Lana stopped running. She dropped her jeans.

Howard, walking toward the fire with Angela holding his arm, watched Lana's vague shape hop on one leg, then the other as she pulled off her shoes. She picked up the jeans again and walked down the gradual slope to the shore.

She suddenly jerked rigid and flung out her arms as if she'd been stabbed in the back. Her feet were out of sight, but Howard knew she had stepped into the water.

Behind him, Glen said, "Ouch! God, I bet that's cold!"

She waded farther out. Her legs looked as if they'd been cut off at the knees. With each step, the black climbed higher. Then all that Howard could see between the surface of the lake and the dark back of her jacket was the faint, pale blur of her rump. The pale area stretched upward as she lifted her jacket and shirt.

Doris moved sideways on the shore, blocking his view.

I shouldn't be staring anyway, he told himself.

"I'll throw some wood on," Angela said as they reached the fire. "Maybe you and Glen could go and gather more."

"Yeah. Come on, Howie."

She squeezed his arm. "Stay close by, though. OK?" She gave him the flashlight.

This is good, he thought as he wandered away from the fire with Glen. Get plenty of wood now, while everybody's around. Get enough to last through our shift.

He looked again toward the lake. Now, Doris wasn't in the way. He saw Lana wading out, the jeans held in front of her. Keith ran toward the shore with a bundle in his arms.

"Hey, man," Glen said. "Quit watching the show and start grabbing firewood. I don't like it out here."

Chapter Nineteen

"What do you know?" Chad said. "We made it."

Corie, bouncing and rocking in the passenger seat, stared at Lana's Granada as they approached its rear. The head-beams gleamed on its bumper, made the red of its tail lights glow and lit its interior. For a moment, she thought two people were sitting in the front seat. Then she realized she was seeing headrests, not heads. "Well," she muttered, "they're not in it."

"Doesn't look that way." Chad pulled up beside Lana's car. He shut off the engine and headlights. Dark flooded down.

Corie picked up the flashlight and climbed out. It felt good to be standing. She stretched, sighing as a pleasant weariness spread through her stiff, sore muscles.

Though breezes shifted through the trees, she was met by no strong wind. The night seemed chilly, but not frigid.

Chad waited for her beside the Granada. She shone her light through the passenger window. Just as she'd thought, nobody was inside.

"Try calling out," Chad suggested.

With a nod, she turned toward the woods beyond the front of the car. "Hello!" she shouted. "Lana! Howard! Angela! Anyone! It's Corie Dalton! Hello?"

Weird, she thought. Here we are, standing beside another abandoned car, yelling, getting no more of an answer than we did at the other one.

"This is like a rerun," she said. "But we know *they* didn't hike into town."

"I suspect they must've gone on to the lake."

"Which is what you suspected from the start."

"What do you want to do?"

Corie scanned the dark woods. She shook her head. "I don't know."

"It'd be a tough hike to the lake, but we could probably make it in a couple of hours. Two or three," he added. "If we don't stray off the trail or fall off the mountain or something."

She smiled. "I can tell you're just rarin' to go. Gonna have to disappoint you, though. I'm too beat, myself. I couldn't make it. I wouldn't even want to try. Not tonight."

"Thank God."

Laughing, she said, "Contrary to popular opinion, I'm not a masochist."

"Could've fooled me."

She nudged him with her elbow, then walked past the front of the car and swept her light across the area ahead. Its beam found a wooden sign—a pair of narrow planks atop a post—off to the left.

"Must be the start of the trail," Chad said, following her.

She stopped in front of the sign and read aloud. "Shadow Canyon Lake, four miles. Calamity Peak, nine miles." The points of the redwood boards were aimed at an opening in the trees, and Corie's flashlight illuminated a narrow footpath.

"Why don't we just take a little walk up that way?" she said. "Without our packs. You never know, we might run into the kids. Maybe they just wanted to get away from where they parked."

"Possible," Chad said, following her onto the trail.

"We won't go far."

"Hope not. I'm owed a certain reward for getting us here."

"Looking forward to it."

They walked along, Corie shining her light on the trail just ahead but peering often into the heavy woods on both sides. She looked for the glow of a campfire. She listened for voices. But she saw only darkness and flecks of moonlight among the trees, and heard only their own footfalls, the squawk and chirp of night birds, the papery sounds of the piny limbs stirred by breezes and sometimes quiet, skittery sounds of small animals scurrying nearby.

"I guess this is far enough," she finally said. She called out, but no answer came.

"We'll get an early start in the morning," Chad said.

She turned around and took his hand. Together, they walked back to the roadhead.

Chapter Twenty

Howard sat with the gun on his lap, his back to the fire. Angela, beside him on the log, faced the fire. Positioned this way, they had a full field of vision, their sides touched, and they were able to talk quietly and sometimes look at each other.

"What time is it?" Angela asked.

Howard checked his wristwatch. "Five till twelve."

"Only an hour and a half to go. This isn't so bad, is it?"

"I don't think I'd be able to sleep, anyway."

"I wonder about the others."

"I don't know." He looked over at the tents. Earlier, he'd been able to see a faint disk of light through the front of Lana's tent. Now, it was gone. Both tents were dark. "I bet they're all asleep."

"Speaking of bets," Angela said, "do you think Keith got to lay his pipe?" She laughed softly.

"Yeah, do you?"

"Yeah. Poor Lana was freezing. If nothing else, she would've done it just to warm up."

"You think so?"

"Sure. And it'd take her mind off what happened, too."

It felt strange to be talking with Angela about other people having sex. It felt strange, but good. We're talking about them, Howard told himself, but we're thinking about us.

At least I am.

"What about Glen and Doris?" he asked.

"That I doubt."

"Me too. But she did let him into the tent."

"She's scared, that's all."

"But who knows, once they're together in there? I think Glen likes her."

"It would be awfully nice if they got together."

"Might make a new woman out of Doris," Howard said.

"Put a smile on her face."

"If they tried making it, though, somebody'd end up squashed flatter than a bug."

Angela laughed and bumped against him. They both turned their heads. Her face was rosy, a little sunburned from the day's hike, ruddy from the night's cold and the glow of the fire. She had a smudge of soot on one cheek, another just above her right eyebrow.

Their eyes met. Howard was surprised to see how solemn she looked. She leaned back a little, eased sideways, and kissed his mouth. Her lips felt cold at first, then warm. Her breast was pushing against his arm. He got breathless and hard. He caressed her hair.

She moaned softly, her lips vibrating and tickling him for a moment before they went away. "We'd better keep watch," she whispered.

"You started it."

A big smile bloomed. "That's right, I did." She sat up straight and grinned over her shoulder at him. "Impetuous me."

"God, Angela."

"What?"

"You've changed so much. And so fast. It's almost as if you're a different person. Ever since last night . . ."

"Last night you finally noticed me." Her smile slipped a bit. "I think it had something to do with the removal of a certain garment."

"Well . . . maybe."

"I haven't changed all that much. Not really."

"You used to be so . . . introverted."

"Well, we were almost like strangers. I guess you always thought I was pretty odd."

"I just . . . yeah. In your own world, kind of."

"You were scared of me." She looked over her shoulder at him and smiled. "Still are, at least a little bit."

"Not so much anymore. And it's not the same."

"Not the same how?"

"Jeez."

"Come on."

He sighed. "I don't know. Before, I thought you were sort of peculiar."

"A weirdo."

"But you're not. Not really. I mean, now that I know about . . . the way you've been living . . . I can see why you kind of kept to yourself and always seemed so . . . preoccupied."

Angela was silent for a moment. Then she said, "The fire's getting low."

Howard went shaky in his stomach.

Now I've done it, he thought. Why didn't I keep my mouth shut?

He leaned over, picked up a few sticks, then straddled the log with his back to Angela, reached out sideways and added them to the fire. Flames licked around the wood. Remembering that he was supposed to be keeping watch for the creep, he looked over at the tents and scanned the darkness beyond them.

"I was all Skerrit had," she said. "He didn't want me to have any friends. Neither did I, for that matter. I mean, I *wanted* friends, but I couldn't have them. I was always afraid someone might find out I was living with him. How was I supposed to explain something like that? Unless I lied.

205

I could've said he was my father, I guess. But what kind of a relationship's that, if you have to tell lies?"

Howard swung his leg over the log and sat again with his back to the fire, his side touching Angela.

"The thing about you," she said, and hesitated. "You know about it and you haven't . . . acted as if I've got the plague. It has to bother you, though."

"Yeah." His heart was thumping hard. He feared she was ready to tell him things he ached and dreaded to know. "I don't really understand it—how you could stay with a man like him? I know you couldn't afford a place of your own, but . . ."

"It was a lot more than that. He paid my tuition, he paid for everything."

"But why?"

"We had a deal. I agreed to live with him and take care of him, and he agreed to put me through college."

But he messed with you! How could you let him do *stuff to you?*

Those thoughts raged through Howard's mind, but he kept silent.

"There was more to it," she said. "In case you hadn't already figured that out. I guess you might say I was his mistress."

"He molested you?"

"I don't know. 'Molested' kind of sounds right. But I'm not going to lie to you, Howard. He didn't actually rape me. I was with him by choice. I didn't want any sex with him, but I let him do what he wanted. Usually. He had to force me to do some of the stuff, but usually I just went along with him. It wasn't so bad."

"God," Howard muttered.

It was worse than he'd imagined. A lot worse. Almost beyond belief.

"I'm sorry," Angela said.

"How could you?"

"I wanted my education. He wanted me. I guess we were using each other."

"But . . . it's *disgusting*."

"I know. The thing is, he wasn't all that bad to me. Most of the time, he treated me OK."

"Well, sure he did. You were putting out for him."

"Hey, come on." She sounded hurt. Howard looked around as she hunched forward. Elbows resting on her knees, she lowered her head and seemed to gaze at the ground. "So now I'm a whore or something," she muttered.

"I didn't say that."

"It's what you're thinking. I don't blame you. I guess I am. Maybe I shouldn't have told. But I don't want to have secrets from you."

"It's all right," he said. He put his hand on her back.

"Skerrit was so much nicer to me than the others. He loved me, he really did. And he didn't hurt me often. When he did, it was only because he cared so much. He was so afraid of losing me." She shook her head. "I shouldn't have left him. He must think I'm gone forever. God, I hate to think what he must be going through."

"You're not going back to him, are you?"

"Maybe that's where I belong."

"No!"

"It wasn't that bad. It really wasn't. Skerrit's an *angel* compared to the others."

"What others? You keep saying that."

"You don't want to know."

"I do." He rubbed her back. "I want to know everything about you," he added, surprising himself. He hadn't expected to speak those words, but when he heard them he knew that they were true.

She sat up straight and looked back at him. She wasn't crying, but she looked sad and weary. "OK," she said.

"OK."

"But let's not forget to keep our eyes open."

"That guy's probably long gone. Now that he knows we've got a gun . . ."

"He won't give up. I've known men like him. He won't quit till he gets what he wants."

"What do you mean, you've known men like him?"

"My stepfather, for starters. Charlie. And his boys. He had twins, Jack and George. All three of them were . . . horrible. They kept me after Mom was killed."

"That's when you were four?"

"Yeah. The twins must've been nine or ten."

"They were your brothers?"

Angela shook her head. "They were Charlie's sons. I don't know who their mother was. Not Mom, though. And I don't know how Mom got mixed up with Charlie. Maybe she didn't have a choice. That's what I like to think, that he took her prisoner or something and she couldn't get away from him. But they got married. At least I think they did. I had his name, Carnes."

"Carnes? I thought it was Logan."

"I was Angela Carnes till I got away from him. Then I changed it. I'd read this book, *Logan's Run*. I liked the name, so I took it. Anyway, I'm pretty sure Mom was married to Charlie. I don't know why she'd do something like that unless he forced her into it. Unless Mom was some kind of an awful person and she actually *fell* for him. I hate to think she was that way, though.

"If she'd lived, maybe she would've gotten me away from those guys. Or maybe not. Maybe she would've just let it all happen, anyway. I guess I'll never know.

"Anyway, it's a long story. I was thirteen before I got away from Charlie and the twins. We lived in a van most of the time. When we weren't on the move, we'd be parked out in the middle of nowhere. In forests, in fields. Charlie didn't want people around.

"I never went to school the whole time I was with them."

"Never? How did you learn to read?"

She shrugged. "*They* sure didn't teach me. I must've learned how from Mom. At least enough to get me started. I read everything I could get my hands on while I was with those bastards. It was great. It's probably what kept me from going crazy. When I was reading, I was living other people's lives. Theirs were always better than my own—

even when they were in hot water. Books were really what kept me going, I think. Books, and my daydreams.

"We'd drive past schools, sometimes, and I'd see all those kids . . . The thing I wanted most in the world, I think, was to go to school. I used to dream about how it might be. But I couldn't go to school like other kids, so I was determined to grow up and be a teacher. That got to be the most important thing to me—to be a teacher. And to teach about books. I knew it would happen someday if they didn't kill me first."

"You thought they'd *kill* you?"

"It's just a miracle they didn't."

"Jesus," Howard muttered.

"They were madmen, crazy. They were like this guy who's been attacking us, but probably worse."

"What did they *do* to you?"

"What *didn't* they?"

"But you were only a kid."

She shrugged. "That didn't stop them. But they got a lot more . . . active . . . when I hit nine or ten. And then when I started to get breasts . . . It wouldn't have been so bad, I guess, but they had to always be *hurting* me. Not because they were angry, either. They did it for kicks. It . . . turned them on. They'd get my clothes off and tie me up. Sometimes, they used handcuffs. They'd do things like hang me by my wrists from a tree limb or whatever else was handy, and whip me with their belts or sticks or electrical cords . . . God, I've been whipped with just about everything you can imagine. When they weren't doing that, they'd use pliers on me, or . . . anyway, they'd get themselves worked up into a frenzy by torturing me, and then they'd . . . you know, rape me."

Howard felt as if his mind had been stunned numb. Men had done those things? To Angela? To the girl sitting right here beside him?

He frowned at her. "They really *did* that stuff?"

"Yeah. It wasn't just to me, either. Plenty of times, they got strangers. They'd give a ride to a hitch-hiker, maybe, and then she'd be the one they used. Sometimes, they'd even run a car off the road if there was a woman in it."

"My God," Howard murmured.

"I suppose some of them must've ended up dead. But I never saw anyone get killed. I'd go into the van and hide while they did what they were doing. And I'd hear the woman's screams. And them laughing and squealing and having a great time. And I'd be glad it was her and not me."

Angela stood up. Turning around, Howard watched her rub the seat of her pants. Then she stepped past him, picked up some wood and added it to the fire. She looked back at him. "Want to walk around some?"

"Sure."

"My butt's starting to hurt." She managed a crooked smile, then turned on the flashlight.

Howard stood, loosened his belt one notch, and pushed the barrel of the revolver under his buckle.

Side by side, they walked slowly toward the tents. In a quiet voice, Angela said, "I bet you never expected to hear a story like that."

"It's . . . terrible. God. How could people get away with stuff like that?"

"They were always on the move, for one thing. I suppose we were usually miles away by the time cops even realized anyone was missing. We were on back roads most of the time. We stayed away from towns except when we needed supplies."

She stopped talking as they stepped behind the tents. She flicked her light against the back of each, then swept it through the woods.

"How did you get away?" Howard asked.

She waited until they were a distance from the tents, walking along the edge of the clearing.

"They killed me."

"What?"

"It was when I was thirteen. We were somewhere in Oregon, and they stopped to pick up this hitch-hiker. She was just fifteen or sixteen, I guess. Anyway, she was about to get into the van. I just couldn't stand the whole thing anymore. So I yelled and warned her and she ran off. She got away. So they took me to a field. They spent . . . I don't know, hours . . . working on me. They thought they'd killed me. When I woke up . . . Well, what they'd done was bury me."

"Buried?"

"One of those 'shallow graves' you hear about. Lucky for me, they'd put me in face down. So I could breathe. And there wasn't much on top of me—a little dirt and a few big rocks, but mostly leaves and junk. I got out. And they were gone. I've never seen them again." She shrugged. "For all I know, the three of them might be dead by now. Or in prison somewhere."

"I hope they're dead," Howard said.

She took his hand and squeezed it. "You're not the only one."

Their wandering had taken them along the far side of the campsite, and on toward the lake. Angela played the beam of the flashlight over the rocky shoreline. Then she turned to face the camp.

"What happened after you escaped?"

"I got to a road and some people picked me up. I spent some time in the hospital."

"Did you tell the police about everything?"

Angela turned to him. She shook her head. "I pretended I had amnesia."

"What?"

"I was so scared, Howard. Charlie and the twins, they thought I was dead. I was terrified they might find out I was alive and come looking for me. So I pretended I couldn't remember anything, not even my name. And it worked. Pretty soon, the cops stopped bothering me."

"If you'd told, they might've been caught."

"I know. But I was just too scared to take the risk. You just can't imagine how it was. They kept me nine years, *nine years*, Howard. I lived every day of that with madmen who did whatever they wanted with me. And some of it was a lot worse than what I've told you. But suddenly I was free. Really free. Because they thought they'd killed me. I would've done anything to keep them from finding out I was alive."

Letting go of his hand, she wrapped her arms across her chest. "I know it was wrong not to tell the cops. But I couldn't. I just couldn't."

"Should we go back to the fire?"

"Yeah. I'm getting the shakes."

They returned to the campfire. Instead of sitting down, they stood side by side, close to its flames. Angela put her hands out. "Feels good."

"Yeah."

"Do you want me to go on?"

"Jeez, I'm not sure."

She let out a weary sigh. "Well, the worst is over. I ended up in a foster home, and I finally got my wish about going to school. I stayed with the same family all through high school."

"They treated you all right?"

"Better than Charlie and the boys, that's for sure. But it wasn't a picnic."

"Are you kidding?"

"They weren't actually brutal. Dennis and Mindy, the pious, middle-class, all-American man and wife. They didn't want to mark us up, for one thing. Also, they had two other female wards, so the abuse got spread around. I wasn't always the target. But Mindy had a real thing for me, so I got more than my share."

"She had a *thing* for you?"

"She thought I was cute. She liked to tie me down on her bed." Angela let out a deep breath. "But, hey, those two were easy after Charlie and the twins. And Skerrit—he was a really big improvement on all of them."

"How did you wind up with him?"

"He was Mindy's father. He'd come up for visits a few times. I wanted to attend Belmore and he lived near it. A deal was made. I guess Mindy wanted to keep me in the family, come to visit on parents' weekend and that sort of thing." Angela smiled into the fire. "Dennis and Mindy went down in an airplane during my freshman year. They went down and stayed down."

"God."

"I suppose I shouldn't gloat. They weren't the worst people in the world. But I hated them."

"You don't hate Skerrit, though?"

She shook her head. "I feel sorry for him, mostly. He's awful in some ways. Perverted. But I can't loathe him. He's too lonely and pitiful for that." Turning her eyes to Howard, she said, "I guess now you see what I mean about attracting madmen, huh?"

"And women," he muttered.

"Just Mindy."

"But that makes six altogether."

"You kept score, huh?"

"It's unbelievable."

A corner of her mouth trembled. "Maybe I'm cursed. What do you think?"

"God, I don't know."

"And now there's the wild man of the mountains running around. He's gone after Doris and Lana. My turn next."

"He won't get you."

"Better him than Butler, I guess. At least he's flesh and blood. He couldn't do anything to me that hasn't been done before. Except kill me."

"Nobody's going to kill you. Nobody's ever going to hurt you again, not while I'm around." He pulled the revolver out of his belt and pushed its barrel down the rear of his pants. Then he took Angela into his arms.

She squeezed herself tightly against him, pressed her face to the side of his neck.

He caressed her hair, her back. He felt her soft breathing on his neck. He felt her breasts, her belly, her pelvis, her thighs. All snug and warm against him.

But he wasn't aroused.

He wanted to push her away.

213

Her back gave a hitch, and she made a quiet gasping sound. It happened again, then again.

What's she doing? Howard wondered.

Either laughing or sobbing.

He knew which.

"What's wrong?"

"I've ruined everything."

"What are you talking about?"

She shook her head. Her face was wet and slippery, and her eyelashes flicked against the side of his neck.

"What?" he asked again.

"Nothing."

"Come on."

"You can let go of me now. You can stop pretending."

"Pretending what?"

She pushed him away.

He clutched her shoulders. "Angela!"

"Leave me alone." Knocking his hands away, she lurched past him and ran from the fire. Out of its ruddy glow. Into the darkness. Toward the lake.

Chapter Twenty-one

Howard sat with the gun on his lap, his back to the fire. Sometimes, he glanced over at the tents. Most of the time, he watched Angela.

She was sitting near the shore, probably on the flat surface of the boulder she had called "our rock." Only her head and back were visible. They were dim blurs. Howard figured she must be awfully cold.

Awfully miserable.

When she had first run off, he'd taken a few quick steps in pursuit. Then he'd halted and returned to the fire. She didn't want him chasing her. She wanted to get away from him. That's why she'd left.

He would wait her out. He would just sit here and watch over her, make sure she didn't do something weird like jump in the lake, protect her if the crazy man should make a try.

He felt sorry for her. Sorry for himself, too. He wanted things to be the same as they'd been before she told her awful, incredible story. But when he'd embraced her there at the end, he'd felt revulsion. As if she were tainted, spoiled. Filthy. As if she reeked of all the others, their sweat and semen.

Somehow, she had sensed his reaction.

I don't want it to be this way, he told himself. Besides, it's stupid. She's still Angela. She's no different than she was when we started talking. She didn't seem *dirty*, then. And nothing happened to change her. She spoke. Air went past her vocal cords. She made words. That was all. She didn't turn rotten and smelly. All she did was speak.

It was words. Just words.

It's just words, Howard thought, if somebody says he spit in your soup.

You might've been slopping the stuff up, enjoying the hell out of it. A few words. *Guess what, I hocked a loogie in your gumbo.* Suddenly you can smell the sweetish stench of saliva and just the idea of one more spoonful is enough to make you heave.

It's not the same thing, he told himself.

Close enough.

No. They're two different things, entirely. She's clean. Nothing's still on her from those people. Nothing's *in* her. You go to restaurants, you're always eating off dishes other people have used. You don't even think about it, just as long as they've been washed good. It doesn't matter how many people have used them.

It doesn't *matter* how many people have fucked Angela.

It shouldn't.

It's stupid for it to matter.

Howard fed the fire and scanned the campsite and watched Angela. Maybe he should've gone after her. Maybe that's what she'd wanted. It would've showed that he cared.

I *do* care, he told himself.

Then why didn't I go over there? Why have I just been sitting here like a jerk all this time?

He checked his wristwatch. One-twenty. Their turn at guard duty would be over in ten minutes.

He stood up, stuffed the revolver's barrel down the rear

of his pants, and walked away from the warmth of the fire. Angela didn't turn around as he approached. He stepped onto the rock. "It's just me," he said.

"I know."

"Aren't you freezing?"

"It's not so bad."

He crouched behind her. He stroked her hair, but she continued to face the lake. "I guess you're mad at me, huh?"

"I'm not angry with you."

"Correcting my grammar?"

"Don't try to be funny, all right?"

"Sorry." He stood up. "Why don't you come back to the fire now? You must be freezing. Besides, it's almost time to wake up Lana and Keith."

She nodded, got to her feet and turned around.

Howard led the way. They returned to the fire in silence and Angela squatted close to it. He could see that she was shivering.

"I don't know what to say," he told her.

"It's not required that you say anything."

"God, Angela. What'd I *do*?"

"Nothing," she muttered.

"I thought we were friends. You know?"

"We can still be friends. But I guess it stops at that."

"Why?"

"You know why."

"No, I don't."

She stared into the fire for a while. Then, without looking up at him, she said, "I'm not exactly what you had in mind, am I?"

He shrugged. "God, I don't know. I never . . . expected you were a virgin. I mean, who is?"

"Probably you."

A blush heated his skin. "It sure isn't by choice," he said, and let out a nervous laugh.

"It isn't by choice that I'm not."

"I know."

"But that doesn't count, does it. What counts is that I'm

217

damaged goods. Damaged beyond your wildest expectations. You can't even touch me, now, without thinking about all those people who've done stuff to me. And being disgusted."

"That's crazy."

"Don't lie. It's true, and you know it."

"It's not true."

She stood up and sighed. "Is it time to get the others up?"

Howard checked his watch. "Yeah."

"Do you want to get them, or should I?"

"We don't have to do it right away."

"We might as well."

"OK. You can stay here and keep warm, I'll wake them up." He walked toward Lana's tent. He felt sad and confused. He wanted to make things right, but he didn't know how. If only she'd kept her mouth shut about Charlie and Skerrit and everyone. If she hadn't *told* him so much.

Spit in the soup.

Damn it!

He stopped in front of Lana's tent. "Hey, guys," he said. "This is your wake-up call."

"Get fucked," Keith replied.

"It's one-thirty."

"Coming," Lana murmured, her voice groggy.

Howard heard soft rustling sounds from inside the tent. Soon, the flaps parted. Lana crawled out, the bundle of a coat clutched to her chest. She was wearing a hooded sweatshirt and sweatpants. She stood up. As she struggled into the coat, her breasts shook inside the loose, baggy sweatshirt.

No bra.

Howard felt a warm stirring in his groin.

Here I am, getting turned on, he thought. Keith probably screwed her an hour or so ago. If he didn't use a rubber, she's probably got his gunk in her. So how come *that* doesn't disgust me?

She pulled the zipper up. "I take it nothing went wrong," she said.

"No problems."

"Great. The shit would've tried something by now, if he was going to."

"You'd think so."

Keith came out of the tent and stood up, hugging his chest and gritting his teeth. A flashlight was gripped in his hand. "What're we standing here for?"

They hurried over to the fire. Keith hunched down close to it. Lana added some wood to the blaze. "Why don't you guys go ahead and use our tent? You might as well. We won't be needing it for the next three hours. When it's time for the next watch, maybe Glen'll let you move over into his tent. It'd beat trying to sleep out here."

"Just use your own sleeping bags," Keith said. "I don't want your cooties."

Howard looked at Angela. She shrugged.

"OK," he said. "Thanks. Are you sure you don't mind?"

"I wouldn't have offered if I minded."

"Well, great." He handed the revolver to Keith.

Angela followed Howard away from the fire. They gathered their sleeping bags and backpacks, and went to the tent. "This will be a lot more comfortable," Howard said.

Leaving their packs just outside the flaps, they crawled inside. Lana and Keith had left their sleeping bags spread out, sides touching each other.

"Should we move them out of the way?" Angela asked.

"Let's just put ours on top. It'll make the ground softer."

Angela held the flashlight while Howard unrolled their sleeping bags on top of the others. When he was done, he said, "I guess I need to brush my teeth. Do you want to come along?"

"I think I'll wait and do it in the morning."

She gave him the flashlight. He crawled outside and took his toothbrush and paste from a side pocket of his pack. He grabbed his canteen. Lana and Keith were sitting near the fire. Keith had his arm around her back. Howard turned away from them and stepped into the trees behind the tent.

He didn't go far. He brushed his teeth quickly, thinking about the creep.

Though he suspected that the guy was only interested in girls, Butler had said otherwise.

Done with his teeth, he wandered farther from the tent so Angela wouldn't hear him. When he thought he'd gone far enough, he tucked his brush and paste into a pocket, clamped the canteen and flashlight under one arm, and un-zipped his pants. Before freeing his penis, he looked all around. He could still see the glow of the campfire. But it was way off in the distance, mostly blocked by trees.

If something happens . . .

Let's just make it quick.

He dug himself out of his underwear and started to go. The chilly air felt good down there. His splashing sounded loud, but he was sure Angela couldn't hear it. He thought about her back in the tent. She was probably taking the opportunity to change clothes—put on whatever she planned to sleep in. Sitting cross-legged on her sleeping bag, reaching up behind her back and unfastening her bra, taking it off.

The limp penis between his thumb and forefinger grew and stiffened.

Guess she's not so disgusting, after all.

He was half erect by the time he shook off the last drops. He had some trouble forcing it back inside his briefs.

Maybe I'm getting over the shock, he thought as he started back toward camp. Maybe the revulsion was just some kind of temporary reaction.

At the front of the tent, he put away the toothbrush and paste. Searching through his pack, he found his sweatsuit and a fresh pair of socks.

He hesitated, wondering if he should put them on before entering the tent.

"Is that you?" Angela asked.

"Yeah."

"What're you doing?"

"I'm gonna change clothes."

"Out there?"

"Well . . ."

"You'll freeze. Come on in. I won't peek."

"Well, OK."

Holding the canteen and clothes against his chest, he crawled inside. Angela squinted and turned her face away from the flashlight's beam. She was in her sleeping bag, braced up on her left elbow. She wore her sweatshirt. Its wide neck hung off her shoulder. Howard didn't see any strap.

He shut off the light and sat down on his sleeping bag. His back to Angela, he began to undress. She had promised not to look. The tent was dark. But he felt breathless and shaky when he drew his corduroys and underwear down. The nylon cover of the sleeping bag was cold under his bare rump. He started getting hard again.

What if she sits up and reaches around and *touches* me?

She didn't.

He pulled the sweatpants up his legs, raised himself a bit and brought them up around his waist. Quickly, he got into his clean socks, stripped off his jacket and shirt, and pulled the sweatshirt down over his head. After rolling his clothes into a bundle to use as a pillow, he got to his knees and turned around.

Angela was still propped up on her elbow. Had she been watching, after all? She said nothing as Howard scurried into his sleeping bag.

He rolled onto his side. Her face was a vague blur. Her shoulder was still uncovered. It must be cold, he thought.

"Are you warm enough?" he asked.

"Fine."

"Nice of them to let us use their tent."

"Yeah."

He wondered why she was staying braced up that way instead of snuggling down into her bag. After a while, he said, "Do you want to come over?"

"And contaminate you?"

"Jeez," he said.

221

"Go to sleep, Howard." With that, she sank down and settled on her back and turned her face away.

Later, he heard her sniffing. A runny nose? No. She was crying. Softly so he wouldn't notice.

In his mind, he eased out of his sleeping bag and crawled over to her. He kissed the tears from her cheeks, her lips. And she kissed him. Feverishly. Desperately. *Make it all right*, she whispered, and opened her sleeping bag to him. He slipped inside. They embraced, the sweatclothes soft between them. *I want you*, she gasped. *I want you so bad.* She lifted her sweatshirt, pressed his hands against her breasts. He had never touched anything so smooth. He fondled them, squeezed them, kissed them. And as he did that, Angela's hand crept down and went inside his sweatpants. Her cool fingers curled around him. *Ooo, so big*, she said. *In me. I want you in me.*

He touched himself through the front of his sweatpants. His penis felt like a hot bar of iron.

Quit thinking about her and get over there! She's crying. She's lonely. She *needs* you. Get over there and kiss her.

Right. With a hard-on?

Why not? It shows you're not turned off by her. That's what she needs to know. That's the main thing she needs to know. It'll show you don't care about all the others.

She probably won't notice, anyway.

Just crawl over there and kiss her.

Slowly, Howard began to lower the zipper on the side of his sleeping bag. He was trembling, his heart slamming. The zipper made quiet clicks.

He was still easing it down when Angela snored.

What?

He listened. She was snoring, all right. Not loudly. Just a soft, peaceful sound.

Go over anyway? he wondered.

Wake her up, she might think she's being attacked. Could give her an awful scare, especially after everything that's happened today. She'll think the creep's gotten into the tent and it's rape-time again.

Surprise, it's only me.

What'd you wake me up for?

Howard slid the zipper up, settled onto his back, and shut his eyes.

He was running through darkness, running toward screams. Need my knife, he thought. He reached down. Instead of finding his pants pocket, his hand slid over bare skin. Shit! Where are my clothes? Where's my knife?

Then he realized he had something better than his puny little Swiss Army knife. In his left hand was a machete! He brandished it and yelled, "I'm coming!"

He was answered by shrieks of agony.

He raced around a bend. The tunnel ahead shimmered with firelight. A sweaty old hunchback smiled over his shoulder. His eyes were hidden behind sunglasses. He wore nothing but a jockstrap. In his right hand was a whip. A six-foot, living snake. He held it by its tail. The beast writhed and raised its head and bared its fangs.

"Drop it!"

Skerrit lashed out with the snake.

But not at Howard.

At the girl suspended by her hands from the tunnel's ceiling. The living whip smacked against her back. She shrieked and flinched. The fangs dug in, gouging thin bloody trails down her skin before Skerrit jerked the snake back and swung it overhead.

He grinned at Howard. "Want to give it a try?"

"No!"

"Sure you do." The deformed old man lumbered toward Howard, holding out the snake.

The girl strained her head sideways and looked over her shoulder.

Angela. She had tears in her eyes. She looked more beautiful than ever before.

"It's all right if you want to," she said. "I don't mind."

"Besides," Skerrit said, "it's your turn." He tossed the snake to Howard. It flew at him head first, mouth gaping.

A swift chop of the machete decapitated it.

"Now look what you've done!" Skerrit shouted. "Ruined a perfectly good whipper-snapper."

"Dirty bastard!" A downward blow split Skerrit's head and knocked his sunglasses to the ground. Howard whirled toward Angela.

She gazed over her shoulder at him. She sniffed.

"Are you all right?" Howard asked.

She nodded. "You saved me."

He tossed the machete onto Skerrit's corpse. He stepped up behind Angela. He caressed her back. It was slippery with sweat and blood, criss-crossed with welts and fang trails. "Does this hurt?" he asked.

"Oh, no. It feels good."

He kissed her wounds. He licked them. She moaned and squirmed. Moving closer, he kissed the nape of her neck and rubbed himself against her back. Her buttocks flexed, squeezing his erection.

"Make love to me," she whispered.

"Right here? Right now?"

"Yes, yes."

Stepping back, he swiveled her around. Snakes dangled from her breasts, fangs buried in her nipples. She stretched her mouth wide and a snake shot out and darted straight toward Howard's mouth. Another slid out of her vagina, reaching for his penis.

He gasped and jerked away and woke up breathless to find the blur of Angela's face above him. The tent was dark. His head was on her lap. She was gently stroking his hair.

"It's all right now," she whispered. "It's all right."

"Oh, God," he gasped.

"Must've been horrible for you."

"You . . . you had snakes . . . on your breasts."

"Snakes, huh? I wonder what Freud would have to say about that."

"It was awful."

"Just a nightmare. Nothing but a dream." She lifted her sweatshirt. "See? No snakes."

This can't be happening, Howard thought. He wondered if he might still be dreaming. He didn't think so.

He stared up at her breasts. They looked gray in the darkness. The nipples looked black.

Angela lifted one of his hands to a breast.

He had never touched anything so smooth.

"This is all my fault," she whispered. "If I hadn't told you those things . . ."

"Those things don't matter," he said. "Maybe they do. I don't know. But . . ."

"Do you want me?"

"Oh, my God."

She took the sweatshirt off. Still fondling the breast, Howard rubbed his cheek against the silken warmth of her belly.

She eased out from under his head. Sitting down beside him, she peeled her socks off. Howard turned onto his side. He watched as she pulled the sweatpants down her legs. He unzipped the side of his sleeping bag.

Angela slid in beside him.

She tugged his sweatshirt up. He struggled with it, got it off and tossed it aside. As Angela snuggled against him, she hooked his sweatpants down around his thighs. She worked them lower by rubbing them with her feet.

Then there were no clothes in the way and Angela was all long and slim and warm and smooth. She guided Howard onto his back. On top of him, she kissed his lips. A tongue, not a snake, slid into his mouth. He sucked it. His hands glided down her back. No welts, no blood. Only smooth, wonderful skin. He curled his hands over the small mounds of her rump, slid them down the backs of her thighs.

Her legs were resting on his, parted just a little, lightly touching the sides of his penis. It was tight against the heat between her buttocks. She closed her legs, squeezing it. As he gasped into her mouth, her legs opened and rubbed down against his thighs. She lifted herself.

On elbows and knees above him, she caressed his mouth

with her wet lips. She brushed his chest with her nipples. She stroked the tip of his penis with slippery open flesh. Then she slid down, easing him slowly into a sheath of tight, hugging heat.

Chapter Twenty-two

"Yo! How about a break?"

Chad swung around as Coreen staggered to the side of the trail. She leaned back until a boulder took the weight of her pack. Then she slipped out of the straps, made sure the pack was steady, and stepped away from it.

"Oh, man," she muttered. She rolled her shoulders, arched her back, rubbed her neck. "God, I hate these switchbacks. Up up up. Jeez." She slipped the red bandanna off her head and rubbed her sweaty face with it. Chad watched her slide the wadded cloth down her neck and inside the top of her shirt. "Why don't you take a load off? I'm sure not going anyplace for a while."

"We won't catch up to the kids this way."

"Tough." She sat down on a low slab of rock and stretched out her legs.

Taking off his pack, Chad said, "We didn't exactly get off to an early start." As he propped it up beside Coreen's pack, he heard a soft chuckle from behind him. "Not that I'm complaining or anything."

"Better not be, buster."

He stepped across the trail and sat down beside her. "What a way to start the day."

"Yes and no."

"What's this 'no' business?"

She scowled at him. "You yucked me all up."

He laughed. "Comes with the territory."

"Some of it *stays* with the territory. Not that I'm complaining or anything."

"Doesn't sound like it."

"Somebody oughta dump some glue in your skivvies, see how you enjoy it."

"Might feel good."

Coreen smiled. "Well, it does and it doesn't. A nice souvenir, but it's a trifle sticky."

"There'll be a lake when we get to the top."

"Something to strive for. How much farther, do you think?"

"Well, I'd say there's more mountain below us than above us."

"What an optimist." With the bandanna, she mopped away the specks of sweat under her eyes. "I can't imagine some of those kids making it up this trail. Especially Doris."

"Is she the chunk?" Chad asked.

"Don't be cruel. But yeah, she's the chunky one. So's Glen. But he and Keith are football players. I doubt if they had much trouble. And Lana's in good shape."

"I'll say."

"Jerk." Coreen bumped him with her shoulder.

"Don't worry, she's not my type."

"She's every guy's type."

"Only one girl for me," he said, and rubbed her back. Her shirt was hot and damp under his hand.

She slipped the bandanna around her head, frowned at the trail for a moment, then looked at him. "You aren't gonna go running off on her again, are you?"

"What do you think?"

"She'd hate to wake up some morning and find you gone."

"You don't have to worry about that."

"I'd sure *like* to not worry about it." She stared into his eyes. "But I can't get it out of my head that you might be here on temporary loan. Like a library book."

"In a way, we're all here on temporary loan."

"I'm gonna bop you. I'm serious about this. The last time you took off, I was ruined. I felt as if I'd been abandoned by my best friend or my brother or something. But now we've gone so far beyond that."

"There isn't a chance in hell I'll leave you again."

"You say that now, but . . . I get this awful, empty feeling sometimes. Even when we're making love. Especially then. It's like, things won't always be this way, I'll lose you, I'll be alone again."

"I get those same feelings."

"Maybe they're contagious."

He shook his head. "They're just normal. But rare."

"Rare for you, maybe. I've been getting them all the time since you came back."

"Good."

"Good, my ass. Just when I should be . . . I'm going through some of the most terrific moments in my life . . . or what *should* be . . . and then they're all messed up because I picture how it'll be without you."

"And the same thing happens to me."

"I didn't abandon you for five years."

"But you'll get older. We both will. We'll die."

"Oh, terrific. That's just what I wanted to hear. Get morbid, why don't you?"

"The thing is, it's the times when we get that sad, empty feeling that are the most precious. Because we want those times to last, to never go away, but we know they will."

"Remember I called you an optimist? I take that back."

"You never get that feeling when you're hungry, you know. Or cold or tired or in pain. Or when you're grieving or when you're lonely. You don't get it when you're bored or when your bank account's empty or your drain is stopped up. There are a million different ways to be miserable. And when you're that way, you never once feel any kind of ache in your heart because you know the moment is going to pass and be lost. You only get that at the best of times. It's a signal that things are going damn good."

Coreen gazed at him. A corner of her mouth tilted upward. "When did you turn into such a philosopher?"

"And pedant?"

"That, too."

"Solitude. It does that to you. Living alone in the mountains. It turns you into a philosopher or a madman, one or the other. Sometimes both, maybe."

"Let me make sure I've got this straight, OK?" Her eyebrows lifted high. "I shouldn't be concerned about my blues. I should view them as pretty blue ribbons on my precious gifts of happiness."

"Sums it up nicely."

"What a crock." With a laugh, she leaned sideways and kissed his mouth. "But I love you, anyway. Come on, we'd better hit the trail. Life's so transitory, we may never catch up with those rats if we don't really haul some ass."

They stood up, got into their backpacks, and resumed the hike. Chad had been leading the way, but now he slowed his pace to stay beside Coreen. They trudged up the trail in silence for a while. Then she said, "What does the philosopher think about the institution of holy matrimony?" She gave him a playful smile, but the look in her eyes was intense.

Chad gazed at her, stunned. "You want to get married?"

"Don't you?" she asked.

"Well . . . *sure*."

"Me too. Someday. When the right man comes along."

"Huh? What about me?"

"Wouldn't want you to be left out in the cold. We'll have to find just the right gal for you. She'll have to be deep, of course—someone who can appreciate the depth of your thinking. An egghead. I don't think you'd find yourself happy, over the long run, with a mindless bimbo. However, she ought to have a certain amount of bimbotude, since you're such a sex fiend."

"The more bimbotudinous, the better."

"An egghead who enjoys a good fuck. What other characteristics would you want to see in your spouse?"

"I like a woman with a sense of humor."

"A smart bimbo that cracks wise. What else?"

"She has to be beautiful."

"Jeez, you're a tough guy to please. No wonder you're still a bachelor."

"If I'm going to spend my life with this gal, she has to be perfect."

"Perfect, huh? That lets out just about everyone I know. Can you think of anybody who has all that going for her?"

"Nope."

"In that case, I guess you'll just have to go screw yourself."

He grinned. She stuck out her tongue. "What are you looking for in a guy?" he asked.

"Fabulous wealth."

"Is that all?"

"Well, I like my men short, skinny, bald and dumb. Preferably at least ten years older than me."

"I guess that leaves me out."

"I guess that makes us even."

"You're mean," he said.

"Yep."

"Do you want to marry me?"

She stopped walking. They faced each other. "Do you mean it?" She laughed softly. "Dumb question, huh?"

"Dumb question."

"So this is it."

"Yeah."

She caught her lower lip between her teeth. Her eyes glimmered. She turned her head slowly, looking around. "Right here on a mountainside."

"We could wait, and I'll ask you in a nice restaurant. With soft music. And an engagement ring."

She met his eyes. "Here's just fine."

"I love you."

"I know. And I love you."

"But?" he asked, going suddenly cold inside.

"But what?"

"I don't know. But what?"

"But we have no champagne?"

"Does that mean yes?"

"Yes. Of course it means yes."

"Oh, man." He stepped up close to her. They both leaned forward against the weight of their packs, and kissed.

"Dalton," she said as they made their way up the trail. "Coreen Dalton."

"What are you doing?"

"Seeing what my name will sound like when we're married. Sounds good, don't you think?"

"Sounds great. Hate to mention this, though, but it's already your name."

"Jeez, you're right. This is gonna save on a lot of paperwork. I won't have to get the name changed on my driver's license, credit cards, magazine subscriptions, letterhead . . ."

"You can't marry just anyone and get a deal like that."

"I know, I know. This'll work out terrific."

They came to the end of a switchback. Instead of a hairpin turn and more trail slanting up the face of the mountain, they found a level footpath that curved into a wooded pass.

"Does this mean what I hope it means?" Coreen asked.

"I think the lake should be just through those trees."

"Fantastic." She quickened her pace.

Chad followed, dropping back far enough to have a view of her buttocks flexing under the dirty seat of her shorts, her long slim legs striding out.

My wife, he thought. She's actually going to marry me.

It seemed unbelievable.

His first night back, when they were done making love in the hallway, he'd wondered whether she would agree to marry him. He'd told himself, then, that she probably would. And he'd grown more sure of it with every moment they spent together.

She loved him. She wanted him. If he asked her to be his wife, she would probably say yes.

Now he had asked, and she had said yes (you didn't *really* think she would), and he felt stunned and astonished.

It's too good to be true, he thought.

But it is true.

We're not married yet.

That's beside the point, he realized. What matters is that she said yes. She loves me that much. She wants to spend her life with me.

Incredible!

He followed her through the shadows. He smiled and shook his head as he walked.

Coreen's perfect. The day is perfect. Everything is perfect.

The shit has probably already been launched toward the spinning blades of the fan.

Stop it, he told himself. Everything's fine.

"Lake ahead!" Coreen called, pointing up the trail.

Chad peered into the distance and saw pale blue patches beyond the trees. "Must be it," he said, catching up to her.

"I almost hope the kids aren't there," she said.

"I thought the whole point was to find them."

"It is."

"But you're hoping they're gone."

"Well, we don't need to find them this instant, you know. Later today would be just fine. What would be nice for the immediate future would be a little privacy so we can have a celebration and go for a swim and things. Don't you think so?"

"Sounds great to me."

They walked only a short distance closer to the lake before spotting a swath of red.

"What do you think that is?" Coreen asked.

233

"A tent, maybe."

"Damn."

"It might not be the kids."

"It has to be someone's. So much for having the lake to ourselves."

Chad took over the lead. "Just stay close," he said, "and don't call out or anything. Let's find out who's here, first."

"It must be the kids."

"You never know till you know."

"I'm marrying Yogi Berra."

They approached the campsite in silence, Chad walking slowly and listening. He heard no voices, no sounds of movement. At the edge of the clearing, he halted.

Two tents, a red one and a green one. A fire circle, but no fire burning within it. Other than the tents, there was no camping gear in the area. And he saw no people.

He scanned the sparse woods around the clearing. He checked the shoreline, the surface of the lake, the wall of tumbled granite along its far side.

"What do you think?" Coreen whispered.

"Looks like you got your wish."

"Should we check inside the tents?"

"Guess we'd better." Gesturing for Coreen to stay behind, he hurried to the red tent. Its flaps were zippered shut. Attached by a safety pin to the zipper tab was a small sheet of paper. It looked as if it had been ripped out of a spiral notepad. "Somebody left a message," Chad called.

"What does it say?"

He bent closer to the paper, and read aloud. "Dear Creep, Mess with our tents at your own risk. Their fabric has been treated with a secret substance known as KAQ which penetrates the skin tissues and Kills Assholes Quick. That means you. Hands off or you die. Sincerely, The Bold and Fearless Six."

"What the hell's *that* all about?" Coreen said.

"Got me. But it must've been left by your kids—'The Bold and Fearless Six.' " He pulled down the zipper tab and peered between the flaps. "Empty." He went to the other tent and looked inside. "This one, too."

"No gear or anything?"

"Nothing. They must've decided it'd be easier to make the last leg of the hike without the extra weight."

"Then they're planning to be down here again before night?"

He shook his head. "They took their sleeping bags and everything else. I think they just figure on spending tonight under the stars."

"Nuts. I thought maybe we could just wait for them here."

"They'll come back eventually. All we have to do is wait long enough . . ."

"That's no good. We've gotta keep after them. But let's have some lunch first. And then I want to get cleaned up." She swung her backpack to the ground. "What'll it be, mister? Gorp and Kool-aid?"

"No champagne?"

"Alas."

Chapter Twenty-three

"We found it!" Keith shouted.

"What?" Angela called up the trail to him.

"Get over here and see for yourself."

Angela picked up her pace.

Howard hurried after her. He gasped as she stepped on a loose rock. She stumbled. Her side bumped the granite wall on her right. Though the impact didn't look like much, it was enough to make her stagger to the left. Toward the edge of the trail. Howard lurched forward, reached out and shoved the side of her pack, thrusting her away from the edge.

She leaned back against the slope. She looked stunned. She was gasping for breath. Her hands were clasped against her belly. She was shaking so hard that even the flimsy white fabric of her shorts trembled.

"Are you OK?"

She nodded.

"Jesus," he muttered.

Bending over slightly, she rubbed her thighs. And gazed

past the side of the trail. Moaning, she shut her eyes and leaned back.

"It's all right," Howard said. "You didn't fall."

"So close."

"Yeah."

"You probably saved my life."

"I guess so." He looked over the edge of the trail.

No guessing about it, he thought. If she'd fallen, that would've been it.

During the past hour of their hike up Calamity Peak, the terrain had changed a lot. Before, the trail had been several feet wide, slanting gently upward in a series of switchbacks much like the trail yesterday that had taken them to Shadow Canyon Lake. It had made the hike tedious and grueling, but not especially dangerous. A fall would've been painful. Probably not fatal, though. Howard had taken comfort in the thought that if he or anyone else went over the side, the fall would be stopped fairly soon by the trail. One level down.

But they had left that area behind. Now, the trail was not much more than two feet wide. The slope below was nearly vertical, jagged with protruding rocks. He couldn't even *see* the lower level of the trail. He supposed it must be down there. Somewhere. But it certainly was no safety net like the earlier switchbacks. If Angela had fallen, that would've been it.

Feeling a little sick, he leaned back against the wall.

"Maybe that was what Butler meant about protecting A.L.," Angela said.

"Yeah."

"Thanks."

Doris trudged into view around a curve in the trail. She had her right hand against the wall to keep her steady. Her face was red and sweaty. She looked terrified.

"They found something," Howard called to her.

"Hot damn," she muttered.

"Thrilled as usual," Angela whispered. "Ready to go?"

"Are you?"

"Ready as I'll ever be."

"Watch your step, OK?"

"You know it."

Howard kept a hand on the side of her pack as she eased herself carefully away from the wall. She started up the trail, head down. Howard stayed far enough back to avoid tripping her, close enough to reach her—he hoped—if she should stumble again.

Suddenly, she rushed ahead.

"Angela!" he cried out. Chasing her around a bend, he realized it was fine for her to rush. The narrow trail was gone. The precipice was gone. Though the mountain loomed above them on the right, the left was now a broad, gentle slope.

You couldn't fall off it if you tried.

Howard took a deep, shaky breath, and sighed. Stepping to Angela's side, he spotted Keith and Lana near the rim of the slope. They had taken off their packs. There appeared to be a drop-off in front of them, some kind of gap with a steep rise on its other side.

Walking toward them, Howard became aware of a rushing noise. It sounded like a strong wind surging down the mountainside. But he only felt a mild breeze. By the time he and Angela joined them, the noise was a roar.

He lowered his eyes and found its source. At the bottom of the chasm, at least fifty feet below him, a stream was raging through a narrow gorge. Its water raced along, tumbling over boulders, plummeting down falls, a torrent of frothy white pounding its way downward.

Angela took hold of his hand. "Isn't it *glorious*?"

"Yeah," he said. He thought it look wild and dangerous. He took a step away from the edge, pulling Angela along with him.

"Is this your big discovery?" he asked Keith.

"*That* is," Keith said. "Over on the other side." He pointed beyond the gap.

"What? I don't . . ."

"There! There!"

Then he saw it. Someone had left graffiti on a vertical face of a granite block above the gorge. Red paint. The big, red outline of a valentine heart speared by an arrow. Inside the heart was scrawled MARK & SUSAN.

"Mark," Angela muttered. "My God."

"Butler's sign," Keith said, grinning.

"What's the big deal?" Doris asked from behind them.

Howard turned around. Glen had caught up to Doris, and was walking at her side. "Did Glen tell you about our session with the Ouija board last night?"

"She didn't want to hear about it," he said. "Or anything else."

"Well, we got in touch with Butler," Lana explained. "We asked him how to find his mine, and he told us to go 'up to Mark and go with heart.' "

"In his usual cryptic way," Glen said.

"It wasn't all that cryptic, after all." Keith pointed. "Get a load of that."

When Glen spotted the graffiti, he said, "I'll be damned. So where's the mine?"

"We must be close to it," Lana said.

Doris curled her lip. "With our luck, it's probably over there someplace."

"If it is," Lana told her, "we haven't spotted it yet."

"We're supposed to 'go with heart,' " Angela said. "That heart has an arrow through it. Maybe the arrow's pointing toward the mine."

The shaft was piercing the heart diagonally, its tip aiming upward to the right. In that direction, the rugged wall of the mountain curved out of view. "Over there, maybe," Howard said.

"Good chance of it," Lana agreed.

"Terrific," Doris muttered.

"We'll just have to find a way to cross the stream," Lana said. She swung up her pack. Keith held it while she slipped into its straps. Then he got into his own pack.

"We're gonna get ourselves killed," Doris grumbled.

" 'We owe God a death,' " Glen said.

"Fuck you, Falstaff."

Lana and Keith led the way. Howard followed them, Angela close to his side, while Glen and Doris took up the rear. As they made their way along the rim of the chasm, Howard gazed over his shoulder and searched the far wall for openings. It looked very rugged on the other side. There might be a dozen mine entrances hidden among the jumbled mass of boulders. But he couldn't spot one.

"That nice, cold stream would sure feel good about now," Glen said.

"Why don't you take a flying leap and find out?"

"Doris hasn't changed much," Howard said, keeping his voice low. Since Doris and Glen were some distance behind him and the stream was roaring, he doubted that they would be able to make out a single word.

"She hasn't had a smile on her face all day," Angela said.

"Guess they didn't do it."

"Slept together, but didn't *sleep* together."

"Too bad. Might've worked wonders on her disposition."

"Sure improved mine," Angela said, and smiled. "I feel so incredible."

Howard felt a warmth spread through his chest. "Me too."

"Does it bother you that they all know?"

"I kind of like it."

"Me too. We don't have to hide anything, you know?"

"It was a little embarrassing at the time."

She laughed. "I don't think it exactly surprised them."

"They sure surprised me." He smiled as he remembered his shock at being awakened to find himself warm under Angela's naked body and Lana with her head inside the tent, shining her flashlight on them, saying, "Time to rise and shine, lovebirds."

Then Keith was sticking his head into the tent, saying, "Thata way to go, guys. But you're gonna have to unstick yourselves and move over to Glen's tent."

Left alone, they'd scurried out of the sleeping bag, gotten into their sweatclothes and hauled their belongings outside.

Glen and Doris, bundled up, were over near the fire. "Name the kid after me!" Glen had called.

"Don't worry about a kid," Angela had said once they were inside Glen's tent. "I'm on the pill."

"I wasn't worried. But I sure wouldn't have named the kid Glen or Glenda."

She'd laughed at that while Howard, shivering, crawled into his sleeping bag. "Wanta come over?"

Moments later, she was inside his warm down bag, snuggling with him, hugging him tight. They were both trembling. "How about they caught us?" she'd whispered.

"I know. God."

"Somebody probably won five bucks."

Angela broke into his thoughts, saying, "It was the best night of my life."

"Me too," he said, glancing over his shoulder to make sure that Glen and Doris were still out of hearing range. They were even farther back than before.

"I'm awfully glad you had that nightmare," Angela told him. "I heard you over there gasping and whimpering, and pretty soon I just didn't care what you thought of me. All I wanted to do was hold you. It didn't matter if you thought I was . . . damaged goods."

"Well, I don't think that."

"You did. And I am."

"You're great just the way you are. And if . . . things hadn't happened to you, you wouldn't be the same person. You'd be different. You might've turned into some kind of horrible, obnoxious bitch or something."

She shrugged. "Could be."

"Hell, maybe you wouldn't have ended up at Belmore, and we wouldn't even know each other."

She took hold of his hand and squeezed it.

Lana and Keith halted, turned around and waited for the others.

"What gives?" Glen asked.

"This looks to be about as good as it gets," Lana said. She nodded sideways at the chasm, and Howard was surprised to see how the gap had narrowed. The last time he'd looked, it had been at least fifteen feet across. Here, the space appeared to be no wider than four or five feet.

But only here. The granite flared out, extending over the gorge like half the top of a huge around table, then curved inward again. Up ahead, the gap appeared to be impassable until it bent out of sight high on the mountainside.

"You want us to jump that?" Glen asked.

"Nobody has to," Lana told him. "But I don't see how else we're going to get over on the other side, do you?"

Glen approached the edge and stared down. "Shit," he muttered, and stepped back.

"You could climb down if you want to," Keith said.

"Get real."

"Swim the stream, climb back up over there."

"I guess I'd rather take my chances jumping," Glen admitted.

"Some jump," Keith said. "If it was any narrower, we could *step* across." He took a small running start, leaped, and landed well beyond the far edge. Turning around, he grinned. "See? No sweat."

"What do you think?" Glen asked Doris.

"I don't," she said. She folded her arms across the bulging chest of her sweatshirt and shook her head.

Lana leaped to the other side. The weight of her pack seemed to knock her forward, and she staggered off balance for a few steps before Keith grabbed her.

With a glance at Howard, Angela said, "Looks easy enough."

"You want to do it?"

"I don't see much of a choice," she said.

"There's always a choice," Doris told her.

"It's a cinch," Lana called from the other side.

Angela frowned toward Doris. "What about you?"

"Don't worry about me. Nobody else does."

"Will you be able to make it all right?"

"Why don't you stop acting all concerned and jump if you're going to?"

Sighing, Angela turned toward Howard and rolled her eyes upward. She gripped the straps of her pack. "Too bad this isn't a parachute, huh?"

"Yeah. Hey, why don't you take it off? I'll take it across for you."

"Chivalry in full bloom," Doris muttered.

"I don't think it'll be a problem. And you don't need the extra weight."

"No, really . . ."

"See you on the other side," Angela said. She skipped away from him, turned toward the gap, and broke into a run. Howard went sick inside as she dashed closer to the edge. Then she leaped, kicking out far with a long, slim leg.

She was airborne, dark hair streaming behind her, the shiny legs of her shorts fluttering around her thighs.

Howard saw her leading foot come down on air, saw her drop, her shorts bellowing, her hair flowing straight up. The vision of it made his stomach plummet.

No!

Her foot touched down. She stumbled. Lana and Keith grabbed her by the upper arms and steadied her. Turning around, she smiled. "Easy," she called.

"Not so easy to watch," Howard called back.

Then, afraid of what might happen if he gave himself time to think about it, he dashed for the edge and jumped. *Oh Jesus, oh Jesus!* His boot pounded down on the other side, jarring his whole body. His pack slammed against him. He staggered forward into Angela's arms. She hugged him.

"You were right," she said. "Watching's the hard part."

They watched Doris smirking and gesturing at Glen, apparently urging him to go first. With a shrug, he turned away from her, charged the rim of the gorge, shouted "Geronimo!" and sprang into the air.

He made it across with plenty of room to spare, landing solidly on both feet. Turning his back to the others, he waved Doris forward. "Just give it a good running start, you won't have any trouble at all."

"Give my regards to Butler," Doris called. She shrugged

her pack off her shoulders, dropped it to the ground, sat down and crossed her legs.

"What are you doing?" Glen demanded.

"Getting comfortable."

"Oh, for godsake," Keith muttered.

"Come on, Doris," Glen said. "Just jump the damn thing. You're not going to fall."

"I *know* I'm not going to fall. I'm staying right here."

"Why do you always have to be such a pain?"

"It's my nature," she said, tilting her head and smiling as if performing her impression of a cherubic child.

"The hell with her," Keith said.

Glen scowled at him. "We can't just leave her here."

"Why don't you stay and keep her company?"

"Oh yeah, right."

Lana stepped past Glen and halted at the edge of the chasm. "Look," she said, "we can't make you come over."

"I think that goes without saying."

"But do you really want to stay there by yourself?"

The girl's smile faded.

"Have you forgotten about our friendly local wildman? I mean, my God, there's no telling where he might be. What if he shows up?"

Her smile returned. It looked strained. "I'll worry about that if it happens. Just go on and get out of here. I'm not moving."

"Aren't you curious about the mine?" Glen asked her.

"Not in the least."

"Christ," he muttered. "You've come all this way. You don't want to quit now. We're almost to the mine. We're almost *there*! Don't you want to be in on it when we find Butler's loot?"

"If you aren't there," Keith said, "you don't get any."

"Cut it out," Lana told him.

"Well, why should she?"

"Because she's one of us."

"Not if she stays behind, she isn't."

"And she saved my butt last night. Or doesn't that count?"

He let out a loud, hissing sigh of annoyance. "Yeah, OK. Shit."

Lana reached back over her shoulder. She shoved her hand in between her bedroll and the top of her pack, and pulled out the revolver.

"Good idea," Keith said. "Plug her."

"I don't want it," Doris called.

Ignoring her, Lana sprang across the chasm.

Doris looked horrified. "Damn it! Why didn't you just *toss* the fucking thing! I don't need it anyway! What if you'd fallen? Would've been all my fault!"

If Lana said anything, Howard couldn't hear it. He watched her bend down and offer the revolver to Doris. The girl's face was red, her lips pushing out. She yanked the gun from Lana's hand.

Lana leaped once more across the gap.

"You're nuts," Keith told her. "She won't jump the fucking thing *once*, and you do it *twice* just to hand over our gun."

"My gun," Lana corrected him.

"What if *we* need it?"

Grinning, she slapped him on the shoulder. "We've got each other." Then she turned to face Doris. "If there's any trouble, fire it and we'll get back here as fast as we can."

Doris nodded. She was sitting there on the ground with her legs crossed, her head down, the revolver on her lap.

"God, she's pathetic," Keith muttered.

"Shut up," Lana said. "Come on, let's find that mine."

Chapter Twenty-four

Corie felt lazy and comfortable. She was lying on the flat surface of a rock by the shore, a towel under her back. Her eyes were shut against the glare of the sun, her knees up, her hand resting on Chad's bare hip. She didn't want to move.

But she knew they should finish here and be on their way. They'd eaten lunch. They'd made love. She still needed a quick swim to clean off before they could set off to find the kids. And if she remained this way much longer, she would probably find herself with a sunburn in places she'd never had one before.

Groaning, she sat up. Dribbles of sweat ran down her body. A thicker fluid, inside her, began to trickle slowly. She plucked the towel out from under her to keep it from getting messed.

"Ready to go in?" she asked.

"I don't think I can move."

"You were moving pretty good a while ago."

"I'm ruined."

"I guess so." She lifted his limp penis and let it fall. It flopped against his thigh. And started to grow. "Maybe not," she said.

"Look at my knees."

The towel hadn't helped them much. They were red, pitted with tiny indentations from the granite.

"Poor thing." Corie got to her own knees, wincing. "You should've said something."

"I'm tough."

"Yeah." She hovered over him and kissed each of his kneecaps. "Better?"

"Uh-huh."

He flinched when she kissed his penis, moaned as she tongued it into her mouth and sucked it. Corie felt a hand curl around her right breast. She felt some semen starting to roll down her thigh, tickling. She slipped her mouth off him. "You don't seem to be ruined at all. You coming in for a swim?"

"Do I have to?" he asked, a lazy, contented smile on his face.

"Not if you don't want to."

"I'm so comfortable. And the water's freezing."

"That's all right. I'll just be a few minutes." She gave his belly a gentle slap, then stood, stepped down to the shore and walked into the lake. She shuddered. The water around her feet felt like liquid ice. Gritting her teeth, she continued forward.

Chad sat up and watched her. "How is it?" he asked.

"A wee bit chilly. Want to feel?" Grinning, she bent over, cupped up a handful of water and flung it at him. He grabbed her towel to shield himself. As she'd intended, however, the water fell short.

"Missed me."

"Don't get cocky or I might improve my aim."

"I wouldn't *think* of getting cocky."

Corie waded farther out, the frigid water climbing her legs. When it was almost to her groin, she halted. Bending over slightly, she reached below the surface and rubbed her thighs clean. Then she took one more step. She hissed and flinched rigid.

"What's the matter?"

"Is steam rising?"

Chad laughed. "I don't see any."

Gasping and shaking, she cleaned herself. Then she took a deep breath, thought, *I don't really have to do this*, and plunged in. The jolt of cold stunned her, shot pain up the back of her neck and into her head. But as she glided through the water, the pain faded. She slipped to the surface, filled her lungs, and swam toward the middle of the lake. With every kick and stroke, she felt the chill easing its grip. Warmth seemed to be spreading down her arms and legs.

This isn't so bad, she thought. But it'll be wonderful to get out. Sprawl beside Chad on the rock and let the sun dry me.

Maybe give him a big hug, first, while I'm still wet and cold.

Breathless, she stopped swimming. She saw that she'd gone way beyond the middle of the lake. She was nearly to the far side. Treading water, she spotted a low slab of granite that jutted into the lake like a small dock.

For a moment, she considered swimming over to it. She could climb out and get warm. Give Chad something to look at.

Forget it.

Just a couple of minutes in the sun, and re-entry would be a torture.

Turning around, Corie thrust an arm high overhead and waved. She started to sink. She lowered her arm. Using it to keep herself afloat, she scanned the distant shore until she located the rock where she'd left Chad. She saw only the rock. Chad, she decided, must've gotten tired of watching and laid down flat, out of sight. Either that, or he'd wandered off.

She felt a little disappointed. She'd expected him to be watching her.

Isn't every day you get to see your fiancée skinny-dipping in an alpine lake.

With a sigh of regret, she swung herself around and leaned into the water. She arched her spine and kicked, the back of her head submerging as her torso and legs drifted to the surface. Then she went limp and floated. She closed her eyes against the sun's glare. The lake buoyed her up, lapped at her underside with slick cold tongues. It filled her ears with silence. The sun soothed her with its heat.

She felt so peaceful and languid that she didn't want to move. But she knew that she couldn't stay here.

If we didn't have to go after those damn kids . . .

We wouldn't be here at all.

We'll have to come up here again. We've got the whole summer. We'll come back to this lake, maybe spend a week or more . . .

But right now, duty calls.

Staying on her back, she began to kick. The water pushed gently against the top of her head, slid over her shoulders, flowed along her back and rump. It felt like cold silk.

We'll get there when we get there, she told herself.

Raising her head a bit, she found that she was still on course and making progress. She wondered if Chad was watching her now. She hoped so. Her body gleamed with sunlit water. The motion of the kicks was rocking her gently from side to side, swaying her breasts. In spite of the sun's warmth, her nipples were tight and jutting.

If he's watching, Corie thought, he'll probably have a boner the size of a telephone pole by the time I get to him.

Have to take care of that.

Then what, take another dip?

Problems, problems, she thought, and lowered her head again.

She continued to kick along on her back for a while, then rolled over. Still no sign of Chad. He must've dozed off, she told herself. And smiled. He would be in for a big surprise when she flopped down on top of him.

She breaststroked toward the jutting slab. Realizing he

might hear her approach, however, she veered off to the right. She swam as silently as possible, sweeping back the water with gentle strokes, slowly spreading her legs and scissoring them together.

Don't make a sound.

She felt like a kid playing commando.

And doing a good job of it. Except for a few quiet slurping sounds, she made no noise at all as she slipped past the rock. She glanced over her shoulder. The slab was too high out of the water for her to see Chad.

Or for him to see her. Unless he sat up.

Which he didn't do.

So far, so good.

With her hands and knees, she found the rock and gravel of the lake bottom. She eased her way forward, pushing herself up. Water spilled down her body, streaming and dripping. But not very loudly. Chad still didn't sit up and look at her.

Got it made.

She crawled out of the water and made her way to the side of a small, blocky boulder. There, she rose to a squat and turned to see Chad.

He was there on the slab, all right. Sprawled out motionless on his back. Spread-eagled. He had draped the towel over his face to block out the sunlight. He looked as if he must be baking. His skin gleamed with sweat.

This is almost too cruel, Corie thought as she crept toward him. But she was grinning.

Then she rushed, eager to reach him before the sun could warm her ice-cold skin. She bounded onto the rock, dropped to her knees between his legs, and keeled forward. She thrust out her hands to catch herself so she wouldn't crush him. Much. Her wet body slapped against him.

He didn't flinch. He didn't cry out.

He just lay there motionless, his skin hot and slippery under her.

Corie felt her heart lurch.

"Chad?"

She flung the towel away from his face.

His eyes were shut, his mouth drooping open. The hair above his right ear was matted flat with blood, and a thin stream of it trickled along the granite.

"Yes-yes-yes-yes-yes!"

Corie gasped and thrust herself up and thought, *What's going on? This can't be! We're alone!*

Alone except for the man standing ten feet in front of her. Looked as if he'd stepped off the page of a muscle magazine. Hairless, shiny, sunglasses on his face, naked except for a thin band slanting down from his hips to a bulging black pouch. Hissing *"Yes-yes"* as he pitched a rock at Corie.

She hurled herself sideways. The rock nicked the rim of her ear. She hit the slab, rolling, and toppled off. Her back smacked the lake. Even as she submerged, she flipped herself over. She clawed the bottom. Her right hand found a clump of granite. She grabbed it and lunged up, staggering in the knee-deep water.

"Yes-yes-yes!"

He was charging down the shore, rushing straight at her. Instead of pumping to help him run, his arms were reaching for her. Huge arms, corded and bulging. The muscles of his mammoth body flowed and bounced.

Corie hurled the rock.

It clipped a corner of his sunglasses and tore them from his face. His pale blue eyes looked cheery and mad.

She whirled away from him and dived, hitting the water flat, kicking and stroking as hard as she could, thinking, *Gotta move! Gotta go! This is crazy! Where'd he come from? Go! Come on! What'd he do to Chad? Oh Jesus Jesus Jesus! Hope he can't swim. Some kind of fucking maniac! What does he want with me? Don't find out, don't find out. Go go go! Waiting for me. He was waiting for me!*

Something clutched her right ankle.

Something? His *hand!*

It started dragging Corie backward.

No!

She smashed the water with both arms. She squirmed and

251

twisted. She tried to kick at his hand with her free foot. And he grabbed it.

Now he had both her feet, and she knew it was all over.

Just beginning.

She kept struggling, trying to jerk free, trying to grab the water and stop her swift backward slide. But the icy liquid kept rushing up her body.

He suddenly gave her a quick pull that forced water into her nostrils. As she blew it out, she realized he had let go.

Move it! Move it!

She beat the surface and kicked.

Kicked once with each leg before he caught her ankles again.

His grip felt different this time.

He'd reversed it?

Before she could wonder why, her legs were hoisted into the air. From mid-thigh to head, she swept downward through the water. She stretched her arms. Her hands jammed the bottom. She grappled among the rocks, seeking a weapon. But she was being pulled along too fast. Pulled toward shore.

The level of the lake dropped rapidly like a cold garment sliding up her body, baring more and more of her. Her lungs burned for air. But she knew she would soon be able to breathe. The surface was already halfway up her ribcage. Then she felt warm air against the undersides of her breasts.

Good enough!

She bucked hard, bending at the waist. Water surged over her face. A moment later, she broke the surface, gasping and blinking.

He was holding her feet up higher than his shoulders, grinning down at her like a crazed bully hoping to shake coins from the pockets of a kid who had no pockets.

Still lunging upward, Corie clamped her fingernails into the solid flesh of his rump. She tugged herself at him, driving her forehead toward his groin.

His knee shot up and smashed against her shoulder. The blow knocked her swinging backward. Her head went under. And stayed under. He was holding her just high enough so that the surface of the lake lapped against the tops of her shoulders. Corie held her breath.

He isn't going to drown me, she told herself. He'll let me up pretty soon.

She began to ache for air.

She remained completely motionless, waiting, staring at the man's blurred, sunlit body through several inches of water.

I'll kill him!

Her heart felt like a sledgehammer pounding thunder through her body. She had fire in her lungs.

Let me up, you bastard!

Enough!

She curled herself toward the surface. The man drove her straight down by the ankles, ramming her at the bottom. She flung her arms across the top of her head. Just in time. Something near the bottom struck her right forearm.

A moment later, she was hoisted high.

"You tried to hurt me," the man said. Frowning, he gave her a shake. "Don't ever try to hurt me or I'll make you dead."

Corie sucked air into her lungs, wheezing.

"I don't want to make you dead. You wouldn't stay pretty."

He turned around. Carrying Corie upside-down in front of him, he waded ashore.

Chapter Twenty-five

Howard was sitting on a throne of granite, feet dangling, Angela leaning back between his knees while he massaged her shoulders.

"I sure hope nobody's in there," she said.

He looked at the mine entrance a few yards in front of them, and felt a mixture of excitement and dread. "Me too. Just a fabulous treasure."

"Butler *said* he'd meet us at the mine. Remember? Just before Dr. Dalton's friend showed up at the door."

"Don't worry about it. I'll protect you."

Howard hunched over, pressing his lips against her soft damp hair and sliding his hands down until they cupped her breasts. He squeezed them gently through her T-shirt.

Squirming, she murmured, "Not right now, OK?"

"Nobody's here."

"Maybe and maybe not."

Howard returned his hands to her shoulders. Twisting around, he spotted Glen at the top of the outcropping, his back to them as he kept watch for Lana and Keith. "Glen's

254

looking the other way. And even if he turns around, he won't be able to see much."

"All the same . . ."

"Afraid Butler might be peering out at us?"

As he felt Angela shrug, he wished he hadn't said that. He lifted his gaze to the door-sized hole in the granite wall. The light from outside reached only a few feet into the mine, revealing a rough gray floor of rock. Someone *might* be lurking inside, just beyond the dim spill of light. Staring out at them.

A chill crawled up his back. The skin on the nape of his neck went tight and prickly.

"Nobody's in there," he said.

"Don't count on it."

"Hey, come on. I'm starting to get the creeps."

Angela patted his shins, then stroked them. He saw her head lower. "You do have goosebumps, did you know that?"

"I had a sneaking suspicion."

She rubbed his legs more vigorously. "I'll make them go away," she said. "It's too bad we don't have the gun. Maybe they'll come back with it. For that matter, maybe Doris'll be with them."

"I don't think they would've gone all the way back there."

"It isn't really so far. Not from where we left the packs."

"Yeah, but they're not going to bother with her. They want to get back here and explore the mine. They'll just grab their flashlights and . . ."

"Here they come," Glen called from his perch on the outcropping. He started to climb down.

Angela gave Howard's legs a quick squeeze, then stepped away. He hopped to the ground. They watched Glen descend into the shadows of the narrow gorge. Near the bottom, he leaped from a boulder and landed with a jolt. "All set for fun and games?" he asked.

"Maybe Doris had the right idea," Angela said.

"You're not gonna wuss out on us, are you?"

She shook her head. "I've come this far."

"Good gal. Besides, we might need you in there. Butler says you're the one who'll lead us to the loot."

"She got us to the mine," Howard pointed out.

Glen reared back his head, doubling his chin. "Hey, I'm the guy that found it."

"It was Angela's idea to go in the direction of that arrow."

"Yeah." Nodding, Glen said, "Think that was all Butler meant?"

"Who knows what he ever means?"

"True. The bastard talks in riddles."

A corner of Angela's mouth turned up. "You'd better be careful what you say about him. We might be meeting him in a few minutes."

Glen laughed, but it sounded a little nervous. He eyed the mine entrance. "If he's in there, he's dead. Right? He's been communicating with a Ouija board, so he's gotta be dead."

"Who knows?" Howard said.

"Come on, man. It's common knowledge. You use the damn things for talking with spirits. Butler's beyond the veil, over there on the other side, all that crap."

"Hope so."

"He said he'd meet us at the mine," Angela said.

"He probably meant it figuratively. Anyway, if he *is* in there and he's not a stiff, there's five of us and one of him." Glen patted the knife sheathed on his hip. "He'd better not try anything unless he likes the taste of cold . . ."

"Ready to do some exploring?" Lana asked, striding through the gap at the end of the broad passageway. Keith was hurrying along behind her. They both looked breathless and sweaty.

Lana carried a flashlight in one hand. Looped over her right shoulder was a coil of rope—the line that she'd stretched from tree to tree, back at camp that morning, to dry her clothes in the sunlight while they prepared breakfast. The coil pulled at her shirt, spreading its front enough for Howard to see the top of her breast, a dusky sheen against the stark white of her bra. The shirt was unbuttoned, held together by a loose knot just below her breasts, leaving her bare to the waistband of her shorts. The shorts hung lower on one hip than the other, dragged down by the weight of the hatchet dangling from her belt.

"Planning to chop some wood?" Glen asked.

"Thought we . . . might need a weapon." Howard watched her chest rise and fall as she gasped for air. "Never know . . . what we might run into. Brought some rope, too." She patted the coil, sending a little shimmer down the slope of her breast. "Just in case," she added.

"You didn't happen to pick up the gun?" Angela asked.

She shook her head. "I saw Doris, though. She's still sitting there. Reading a book." Lana pointed the flashlight at her face and thumbed its switch. A faint disk of brightness lit her chin, moved up her lips and nose, and swept from eye to eye. She switched it off. "I'd like to've gotten the gun back from her. Couldn't do it, though. She'd be defenseless."

"She'd have her mouth," Keith pointed out.

"Quit it," Lana said. She took a deep breath. "OK, I guess I'm ready. Everyone else ready?"

They all looked at each other.

"I'll take the lead," Lana said.

"Good idea," Keith said. "Ladies first."

"You stick close to me." She pulled the hatchet out of her belt and handed it to him. "Stay ready with that, but make sure you don't whack any of *us*."

"Who, me?"

"Just be careful with it. Glen, why don't you take up the rear? Give him your flashlight," she told Keith.

They followed her to the mouth of the mine. There, she halted and turned on her flashlight again. Howard watched its beam sweep through the darkness. The tunnel looked as if it had been chiseled straight into the mountainside. But only for about thirty feet.

"I don't see any loot," Keith muttered.

Neither did Howard. All he saw were the rough walls and ceiling, some rubble on the floor, and what appeared to be a dead end. There were no support beams, but he supposed that a mine bored into solid rock didn't need them.

"Maybe we'll have to dig for it," Lana said.

"Right. A buried treasure. Shit. Maybe it's still in the *walls*—like a vein of gold—and we're supposed to whack it out a piece at a time. Butler should've warned us to bring along our picks and shovels."

"We might have the wrong mine," Glen said. "If prospectors were working this area, there could be some others nearby . . ."

"Let's check it out, anyway," Lana said.

Crouching slightly, she stepped through the opening. Keith followed, holding the hatchet low at his side. Though Angela had plenty of headroom, she ducked as she entered. Howard went in after her.

The mine wasn't chilly, as he'd expected. Instead, its stale air was hot and dry. Heavy. Stifling.

He took only a few steps before the light from outside faded. He could see nothing except the dim, pale back of Angela's T-shirt. He reached forward and put a hand on it.

"Who turned off the fuckin' air conditioning?" Keith said.

Behind Howard, Glen's flashlight came on. Its beam shifted from wall to wall, then lowered, casting its glow along the rough gray floor. It skidded from side to side as if searching for a way past Howard's legs to light the area ahead for Angela. "Is that helping?" he whispered.

"A lot," Angela said. "Thanks."

"Looks like we're in luck," Lana said. Her voice reverberated through the tunnel. "It doesn't stop, it turns."

"Terrific," Glen muttered.

"Hey, daylight." Keith's voice.

A moment later, Lana said, "Uh-oh."

"What the hell?" From Keith.

"I'll be . . . *shit*!" Lana.

"Oh, man!" Keith.

Glen's beam shot to the side, lighting the corner of the wall just in front of Angela. She took another step, then turned her head toward the passageway, gasped and lurched back against Howard's hand.

"What *is* it?" Glen blurted. He shoved against Howard, trying to squeeze by.

"Quit it!"

"Let me . . ." He shouldered Howard out of the way, side-stepped past Angela, and lunged around the bend. "Oh, my *God*! Let's get out of here!"

"Cool it," Lana said. "Just cool it."

"Never seen a stiff before?" Keith asked.

Howard's stomach went cold. He wrapped an arm across Angela's shoulders, swung his head to the right, and saw the others. Glen, just beyond the turn, stood rigid in a gray spill of light from above. At his feet were the remains of a campfire: a pile of ashes and charred wood and bones. Someone, Howard realized, must've been living here—and eating small animals.

Lana and Keith stood close together a few yards farther up the tunnel. On the other side of a rumpled blue sleeping bag that was spread out beside the dead fire. On the other side of the skeleton sitting upright beside the bag.

Lana and Glen both had their flashlights aimed at it.

The skeleton sat with its back and head resting against the wall, hands folded over its pelvis, fleshless legs stretched out.

At least it's not gross, Howard thought, fighting the cold numbness that seemed to be flowing outward from his stomach. Could've been worse. Not a rotting corpse. Just a skeleton.

A dead person.

"Jesus," he muttered.

"It must be Butler," Angela whispered.

Glen stepped over the legs, apparently in a hurry to join up with Lana and Keith. "Hey, what?" He kept his flashlight aimed at the space between their bodies. They moved farther apart.

"It's the rest of his stuff," Lana explained, shining her own light onto the scattered gear behind her.

"Who's stuff?" Glen asked. "The dead guy's?"

"Who knows?" Keith said.

"Come on," Howard said. Taking Angela's hand, he led her around the campfire. He stepped on the sleeping bag. Its thickness was springy under his shoes. A down-filled mummy bag. "Pretty good stuff," he said.

"Maybe this is our big jackpot," Keith said.

"Butler's loot?" Lana asked.

"We oughta go through all this," Glen said.

"Yeah," Keith said. "Might be a million bucks in the backpack."

"Could you shine one of those flashlights our way?" Howard asked.

"Sorry." Lana turned around and trained her light on the skeleton's legs.

"Thanks," Howard said, stepping over them. When he was clear, he looked back.

Angela halted, let go of his hand and crouched beside the legs. "Did you notice this?"

"What?" Howard asked.

"Lana? Everyone? Come here. Look at this."

The others returned, gathering close to the skeleton and shining the flashlights on it. Angela pointed at its knees. They were wrapped with strips of leather.

"Yeah, so?" Keith asked.

"And here, and here." Angela pointed to the wrists and elbows. They were bound the same as the knees. "And look." On both sides of the mandible were shoelaces that tied it to the skull.

"Oh, man," Glen muttered.

"It didn't do this to itself," Lana said. She lighted one of the hands as Angela picked it up by the wrist. The collection of bones rattled quietly. From what Howard could see, the hand was complete.

He grimaced as Angela lifted it close to her face. She gazed at it, her nose wrinkling. "All these finger bones and . . . they're tied together with hair." She set the hand down gently, got to her feet, and rubbed her hand across the belly of her T-shirt.

"We're looking at somebody's hobby," Keith said.

"And his sleeping bag is right beside it," Lana pointed out.

"Yeah. Speaks highly of his state of mind, huh?"

"I wonder if he's the creep who's been jumping us," Angela said.

Howard felt his bowels squirm.

"I wouldn't be at all surprised," Lana said.

"Sounds like just his speed," Keith said. "The nut lives with a stiff in an abandoned mine and makes forays down the mountain to attack campers. A wild and crazy guy."

"This is probably one of his victims," Glen muttered.

"It looks like it's been here for years," Lana said.

"Maybe he's *been* here for years," Keith said.

"He didn't look much older than twenty. I don't know that he's old enough to have killed this person."

"Who knows? How long does it take to turn into a skeleton?"

"You got me."

"It could've been here when he moved in," Glen suggested.

Keith let out a nervous chuckle. "Yeah, and he liked the idea of having a buddy. Maybe the two of them decided it'd be nicer around here if they had a babe."

"If this is Butler . . ." Angela began.

"Yeah. He's the one who lured us up here."

"But he said he didn't bring us here because of the guy," Howard pointed out.

"He might've lied," Angela said. "Maybe there never was any loot, and he just used it as bait so they could lay their hands on us."

"Let's get out of here," Glen said.

"Not till we've checked the place out." Lana turned around and aimed her light at the heaps of clothes and gear. "We'll go through his stuff, then search the rest of the mine.

I came here for Butler's loot. The least I'm gonna do is *look* for it."

"It's not worth dying for."

"Nobody's keeping you here."

"Like I'm *sure* I want to stay by myself."

"You could go back and stay with *el chubbo*," Keith told him.

"Fuck you."

"Fuck *you*."

"Cut it out!" Lana snapped. "Look, we've been in here for five minutes or something. The bastard hasn't attacked us yet. That means one of two things. Either he's not around, or he's decided to leave us alone."

"Either way could change damn fast," Glen said.

"So let's look through his stuff fast." Lana hurried over to it, and the others followed. She gave her flashlight and the coil of rope to Keith. "Keep watch," she told him. She toed a bundle, knocking a wadded blanket off the top, revealing a mound of gray fur. She crouched, poked the fur, and picked it up. A coat. It looked like a patchwork of animal skins: squirrels and coyotes. She sniffed it. "This is what he was wearing last night when he grabbed me."

"Are you sure?"

"Yes, I'm sure." She tossed it aside and lifted a pair of pants. Their tops appeared to be regular bluejeans. But the denim legs were gone. In their place were bulky legs of skin attached to the fabric with leather thongs. Lana stuck her arm into one of them. "Fur-lined," she said. "These must be the leather pants you told us about," she said, looking over her shoulder at Angela.

"Probably are."

She flung them. Upright on the rock floor was a pair of high-top hiking boots. She turned them upside-down and shook them. Nothing fell out.

She crawled over to the backpack, pulled it toward her and up-ended it. Out tumbled a towel, a bar of soap, an injector razor, a pair of leather sandals, a leather belt, several pieces of rope and a plastic bottle of insect repellant, followed by an avalanche of brassieres and panties that buried the other items. "What the hell?" Lana muttered.

"This is one weird puppy," Keith said. He nudged the colorful array of undergarments with the toe of his boot. "Anything of yours in there?"

"I think he's gone beyond panty raids," Lana said.

"Yeah. Nowadays, he's after what's *in* the suckers."

She set the pack down on top of the pile, opened one of its side pockets, and reached in.

"Careful what you touch," Keith said.

She brought out a handful of matchbooks, dropped them, and dug deeper into the pocket. She withdrew a Band-aid tin and a toothbrush. She flipped up the lid of the tin. "Just bandages." She emptied her hand, reached again into the pocket, and came out with a leather billfold.

"All right!"

"This might be interesting," she said. Keith bent over, holding the flashlight close to the top of the wallet as Lana opened it. She spread the bill compartment.

"By God, it's our loot!"

"Knock it off," Glen said.

Lana flicked through the bills. There weren't many of them. "Twenty-six bucks," she announced.

"We're filthy rich. Thank you, Butler!"

"You're a riot," Glen said.

"Here's his driver's license."

"No shit." Keith squatted down beside Lana. "He had hair then."

Looking over her shoulder, Howard saw the card inside a clear plastic holder. The small, color photo showed a man with a broad face and curly blond hair. After a glimpse of the license, his eyes were drawn to the glossy slopes of Lana's breasts. He watched a trickle of sweat slide down the side of one and melt into the edge of her bra. Then a drop of sweat fell off his nose and splashed the top of her other breast. "Sorry," he muttered. Apparently unconcerned, she brushed it away with her free hand. Howard stepped back.

263

"It might not be him," Lana said a few moments later.

"It's him, all right. Look at that neck."

"Hubert Orson Elliot."

"Name like that, no wonder he became a hermit."

"A San Francisco address."

Howard lifted his shirt. As he used its front to wipe the sweat from his face, Angela reached around behind him and caressed the bare skin above his hip. He wondered if this was the same hand that had held the wrist of the skeleton. And he realized it was.

And he realized he didn't really care.

Her hand felt good on his side.

She's mine. She'll still be mine after we're out of here, after all this scary mess is just a memory.

If we get out of here alive.

He let his shirt fall. Her hand stayed under it, roaming slowly up and down. He put his arm across her back and rubbed her side and wished he hadn't snuck those peeks at Lana's breasts.

"Look there," Keith said. "The thing expired last year."

"Maybe he got an extension." Lana turned the card over. "Nope. And you have to renew every four years, so . . ."

"He apparently hasn't been a crazy panty-snatching hermit forever. That's good to know, huh?"

Lana looked through the rest of the wallet, then dropped it.

"Hey, let's at least grab the money."

"Forget it. I'm not a thief."

"Well, shit. The fucker jumped you last night."

"That doesn't make it right to steal from him."

"It isn't enough to bother with, anyway," Glen said.

"You're just scared it'll piss him off. Tell you what. Us guys'll split the cash, and you gals help yourself to some nice bras and panties."

"Hilarious," Glen said.

Keith picked up the wallet.

"Don't!" Lana snapped. "I mean it."

"Hey, we came up here for loot. This is loot. Right where Butler said we'd find it."

"This isn't what he meant," Angela said, her fingers pressing into Howard's side.

"Well, it sure ain't much, but . . ."

"Butler said I'm the one who would lead us to it, didn't he? Well, I'm telling you, this isn't it."

Keith tossed the wallet into the pack and stood up. "OK, where is it?"

"I don't know yet."

"Great."

"But I think we should search the rest of the mine."

"Yeah," Howard said. "The treasure might be farther in. We need to explore the whole place."

"We're not done here, yet," Lana said, reaching into the pocket on the other side of the pack. "Glen, why don't you go over and make sure there's nothing in the sleeping bag? The rest of you, help me out. There's plenty of junk right here that needs to be checked before we do anymore exploring."

"My hands are full," Keith said. He held them out as if displaying the flashlight and hatchet, the coil of rope looped over his left wrist. "If it's all the same to you, I'll stand guard and give Hubert Orson Elliot forty whacks if he comes bopping along."

Chapter Twenty-six

Chad opened his eyes. Sunlight came in, stabbing his brain. Groaning, he squeezed them shut.

He didn't know where he was, but he wondered if he'd been drinking last night. Must've gotten really smashed to have a hangover this bad.

His pounding head felt as if it might explode. Maybe it already had.

He raised his arms, planning to squeeze it. And flinched when his right hand met a raw lump above his ear. He jerked his hand away, then brought it back carefully. The knob, matted over with stiff, gooey hair, felt the size of a golf ball. Fingering his way through the hair, he touched a small gouge. Then he brought the hand in front of his face and opened his eyes enough to squint. His fingertips were stained red, speckled with rust-colored specks. Blood. Some dry, the rest nearly dry.

Did I fall? What . . . ?

He started to sit up. Swirling with dizziness, he saw that he was lying naked on top of a rock. Before he could wonder much about it, his stomach turned. He flung himself over and got to his hands and knees. The vomit erupted. He heaved, spasms jolting his body, jamming his head with pain.

When he was done, he sank back onto his haunches and gasped for breath. He saw a towel on the rock just beyond the spreading mess. Bracing himself up with one hand, he reached out and grabbed it.

Pink.

Isn't mine.

Whose is it?

As he settled back and rubbed his face with it, he realized that the towel must belong to Coreen.

Coreen.

I was here with Coreen. Looking for her students. We camped out last night, and today we . . .

Chad's heart started sledging, pumping agony into his head.

. . . made love here, that's why I'm . . .

A clump of ice seemed to drop into his stomach.

. . . *Where is she?*

The lake. Went in to clean up, to swim.

Chad flung the towel down and struggled to his feet. As he turned toward the lake, he lost his balance. He staggered, flapping his arms, and managed to steady himself before stumbling off the edge of the granite slab.

Shading his eyes with both hands, he scanned the ruffled blue surface of the lake. It glinted specks of sunlight that hurt his head. He felt himself swaying a little. But he kept studying the lake and its desolate rocky shores.

Any second, he would spot Coreen swimming in the distance.

Or maybe perched on a boulder on the other side, sunning herself.

But he didn't spot her.

And he pictured her down below, turning slowly in the currents, her skin pale blue in the cold rays of sunlight slanting down through the water, her hair flowing lazily around her face.

"Coreen!" he shouted, blasting pain through his head. "Coreen!"

No answer came. He heard only the hiss of the mountain breezes, bird cries and the soft lapping of the lake as it washed against his stone platform.

I was out cold, he told himself. *Maybe she went to get help for me.*

Why was I out cold? What hit me?

I stood up to watch her, and slipped?

Or somebody clobbered me? Who? There's nobody . . . nobody we saw.

Coreen wouldn't have hit me. No. Not on purpose, anyway. Some kind of accident?

He called out her name three more times, cringing with pain at each shout. Then he turned his back to the lake. He scanned the shoreline, the campsite, the shadowed woods around the clearing. Nothing moved.

He made his way carefully to the edge of the rock, stepped down, and trudged up the gradual slope to the campsite. Both backpacks were still propped against a log by the fire circle. As he walked toward them, he saw that his clothes were draped over the top of his pack. Coreen's clothes were gone.

She hadn't drowned! She must've come back here and gotten dressed and . . .

No. He remembered, and his elation died. He was the one who had stripped down here by the fire and left his clothing on the pack. Coreen had gone into the red tent. She'd come out wearing nothing but the towel wrapped around her waist.

Chad ran to the tent, wincing as each footfall pounded pain into his head. He swept a flap aside. The tent was crimson inside with tinted sunlight. On the floor were her boots and socks, her shorts with a corner of black panties hanging out through the waist hole, her bra draped across her rumpled plaid blouse. Her red bandanna, still knotted to form

268

a headband, formed a hoop around one of the bra's flimsy, collapsed cups.

At the sight of her bandanna, Chad felt his throat go tight. She's OK, he told himself. She's gotta be OK.

She's gone.

She wouldn't have wandered away naked.

She has extra clothes in her pack. Maybe . . .

God, what happened *to her?*

Chad ducked into the tent. The trapped air was hot. Squatting, he picked up Coreen's bandanna. It still felt a little damp. He squeezed it tight, and some moisture dribbled between his fingers. Her sweat. He pressed his fist to his mouth as his vision went blurry with tears.

"I'll find you," he murmured. "Damn it, I'll find you."

He took the bandanna outside with him. He wiped his eyes with it. After the heat inside the tent, the breeze chilled his wet skin. He stood motionless, listening, gazing through the shadows at the sunlit lake. Trembling. Thinking.

She went swimming. She didn't come back here for her clothes. Even if she put on some fresh things from her pack, she would've gotten into her boots if she planned to hike any distance. So . . .

Maybe she was swimming around, got too cold, and climbed ashore somewhere to rest. And fell asleep. She might be sleeping right now. Stretched out on a sunny rock. She just didn't hear me yelling for her.

She'll show up any minute.

No she won't, he thought. She isn't just taking a snooze. Whatever happened to her, it *has* to be connected somehow with what happened to me. Too much of a coincidence, otherwise.

He suddenly realized that she hadn't drowned, either.

Again, that would've been too much of a coincidence.

I fall and knock myself out, Coreen just happens to get a cramp or something and go down?

No way.

Chad felt a little relief. But not much.

Because, if Coreen hadn't found him unconscious and

rushed off to seek help (and that seemed awfully unlikely), he could think of only one way to connect his injury with her disappearance.

He hadn't fallen down. Someone had crept up on him while he sat on the rock watching her swim. Crept up and bludgeoned him. To take him out of the picture. So the attacker could go after Coreen.

He realized that his hands had worked open the bandanna's knot. He stretched the cloth taut, wrapped it around his head, and tied it.

Then he raced for his pack.

A guy, he thought. Had to be a guy. Maybe more than one. Spied on us. Wanted her. Wanted to grab her, rape her.

Maybe she got away.

She isn't *here*, that's for damn sure.

As fast as he could move, Chad got dressed and into his boots. With fluttering hands, he opened a side pocket of his pack. He found his first-aid kit, dug out a tin of aspirin, and downed four pills with water from his canteen. From the pocket on the other side, he removed his sheath knife. He slipped it onto his belt, and took off running as he fastened the buckle.

They didn't get her here.

(Unless her body's just out of sight in the trees—or in the green tent. No!)

They didn't get her.

She made a break for it. Maybe hit the lake. That'd be the smart thing to do. If they can't swim, she's got it made. If they *can* swim, she's probably faster. She's a hell of a swimmer.

Chad halted at the edge of the lake. Swiveled his head. Nobody in the water. Nobody along the far shore. But portions of the lake and shoreline were out of sight along the near side, and there might be hidden coves or inlets.

He went to the right. Though tempted to run, he forced himself to hold back. He walked fast. He scurried up the mounds and blocks of rock as he encountered them. But never too quickly. As he moved along, he peered down at the shallows of the lake. He searched nooks and recesses along the shore. He gazed into the shadowy woods.

He imagined finding her crouched in the water, hiding among rocks close to shore, looking up at him with terror in her eyes, then sighing, saying, "Thank God it's you. Are they gone? Where are they?"

He imagined finding her sprawled face down in a sheltered and sunny space among the boulders, himself rushing to her side, turning her over. And waking up, Coreen smiles at him and says, "Did I fall asleep?"

He also imagined turning her over and finding a horrible slash across her throat.

He imagined finding her among the trees, barely visible in the distance, half buried as if she'd sunken into the soft mat of pine needles, the skin of her back ghastly white in the shadows.

He imagined finding her among the trees, struggling as one man held her down and another tried to mount her and Chad raced at them silently, drawing his knife.

He did not imagine finding Coreen partway up the side of the mountain beyond the other end of the lake, trudging up a switchback, followed by a giant of a man who appeared to be as naked as she was. A giant hanging onto her hair with one hand. A giant with a long, gleaming blade in the other.

But that was what Chad found after he climbed to the top of a high outcropping near the end of the lake. Though he'd known the climb would be exhausting and painful and time-consuming, he'd realized that the summit would provide him with a full view of the lake and its surroundings. And so, full of hope and dread, he'd made his way up.

From his perch at the top, he had looked down into the lake. He had scanned its shores, its little coves, the steep slope of jumbled granite that he would have to cross when he continued his way around the lake, the wooded area surrounding the campsite on the other side. He'd seen the red and green of the tents. He'd seen the low slab of rock where he and Coreen had made love, where he'd found himself unconscious. And near the far end of that shore, he'd seen a stream partially hidden by the trees, a stream emptying its run-off from Calamity Peak into the lake.

He had gazed at the mountain. That's where her students must've gone. Searching for their damn treasure.

Frowning at the rugged wall of the mountain, Chad had wondered if he should go up there and try to find the kids. Get them back down, and they could help him search for . . .

Coreen.

There she is!

Someone. It *must* be her!

Trudging up a switchback, followed by a giant.

Chapter Twenty-seven

Following Angela, Howard stumbled out of the dense heat and darkness. Though the area in front of the mine entrance was now in shadow, the daylight stung his eyes and made him squint. The air felt cool, fresh, wonderful.

Glen, who'd been in the lead, flopped onto his back.

Angela stayed on her feet, but bent over and clasped her knees. Her black hair was matted to her head, and hung in strings past her face. Her T-shirt, pasted to her back, was nearly transparent. Her skin looked pink through the fabric. The thin straps of her bra showed. So did the bumps of her spine and the curving bones of her ribcage.

Seeing the bones reminded Howard of the skeleton.

He felt very glad he had left *that* behind. With any luck, he would never have to see it again.

He staggered past Angela, sank to his knees, turned around and leaned back against the base of the rocks across from the mine entrance. He stretched out his legs.

And realized he was sitting in a position much like the skeleton.

He crossed his ankles to take away the similarity. His legs felt greasy and hot inside his corduroy pants.

Keith stepped out of the mine. He still carried the hatchet. He had looped the coil of rope over his head, and it hung like a necklace against his bare chest. His shirt, tucked under his belt, draped the front of his jeans like a loincloth. He plucked it out and mopped his face with it. After a couple of sidesteps away from the entrance, he settled back until his rump met the nearly vertical slope.

Lana came out, switching off her flashlight. Her face was dripping. Her blond hair clung to the sides of her head in tight, dark curls. She had followed Keith's example and removed her blouse during their long search through the tunnels. It hung at her side, its collar tucked under her belt at the hip. Her bra was very white against her tanned skin. She was dripping with sweat. Though the bra looked sodden, Howard found that he couldn't see through it. He liked what he could see, however, and watched as she joined Keith, leaning against the slope. She tilted back her head and shut her eyes. She was gasping for air. She licked her lips. "Should've brought some water along," she said.

"I'd like to be down at the lake right now," Glen said. He was still stretched out on his back, but his head was lifted, hands cupped behind it, apparently so he could enjoy his view of Lana. "Wouldn't you just love to jump in right now?"

"The stream's a lot closer," Keith said.

"Getting down to it would be a trick."

"There's probably an easy way down. It must be where Hubert gets his water."

"We've got plenty down at the packs," Lana said. She stuffed the flashlight into a front pocket of her shorts. "Maybe one of us . . . oughta go down for a couple of canteens. Then we can look around for another mine."

"I don't think there *is* another mine," Angela said. She was standing up straight, now, hands on her hips. "I mean, I think this is the one Butler meant." She stretched, bending herself backward like a bow. "Don't you think so?" She looked around at the others.

"We didn't find anything," Glen pointed out.

"Shit," Keith said, "we *found* plenty."

"Gimme a break." Glen grimaced, then sat up.

"There wasn't any treasure," Lana said. "Or if it's there, it's too well hidden. If that's the right mine, it's a bust."

"But don't you think the skeleton was probably Butler?" Angela asked.

"Who knows?" Glen said. "Who cares? There wasn't any loot."

"If that's Butler," Keith said, "I oughta go back in and give him a kick in the chops. Put us through all this shit for nothing."

Angela wandered over to Howard. She sat down beside him and crossed her legs.

"What does everyone think we should do?" Lana asked.

"What we *don't* want to do," Glen said, "is be here when Hubie shows up."

"I'll second that," Keith said.

"So . . . should we just give it up and go back down to the lake?"

"Sounds good to me," Glen said.

"We'll have come all this way for nothing."

"Oh," Keith said, "but it's sure been fun."

Glen suddenly turned his head, frowning at Angela. "He said *you'd* know where the loot is."

"Don't go blaming her," Howard said.

"What's . . . the bastard's been lying to us all along?"

"There was always a good chance of that," Lana said. "Coric warned us, remember?"

"But he told us where to find the hundred bucks!"

"He must've had a reason for bringing us here," Howard said.

"Yeah. So we could get nailed by his buddy, Hubie the Hermit."

"Maybe the whole point," Keith said, "was to add some

underthings to the collection. Either of you babes care to donate?"

Lana, frowning, elbowed him hard in the arm.

"Hey!" He kept his smirk as he rubbed his arm and said, "I mean it. Look at the facts. Butler got all three of you gals to show off your bras at Dalton's party. Right? He wanted to check them out. Obviously, he liked what he saw so he tricked us into coming up here. He wants your bras, babes. That was the whole point. The be-all and the end-all, the Alpha and Omega, the *raison d'être* of our pilgrimage to this scenic locale."

"Eat shit and die," Lana told him. She pushed herself off the wall. Striding away from Keith, she tugged her blouse out of her belt, thrust her arms into its sleeves, and started to button the front.

"Now look what you made her do," Glen said.

"Don't you start in," Lana warned him.

He blushed and lowered his head.

Lana finished fastening her buttons. "We might as well get out of here."

"Hasn't it occurred to anyone," Angela said, "that maybe we should ask *Butler* about the loot? I mean, we've got the Ouija board with us. It's in your pack, isn't it?" she asked Lana.

"Yeah." Lana seemed to be frowning and smiling at the same time. "Yeah, it is. I should've thought of that. Who wants to come along?"

"Why don't we all go?" Howard suggested. "We might not have to come back. And it's safer if we stay together."

Nobody disagreed.

They followed Keith out of the recess and into the sunlight, then began making their way along the rough slope, moving gradually lower. Soon, Howard could hear the rush of the stream. Pausing, he turned his head to the left and looked for Doris. Though he could see both rims of the gorge, the narrow place where they'd leaped across was blocked from view by high clusters of rock on their side.

He hoped she was all right.

She has the gun, he reminded himself. She's probably safer than the rest of us.

He moved on, following Angela down the face of a tilted granite sheet. At its bottom, they hopped from boulder to boulder. Howard saw the painted heart just ahead. They'd left their packs in a flat area below it—their starting place for the search.

He looked back again. And saw Doris in the distance, sitting cross-legged a few yards from the rim of the gorge, her head down. She seemed to be reading, though Howard couldn't make out the book.

For a moment, he envied her. She'd just been sitting there the whole time, probably enjoying herself. Not climbing around on a mountainside, not wandering through the suffocating heat and darkness of a mine, not having to see the bones of a dead person. Hell, she was even blissfully unaware that she was sitting no more than a hundred yards from the camp of the lunatic who'd attacked her yesterday.

Howard almost wished *he* had been the one to chicken out and stay behind.

But he wouldn't have liked being alone. She looked awfully lonely, awfully vulnerable sitting there by herself.

Turning away, he saw Angela scurry down to the broad ledge where they had left the gear. The others had arrived ahead of her and were already bending over their packs. By the time Howard joined them, they were gulping from their canteens and water bottles. His own canteen hung against the side of his pack. He untied its strap, twisted off its top, and drank. The water had been ice cold when he'd filled up that morning at the stream at the end of the lake. Now it was warm, but still delicious. He stopped for air, then drank more before knotting the canteen's strap to his pack.

He had left his hat here so it wouldn't get in his way while climbing around to search for the mine. It was stuffed under one of the cords that bound his sleeping bag to the top of his pack. He pulled it free, shook it open, and put it on. The big, floppy brim cast a soothing shadow onto his face.

Angela took the spiral notebook and pen from her pack.

Lana sat down, her back to the rim of the gorge. Legs crossed, she leaned forward and set the Ouija board in front of her. She placed the pointer on the board. "Let's do it," she said.

Glen, Keith and Howard took their positions on the other sides of the board. Angela sat beside Howard. She brought up one knee and held the notepad against it, ready to write. The rest of them leaned closer to the board and placed their fingertips on the plastic heart-shaped pointer.

In a firm clear voice, Lana said, "It's us."

"Again," Keith muttered.

"Butler, are you here? Butler? We found a mine where you said it'd be. Where's the loot you told us about?"

The pointer trembled and began to glide. It stopped over the I, then slid sideways down the curving letters and halted at the M. It kept on moving slowly and pausing, and Glen spoke each letter aloud.

"I-M-B-O-N-E-S."

"I am bones," Angela said.

"The skeleton? You're the skeleton?"

The pointer slid upward from the S to the YES beside the smiling sun.

"You were right," Howard said, glancing at Angela.

"We oughta make sure this is Butler," Glen said.

"Are you Butler?" Lana asked.

"I-M."

"I am," Angela said.

But the pointer didn't stop. It drifted from letter to letter. "A-N-N-A-B-E-L-L-E-B-U-T-L-E-R."

Angela frowned at her notepad. "Ann a bell e Butler. Annabelle Butler?"

"A gal?" Glen said.

"Are you the same Butler who brought us up here?"

The pointer carried their hands upward to YES.

"Butler's a *woman*," Howard said.

"Looks that way."

"So that skeleton up there's a babe?" Keith sounded astonished.

"Must be."

"Could've fooled me."

Howard looked at Angela. She was making odd, gasping sounds. Her left hand fell away from her upraised knee, taking the notepad with it. The pad slapped against the thigh of her other leg. She gazed at the Ouija board. Her mouth hung open.

"What's wrong?"

She shook her head. "It's . . . I don't know . . . Annabelle."

"Yeah?" Keith asked. "So?"

"It was my mother's name."

"Where's your mother?" Lana asked.

"She died. A long time ago."

"This isn't your mother," Keith said. "This is Annabelle Butler, not Logan."

"My name isn't Logan."

"What?" Glen blurted.

"It was Carnes." She spoke softly, staring at the board. "Mom was married to Charlie Carnes."

She's telling.

Howard wondered if Angela was even aware that she was revealing parts of her awful secret. She seemed dazed, almost as if in a trance.

"Well, Carnes isn't Butler," Lana said.

The pointer began jerking across the face of the board, stopping only for an instant at each letter. Angela watched it move, but wrote nothing. The pad remained on the upturned side of her thigh. The fingers holding it there trembled.

"M-A-I-D-E-N-A-M-E," Glen read aloud. "Maiden name?"

"Holy shit," Keith said.

"Is that right?" Lana asked, gaping at Angela.

"I . . . I don't know. I don't know *what* her maiden name was."

"How could you not know something like that?" Glen said.

"She was just a little kid when her mother died," Howard explained.

"Are you Angela's mother?" Lana asked the Ouija board.

The pointer glided up to the YES.

Angela dropped her pen. She curled her hand across her mouth.

"Oh, this is too fucking weird."

Lana cast a sharp look at Keith.

Howard took his hand off the pointer. He laid it on Angela's back and rubbed her gently through the damp fabric of her T-shirt.

"What's her body doing in the mine?" Glen asked.

The pointer began to carry the remaining three hands over the alphabet.

"M-U-R-D-E-R-E-D."

Angela made a quick, startled whimper.

"Did Hubert do it?" Lana asked.

"C-H-A-R-L-I-E."

"Her husband," Keith whispered.

"And Charlie left your body in the mine?"

"T-A-K-E-M-E."

"Take you where?"

"A-W-A-Y."

"Maybe she wants a decent burial," Howard said. He eased Angela close against his side as she began to sob.

"Is that what you want? To be taken out of the mountains and buried?"

The heart started moving again. "H," Glen read. "E. M."

Angela, weeping softly, snatched the pad off her leg and found the pen and began to write.

"A-D-U-K-I-L-L-N-G-E-T-M-E-A-W-A-Y."

When the message seemed to be over, she sniffed and wiped her eyes. She held the pad up so that she and Howard could both study the string of letters.

" 'He mad' . . . ?" she said, her voice trembling.

"Or 'Hubert Elliot mad.' "

"Yeah."

"Maybe not 'mad.' What about 'made a duke"?"

280

"That doesn't make sense," Lana said.

" 'Hubert Elliot mad.' " Angela nodded as if sure of herself. " 'You kill and get me away.' "

Glen moaned. "She wants us to *kill* him?"

"Why do you want us to kill him?" Lana asked.

"4-M-Y-S-A-K-E."

" 'For my sake?' But he isn't the one who murdered you."

"D-E-F-I-L-E-S."

"Shit," Keith said. "What does she mean by that?"

"Use your imagination," Lana told him. "God Almighty. Look, Annabelle, we aren't going to murder anyone. Is that the reason you brought us up here? So we could kill this Hubert guy and take your bones back to civilization?' 'A-N-G-E-L-A."

Her back went rigid under Howard's hand.

"What about Angela?"

"M-I-S-S."

She shuddered with a sob.

"L-O-V-E."

Lana raised her solemn eyes to Angela. "Do you want to talk with her?"

"I . . . Mom? I . . . I love you. Oh, God, this is so . . . I'll take you with me."

"Fun and games," Keith muttered.

"Shut up," Lana said.

"Look, ask her about the fucking loot. Or was that just a lie?"

"Annabelle, you told us there would be loot if we came to the mine. Was that just a trick to get us here?"

"U-G-E-T."

"Where is it?"

"G-O-2-B-U-S."

" 'Go to bus'?"

"What is this shit?" Keith demanded. "What bus? There's no damn bus up here."

"We'll find the loot in a bus?" Lana asked.

"2-M-O-R-R-O-W."

"Where?"

Richard Laymon

"O-F-F-P-U-R-D-Y-R-D."

" 'Off pretty RD?" Keith said. "Who's RD?" He looked around the group.

"Could be the abbreviation for 'road,' " Glen said.

"So we've got to find a pretty road? Terrific."

"A-L-F-I-N-D-S."

"I'll find it," Angela said.

"Where is it?" Lana asked, staring at the board. "Where do we look?"

The pointer didn't move.

"Annabelle?"

It glided slowly downward, past the numbers below the alphabet, and swept across GOOD BYE. Then it stopped.

"Shit!"

"Annabelle? Come on, you've got to tell us more."

The pointer remained motionless.

"That's all we're gonna get," Glen said, and pulled his hand back.

"Looks that way." Lana leaned back, bracing herself up on stiff arms, and looked at Angela. "Do you know what this is all about?"

"No. Not . . . it's so confusing."

"You don't have to talk about it," Howard told her.

She sniffed and wiped her eyes. "Charlie . . . he said Mom was killed in a car accident. That was right after we got home."

"They'd been on a camping trip," Howard explained.

"Where?" Glen asked. "Here?"

"I don't know," Angela said. "I guess it's possible this is where we were. It was in the mountains *some*where. But I'd always thought Mom got home with us."

"You don't *know*?" Keith asked.

Angela shook her head.

"She was only four years old," Howard said.

"Hell," Keith said, "I remember stuff when I was nothing but a baby."

"It's normal to forget nearly everything that happened before you were about five," Lana pointed out. "And there's

282

also a tendency to block out traumatic events."

"But to forget what happened to your own mother . . ."

Angela rubbed her face. She sighed. "I always *thought* she made it back home with us. Charlie said she did. He said she went out for cigarettes and got killed in a car accident."

"Was there a funeral or anything?" Lana asked.

"I don't remember one."

"Did you ever see her actual grave?" Glen asked.

"Huh-uh. We . . . we'd been living in a trailer park."

"Where was that?"

"I don't know. Maybe somewhere near Sacramento? I'm not sure. But right after Mom died, we left and started living in a van. Traveling around. And one time when I was older? I started really missing Mom, you know? So I threw these fits. You know, crying and everything. I wanted them to take me to her and I wouldn't quit bugging them about it."

"Who's *them*?"

"Charlie and his sons. The twins. So anyway, I guess they got tired of putting up with all the tantrums I was throwing, and they said they'd take me to the cemetery so I could visit her grave. I thought they meant it. I was really happy for a while. That's where I thought we were going and pretty soon I'd get to be with her. So one night they woke me up? And we were in a cemetery, all right. Out in the country somewhere. It was a horrible place. It looked like nobody'd been there for years. It was all overgrown. Some of the tombstones were knocked over. And I got led around in the dark while they pretended they couldn't remember where Mom's grave was. But it wasn't there at all. The whole thing was just a trick. They wanted to teach me a lesson."

"What kind of bastards . . . ?" Keith muttered.

"I started getting really scared, you know? The place was *spooky*. And they were acting weird. You know, laughing and stuff. Tripping me all the time. They made me get down on top of a grave, and . . ." She shook her head roughly. She was silent for a few moments, then went on. "They ended up leaving me tied to a tree right in the middle of the graveyard. Just left me there and drove away. And they didn't come back all night. They came back in the morning and I remember Charlie . . . While he untied me, he was laughing. And he said, 'Did you have a nice visit with your Mama?'

"Anyway, after that I pretty much kept my mouth shut about Mom."

Everyone sat there, staring at Angela. Finally Glen murmured, "Jesus."

Lana had a look of revulsion on her face. She said, "You grew up with guys who would do something like that to you?"

"Yeah. They were sweethearts."

"God, that's horrible."

"So I guess now I know what happened to Mom. It was all a lie about the car accident and . . ." Lifting her head, she gazed up the mountainside in the direction of the mine. "Will somebody come with me?"

"Sure," Howard said.

"We all will," Lana said.

Keith and Glen nodded.

Angela got up and went to her pack. The others followed. They stood around her as she removed her sleeping bag and opened the top of the pack. She began to take out her clothes and equipment and her share of the group's food.

Nobody asked questions. Nobody made remarks.

In silence, they picked up her things and found room for them in their own packs.

"That's all," she finally said.

Howard glanced down into the pack. A small stuffed kitten remained at the bottom. "Aren't you gonna . . . ?"

"That's Puffy. She doesn't take up much room. Mom gave her to me and . . . I don't know . . . I think I want to leave her in."

Angela closed the flap. She picked up the nearly empty pack, swung it onto her back and slipped her arms through the straps.

"Let's just leave everything here except the flashlights," Lana said.

"And this." Keith snatched up the hatchet. "In case Hubert shows up."

"Let's get it done," Glen said.

"Hey, all of you."

They faced Angela. She was frowning. Her lower lip was pressed between her teeth. She glanced at Howard, then turned her eyes to Glen, to Keith, and finally to Lana. In a shaky voice, she said, "You're all really terrific."

"That's us," Keith said.

"Well, you are. And Mom promised we'd find the loot tomorrow, and we will."

Chapter Twenty-eight

"Could you let go of my hair?" Corie asked. "You're giving me a headache."

"You'll run away," the man said.

"Here? Are you kidding?" This section of the trail was so narrow that an attempt to run would probably send her off its edge. "Besides, where would I go?

"You've got me, all right? I won't try anything. I promise."

"You might jump."

"I'm not going to jump," she said.

He didn't release her hair, so Corie dropped the matter.

She had decided—it seemed like hours ago—to cooperate with this man. He was just too quick and powerful. And he was obviously crazy. If he lost his temper, he could kill her in an instant with his bare hands. Or with the machete he'd picked up after taking her out of the lake.

Corie was fairly sure that he wanted to keep her alive. Hell, he'd *said* he didn't want to kill her. And once she'd stopped struggling, he had quit hurting her. He'd hardly touched her at all, except for the hand clenching her hair.

That was an annoyance, a mild lingering torment, nothing that would damage her.

The only real damage had been done to her feet by walking.

"Where are you taking me?" she'd asked when he first began to steer her away from the campsite.

"Up the mountain."

"Let me get dressed, OK?"

"You're too pretty for clothes."

"But the sun'll cook me."

"The sun is good for you. It'll turn you to gold like me."

"At least let me put my boots on. My feet'll get torn up."

"It'll make them strong like mine."

"Please!"

"Don't beg. Be strong."

He wants me to be like him. All right. Maybe that means he isn't going to hurt me unless I do something wrong. He's after a companion. A mate. And I'm it. I can live through this. If I'm smart.

She had tried to look back for a final glimpse of Chad, but the man had twisted her hair, forcing her head forward. As they made their way along the shore, she'd prayed that Chad would rush to her rescue. Then she hoped he wouldn't.

Just be alive. Be alive but stay where you are. Don't come after us. He'd kill you for sure.

I'll be OK.

I'll be OK till he decides to fuck me.

He could've done it right away, but he hadn't.

What's he waiting for?

During their trek along the lakeshore and as they'd waded across the icy stream and for a while after they'd started up the mountain trail, Corie had expected to be thrown down at any moment and raped.

When that didn't happen, she'd begun to wonder why not.

He wants to get where we're going, first?

That was the only explanation that made any sense.

287

She'd tried to tell herself that he was gay. After all, he was obviously a body-builder. But she knew that the stereotype was false. Plenty of those men were straight. Besides, he'd left Chad behind. He'd taken her. And he hadn't allowed her to get dressed. He wasn't gay.

Maybe his reasons for wanting her had nothing to do with sex. He might just be lonely.

In your dreams, she thought. You don't get off that easily.

He's violent. He's crazy. If he didn't grab me for sex, there's no telling *what* he's got in mind.

He wants me to stay pretty, that's the thing to remember. He wants me to get tanned the way he is. And he wants my feet to get tough like his. That doesn't sound like someone who wants to eat me or torture me or do God-knows-what. Just stay calm and play along with him.

We might even run into the kids.

This was the Calamity Peak trail. It must be the way they'd gone. Though they undoubtedly had a huge head-start, the weight of their backpacks would slow them down. They couldn't make very good time, not with someone like Doris along. And Angela probably wasn't strong enough to keep up a quick pace.

Sooner or later, Corie thought, we might overtake them.

Six of them. They'd sure have this guy outnumbered. If we all attack him at once . . .

Someone was sure to get hurt, though. Maybe even killed. Unless they took him by surprise.

On the other hand, if he suddenly found himself facing so many opponents, maybe he wouldn't even try to fight them. He might just run off and leave her. It could happen that way.

But what if he chose to fight? With that machete . . .

He must already know about the kids, Corie realized. He'd been at their campsite, seen their tents. Maybe he'd even been waiting for them to return, hoping to grab one of the girls, when she and Chad had shown up.

She suddenly remembered the note on the tent flap. A warning of some kind. The kids had left it. The message had started, "Dear Creep." It must've meant *him*.

What did he *do* to them?

Shocked and alarmed, Corie had come very close to blurting out questions, demanding to know if he'd hurt any of her students. Before she could speak, however, it dawned on her that he hadn't hurt them. Not seriously, at least.

There'd been a frivolous, mocking tone to the note they'd left behind. He'd obviously given them some kind of trouble, but he hadn't seriously injured or killed any of them.

Besides, they were hardly likely to have continued on their stupid, damn search for Butler's loot if the creep had done real damage to any of them. Or even if they considered him a serious threat.

What if he got them after they left the note?

No. That didn't seem likely. If he'd slaughtered them, where were their bodies? Where was their gear? Except for the tents, Corie had seen no trace of the kids. Besides, the creep wouldn't have killed them all. He would've kept one of the girls alive. Lana, probably. He would've grabbed Lana for his companion or mate or whatever . . . and she'd be the one he's taking with him.

It's better this way, Corie told herself. Better that he has me.

Not better for Chad.

She felt a quick surge of agony —guilt and sorrow that tightened her throat and brought tears to her eyes. She'd looked down the mountainside. She could see the lake far below, but the woods surrounding the campsite blocked any view of the rock slab where she'd last seen Chad.

It's all my fault. I got him into this. If he's dead . . .

No, he's not dead. He can't be.

He might be.

No! He'll wake up with a headache and wonder what happened to me. Will he think I drowned? What'll he do?

He'll look for me. He won't stop looking until he finds me.

And then what? He gets his head chopped?

She hurt too much, thinking about what might happen.

Think about the kids, she told herself. They're all right. They must be. And Chad's all right, too. Everything'll turn out fine.

I've just got to play along with this bastard and stay alive no matter what and eventually I'll either get away or be rescued.

But as the afternoon wore on, with the heat bearing down on her, the rough trail scraping her feet raw, her plan to cooperate seemed like less and less of a good idea.

With each painful step, she was moving closer to the place where the creep was taking her. With each step, her dread grew like a ball of ice forming in her stomach. Whatever he intended to do with her, it was going to happen when they reached their destination.

She didn't want to get there.

Even if it meant risking a fall.

And so she had asked him to let go of her hair, promised that she wouldn't try to escape, and been told that she might jump.

I wouldn't jump, she thought. He's crazy if he thinks I'm going to jump.

Crazy.

She heard herself let out a soft huff of laughter.

"What's funny?" he asked.

"You are. You said I might jump if you let go of my hair."

"That's funny?"

"I'm not the type. But look, could I sit down or something? I can't jump if I'm sitting down. My feet are killing me. I'm worn out. If we don't rest, I might just pass out and *fall*. You wouldn't like that, would you?"

"I won't let you fall. Keep moving. We're almost there."

Just what Corie didn't want to hear.

She let her knees buckle. She started to sink forward, arms out to catch herself. The man jerked her hair. She cried out. But she stayed limp. He held her up for a moment, then lowered her slowly until her knees met the trail. "Let go, damn it!"

He released her hair.

She hunched over. On elbows and knees, she clasped the top of her head and rubbed her aching scalp.

She heard nothing from behind her. She knew the kind of view she was giving him. Maybe he was too interested in that to give her trouble about the delay.

I'm really asking for it.

So what?

Let him try it right here if that's what he wants. Get it over with. And maybe somebody'll take a nose-dive off the mountain. And maybe it'll be him.

"Up," he said.

Corie didn't move. "Where are you taking me?" she asked.

"To my home."

"What for?"

"You're mine."

"The hell I am. I'm not yours. I'll never be yours. I'm *mine.* And part of me belongs to that man I was with at the lake, and if he's dead so are you."

For a few moments, he said nothing. Then he asked, "What's your name?"

"Me Jane."

"Get to your feet, Jane."

She scurried forward on her elbows until she was stretched out flat on the trail.

"Get up now."

"Do whatever you want. I'm not going anywhere."

"Do you want to die right here?"

"If you kill me, I'll stop being pretty." Carefully, aware that the trail was not much wider than her body, she rolled onto her back. She propped herself up on her elbows.

The man was standing just beyond her feet. His sunglasses, frames bent by the blow from the stone she'd thrown at him, rested slightly askew across his eyes. His mouth was a tight, straight line. His sweaty skin glimmered in the sunlight. The blade of his machete flashed as he raised it.

"Get up," he said.

Though her heart was thundering and she felt as if she couldn't catch her breath, she managed to say, "What if I don't?"

The machete slashed, whipping through the air above her legs. She knew it was missing her. But she flinched and gasped anyway.

Squatting, he grabbed her right ankle and jerked it up. With the flat of his machete, he smacked the bottom of her foot.

Corie bucked and cried out.

He flung her leg sideways. Past the edge of the trail. It dropped. Corie sucked air, shocked. Her whole leg was going down. The rim scraped the back of her thigh, dug into her buttock. She twisted away, kicking up, and he caught her ankle.

It was all, suddenly, too much. She had kept herself under tight control, she'd used her head, she'd tried to be brave. She'd pushed on, though the sun had seared her naked body and the rocky trail had bloodied her feet and the steep climb had stolen all her strength. She'd fought against her sorrow, her guilt, her terror. But the slap of the machete had hurt too much. The sudden drop of her leg had scared her too much. She broke. She bawled.

She lay flat on the trail, hands pressed to her face, spasms shaking her body as she sobbed and blubbered.

"Stop it," he said.

"Go to hell."

He rose from his crouch and stepped between her thighs. He slipped the leather sling of the machete over his right shoulder so that the weapon hung behind his back. Then he bent down, grabbed her wrists and yanked her up. As she stumbled forward, he threw his arms around her and jerked her hard against him. Their wet bodies slapped together. She felt herself being mashed breathless against his massive chest.

"You will walk," he said. He squeezed her so hard she thought her ribs might snap.

When the awful hug loosened, Corie found that her legs

wouldn't support her. She began to slip down his body. He grabbed her under the armpits and held her upright while she sobbed and struggled for air. Every now and then, he gave her a rough shake that wobbled her head, set her limp arms swinging and jiggled her breasts. She thought he was doing it to punish her.

But then he lifted her off her feet, raised her straight up until she was looking down at the top of his shiny, hairless head. Until her breasts were level with his face. She watched them bounce and sway as he shook her some more. He held her still for a few moments, then brought her closer. He rubbed a bristly cheek against the side of her right breast. Turning his head, he opened his mouth. He licked her nipple. Licked it like a kid with a lollipop.

Corie slammed her open hands against his ears. Roaring with pain, he hurled her away. She saw the sky, the steep slope looming above her. She wanted to reach out and grab the slope, but feared that any contact might throw her away from it and send her plummeting down the mountain. Her heels struck rock. An instant later, her rump hit. She kept her head up as her elbows and back crashed against the trail. A brief skid scorched the skin of her back and buttocks. When she stopped, she let out a shuddering whimper. She hurt all over. But she hadn't gone over the edge!

As fast as she could, she pushed herself up.

The creep was down on his knees, hunched over, clutching his ears, bellowing.

Corie scurried to her feet. She winced and wept. She wiped her eyes. She knew she ought to attack. Right now. Before the bastard could recover enough to defend himself.

Smash his head with a rock. Or grab the machete dangling by his side and chop him. Or even try to shove him off the edge.

One way or another, finish him off.

But she didn't dare. She couldn't force herself to take even a single step toward him. If she got within his reach, he just might . . .

He raised his head. *"You!"*

293

Corie squatted, snatched up a chunk of rock and threw it at him. Though she'd aimed for his face, it struck him just below the collar bone. It gouged some skin and bounced away. She grabbed another chunk as he got to his feet. He took a step toward her and she pitched it. This one slammed his mouth. It knocked his head back. His sunglasses fell off. He blinked his eyes, shook his head, licked his mashed lips, spat out a spray of blood, and lurched toward her.

Corie whirled around. She hurried up the thin strip of trail, jogging at first, sick with the idea of falling. But she heard the man gaining on her. He grunted. Sometimes, he gasped, "Yes!" And the sounds were getting closer.

She knew she would rather fall than let him catch her.

So she dashed. She pumped her arms. She shot her legs out far and quick. The trail was a jolting blur through her tears. Though she could hear him, she couldn't tell how far behind he was. She wanted to look back, but she didn't dare. With the turn of her head, she might mis-step. And if he was still closing in, she didn't want to see it.

She half expected to feel a blade slice down her back. Or maybe he would simply shove her sideways, sending her in a long dive to oblivion.

She slowed a little as the trail curved to the right.

Maybe he'll take the turn too fast, she thought. He's so much bigger, so much heavier. If he tries it full speed . . .

She pictured him sprinting into space like Wile E. Coyote, running on air, OK till he looked down and saw his predicament, then plummeting.

When she rounded the bend, her stomach dropped. Confusion numbed her mind.

A few strides in front of Corie, two hands were gripping the rim of the trail.

Impossible! How did he get ahead *of me?*

Then she thought, *Now I've got him!*

Adios, asshole!

A stride away, she braked her rush. She dropped to her

knees and scurried toward the edge, eager to tear the fingers from their hold.

And found herself staring down into the eyes of Chad.

With a snap of her head, she glanced over her shoulder. Just in time to see the bulk of her mad assailant rush around the bend.

"No!" she shrieked.

"Go!" Chad gasped. "Run! Now!"

She scuttled past him, thrust herself to her feet, but couldn't run away. Turning around, she watched Chad lunge up alongside the trail. He pulled a knife.

The creep was moving too fast to stop. He had a look of puzzlement on his face. Chad dropped across the trail, blocking his path, and he tumbled over Chad's body. His right shoulder pounded the wall. The blow knocked him sideways, but not far enough. Chest first, he slammed the trail, his head at Corie's feet. His left arm dropped over the edge.

"Get *out* of here!" Chad blurted, struggling out from under the legs.

Corie dropped to her knees. She clamped the broad, slick head between her thighs. Squeezing it as hard as she could, she leaned forward and shoved down against the man's back. "Kill him!" she gasped. "Gotta kill him!"

His left arm was no longer hanging. It was on the trail. He started pushing himself up as Chad straddled his buttocks. His head slid up between Corie's thighs. It pushed against her groin. It lifted her knees into the air as Chad raised the knife. The blade flashed downward.

With a quick twisting buck, he threw Chad.

The knife swept across his back, missing him as Chad tumbled away. Corie cried out, "No!" She glimpsed Chad flinging the knife into space, clawing and kicking at the air beside the trail. He was there for an instant, and then he was gone and Corie, thrown toward the edge herself by the sudden buck, only kept safe by the grip of her thighs on the bastard's head, slammed herself down against his back.

He was on his hands and knees. She wrapped her arms around his torso and clung to him.

He started crawling up the trail.

She rode him.

He didn't try to shake her off.

This is mad! It's insane!

Playing horsey. Chad's dead. Oh, God, Chad! Dead.

She knew she could squirm off the man's back and cast herself down the mountainside. She wanted to. Better to be dead, like Chad. Better to put an end to all this. What was the point in living, now? Chad wouldn't be coming back to her. Her future had been wiped out. Why not die, and stop the pain?

And cheat this fucking creep out of *having* me!

But Corie couldn't force herself to do it. She hugged him fiercely, terrified of falling.

And felt ashamed. She had no right to go on living. No reason to, and no right. She'd gotten Chad killed. She didn't deserve to survive.

He tried to save me, she told herself. He wouldn't want me to kill myself.

He loved me. He'd want me to live.

I've got to live, she suddenly realized.

Long enough to kill this murdering piece of shit.

She heard the blade of the machete clinking and clanging as it dragged along the trail beside him. Somehow, through everything, the sling had stayed on his right shoulder. If she let go of him with one arm, she might be able to reach the weapon. And do what with it? Attached as it was, how could she get any leverage into a swing?

Besides, he wouldn't *let* her get a hand on it. The moment he felt her starting to let go, he would know she was up to something. She wouldn't stand a chance.

Corie had kept her eyes shut ever since fastening herself onto the man. Now, she opened them. Her right cheek was pressed against his back. She raised her head.

The movement didn't seem to bother him. He continued crawling along slowly.

His black waistband was just in front of Corie's eyes. A strip in its center passed between his buttocks. She realized that his rump was not only flexing, but swaying slightly from side to side. He was making himself squirm so that his back would slide against her. His head, trapped between her trembling thighs, was rubbing her groin.

You killed my Chad, you bastard, and now you're doing this to me?

She felt used and dirty. As much as she hated him, she hated herself more for riding him and giving him pleasure.

You'll pay for this, she thought as he carried her around a bend in the trail. You'll pay for everything.

Then she saw the wall of the mountain recede. Perplexed, she looked the other way. Where the edge of the trail had been, there was now a gradual slope.

No more narrow trail.

They had reached a level area, a place where it would be safe for him to remove Corie from his back. But still he crawled along.

Enjoying himself too much to stop now.

Maybe he wasn't even aware that they'd left the hazardous strip of trail behind.

But Corie was aware. She felt like a tightrope walker who had finally stepped onto a solid platform. Released from the fear of falling, she began to caress the man.

He didn't seem to mind. He kept on crawling.

She writhed on his back. She eased the grip of her legs. Her hands roamed up his chest, down his sides and belly. When she fingered the band at his waist, he stopped moving. She traced its path up his hips. Curled her hands over the hard mounds of his rump, slid them down the backs of his thighs, stretching as she reached. She felt him begin to tremble under her body. She brought her hands up again, over his rump to his hips. She hooked her thumbs under the thin band. She drew it down halfway to his knees.

Doesn't he even suspect? she wondered. Is he too far gone to care?

Or is he just so damn confident that he doesn't think I'd try something?

A trick?

Maybe he plans to stop me at the last moment. Let me think I'm getting away with it. All the time, he's just using me, enjoying himself, waiting for the right moment to throw me off and nail me.

I don't care.

This is my move and I'm making it.

His belly flinched a bit when Corie touched it this time. He shuddered and moaned when she wrapped her left hand around the thick post of his erection. She slid her fingers lightly down the length of it, and up again.

Got him, she thought. He won't stop me now.

Her right hand cupped his scrotum.

You're history, asshole.

But even as she clamped her hand shut, she felt her wrist being grabbed and jerked down. Her fingertips hit his testicles. Didn't squeeze them. Didn't crush them. Only tapped them, maybe bumped them together, as her hand was shoved away.

Still, he jerked and choked out a gasp. Releasing her wrist, he reared up on his knees.

Corie slid down his back. She flung her hands against the ground. Her legs flew high. She curled her back, rolled away from him with a quick somersault, and landed sitting up. As she scurried to her feet, she turned to look at him.

He was still on his knees, doubled over as if he had a bellyache.

Corie ran at him. She brought up a foot and rammed it against his lower back, slamming him to the rocky ground. But as she stooped, reaching for the machete, he rolled out of the way with such quickness that she staggered backward. The long blade swept through the air above him and clanked down. An instant later, he was clutching its handle. He shrugged the strap off his shoulder. He lurched onto his side and swung the machete at Corie. The blade hissed past her shins, missing by inches.

With a grunt of despair, she spun around and ran.

Blew it, she thought. I had him and I blew it. How did he *know*?

He can't be stopped. He's gonna get me, and . . .

Not if I can outrun him.

He's hurt. I've got a chance.

She seemed to be on a broad slope, a pass of sorts that slanted gradually upward between two bluffs. Off to the left, there seemed to be a gap. She dashed toward it. She couldn't tell how wide it might be. But if she could leap to the other side, she might have an advantage. She might be able to defend that side. At least she would have *something* between her and the madman. Maybe she could nail him when he tried to cross.

As she raced closer, she heard a rushing sound. Like a strong wind. With every stride, it grew louder. It was a roar by the time she saw that the gap was too wide. She wouldn't have a chance of jumping to the other side.

She halted at its edge and glanced down. The view of the wild stream, so far below, made her stomach drop. She jerked her head around.

The bastard was coming. Hobbling a little. His black pouch in place. His left hand cupping it, holding on to his nuts while his right hand waved the machete overhead. The area around his mouth was a bloody mess.

Corie turned her back to the gorge.

She waited for him.

Don't! Are you nuts?

You'll never outrun him anyway. Sooner or later, he'll get you.

She spread her feet, bent over slightly and opened her arms wide as if preparing herself to wrestle with him. "Come on, you bastard!" she yelled.

So far, he wasn't slowing down.

Keep it coming!

He dashed closer and closer. All slabs and bulges of bouncing muscle. With each stride, he made sobbing, growling sounds that Corie could hear through the roar of the stream.

"You want me?" she yelled. "You *want* me?"

He grinned, bloody lips stretching away from his teeth. He was close enough, now, for Corie to see that some of his front teeth were broken stubs.

Three strides away.

Two.

She threw herself sideways. She hit the ground, rolled onto her back, and saw that he'd braked himself at the rim of the gorge. Momentum seemed to be shoving him forward. Bending at the waist, he flapped his arms.

And found his balance.

And turned to Corie.

He sneered down at her. "You sure sink you're tricky," he said.

Something smacked his chest. Corie heard a blast. A gunshot? His left pectoral jumped and she glimpsed a neat round hole a few inches above his nipple. Only a glimpse before the impact twisted him sideways. He flung his right foot across his left to catch himself.

He was bent over as if studying the stream at the bottom of the gorge when the second bullet came, slicing a furrow across his back. With a squeal, he stumbled forward into space. He dropped, turning, and disappeared below the rim.

Corie rolled over. As she pushed herself up on hands and knees, she saw a fat girl in a gray sweatshirt and shorts jogging toward her. A fat girl with a revolver.

"Doris!"

The girl's mouth dropped open. "Dr. *Dalton?*"

Corie stood up, staggered toward Doris, and threw her arms around her.

"My God!" Doris gasped. "What're *you* doing here?"

"You got him," Corie blurted. "You got him. Did you get him?" She pushed herself away from Doris. She snatched the revolver out of the girl's hand and hurried back to the edge of the chasm.

She spotted the bastard.

Way down there. Floating face down in a pool of surging white water, arms stretched out as if he'd been crucified.

She took careful aim and squeezed the trigger.

The blast stung her ears. The gun jumped in her hand. She couldn't tell whether she'd hit him. She fired again.

The third time she pulled the trigger, there was no explosion. Just a hard metallic clack.

The body turned slowly in the current and began to race downstream.

Chapter Twenty-nine

Corie knelt near the edge of the gorge, set the gun down beside her, curled over and buried her face in her hands.

It's finished, she told herself. He's dead and I'm alive. It's finished. He didn't get me. He never will.

She kept seeing the bullets hit him, kept seeing him step off the rim and drop, kept seeing him sprawled in the water down there and scooting away on the quick current.

She kept seeing Chad fall from the trail.

She couldn't stop shaking.

She felt as if she might rear up on her knees and howl with wild joy for her own survival, with agony for Chad and all that might have been.

I've got to go to him, she thought.

But she couldn't move.

She heard quiet footfalls approaching from the rear.

"God, your feet." Doris's voice.

"I'm all right," she murmured into her hands.

"I brought my things over. Do you want to put on some of my clothes?"

"He killed Chad."

Silence. A hand gently stroked the back of her head.

"I'm awfully sorry," Doris said. "But don't you think you ought to get dressed? The others must've heard the shots. They'll be coming back any minute. You wouldn't want them to see you like this. You know Keith and Glen."

"I've gotta find Chad."

"I'll help you. But first you'd better put something on."

Corie rubbed her face. Straightening up, she turned around on her knees. Surprised to find herself embarrassed after all that had happened, she pressed an arm across her breasts and dropped a hand between her legs. She was suddenly upset by the thought that Doris might have seen her on top of the man, stroking his penis.

"Did you see us . . . fighting back there?" she asked.

Doris shook her head. Turning away, she reached into her pack. "I didn't notice anything until I heard you yell at the guy. Then I saw you down here, and him running at you with that big knife. I didn't even realize it was you. But I sure recognized him."

"Thank God you were here," Corie said. "He had me . . . all afternoon. I couldn't get away from him. He would've killed me just now if you hadn't shot him."

"He almost got *me* yesterday." Doris dragged a big, gray sweatshirt out of the pack and handed it to her. "He grabbed Lana last night."

Corie pulled the sweatshirt down over her head. It was huge and baggy. Its thickness seemed to trap the heat of her skin. The abrasion on her back felt like liquid fire.

"I shot at him then, and he dropped Lana. We've been keeping an eye out for him ever since. Do you want shorts or sweatpants?"

"Shorts, I guess."

She pulled out a wide pair of red gym trunks. "They'll be a little big on you. I've got some safety pins here somewhere. You'll probably need one."

While Doris searched for the pin, Corie sat down and

drew the shorts up her legs. The elastic band was loose around her waist.

"Here we go."

Doris handed a safety pin to her. She pinched in a tuck at her right hip, and fastened it there.

"He never showed up again after I shot at him," Doris said, and started searching her pack again. "We figured the gun must've frightened him off. Where did he get you?"

"Down at the lake. By your campsite."

"Jesus. So he hung around. God, if only I'd hit him last night." She lifted out a pair of white crew socks and blue sneakers. As she set them down beside Corie, she said, "You two came looking for us?"

"What do you think?"

Doris looked at her with stricken eyes.

"I'm sorry," Corie muttered. "Is everyone OK?"

"Yeah."

She put on one of the socks. It clung to the sticky bottom of her foot. "Where are they?" she asked, pulling on the other.

"Over on the other side. Looking for Butler's mine."

"Butler's mine," she muttered.

"God, it's all our fault."

"It's my fault. I let you people mess with the Ouija board. I knew better." She put on the sneakers. They were a little too big. She laced and tied them. "You'd better wait here for the others. I'm going down the trail. I've gotta find Chad."

"Where . . . ?"

"I don't know," she said, her voice faltering. "Over there someplace. Where the trail is."

Corie stood up, wincing, wondering how she'd been able to walk at all on her ruined feet, much less run. The pain had seemed bothersome before. Now, it was torture in spite of the socks and shoes.

"Are you sure you shouldn't wait here? They must've heard the shots."

Corie shook her head. She began to limp away, going

down the gradual slope and angling toward the steep wall of the mountain. Each step sent pain shooting up from her feet. The clothing bothered her. The sweatshirt was too hot and it stuck to her back. The shorts kept slipping down her hips and rump. Every few steps, she had to pull them up.

Finally, she stopped to fix the shorts. She lifted the sweatshirt and tucked its bottom edge under her chin. The air cooled her wet skin. She sighed with relief. And thought how strange to be concerned about her physical comfort. Chad was dead, and she was worried about being too hot. But the air did feel good. It felt cool and wonderful. She unclipped the safety pin, made a larger tuck in the waistband of the shorts, and pinned it.

She realized that she was standing near the place where she'd made her move against the man. Stroked him. The memory of it sickened her.

How could I've *done* that?

It hadn't seemed so horrible at the time. Just a . . . necessity.

That's what saved me, she told herself. That's how I got away from him.

But he would've gotten me, anyway, if Doris hadn't shot him.

Turning around, she looked for Doris. The girl was out of sight.

She didn't see me do it.

Nobody'll ever know.

Corie let the sweatshirt drop. She rubbed both hands against the front of it and wondered when she might get a chance to wash them with soap and water.

I'll have to wash a lot more than my hands, she realized.

She started walking again. The last time here, she'd been riding the bastard's back. He hadn't carried her as far beyond the end of the trail as she'd thought. Probably no more than fifteen or twenty feet. It had seemed like a hundred yards.

She stepped onto the trail, saw how narrow it was, saw the broad deep valley past its edge and felt a sickening sweep of dizziness. She placed her left hand on the granite wall to hold herself steady.

She didn't want to venture out onto that thin ledge.

That's ridiculous, she told herself. You not only walked along it before, you *ran* on parts of it.

She took a step onto it and her knees went weak.

She sank down and began to crawl.

This is better anyway, she thought. It'll help me figure the distance. *He* was crawling all the way from the place where Chad went off.

Oh, God, Chad, how could this've happened?

The stone surface of the trail hurt her knees.

She remembered the way Chad's knees had looked, not so long ago. Down by the lake. Only minutes before everything normal and good had come to such a horrible stop. They'd been red and dented from the granite slab. They'd gotten that way while he was on top of her, joined with her so wonderfully and for the last time.

We never should've come here.

The kids didn't need to be rescued. They took care of themselves. And we ended up the victims.

Corie winced as her right knee came down on a loose stone. Stopping, she lifted her head. A few yards in front of her, the trail curved out of sight.

That's where he came at us. She could see him clearly in her mind, charging around the bend. She'd just been peering over the edge, stunned to find Chad looking up at her.

She remembered, now, that her own red bandanna had been knotted around Chad's head.

He'd come for her like a gallant knight, bearing his lady's colors.

Climbed straight up the slope, scaling the mountainside to intercept them.

Only to get himself killed.

Why didn't you stay at the lake! You should've let him have me!

The trail ahead was blurry. She lifted her right arm and

rubbed her eyes dry on the sweatshirt's sleeve. Then she crawled a little farther forward.

This is where it happened.

She eased down against the trail and worked her legs sideways until the wall blocked her feet. On her elbows, she squirmed to the edge. There, she lay down flat. Hands clutching the rim, she pulled herself forward and looked down and saw Chad and forgot her despair and her fear of falling and thrust herself up to her hands and knees and shouted his name.

"Coreen!" he called back. He raised an arm, then let it drop across his belly.

He was on his back on a slim shelf of rock no more than twenty feet below Corie's eyes. His left side was pressed against the sheer face of the mountain. His right leg was bent beneath him, its foot out of sight under his rump.

"Are you all right?" he called up to her.

Am *I* all right? Corie laughed and wept.

"Where's that guy?"

She couldn't answer. She shook her head.

"Hey, stop blubbering and talk to me."

Finally, she was able to say, "He's . . . he's dead. Doris shot him."

Chad was silent for a moment, then said, "Did he hurt you? Are you OK?"

"I'm . . . fine. Jesus! You're *alive!*"

"Portions of me aren't feeling too swift. Took a little fall."

"God, Chad, quit joking around."

"A lot of good I did you in the hero department."

"Where are you hurt?"

"All over. But mostly my leg. It's busted pretty good. I think I'm stuck here."

"We'll get you, don't worry."

"Rotsa ruck."

"Somehow," she muttered. She realized it wouldn't be easy. The mountainside, right here, was nearly vertical and had no switchbacks.

Chad must've plummeted straight down. If he hadn't

landed on that thin jutting lip, he would've dropped another hundred feet or more.

She supposed it would be possible to reach him either by climbing down or by coming up to him from below. The face of the slope was rough enough to provide handholds and footholds. It even had some other ledges and outcroppings not far from his perch. Hell, *he'd* climbed it.

But getting to him was one thing. With his broken leg, he would have to be carried. And that looked impossible.

"Just don't move," she called.

"I appreciate the advice."

"God, it's a miracle you landed where you did."

"I planned it this way."

"I'll go and get the kids. Maybe they've got a rope or something."

"I'll be here."

Corie crawled backward, got to her feet and hurried over the trail. She thought how ironic it would be if she fell now after finding Chad alive, but the thought didn't slow her down.

Alive. A miracle.

Chad hadn't been meant to die.

Nothing can stop us now. We'll get him off that ledge and carry him down to the lake. Maybe spend the night there. Hike out in the morning . . .

She strode off the end of the trail and stopped as she saw all six kids coming down the gentle slope, Doris in the lead. She waved both arms. She shouted, "Over here!"

They spotted her and quickened their pace. They hardly looked like the students who'd been at her party Friday night. They seemed weary and solemn as they trudged along under the weight of their packs. Their clothes were grubby, their skin glowing with sunburn. Lana had always been so tidy and neatly groomed, but now her hair was tangled and her blouse was untucked and half unbuttoned. Keith was bare to the waist, his shirt draping the front of his pants. Glen, big Glen, appeared to have shrunken. Probably, Corie thought, because she'd seen so much of that crazy bastard who was so much larger than Glen. Howard wore a ragged, floppy hat. Its brim hid most of his face. Angela, in a T-shirt and fancy gleaming shorts, looked grim but bore little resemblance to the sheepish and pallid girl Corie remembered. Her face was ruddy, her arms and legs burnished by the sun.

They came toward her in silence.

Doris, she realized, must've told them that Chad had been killed.

"Chad's alive," she said. "He's got a broken leg, but he's OK."

"That's great," Lana said.

The others nodded and muttered agreement. They seemed a little relieved, but not overjoyed.

Why should they be? Corie asked herself. They hardly know him. They're just glad he's alive for my sake.

"How are *you*?" Howard asked.

"I've been better."

"Did that dirty creep hurt you?"

"He made me walk barefoot. That's about the worst of it."

"We should've hunted him down yesterday and killed him," Keith said. "None of this would've happened."

"It wouldn't have happened," Corie said, "if you kids had stayed home."

"We didn't know you'd come after us," Lana told her.

"You're my responsibility. It was my Ouija board. Anyway, the hell with all that. I'm just glad everyone's OK. But Chad's stuck on a ledge. Do you have rope?"

Nodding, Lana swung her pack to the ground. As she opened it, she asked, "How far down is he?"

"Maybe fifteen, twenty feet."

Lana removed a coil of clothesline.

It was dirty gray, and not much more than a quarter-inch thick.

"I don't think that's gonna do it," Corie said. "What about the rest of you?"

The others shook their heads.

"Let's go and take a look," Lana suggested. She swung up her pack and pushed her arms through its straps.

Corie led the way. "Be very careful," she warned. "This part of the trail's treacherous."

"We came up it earlier," Keith said.

As she started along it, she asked, "Did you have any luck finding Butler's loot?"

Lana, just behind her, said, "We found the mine. It was that asshole's camp."

"Hubert Orson Elliot," Keith called.

"That was his name? The guy . . . ?"

"Mr. Universe," Lana said.

He must've been taking me there, Corie realized. To his "home." A mine.

"We'll have to give Doris a prize for marksmanship," Keith called.

"You didn't find any treasure, though?"

"Nope," Lana said. "Not unless you count his collection of ladies' undergarments."

"You're kidding."

"Nope. His backpack was full of the things. We figure he must've spent a lot of time sneaking into people's camps."

"Maybe he took them off babes he grabbed," Keith said.

"Damn lunatic," Corie muttered. Then she saw the bend ahead. She took a few more steps, stopped, sank to her hands and knees, and looked over the edge of the trail. Chad smiled up at her. "Back with the troops," she told him.

"Everyone accounted for?" he asked.

"They're all here. You're the only casualty."

"Lucky me."

Lana, kneeling beside her, stuck out an arm and waved.

Keith stepped right to the rim and peered down. "Holy shit," he said.

Corie saw Glen on the other side of Keith. Not so brave, he had taken off his pack and crawled to the edge. Doris stayed behind him.

Howard and Angela, also without their packs, stepped

around Corie. They got down on their hands and knees and inched forward to look at Chad.

Howard, turning his head, grimaced at Corie. "How'll we get him up here?"

"I don't know."

"Let's just haul him up," Keith said.

"I wonder if the rope's strong enough," Corie said.

"Might as well give it a shot," Lana told her. She removed the clothesline from her shoulder. Holding onto one end, she tossed the rest over the edge. The coil dropped, un-looping. Even as it fell, Corie realized it was plenty long enough to do the job. Her stomach gave a nervous flip when Chad reached up to grab it. He caught the line just above its end. Slack tumbled down on him, draping his face.

"So far so good," Lana said.

"I don't like this," Glen said.

You're not the only one, Corie thought.

Lana called, "Can you tie it around yourself?"

"It's not much of a rope," he said.

"It's all we've got."

"This is too risky," Corie muttered.

Chad arched his back, turning slightly away from the mountainside as he tried to shove the rope underneath his body.

Corie squirmed and gritted her teeth. She yelled, "For godsake, be careful!"

He twisted the other way. He shoved his right hand under his back. A moment later, his hand reappeared gripping the end of the rope. He tugged at the line, drawing more of it through the tight space between his back and the slab. Then he brought its end up. He knotted it above his chest to the vertical side of the rope. When he was done, he squirmed and worked the loop upward to his armpits.

"That oughta do it," he said.

Lana slowly pulled in the slack. On her knees, she backed away from the edge. "OK, guys."

Glen took the rope from her. He stepped backward until he was leaning against the slope at the far side of the trail.

311

He had a look on his face as if he were smelling something awful. "If this thing breaks . . ." he muttered.

Howard moved in beside Glen. He grabbed the rope just in front of Glen's hands. Keith joined them on the other side and took hold.

"Just go easy," Corie told them. Scooting sideways, she wrapped her hands around the rope just above the rim of the trail. She gazed down the taut line. "Ready?" she called to Chad.

He clutched the loop. "Have at it."

"Go ahead," Corie told the boys.

They started pulling. The rope went hard and vibrated in her hands. She saw Chad's head and shoulders begin to rise. The line appeared to be stretching, getting thinner.

It's gonna snap!

"Stop!" she shouted. "Lower him."

"What's wrong?" Keith asked.

"It won't hold him."

"Are you sure?" Lana asked. Crouching at the edge, she stared down. "It'll probably hold."

"It's not worth the risk," Corie said. "It wasn't made for this kind of thing. What if we get him halfway up and it breaks?"

Lana, frowning, looked over her shoulder and said, "You'd better let him down."

As the rope inched through Corie's hands, she watched Chad settle down on the ledge.

"What gives?" he called to her.

"I'm just afraid the rope won't hold you."

"You and me both."

"Don't worry, we'll think of something." She backed away and got to her feet. Most of the kids' packs had a variety of belts, cords and straps used to hold their sleeping bags in place. A combination of those, plus trouser belts . . .

No. Something like that would be too flimsy. If they were all attached, there would be a dozen knots or buckles holding them together, any of which might give way.

She noticed one pack that had two sleeping bags strapped

to its top, and the pack beside it had no sleeping bag at all. The cover flap of that one was stretched over a high bulge in a way that made her wonder for a moment if the kids had brought grapefruit along. If only they'd skipped the fruit, she thought, and brought a decent rope.

"What've you got in your backpacks?" she asked.

The kids exchanged odd, troubled looks. It crossed Corie's mind that they had found something, maybe in the mine, that they didn't want her to know about. Butler's loot?

She didn't care. All that mattered was getting Chad to safety.

"Just food and clothes and things," Lana said.

"None of you has *anything* we might use to pull him up?"

"Tie some clothes together?" Howard suggested.

Corie shook her head. "What about back at the mine? Did you see anything there?"

"Some clothes, a pack, a sleeping bag," Lana said. "I didn't see any rope."

"No," Keith said. "And we searched the whole mine."

"Anything in your car?" she asked Lana.

"Jumper cables. A blanket. No ropes or chains."

"Same here," she muttered.

"There's plenty of stuff here we could probably attach together," Howard said.

"Whatever we attach might come apart." Sighing, Corie stepped across the trail. She leaned back against the slope and folded her arms. "He's OK where he is, that's the thing. If we try to pull him up . . . I just don't want to risk it unless we're a hundred percent sure it'll work. It's a miracle he landed on that ledge in the first place. That isn't likely to happen twice."

"So what do you want to do?" Lana asked.

"I don't know. If nobody has any better idea, I guess we should leave him where he is until we can get some real help. A mountain rescue team."

"I was thinking the same thing," Glen said.

"What do you have in mind, sending up smoke signals?" Keith asked.

"There's a town called Purdy only about ten miles north of the turn off," Corie explained. "You make a right at the end of the dirt road, and . . ."

"Purdy?" Keith asked.

"Yeah. It shouldn't take you more than half an hour to get there after you hit the turn-off. It's probably not much of a town, but it's bound to have a police force and they'd know what to do."

"It's a two-day hike just getting back to the car," Doris said.

Lana shook her head. "It won't take that long. For one thing, we only spent a few hours hiking each day. And going back it'll all be downhill. If we really haul ass, I bet we can reach the car in five or six hours. A couple more hours to drive out to the main road." She looked at her wristwatch. "It's almost five, now. Figure eight or nine hours, and we'll be in Purdy. That'd make it . . . one or two in the morning."

"So you should be able to get a rescue team out here sometime tomorrow," Corie said. "That's not bad."

"Do you think Chad'll be able to make it through the night?" Lana asked. "It'll get awfully cold."

"I'll need some warmer clothes."

"You're coming with us, aren't you?" Howard asked.

"I'm staying."

"Here? All by yourself? I'll stay with you." He looked at Angela, and she nodded. "We'll both stay. We can help."

"Forget it, Howitzer."

"Do you think you'll need them?" Lana asked.

It would be nice to have the company, Corie thought. She didn't relish the idea of spending the night alone on the mountainside. "Is there any reason they shouldn't stay with me?"

The kids all looked at each other.

"What's going on?"

"Howard can stay with you," Lana said. "But I think Angela would rather come with us. Wouldn't you?"

"I want to be with Howard," she said.

"You want to be on Purdy Road tomorrow," Keith told her. "Don't you." It wasn't a question.

"Well . . ."

"There's no reason to bully her," Corie said. "What's the problem? What's this about Purdy Road?"

"It's where we're supposed to find the treasure," Howard explained.

"Good going, Howitzer. Shit!"

"*Angela's* supposed to find it. The Ouija board said she'll take us to it."

"The Ouija board!" Corie blurted.

"We've come this far," Lana said, her voice calm. "If Angela isn't with us tomorrow on Purdy Road, we might miss our chance. Maybe we won't find it anyway. But maybe we will. If she stays here, it could ruin it for all of us. We went through a lot, trying to find Butler's loot."

"Yeah," Corie muttered. "And look what Chad and I went through because of it."

"We didn't know anybody'd get hurt."

"When you mess around with a Ouija board, somebody *always* gets hurt."

"Ask Angela if she's sorry we messed with it."

"We found my mother's body," Angela said. "In the mine. That guy . . . he'd been *living* with it." She stepped over to one of the packs. The one without the sleeping bag. The one with the bulging top. She unfastened the flap and pulled it back.

Corie felt her breath rush out as she found herself looking at a skull. The entire head, perched high on the stalk of its spine, protruded from the pack as if it were peering out to survey the scenery. Hairless, fleshless, eyeless, its jaw hanging.

Doris, gasping, flung a hand across her mouth.

"Jesus," Corie murmured.

"It's my mother," Angela explained. "She's Butler. It was her maiden name."

"*She's* the spirit of the Ouija board," Lana said. "She got

315

us up here to find her body. And to reunite her with Angela."

"And to nail Hubert Orson Elliot," Keith added.

"And she's the one who says we'll find the treasure tomorrow. I don't think it's some kind of malicious Ouija board trick. I think she's sincere."

"Your mother?" Corie asked, gazing at Angela.

The girl looked as if she might start to weep. Lips pressed tightly together, she nodded.

"We're taking her down so she can have a proper burial," Lana said.

"My God," Corie murmured. She stepped closer to the pack and peered down into it. From what she could see of the skeleton, it appeared to be sitting upright, intact except for its legs. The leg bones were stuffed in alongside the ribcage, the upside-down feet resting across its shoulders.

She lifted the flap forward to cover it.

Turning to Angela, she said, "You'd better go along with the others."

"Not if Howard's gonna stay."

She put her arms around the girl. Angela hugged her, face pressing the side of her neck. To the others, Corie said, "I'll be fine here by myself. Just don't go looking for that treasure until you've been to the authorities about all this. I want a rescue team up here tomorrow."

"We'll take care of that first thing," Lana said.

"Can you leave us a couple of sleeping bags? We'll need some food and water, too. And the rope, of course. We'll be all right."

Chapter Thirty

They descended the mountainside into shadows. When they reached their campsite by the lake, Lana suggested they take a rest and eat.

Howard left the others and walked over to the shore. He looked for Dr. Dalton. Trees were in the way. From here, he could only see the very summit of Calamity Peak. It was tipped with gold by the last of the evening sunlight, and the few scattered wisps of cloud above it were ruddy.

He supposed he had done the right thing, coming down with the rest of them. But he hated the thought of Dr. Dalton up there alone on the narrow trail.

She's not alone, he told himself. She's with Chad.

And I'm with Angela. That's the way it ought to be.

But he knew that he still loved her, even though so much had changed, and he felt as if he'd left part of himself high up there on the mountainside. She was undoubtedly out of the sunlight, now. Chill winds were rushing through the valley, and they were probably stronger, colder, where she was.

He and Doris had left their packs with her. He'd taken nothing, not even a sweatshirt, leaving everything for Dr. Dalton. He wondered if she had put his coat on yet. It made him feel better to imagine her wearing it. Maybe she would use his sweatpants, too. They would fit her better than whatever she might find in Doris's pack.

Angela came up behind him and wrapped her arms around his waist. "Are you wishing you'd stayed with her?"

"Not without you."

She squeezed him. He felt her breasts push against his back. "I sure hope they'll be all right up there," she said. "This whole thing's my fault."

"Nothing's your fault."

"It all is. We wouldn't have come here at all except for Mom. It's like she was using everyone else, you know? Just to get me here."

Howard turned around. Angela wore the windbreaker that he'd bought for her. Its front was open. He reached underneath it and pulled her up against him. The back of her T-shirt felt a little damp.

Off in the clearing, Lana was bent over her open pack, searching for something. Keith, nearby, was watching her. Glen was sprawled on his back, Doris sitting beside him and ripping open a package of cookies.

Nobody was watching, so he kissed Angela on the mouth. She moaned softly and rubbed herself against him. After a few moments, he eased his mouth away. "Do you know what?" he asked.

"What?"

"I've been thinking a lot about everything. All the way coming down the mountain. This whole business is very strange."

"You're telling me."

"I mean particularly about Butler. Do you remember all that 'you give' business at the party? Butler had you take off your blouse. Right in front of everyone. That's pretty weird when you figure she's your mother."

"I'll say. It doesn't make sense."

"I thought at first that she might've done it to throw off suspicion. To make it look like you're a victim, so nobody would suspect she was on your side. But then something else occurred to me. Do you know why I think she did it?"

"Why?"

"To get me involved. So I would . . . finally notice you."

Angela laughed softly, and he felt her shake against him. "So you could see me in my bra?"

"Yeah. Hell, it worked. Up till then, I hadn't really thought of you as . . ." He felt himself starting to blush. ". . . someone I might want to . . . have as a girlfriend."

"You think she was playing match-maker?"

"Yeah. I really do. I think she knew how lonely you were. Maybe she even realized I'm the guy who . . ." He shrugged. "Maybe she knew we'd be good together, so she helped things along. And that isn't the only thing. It's all because of coming up here to look for the loot that she got you away from Skerrit."

Howard felt her body stiffen.

"Did you have to mention him?" she muttered.

"You're not going back to him. I won't let you. From now on, you're going to be with me. No matter what. So don't worry about him, OK? This is all part of your mother's plan. She wanted us to fall in love, and I'll bet she wants you to live with me and never see Skerrit again."

"Should we ask the Ouija board about all this?"

"What we'd better do, maybe, is go over and get something to eat."

"OK." She gave him a quick squeeze, then took his hand. Together, they walked up the slope and joined the others.

"You two playing smoochie again?" Keith asked, and broke off a hunk of chocolate bar with his teeth.

"Every chance we get," Angela said.

Lana, hopping from foot to foot as she stepped into her blue jeans, said, "Hang on, we'll dig out some stuff for you." Her shorts were on the ground. The hanging front of her shirt prevented Howard from seeing what she was wearing. If anything. He forced himself to look away.

"Have some cookies," Doris said.

"Good stuff," Glen said, crumbs flying from his mouth.

They went over to Doris and took a couple of the huge sugar cookies from the offered pack.

"What we oughta do," Keith said, "is break into *their* stockpile." He poked a thumb over his shoulder as if hitching a ride. Some distance behind him, two packs were propped against the log that Howard and Angela had used as a bench last night when they sat by the campfire.

"We've got plenty," Lana said. Howard risked a glance at her, and was glad to see that her pants were on. She was zipping the fly.

"So what? It'd be fun to see what they've got."

"It's none of our business."

"Shit, they've got half *our* stuff."

"Shut up and eat," Lana told him. She crouched over her pack and took out a plastic bag full of Tropical Chocolate bars. After taking one for herself, she tossed the bag to Howard. Then she resumed her search of the pack. "Got some freeze-dried apricots and shit in here. Any takers?"

"No shit for me," Glen said.

"You're already full of it," Keith told him.

"I'll have some of them 'cots."

Lana flipped the bag to him, then pulled out a pack of trail mix. "Ah, the good stuff." She turned to the others and frowned. "You know, we *could* have a real meal. It's not as if we've gotta rush off. As it is, we won't be getting into Purdy till after midnight, and they aren't about to send out a rescue party before dawn."

"We'd have to build a fire," Glen said.

"Screw that," Keith said.

"And we'd have to do *dishes*," Doris added.

That comment won her a smile from Glen. She returned a smirk, but reached into his bag of apricots and took a handful.

Lana, still on her feet, gazed toward the lake as she tore open the trail mix. "It's a shame we got here too late for a swim. An hour ago, I was really counting on it."

"Go on in," Keith told her.

"Right, and freeze my buns off. I've been *in* that lake after dark."

"It's not dark yet."

"Close enough. No way."

"Man," Glen said, "you wouldn't get me into that lake for anything. I wouldn't jump in there if I was on fire."

"Isn't that a trifle extreme?" Doris asked.

"How would you like to be swimming around and bump into your old friend Hubie?"

Doris stopped chewing. She looked sick.

"I hadn't thought of that," Lana muttered, wrinkling her nose.

"I thought of it the minute Doris told us he'd taken a nose-dive into the stream. It feeds this lake. He might be floating around out there right now." Glen glanced from Angela to Howard. "You guys didn't happen to see him, did you?"

"They were too busy playing kissy-face," Keith said.

"There's a good chance he didn't make it down this far," Lana pointed out. "He could've gotten hung up on rocks, or something, upstream."

"Could be," Glen said, and poked another wrinkled disk of apricot into his mouth. "On the other hand, he might be bobbing around out there."

"He *might* be swimming around out there," Keith said. "Who's to say he's dead?"

"I shot him twice," Doris said, looking as if she'd lost her taste for food. "And he fell all the way down there. And Dr. Dalton shot at him a couple of times."

"Did she hit him?"

"I don't know."

"So how do we know for sure he's dead?"

"I'm sure," Doris muttered.

Heads began to turn toward the lake.

But Howard stared at the ground in front of him. Until now, there'd been no doubt in his mind that Hubert was dead. Doris had *told* them he was dead.

321

If the bullets didn't kill him, the fall probably did. If he was still alive when he hit the stream, he probably drowned or got smashed to death against rocks when he went down the rapids.

He's *got* to be dead, Howard told himself.

But what if he's not?

"Come on, guys," Lana said. "Nobody could've survived all that." She didn't look as if she believed her own words.

"Ever hear of Rasputin, the mad monk?" Keith asked. "They poisoned that son of a bitch, shot him full of holes, stabbed him a couple of million times, and he still didn't go toes up."

"Took a licking but kept on ticking," Glen said.

A moan escaped from Howard, and the others looked at him.

"What's the trouble, Howitzer?"

"Maybe a couple of us should go back up and stay with Dr. Dalton."

"Get real," Keith said.

"What if the guy's alive?"

"If he is," Lana said, "and I doubt it—he certainly isn't in any condition to climb all the way up the mountain."

"But you can feel free to go back up there if you want to," Keith told him. "Angela stays with us, but you can go."

"It would be a waste of time, anyway," Doris said. "The man's dead and I killed him."

"You sound like it bothers you," Keith said.

She scowled at him. "I'm not in the habit of taking human life. How many people have *you* killed?"

"This guy got what he deserved," Lana said.

"Easy for you to say; you aren't the one who shot him."

Glen set the bag of apricots on his lap, reached over and took hold of Doris's hand. Howard expected her to jerk it away from him and make a cutting remark. But she met Glen's eyes. Her hand remained in his, and her mouth remained shut.

"You had to do it," he said.

"I'm aware of that. It still makes me feel horrible."

"He was a scumbag," Keith said. "If he's dead, you did the world a favor."

"Yeah, sure."

"You did the right thing," Glen told her. "It's just damn lucky you were there and had the gun. If you'd been with us, he probably would've killed the Prof. And then he would've gone on to his mine and run into the rest of us."

"Then *we'd* have had to nail the bastard," Keith said.

"But he might've gotten some of us first," Lana added.

"I suppose."

"We really owe you," she said.

"Maybe we oughta vote Doris a bigger share of the loot," Glen suggested.

"I'll go along with that," Howard said.

Angela nodded. "Me, too."

"I don't want more," Doris said. "Not for killing a person."

"Good thing," Keith said. "All this generosity makes me want to barf."

When they finished eating, Lana got to her feet and said, "I guess we'd better take the tents with us."

"They'll slow us down," Keith told her.

"You don't want to leave *your* tent, do you Glen?" she asked.

"I don't suppose so."

"We might never see them again."

"Aren't we coming back with the rescue party?" Howard asked.

"Who knows? They might not let us. Or they might come in on a different route."

"Maybe they'll chopper in," Glen said.

"At any rate, they aren't going to be bothered with picking up our tents, and I'm not exactly eager to hike back in here to retrieve the things."

"What about those?" Angela asked, nodding toward the two packs. "If we might not be coming back, shouldn't we take them with us?"

"Forget it," Keith muttered.

"Doris and I aren't carrying anything," Howard pointed out.

He expected Doris to protest, but she said, "I wouldn't mind. I'll take Dr. Dalton's, if you'll take Chad's."

He wanted to be the one with Dr. Dalton's pack. It would be a pleasure to carry her load on his back, and to do the favor for her. But if he argued about it, he'd look like a jerk. "I'll take whichever pack is heavier," he said.

"Fair enough."

"Let's think about this for a minute," Lana said. "It might not be such a good idea. What if Corie needs something out of her pack and comes down to get it?"

"We left her with plenty of stuff," Glen said.

"Yeah, but who knows? Maybe there'll be a delay getting them out, and they run out of food. It isn't likely, but it could happen. If we leave the packs here, at least there'll be supplies and things she can get to."

"Good point," Keith said.

"We'd better leave them," Angela said.

Nodding, Howard muttered, "Yeah." He hadn't considered the possibility of the rescue hitting a snag. But he supposed that anything was possible. A bad storm might show up out of nowhere and force a delay. Or the rescue team might be too busy with other emergencies to come in tomorrow. If it comes in by air, the helicopter might crash.

We might crash in the car on the way to Purdy. What if all of us are killed in a head-on before we even get a chance to reach help for them?

Howard knew he was letting his imagination run wild. None of that was likely to happen. But anything *could* happen.

As he got up and went to help with the tents, he imagined Dr. Dalton waiting on the mountainside, waiting for help that never arrives. Finally, Chad dies of exposure. She comes down the trail, out of food by now, starving and grieving. She reaches the lake. Her pack is right here where she left it. Grateful, she sits down to rest and eat. And Hubert comes out of the lake behind her. He is dripping wet, all naked except for that little pouch. Just as he grabs her, Howard shows up and attacks Hubert with his Swiss Army knife. He slashes the bastard's throat. And Dr. Dalton, sobbing with relief, throws herself into Howard's arms.

That's about as likely to happen as the car crash, he thought.

But wouldn't it be neat?

What about Angela?

He looked at her. She was crouched beside him, tugging at one of the tent stakes. She turned her head. Her eyes met his. And he knew that Dr. Dalton was just for fantasies. Angela was for real life, and his.

"Hold it a minute," Lana said. "Somebody's been inside. The zipper's open." She had already pulled the guy line stake. She hung onto the taut cord, keeping the tent upright. "Howard, you want to grab this? I'll take a look."

"Maybe Hubie's in there," Keith called from behind the tent.

"I'll look," Howard said.

Alarm filled Angela's eyes.

"Hubert's dead," Lana said.

Glen and Doris stopped working on the other tent. They turned to watch Howard.

He hesitated, tempted to pull out his Swiss Army knife.

Not in front of everyone, he thought. You'll look like a dork.

Crouching, ready to lurch back, he lifted one side of the hanging flaps. And felt weak with relief.

No Hubert, crouched to pounce.

"There're some clothes," he said.

"Well, get 'em," Lana said.

He ducked through the opening and knelt over them.

The flaps had fallen shut behind him. The tent was nearly dark.

In spite of the deep gloom, he could see enough to send a secret thrill through him.

There were hiking boots, white socks, a plaid blouse with a flimsy black bra draped across it, and black panties hanging outside the waist of a pair of shorts as if the two garments had been pulled off together.

Dr. Dalton's clothes.

Coreen's.

What were they doing here? Is this where Hubert had caught her?

He felt a rush of hatred. And envy. And guilt as he imagined himself in the tent with Coreen. Himself, not Hubert, stripping her.

Kneeling in front of her, reaching behind her back, unclasping the bra and lifting it away. But then he realized that her breasts were the same as Angela's. Small, pale globes, nipples large and jutting. He looked at the face, and it was Angela's face. His guilt faded. He was breathless and hard with desire, but somehow it seemed all right, just fine, not sneaky or dirty or any kind of betrayal now that Angela had taken Coreen's place in his mind.

As he tucked the socks into the boots and rolled the clothing into a bundle, he wondered when he would get to be alone with Angela again.

Maybe later tonight. Maybe after getting to Purdy and going to the police, they would all check into a motel. Maybe he could get a separate room, just for himself and Angela.

With the boots in one hand, the bundle of clothes hugged to his chest, he scurried out of the tent.

Chapter Thirty-one

"What're you doing?" Chad yelled up to her.

"It's visiting hour," Corie called, lowering her legs over the side of the trail.

"Are you nuts? Stay where you are."

"Don't worry."

"My God, don't try it!"

She squirmed backward, the granite edge rough against her belly, rucking up the sweatshirt. The wind was cold on her back and sides, but the rock against her belly still held some of the sun's warmth. She lowered herself some more. Clinging to the rim of the trail, she swung her right leg across the face of the slope until she found the foothold that she'd spotted before starting her descent.

"Coreen, please."

"I know what I'm doing."

She *hoped* so, anyway.

The idea of climbing down to be with Chad had occurred to her shortly after the kids left. But the idea had frightened her. She'd pushed it to the back of her mind and busied herself with taking care of Chad.

She had asked him to untie the rope. Then she'd pulled it up and lowered a canteen to him. After drawing up the rope again, she'd prepared him a care package: trail mix, cookies, a bacon bar, chocolate bars, an assortment of freeze-dried fruit, all wrapped tightly in a shirt from Howard's pack. Once the bundle had settled safely onto Chad's chest, she'd brought up the rope and stretched out flat and talked to him while he ate.

And studied the slope, seeking a way down.

Finding possible routes.

But still reluctant to try it.

Why take the risk? She could see him from here, talk to him.

The next best thing to being there.

Not at all the same as being there.

He was twenty feet below Corie. She felt as if he were in a far-off country.

From which he might never return.

The sun had already dropped behind a distant ridge. Night would be here soon. If she kept procrastinating, darkness would kill her chance.

She knew it was foolish to climb down for a visit. Idiotic. It would accomplish nothing. But she also knew that, if she didn't, she would spend the long dark night alone on the trail regretting her lost opportunity.

And what if something happened during the night?

She didn't want to think about that. The night would pass. Dawn would come, the sun warming the mountainside. And he'd be there, alive and well—though hurting—on his narrow ledge.

But you never know.

Things happen.

She knew that she had to go down to him. Now. If only for a brief visit. Just to be *with* him for a few minutes.

Before starting down, she'd taken the precaution of rigging a safety line. She didn't trust the rope, doubted that it could bear her full weight without snapping, but figured it might be useful in case she should find herself without a handhold.

She'd secured one end to a small knob of rock a few feet up the trail from where Chad had gone over, then drawn the other end around her back, under her armpits and over her breasts. She'd tied it. To keep the rope out of her face, she'd slid the knot sideways to her right shoulder.

She'd coiled the slack and set it at the edge of the trail hoping that it would pay out slowly during her descent. If she found herself needing the rope as a handhold, she would simply pull it all down and make it taut. In the meantime, however, it wouldn't be in the way.

On her belly, she'd scooted backward and lowered her legs over the side.

And kept on working her way down the steep face of the mountain in spite of Chad's protests. The slack payed out according to plan. Until something thumped the top of her head. Startled, she gasped and hugged the slope. For just an instant, she thought that a snake had dropped onto her. It *felt* like a snake. A very long one. But then coils slipped down her head. Dirty gray rope fell past her eyes, brushed the tip of her nose, her chin, and came to rest across the tops of her breasts.

Most of it landed there.

She could feel one loop encircling her neck.

"Shit!" It wasn't her voice. It was Chad's. "Don't move."

"What do you mean, don't move?"

"I think some of it's wrapped around your neck."

"Shit." This time, it was Corie who said it.

But with so much slack piled on her chest, she figured there wouldn't be much of a problem.

She eased herself a bit lower.

"Careful!"

The rope tightened like a noose. She gasped. Her heart sledged. Every muscle in her body suddenly seemed to be shuddering. They shivered with fear. They shook with the effort of holding her spread-eagled against the mountainside.

"It's all right," Chad said.

"Oh yeah sure it is!" Her voice came out squeaking.

"Just don't panic."

"Who me?"

"You'll be OK if you climb *upward*."

"I can't move."

"Sure you can. You're scared, that's all."

"That's all."

"Just loosen up, calm down, you'll be fine."

"The damn rope was supposed to keep me safe, not string me up."

"Well, hang in there."

"Is that supposed to be funny?"

"Just a little gallows humor."

"Ha ha. If you ask me how it's hangin,' I'm gonna come down there and brain you."

"At least this should cure your penis envy."

"Chad!"

"Now that you're so well hung."

"Oh, you're a riot. You're hilarious. I know why you're doing this, you know. You're just trying to take my mind off my fucking *predicament*."

"Is it working?"

"No!"

"Well, I might be able to reach your foot and give you a little boost."

"Am I that close?"

"Not hardly. But I'm gonna stand up and try in about two minutes."

"Oh Jesus." With her right hand, she let go and reached up and grabbed the rope above her head. Pulling on the taut line, she thrust herself a little higher. The noose loosened. With some slack between her hand and neck, she dragged the rope across the back of her head and jerked it forward. It scraped and bent her ear. It scorched her cheekbone, the side of her jaw. When she yanked it past the front of her face, the rope abraded her nose and chin.

But then the noose was gone.

"It's OK," she said. "I got it."

"Thank God. Now, please, climb back up to the trail before something else goes wrong."

She didn't answer. She released the rope and clutched her solid handhold on the slope. She waited until her breathing and heartrate were no longer out of control. Then she resumed her descent.

"Coreen!"

"Loosen up," she said.

"Why are you doing this?"

"I feel like it."

Soon, she saw Chad over her right shoulder. His head was strained back so that he could look up at her. She was above him, her feet probably at the same level as his body. She was over to the side, though. Just as planned.

Making her way lower, she found the narrow ledge that she'd spotted from the trail. It was about a yard below the shelf that had stopped Chad's fall, and only a few inches wide. But wide enough to stand on.

She sidestepped carefully.

"You're out of your mind."

"You looked lonely down here. And I know I was sure lonely up there."

She found a good handhold on the wall above his face. Grabbing it with her left hand, she twisted and bent down, braced her right palm against the corner of the shelf above his shoulder, and lowered her face over his.

"You're cute upside-down," she said.

"You're gonna fall, damn it."

"No, I'm not." Straining downward, she kissed him. His lips felt dry and cracked. Corie's body shook from the effort of holding herself in such a precarious and awkward position. But she felt his warm breath enter her mouth. And she was glad that she'd made the journey down to him.

She kissed the end of his nose.

She kissed his eyes, feeling the lids flutter against her lips. Then she pushed herself upright.

"Did I make you all better?"

"My God, Coreen."

She remembered that she had kissed his knees, down at the lake. So long ago. Only this afternoon.

She'd kissed his penis, too.

"I wish I could kiss you everywhere," she said. "It might be a trifle tricky, though. Short of climbing up there on top of you."

He smiled. Or grimaced. Corie wasn't sure which. "I was just about to suggest it."

"Sure."

"I'm serious."

"Don't you think our amorous proclivities had better be postponed till . . . ?"

"It's my leg."

"Bad?"

"Doesn't hurt much. It's numb and I can't move it."

Corie nodded. His right leg was bent at the knee, calf tight against the back of his thigh, ankle and foot trapped under his left buttock.

During earlier talks, Chad had told her that his tibia and fibula were probably broken. He'd been able to reach them with his hands and explore. "Simple fractures," he'd said. "I haven't got bone ends poking out my skin, nothing like that." Corie had assumed that the injury wasn't extremely serious except for the fact that it rendered him incapable of climbing to safety.

Now, she was worried.

"What do you want me to do?" she asked.

"Straighten it out. Get it out from under me. If you can. The way I'm on it, I'm cutting off my circulation."

"Why didn't you tell me?"

"You might've tried to come down."

"I should've figured it out for myself. Now, how are we gonna work this?"

"Very carefully."

"Oh, boy." The slack of the rope was hanging to her waist. With her right hand, she picked it up and stuffed it down the neck of her sweatshirt. She tucked it under the loose cinch made by the loop. Satisfied that it wouldn't fall out and tangle her, she leaned closer to Chad.

On each side of his head, there was room for one knee. His left shoulder and hip were flush against the vertical slope. On his right, next to his hip, she could see about two inches of flat rock.

Her right hand could go there.

"Maybe you'd better not try this," Chad said.

"I know," she said, and her stomach seemed to drop out from under her as she abandoned her perch and scurried onto Chad's shelf. She heard herself suck air, make a whinnying sound.

Knees on granite, she wobbled. She felt Chad grab her thighs. She ducked forward. Her left hand clutched his left hip. Her right palm thrust against the rock edge to his right.

"*Jesus Jesus Jesus!*" she gasped.

"You're OK. You're fine."

She panted for air. She muttered, "Holy smoke."

"You OK?"

"I guess so. But we'd better make this quick."

"Will it help if I raise my knee?"

"Yeah."

"It won't hit you, will it? I can't see anything but sweatpants."

"Just do it slowly."

His left knee came toward Corie's face. Letting go of his hip, she clutched his upraised thigh. She squeezed it hard. She darted her right hand from the ledge to his right ankle, grabbed hold and tugged his foot out from under his rump. He flinched and gasped. His fingers dug into the backs of her thighs.

Easing down until her shoulder met the top of his knee, she pushed at his right leg and stretched it out straight. Then she planted her right hand against the granite beside his thigh.

"That's got it," she said. "Should I do something else? Splint it?"

"With what?"

"I don't know. My shoes? I could use your belt . . ."

"No, don't bother. This is fine. It doesn't matter, I won't be walking on it. You'd better get back up to the trail while there's still some light."

She raised her head. From the looks of the sky, the darkness of night was looming. Fifteen minutes, maybe, before full darkness. The mountain's wall was a deep and somber gray.

She knew that she'd better start climbing soon.

But she didn't want to leave.

If she stayed, she supposed she could manage to turn herself around and lie down flat on top of him. But if either of them rolled during the night . . . No, it was out of the question. Aside from the strong possibility of falling, there would be her weight on his broken leg. And the cold. They both needed sleeping bags, and her plan from the start had been to lower one with the rope. That had to remain the plan.

"Is there anything else I can do for you?" she asked.

"Considering our positions, there's a lot. But you'd probably fall trying to get my zipper open."

"Probably."

"I've been sorely tempted to try something from my end."

"To my end?"

"You don't need the distraction." His hands moved up the backs of her legs and gently squeezed her buttocks through the thickness of the sweatpants. She expected to feel his head rise between her thighs, to feel his mouth. But his head stayed down. "You'd better go," he said.

"Easier said than done."

"Can you get your feet where your knees are, and stand up?"

"I can try."

"Maybe hang on to my knee and your rope."

"Yeah. Damn it."

"What?"

"I don't want to leave you."

"You've got to."

334

"I know."

"You go, Maria, my crop-haired one. You go and I will go with you. We will go together."

"Cut it out."

"Huh? You don't like my Cooper impression?"

"Robert Jordan died."

"I'll be fine. I'll be *really* fine once you're back up there where you belong."

"I love you."

"I love you, too." He gave her rump a soft pat.

"We'll be married before I've got the cast off my leg. Now go, OK?"

"OK."

She reached high with her right hand and grabbed the robe. She pulled it tight. Not trusting it to do more than hold her steady, she pushed against Chad's upraised knee. She brought up her own right knee until the ball of her foot found purchase on the slab. Then she did the same with her left.

She came out of her squat.

Reluctantly, she let go of Chad's knee and reached for the wall. Nothing there to grab, but she pressed her hand against it, anyway, as she stood up straight.

She felt as if she were towering above Chad.

His face was far below, between her feet. He looked solemn, worried.

"I'll send a sleeping bag right down," she said.

"Sleep tight, OK?"

"You, too. But not till we've got you tied."

"Be careful."

"You, too. Do you mind if I step on you?"

"My pleasure."

On her left foot, she pivoted toward the wall of the mountain. She brought her right foot down on his shoulder, but only for a moment. Then she raised it to a crevice and began her climb.

Chapter Thirty-two

Howard sank into the backseat of the car, and sighed. It felt wonderful to be off his sore feet, off his aching legs, sitting down finally—and on a soft cushion, not on a log or the ground or a rock.

Angela slid in beside him. After she pulled the door shut, he put an arm across her shoulders.

"I didn't think we'd ever make it," he muttered.

"It wasn't fun."

"I guess it went pretty fast, though."

The hike from the lake to the car had been mostly down-hill, the group urged along the moonlit switch-backs by gravity. Howard had felt as if someone were pushing at his back, forcing him to take longer and quicker strides than he liked. He'd constantly needed to slow his descent. Otherwise, he would've found himself rushing down the trail and probably taking a running leap into space. The braking had taken a heavy toll on him. It had jammed his toes into the fronts of his boots. It had reduced his thigh muscles to weak, shaking jelly.

He knew that the hike must've been even worse for those with packs bouncing against their backs. Several times, he'd offered to carry Angela's, only to be turned down. Knowing what was in it, he'd been relieved. Even though the skeleton *was* Angela's mother, he got the creeps just thinking about it. But he'd felt guilty about making the descent without a burden. He had offered to take Lana's pack, but she only thanked him and said, "I'm fine."

Naturally, Glen and Keith had been quick to suggest he carry *their* packs. His guilt didn't go that far. Laughing, he'd told them to take a hike.

Those two had actually *run* down the final stretch of switchback to the level ground at the base of the mountain. So much for needing help. Of course, maybe they'd been too worn out, by then, to bother fighting the pull of gravity.

"Have you ever noticed," Angela asked, "that when you're returning from somewhere it *always* seems quicker?"

"It *was* a lot quicker."

"Yeah. That's for sure." She laughed softly. "I think my toes got pushed in."

"I wish you would've let me carry your pack."

"It wasn't all that heavy. Besides. You know. It was my mother."

Lana, Keith and Glen, done with loading the car, piled into the front seat. "Let's just hope this baby starts," Lana said. The engine grumbled and died. Then it caught. She gunned it, and it roared.

"Where's Doris?" Angela asked.

"She went off to take a leak," Lana said.

"Here's our big chance to lose her," Keith said.

"Fuck you, man," Glen snapped.

"Hey, I was just kidding."

"Well, fuck your kidding, OK? She saved Lana's butt last night, and she saved Dalton today. She's all right. She's *better* than all right. She deserves some respect."

"Methinks you're hot on her, that's what *me*thinks."

"So what if I am? You got a problem with that?"

"Who, me?"

"Just lay off the cracks. From now on. You got it?"

"Sure sure sure. Christ."

"All right, then."

Moments later, Doris returned. She climbed in beside Howard. Even as she pulled her door shut, the car began to back up. It swung past the end of Coreen's car, then started forward and turned away.

Twisting around, Howard looked out the rear window. The car was a black, huddled shape in the darkness, not even touched by moonlight.

"They'll be all right," Angela said.

"Some of us should've stayed," Howard muttered.

"You had the chance, Howitzer."

"This time tomorrow night," Lana said, "Chad and Corie'll be shacked up in a cozy motel somewhere getting it on."

"Playing a little hide-the-salami," Keith said. "Dalton'll have to be on top, of course."

"You're such a cretin," Doris told him.

"Hey, Glen wants me to be nice to you. Don't make it any more difficult."

"Then cut out the crass remarks. You're not amusing."

"I was only attempting, in my singularly cretinous way, to allay Howitzer's concerns about the Professor's safety."

"Yeah, well, you shouldn't talk about her that way," Howard said.

"Screw you."

"Screw *you*."

"Why don't we all shut up for a while?" Lana suggested. "You're giving me a headache. Or this road is. Something is. Let's have some peace and quiet."

"You heard the lady," Keith said, looking over his shoulder. "You people quit your belly-aching back there." He turned to the front again. Laughing softly, he settled down in his seat.

Angela squeezed Howard's leg. He looked at her. The vague blur of her face, bouncing and wobbling with the rough jostles of the car, seemed to be grinning. He pulled her closer against him. She raised her arm out of the way, put it behind him, and caressed his side. They bobbed and swayed and bumped each other.

After a while, Howard heard snoring from Doris.

Amazing. How could anyone fall asleep while being pounded and shaken this way?

He felt dead tired, himself. He wished he could sleep. But if he had to be awake, this wasn't so bad. The car was dark and warm and he was holding Angela.

They tried to kiss, but their mouths collided.

"You OK?" he whispered.

"I think so. How about you? Split lip? Broken teeth?"

"I'm all right."

"Try here."

She pointed. Howard brushed his lips against her cheek. The skin was smooth and warm, vibrating slightly. With a sudden lurch of the car, her cheekbone punched his nose.

"Oooo. Are you all right?"

He held his nose. His eyes were watering.

"Is it bleeding?"

He sniffed. He wiggled his nose. He fingered his nostrils. "I don't think so."

"We'd better stop."

He looked away from her. Nobody was watching. Though Doris continued to snore, he wondered if anyone in the front seat had been able to hear their conversation. Maybe not. The engine was making plenty of noise. The car squeaked and thudded as it bounced. Rocks crunched under the tires. Snaps and pops came from twigs, branches, pine cones, whatever else was being run over.

"Let's not," he whispered.

"Let's not what?"

"Stop."

"I don't want you to get hurt."

"We'll be careful."

Angela nodded. Leaning forward, she struggled to take off her windbreaker. Howard helped pull the sleeves down

339

her arms. While he held the jacket, she reached under the back of her T-shirt. Howard realized what she was doing. His breath snagged and his heart quickened.

She brought her hands to the front, slumped back against the seat, and took the windbreaker from him. She spread it open and draped it from her shoulders.

Twisting himself sideways, Howard eased his left arm behind her head. His right hand slipped beneath the nylon cover. It met Angela's hands as they plucked the T-shirt free from the waistband of her sweatpants.

They not only untucked the shirt, they lifted it out of his way.

Howard roamed the silken, warm skin of her belly. He tried to caress it gently. Sometimes, the motions of the car made him lose the feel of her. Other times, a jolt thrust her up against his hand, or jarred him so that his hand slid abruptly across the smoothness.

Slowly, he made his way higher.

So did Angela's hand on his thigh.

Trembling and breathless, he caressed her beneath the left breast. He ached to feel the breast, but he didn't dare.

Stupid, he thought. I made love to her last night. We went *all the way*.

But the breast was like a secret treasure. He was afraid to touch it.

She wants me to, he told himself. For Godsake, she covered herself so I could do it. She even unfastened her bra. Can't be more obvious than that.

Still, he hesitated.

Until Angela's hand pressed his groin, rubbed his penis gently through the corduroy.

He squirmed and tried not to moan.

He curled his hand against the underside of her breast. So smooth. So warm. Cupping it lightly, he felt the slope jiggle. An abrupt sharp bounce of the car patted it against his palm and fingers.

This is so incredible, he thought. Doing this to each other. Right here in the car. Nobody else knowing.

Angela's hand, he noticed, was no longer rubbing him. He wondered why she'd stopped. He thought he knew why; she was too involved, just now. Distracted by her breast and his hand.

Or maybe she sensed how close he was to losing control. Good thing.

As if reading his mind, she lifted her hand away and began to caress his thigh.

Another bounce of the car slapped her breast softly down against his palm.

Angela moaned as his thumb moved forward along the slope and met a curving ridge of firm, puckered flesh. He traced a semi-circle, following its edge, then slid his thumb up onto it. A rumpled, turgid cone rose steeply until it jutted straight out like a post. He stroked slowly upward, found the rounded top, caressed it, pushed on it, felt it bend like a rubber tube as Angela gasped and flinched and clutched his leg. A little alarmed, he stopped pushing. The nipple sprang up straight again.

"Did that hurt?" he whispered.

"No. God, no. It was wonderful."

This is almost better than last night, he thought, bringing up his forefinger and using it along with his thumb to savor and tease the nipple.

Last night had been great. Better than great. But it had been frenzied and rushed and quickly over. This was so very different—a slow exploration of contours and textures and responses Nothing to do *except* touch each other secretly. Not here in the car with the others present. So it might go on forever. Or at least until Doris woke up or someone in the front seat looked around. With luck, it might last until they came to the main road.

That should still be more than an hour away.

A whole hour, probably longer.

A long time. But not so long, really. He supposed he could gladly spend that much time lingering over just this single breast. But there was another. And there was the deep juicy cleft between her legs.

Would she let him slip his hand down there?

Probably.

And what would she do to him? What would she dare?

He closed his hand over the soft mound, the nipple jutting out between his open fingers. When he gently squeezed, her back arched. Her breath hissed in. Her fingertips dug into his thigh.

As the car rocked and bounced over the rough dirt tracks, Howard continued to fondle Angela's breast. He roamed it, caressed and squeezed it, held it lightly in his palm to feel its smooth weight shake and bob with the car's motions, gently pinched and pulled the nipple. Sometimes, Angela shut her eyes and sat still. Other times, she gasped and writhed. She kept her hand away from his groin as if knowing that a touch from her might be too much.

Just the feel of her breast was almost too much for Howard to bear. Every so often, nearing the brink, he took his hand away until he could calm down a little.

Aware that time was passing, he switched his attentions to her right breast. Though it felt very much like the other, its curves and textures were fresh, thrilling magic to Howard. And it was closer to him, easier to reach. He realized how heavy his arm had become, stretching across her body to the farther breast. This was much better.

He was cupping it, feeling it joggle inside his hand, when Angela reached up and drew the windbreaker aside just enough to uncover his hand and the breast beneath it. A glance toward the front seat assured him that no one was looking. Behind him, Doris continued to snore. He looked at the blur of Angela's face. He couldn't see her expression, but he saw her nod.

He lowered his gaze. Angela's T-shirt, the bra hidden inside it, formed a puffy roll just above her breast. His hand appeared very dark against her pale skin. He slid it down against the underside. There, he could feel her without obstructing his view.

He stared and stared at the creamy mound, its dark cone

and pillar. He watched it jitter, felt it bounce against his palm. He watched his fingertips glide up its slope. He watched them push, felt the flesh yield but then spring up when he eased the pressure.

If only there was more light, he thought.

If only we were alone.

It's nothing but a pouch of skin filled with fatty tissue, he suddenly thought. How can it do this to me?

He didn't know how. He realized he didn't care how. All that mattered was to have it, to be holding it and seeing it, and to know that Angela cared so much about him that she was willing to let him.

Bending down, he pressed his cheek against the rumpled nest of her shirt and bra. He kissed the top of her breast. Then he turned his head and strained lower. He licked the nipple, tongued it into his mouth, squeezed his lips around it, sucked. Angela, shuddering, pushed her fingers into the hair on the back of his head. She pressed him hard against her. He took more of the breast into his mouth. It filled him. He probed it with his tongue and teeth. It was springy and warm, slick with his saliva.

He felt as if his trapped penis might throb and pump.

Not yet!

You haven't gotten *down there* yet!

He slid his hand down her belly, under the elastic band of her sweatpants. As he tried to work his fingertips under the thin band of her panties, she clutched his hair and pulled his head back and whispered, "No, don't." The breast came out of his mouth with a wet slopping sound.

Confused and hurt, Howard suddenly lost his agony of desire. He sat up. And watched as Angela pulled the windbreaker sideways to cover her breast.

"What's wrong?" he whispered.

She shook her head.

"Angela?"

"I'm sorry."

"What did I do?"

Again, she shook her head. Then she turned to him. The

wind-breaker fell from her shoulders, dropped into her lap. Howard saw that she had already pulled her T-shirt down. The bra made it bulge oddly above her breasts.

She put her hand behind Howard's head and drew him closer. She pressed her cheek to his cheek. "I'm really sorry," she whispered, her breath tickling his ear. "I didn't want to stop you. I loved it all. I love *you*. But . . . this is really embarrassing."

"What?"

"I was afraid . . . I couldn't let you touch me. Not there."

"It's OK," he whispered.

But he felt crushed. What had gone wrong? She hadn't complained last night. They'd *made love*, for godsake. So why, all of a sudden, was he not supposed to touch her there?

Because the others might find out?

How could that be it? She'd actually *showed* her breast. If she was afraid of Keith or Glen turning around, why did she do *that*?

"Are you awfully disappointed?" she whispered.

"No."

"I'll make it up to you."

"It's all right. Honest."

"The thing is . . ." She hesitated. "I was afraid if you . . . I've gotta pee something horrible."

"What?"

"That's why. It's all I can do to hold it."

Relief swept through Howard and he laughed. Angela squirmed. Her hand came up in front of his face and rubbed her ear.

"It's not funny," she whispered.

"Let's have them stop the car."

"I don't want to make a big deal out of it."

"But if you've gotta go . . ."

"I can wait a while longer. We must be almost . . . it won't be so bad once we're on a smooth road. Maybe I can wait till we get to the town."

"You oughta take care of it now."

"The guys'd make fun of me. You know that."

"If that's what you're worried about, I'll say I'm the one who's gotta go."

"Let's just . . ."

A jolt bounced them. Angela groaned and held on to Howard as they were flung up and came down so hard the seat cushions squeaked under their weight.

"Are you OK?" he asked.

"Hanging in there."

"I'll tell them . . ." He felt the car make a right turn, felt a sudden, surprising calm. The bumps and lurches were gone. Looking over the top of Keith's head, he saw that they were riding on the smooth asphalt surface of the main road.

"Thank God," Angela gasped.

"Do you want to try and wait for town? It's supposed to be about ten miles."

"I think I'd rather. If I can."

Behind him, Doris snorted. Then she let out a small gasp and murmured, "Huh?"

Angela let go of Howard. She pulled the windbreaker up as they both settled back against their seat. Howard looked over at Doris. She was rubbing her eyes with her fists.

Amazing, he thought. She'd slept her way through the rough part of the ride, only to wake up the moment the turbulence stopped.

She stretched, then twisted around to peer out her window.

Howard turned to Angela. The windbreaker draping her front was alive with moving bulges as she reached up beneath it and pulled her bra into place. Her hands went away. Twin mounds remained. They pushed up against the fabric while she arched and struggled to fasten the clasps behind her back. Finished, she slumped against the seat. She patted his thigh.

"I think we'd better . . ."

"Hey," Keith said, "there's somebody who ran shit outa luck."

345

"They didn't have a trusty, indomitable vehicle like mine," Lana said.

"Flat tire," Glen said.

Howard looked past Doris's head as they sped past the dark shape of a car at the side of the road.

"Thank God *we* didn't get a flat," Lana said. "I'm surprised we have any tires left at all, after that cute piece of road."

"Could we pull over?" Howard asked. "My teeth are floating."

"Hang it out the window," Keith suggested.

"I'm serious."

"I could use a pit-stop myself," Lana said. The car slowed, glided to the right, and tipped slightly as its side dropped from the pavement to the ground. It crunched forward a few feet, then stopped.

"Anybody who needs to go," Lana announced, "should do it now. It'll probably be twenty minutes or so before we hit town."

All four doors of her Granada swung open.

Howard climbed out behind Angela. While she thrust her arms into the sleeves of the windbreaker, he swung the door shut and saw Lana scooting across the front seat. Then Angela was pulling him by the hand, leading him in a rush toward the other side of the road.

"You don't have to watch," she gasped. "Just stay with me."

"Where are you guys going?" Lana called.

Howard glanced back. She was standing beside the car, peering over its roof at them. Doris was waiting beside her. Keith and Glen, walking past the front of the car, looked over their shoulders.

"Perverts!" Keith yelled.

Glen laughed and shook his head.

"The hell with them," Angela said. Still clutching his hand, she plunged through undergrowth beyond the edge of the road. The nearest group of trees was off to the left.

346

She headed that way, running, Howard racing along at her side.

Almost there, they leaped over a channel of tire ruts, each landing with one foot on the center rise and bounding over the second rut.

Then Angela released his hand. She dashed to a nearby tree and ducked behind its trunk. Not quite out of sight. The trunk was narrow.

He could see her right side, gray and flecked with moonlight, as she yanked the sweatpants down to her ankles and leaned back and sank to a squat. The trunk rucked up her windbreaker. He glimpsed the pale curve of her rump, the side of her bare, bent leg. When he heard her stream start splashing the ground, he turned around.

He unzipped and pulled out his limp penis.

Though he knew Angela was close enough to see and that her pants were down, though he could hear her, he didn't feel aroused.

Too pooped, he thought, and began urinating. He aimed his stream toward the closer of the tire tracks.

It was up so long, he thought, it's all worn out.

He finished, shook off the final drops, tucked himself away and zipped up.

Angela was *still* going.

He kept his back toward her. He had no urge to look, and that seemed strange to him. Right now, he felt no sexual desire for her. Instead, there was a strong feeling of tenderness. And intimacy. As if she were his best pal, not his girlfriend. They were a couple of buddies who'd simply rushed into the woods together for a quick leak.

"All done," she said. Howard heard her footsteps approaching. "Boy, do *I* feel better."

She patted his rump, and he grinned at her. "Good thing we stopped when we did."

"Just in the nick of time, I'd say."

They turned to each other. Angela wrapped her arms around him. He hugged her hard, kissed her open mouth. She was trembling.

347

"Cold?" he whispered.

"It's not so bad now. Do you want to . . . ? You know."

"Here?"

"Yeah."

"Jeez."

"If we do it fast."

"How fast?"

"Very fast. The others, they'll start wondering about us."

"I don't know. I want to, but . . ."

"Maybe it's not such a hot idea."

"We'd have to really rush. It'd be nicer if we can take all the time we want."

"In a warm place."

"With a bed."

"I can wait if you can."

"Maybe we can get into a motel tonight."

"I hope so. It's pretty late. What time is it, anyway?"

Howard released her and stepped back. He fingered a button to light the face of his wristwatch. "Twelve-fifteen."

"We made pretty good time."

"And *had* a pretty good time."

"The last couple of hours were sure great." She took his hand and squeezed it. "I guess we'd better go back to the car, huh?"

"Guess so."

She took a step toward the nearer rut of the tire tracks. Howard pulled her sideways.

"Puddle," he said.

"Oh." She laughed softly.

He led her past the wet area.

"Safe now?"

"Probably."

She walked down into the rut, then onto the higher ground of the center strip. Howard, staying at her side, strode along the worn path.

"Do you like me tall?" she asked. Her eyes were level with his.

"Different. But I wouldn't want anything changed about you."

"Nothing?"

"You're perfect just the way you are."

"My boobs are too small."

"I love them."

"Maybe when we find the treasure and we're rich, I could get implants. You know, get them enlarged."

"No! Are you kidding?"

"Wouldn't you like . . . Weird."

"Weird, all right. They're . . ."

"Not that." Halting, she raised his hand with hers and thrust it forward as if pointing. "Look."

He turned his head to the front.

No more than ten feet farther ahead, the tire tracks seemed to end. Howard hadn't paid much attention to them before, but he'd thought they would lead back to the main road. Just at the edge of the woods, however, a tangle of limbs and bushes blocked the way.

"We can circle around," he said. He pulled Angela's hand, but she resisted.

"No. Wait. Don't you think this is *strange*?"

He shrugged.

"Let's take a look." Releasing his hand, she rushed to the obstruction. She crouched and tugged at a branch. It slid toward her feet. Leaning forward, she lifted a small bush from the pile. She tossed it aside.

"What are you doing?"

She stood up and faced him. "I bet this is it." Her voice was hushed, excited.

"This is what?"

"Somebody put this stuff here. To hide the way in, you know?"

"So?"

"The treasure. It's supposed to be off Purdy Road, right? Well, this is off Purdy Road."

"Yeah, but there must be dozens of other . . ."

"Somebody took the trouble to *hide* this one."

349

Angela turned her head. Howard did the same. The pair of tracks stretched away and faded into the darkness of the forest.

"If we follow it far enough," she whispered, "I bet we'll find the bus."

Chapter Thirty-three

Groaning, Corie lifted her face off Doris's rolled sweatpants. The trail in front of her was so bright that, for just a moment, she thought that dawn had come.

Only moonlight.

She muttered, "Shit."

This had to be ranked up there as one of the longest nights of her life.

She felt as if she'd been in the sleeping bag forever.

Though it kept the cold out, it provided little relief from the hard surface of the trail in spite of the coat and other garments she'd spread out beneath it.

If she lay on her side, the ground punished her hip and shoulder and quickly squeezed her arm numb. If she lay face down, it hurt her knees, shoved against her ribs and mashed her breasts. On her back, she might've been able to find a little comfort if not for her injuries. Her shoulder blades and buttocks cushioned her somewhat, but they'd been scraped raw when Hubert hurled her away and she'd skidded on the rocks. A few minutes on her back, and the abrasions would begin to sting.

So, over the hours, she'd adjusted her position countless times. Very carefully. Always aware of the precipice close to her side.

She wasn't sure if she had slept at all. Maybe for a few minutes now and then.

But she felt as if she'd been awake the whole time, sometimes able to think clearly, often finding her mind drifting into a nasty, surreal realm that confused and terrified her. A realm where she was being pursued over strange landscapes by Hubert. He was naked and gleaming and laughing.

Sometimes, he caught her.

Once, he had picked her up overhead and hurled her off a cliff. Plummeting down, she'd passed Chad on his narrow shelf and called out "Good-bye" and he'd returned a forlorn last wave.

Another time, after catching her, Hubert had lifted her by the ankles. Higher and higher. Until she was looking down at his face and his mouth spread wide—too wide— and he lowered her. The top of her head went into his mouth. His teeth pressed into the flesh above her ears. Squeezed. She'd grabbed her head to stop her brains from bursting out, and that had put an end to that particular episode.

But it had soon been replaced by another, one in which he chased her over dunes that trapped her feet and slowed her down. He kept gaining on her. Glancing back in terror, she saw that he wore snowshoes. "That's not fair," she'd shouted. "Yes-yes-yes!" he'd answered, and twirled his machete. Finally, trying to climb a hill of sand, she'd lost her balance, fallen backward and slid down the slope and come to a stop at Hubert's feet. The machete flashed twice. *Whiss whiss.* Lopping off her breasts.

Flinching back to reality, she'd found herself stretched out face down in the sleeping bag, her breasts mashed painfully against her chest.

Onto her back she'd turned for another try at sleep, another brief visit from Hubert. She soon was sliding down a steep wall of granite, feet first, the rough surface ripping the flesh from her rump and back. She left a wet red path as she descended. A path strewn with patches of her skin. Beyond her feet and far below, Hubert waited. His machete waited. "Spread 'em wide, Jane! Slide right on." She skidded closer, closer to the blade. She kicked at it, kicked at the sleeping bag, realized what she was doing and rolled over again.

And began to sob against the soft pillow of Doris's sweatpants.

He's dead. Why won't he just leave me alone?

It'll be over soon, she told herself. Dawn will come. Everything'll be all right.

Why am I even trying to sleep? Why don't I sit up, or something?

She crawled out of the sleeping bag, crawled away from it, crawled until her head bumped into bare shins and Hubert picked her up by her hair until she dangled in front of him. "Can't get away from me that easy," he said. "Fuck you!" she shrieked, and stabbed her fingers into his eyes. The eyeballs popped, squirted. Both fingers went deep into his sockets. He blinked. His lids snapped shut like jaws. She screamed and jerked back her hand. The two stubs spouted blood.

"No!"

The sound of her voice broke the spell.

No is right, she thought.

Didn't happen.

She hadn't crawled out of the bag, had only thought about it.

She groaned, lifted her face off Doris's rolled sweatpants, saw the moonlit trail, muttered "Shit," and wondered if the night would ever end. Her eyes and cheeks itched from the tears. She rubbed them with a sleeve of her sweatshirt. Then she lowered the zipper at the side of Doris's sleeping bag, pushed herself up to her hands and knees, and crawled out.

The cold clamped her. Her sweatsuit, sodden after the series of horrible dreams or hallucinations or whatever they'd been, was clinging to her body and twisted askew. The wind chilled its moisture, passed through the heavy fabric, wrapped her skin like ice water. Clenching her teeth, shuddering, she tugged Howard's coat out from under the sleeping bag and put it on.

The coat helped a lot, but not enough. From the waist down, she was frigid. Her feet felt like clumps of ice.

With a quick search of Doris's pack, she found two more pairs of socks. She sat on top of the sleeping bag and crossed her legs. She wanted to take off the wet socks she was wearing. But they felt as if they'd been glued to the bottoms of her feet. Their white cotton, distinct in the milky moonlight, was blotched with blood. No telling what damage she might do, trying to remove them.

"Thanks for everything, Hubert," she muttered, her voice shaking.

She pulled two fresh socks over each foot. Better. Much better.

She unrolled the sweatpants that she'd been using for a pillow, and pulled them up her legs. The extra layer blocked out most of the wind. She let out a trembling sigh.

Hands stuffed into the coat pockets, she remained on the sleeping bag and took slow breaths, trying to calm herself and control the tremors.

"Not so bad," she finally said.

One hell of a lot better that staying in the bag, tossing and turning, having those damn visions.

Getting to her knees, she turned herself sideways. She bent over and pressed her hands against the edge of the trail. Easing forward, she peered down the bright, moonlit slope. The rope, directly under her face, angled sideways. It looked like a solid gray rod leading down to Chad. She could only see the very top of his head. The rest of him was hidden beneath the dark oblong of Howard's mummy bag.

"And I think I've got it rough," she muttered. "God, Chad."

Though he'd tied the rope securely around his chest and was probably in no great danger of falling, he had nothing but the clothes on his back to cushion him from the granite shelf. He hadn't been able to get inside the sleeping bag. Not by himself. Not without too much risk of tumbling from his perch. And he'd threatened to shove the sleeping bag into space if Corie tried to come down and help.

Must be awful, she thought, gazing down at him.

She wanted to call out, to talk with him.

For all she knew, however, he might be asleep.

It seemed unlikely. How could *anyone* fall asleep under such conditions?

But if somehow he was asleep, it would be an unforgivable cruelty to wake him.

What if he's not all right?

What if he's dying?

"Is that you?" He sounded . . . cheerful?

"How are you doing?"

"This isn't the most pleasant night I've ever spent."

"I should think not. Are you freezing?"

"It's not too bad. I seem to be out of the wind."

"That's wonderful. I'm not."

"What are you doing up?"

"I couldn't sleep. How about you?"

"I just woke up a few minutes ago. And boy, was I pissed. I was right in the middle of a great dream. Starring you."

"Lucky you."

"Well, I was *about* to get lucky, but then I woke up."

"Too bad. Look, is there anything I can do for you?"

"Yeah. Find someplace comfortable for yourself. You don't have to spend the night on that damn trail. You said it widens out up ahead. Why don't you move over to that area? Maybe you can find yourself some shelter. At the very least, you won't have to worry about rolling off."

"I'd rather be here with you."

"Frankly, it makes me nervous thinking about you up there. I'd feel a lot better if you got yourself someplace safe."

"Well, maybe I'll check it out. Are you hungry or anything?"

"I'm fine. Really."

"How's the leg?"

"Not so bad that it kept me awake. I'm sure glad you got it out from under me, though."

"Glad to be of service."

"I guess this screws up my idea of a backpacking honeymoon."

"*What* idea of a backpacking honeymoon?"

She heard him laugh.

"Oh, I wouldn't have done that to you," he said. "But it did sort of run through my mind this afternoon. While I was watching you swim."

"I hope it ran right out again."

"Things were pretty great until that bastard showed up."

"That's true," she said. "I remember thinking, myself, how nice it'd be to come back. Just the two of us. Just to have fun and not go chasing after the kids. I don't think I'd want it for the honeymoon, though."

"Softy."

"I'm just trying to be considerate of your knees."

Chad was silent. Corie wondered if he was trying to think of a witty comeback. But she waited, and he said nothing.

"Chad?"

"This won't . . . that damn maniac . . . I've been all over these mountains, never had any trouble. Not till now. This was a real fluke. I just hope you won't be afraid to give it another try."

"I don't know. We'll see."

"It was awfully good before he got to us."

"It couldn't have been much better."

"And there's no such thing as being completely safe."

"I know."

"You could run into a guy like that anywhere. Most of them aren't in the mountains. They're out in civilization, not in places like this. They're where the people are."

"I never said I wouldn't come up here again. But right now, it doesn't sound like the neatest idea in the world. I'm cold, tired, sore, scared . . . you name it. If it's lousy, I'm feeling it."

"Lonely?"

She thought about that. "Yes and no. Talking's OK. But I wish I could hold you."

"You and me both. But don't even think about trying to come down here."

"Can we keep on talking?"

"I'm not going anywhere."

"Am I keeping you up?"

"You might be keeping me from a great dream, but that's OK. The real you's better, anyway."

Chapter Thirty-four

"Shit, look at this." Crouching over the pile of limbs and bushes, Keith lifted one end of a long two-by-four. Its length was spiked with jutting nails. "Almost porked myself," he muttered.

"Could've had the fun of a tetanus shot," Lana said.

Keith picked up the rest of the board, swung it around and hurled it aside.

When they finished clearing the barricade, Lana rubbed her hands against the front of her sweatshirt and said, "OK, let's check it out."

"What do you mean?" Howard asked.

"Take a little ride down there and see if we can find the bus."

"Now?"

"No time like the present."

"We can't do that," Doris said.

"Sure we can," Keith said.

"It won't take long."

"We shouldn't do *anything* until we've been to the police," Doris protested. "It's our obligation to Dr. Dalton and . . ."

Lana shrugged. "Another half hour or so isn't gonna make any difference to them. It's the middle of the night. Nobody's about to send out a rescue party before morning."

Turning around, she stepped onto the pavement. Keith joined her. Together, they walked at an angle away from the abandoned car directly across the road, heading for Lana's Granada.

The others followed.

This is crazy, Howard thought.

Angela took his hand.

He looked at her and shook his head.

"I know," she muttered. "We shouldn't do it."

Why did we show them the dirt road? Howard thought. That was the big mistake.

Even when they'd started clearing the debris that blocked its entrance, Howard hadn't thought that anyone would seriously consider traveling down it *tonight*. They would drive on into town, take care of reporting Coreen and Chad's situation to the authorities, then find somewhere to spend the night. A motel, if they could get into one so late. A motel where he could be alone with Angela. It would be wonderful. In the morning, they would get together again and come out here to search for the bus.

In the morning.

They climbed into Lana's car and she started the engine. But she didn't start driving. She looked over her shoulder. "OK, everyone, what's it gonna be?"

"I already expressed my views on the matter," Doris said. "I'm certainly interested in finding the treasure, but our first duty is to Dr. Dalton. We can always come back here tomorrow. Also, I might point out that tomorrow is when Butler told us we'd find it. Tomorrow, not tonight."

"In case you haven't noticed," Keith said, "this *is* tomorrow. Butler didn't say anything about daylight."

"I'd rather wait for daylight," Howard said.

"Yeah, well, you always were a wuss."

"Cut it out," Lana said.

"I'm not real eager to go down that thing in the dark, either," Glen said. "But I think maybe we should. I get the feeling this is when we're meant to go for it. Look at the facts. This is tomorrow. The bus is supposed to be off Purdy Road and Angela's supposed to be the one who finds it. Well, she's the one who found those tire tracks. Everything's set up just right."

"Right on," Keith said.

"If we weren't meant to go looking until tomorrow morning," Glen continued, "I think Angela wouldn't have stumbled onto the dirt road until then."

"Excellent point," Keith said.

"Angela, what do you think?" Lana asked.

Howard felt her shoulder lift and lower slightly against his arm. "I don't know. I don't want to miss out on finding the treasure, but . . ."

"It might not be there in the morning," Keith pointed out.

"It's not as important," she went on, "as helping Dr. Dalton and Chad."

"It's not an either/or situation," Glen said.

"I tell you what," Lana said. "We'll give it five or ten minutes." She began pulling the car forward, swinging it into a slow U-turn. "We'll just make a short run up that road and if we don't find something quick, we'll head on into town and come back in the morning for a thorough search. How does that sound to everyone?"

"Perfect," Keith said.

Glen nodded his approval.

"OK, I guess," Angela said.

"All right," Howard said.

"Bullshit," Doris muttered.

"You're outvoted," Keith told her.

The car rocked and bounced as Lana steered onto the dirt road. "It's no big deal," she said. "Fifteen or twenty minutes, one way or the other, won't make any difference to Corie and Chad."

Howard put his arm across Angela's back and pulled her

close to his side. Together, they shook and swayed with the rough motions of the car. This seemed very much like the earlier part of the trip. But terribly different.

We shouldn't be here, he thought.

He supposed that Lana was right about Coreen and Chad. A brief delay shouldn't matter much.

But he didn't like this road.

Not at all.

Somebody had tried to conceal its entrance.

The barricade had been their clue that this was *the* road. But didn't it bother anyone that somebody had put it there? Somebody who didn't want visitors?

And what about the abandoned car?

It had a flat tire.

And there'd been that board with nails in it.

This is really bad, he thought.

Butler is Angela's mother, he reminded himself. She wouldn't be sending us into trouble.

Oh, no? What about Hubert? She ran us into him.

Maybe she doesn't care what happens to any of us but Angela.

Who knows what she's really up to?

Back there in the trunk, plotting.

In the trunk. Howard had been aware, all along, that they were riding with the skeleton of Angela's mother in the trunk. Until now, it hadn't bothered him.

Now, he found himself spooked.

The fleshless bones. The grinning skull. Jammed inside Angela's pack. Along with that tattered, stuffed kitten.

If the seatback weren't in the way, she would be near enough to touch.

A dead, horrid passenger riding along with them in silence, but leading them.

Leading them deep into the woods in the middle of the night for reasons known only to her.

"It's been more than five minutes," Doris said.

"No place to turn around," Lana said. "I'm not about to *back* all the way out to the road."

A pretty lame excuse, Howard thought. He could see past the side of Keith's head and through the windshield. Though trees bordered the twin ruts, they were far enough back for Lana to turn the car around if she wanted to.

"We're not exactly hemmed in," Doris said.

"Give it a rest," Keith told her.

"Just a little farther," Lana said. "Then we'll . . . Jesus!"

Howard glimpsed a clearing ahead. Then the bright pale beams of the headlights vanished as if sucked back into the car.

Lana jammed on the brakes. The car lurched to a stop.

"Holy shit," Keith muttered.

Glen said, "Oh, man."

"That's it," Lana said.

Howard saw it.

A bus.

He *guessed* it was a bus. At the far end of the moonlit field. Maybe a hundred yards away. But all he could see of it was a long row of rectangles that seemed to hover above the ground. Its passenger windows. Faint, glowing patches of crimson. Apparently, the windows were shrouded with red curtains.

"Looks fuckin' creepy," Glen whispered.

"What the hell's it *doing* out here?" Lana asked.

"We've found it," Doris said. "Now let's turn around and leave."

"No way," Keith said. "This is it. This is what it's all about. We can't quit now."

"I don't know," Lana muttered. "Looks like somebody might be in there."

"If it didn't have lights on, we couldn't have seen it. They're on for us. Right, Glen? It's all part of the same deal. Butler had to make it so we could spot the damn thing."

"I don't like this," Glen said.

"That shows you've retained a modicum of good sense," Doris pointed out.

"Maybe we'd better wait for daylight," Lana said.

"It might not *be* here. Look, let's just leave the car and

sneak up on the thing. We'll check it out. We don't have to go inside, but we've gotta at least take a closer look. I mean, our treasure's supposed to be in there."

"I guess as long as we're careful," Lana muttered.

"*I'm* not going," Doris said.

"Gee whiz," Keith said, "that comes as a mighty surprise."

"Howard, why don't you take care of the courtesy light? We don't want it coming on when we open the doors."

He reached up to the ceiling and tugged at the light's plastic cover. One end snapped loose. Fumbling underneath it, he twisted the bulb and plucked it free. "Got it." He stuffed the bulb into a pocket of his corduroys.

"Let's go," Lana said.

Three of the doors swung open. As Howard scooted across the backseat, he glanced around at Doris. "See you later," he said.

"You're as big a fool as the rest of them."

So much for being nice to her.

Climbing out, he noticed the quiet way Lana shut the driver's door. He shut his door gently, pushing until it latched. Keith, who'd followed Glen out the other side, also took care when he closed his door.

Not a single good slam, Howard thought.

We're all scared shitless.

They gathered around Lana at the rear of the car. Her keys jangled. Finding the one she wanted, she bent over the trunk and slid it into the lock.

"What're you doing?" Glen whispered.

"Flashlights and weapons." Lana turned the key. A quiet clack. The lid of the trunk slowly rose. She leaned into the darkness, lifted a pack, turned around, and offered it to Angela. "Just keep it for a minute."

Angela took the pack. She stepped back, set it down at her feet, and tipped its frame so it rested upright against her legs. A milky patch of moonlight shone on its top as if for the sole purpose of illuminating the bulge for Howard's benefit. The bulge made by the top of the skull.

It's not some horrible thing, he told himself as goose-bumps crawled across the nape of his neck. It's Angela's mother.

He wished it was locked away in the trunk.

The other three packs were now on the ground, being opened.

"Get your flashlights," Lana whispered, "but don't turn them on."

"I'm bringing along this baby," Keith said, pulling the hatchet out of his pack.

"Wanta trade?" Glen asked, and held a sheath knife toward him.

"Bite my shorts."

Lana took out her revolver.

"You've gotta be kidding," Keith said. "The fucker's empty."

"Nobody knows but us."

"Can't shoot anyone with an empty gun."

"Maybe not, but you can sure worry them." Reaching behind her back, she lifted her sweatshirt out of the way. Howard saw a band of pale skin above her belt as she shoved the barrel down the seat of her jeans.

"I don't know about this," Angela muttered.

"What don't you know?" Lana asked.

"Look how you're arming yourselves. If it's going to be so dangerous, shouldn't we forget about it?"

"We're just taking precautions. If I honestly believed we'd be running into trouble, I wouldn't go anywhere near that bus."

"It can't hurt to be prepared," Glen added.

Howard realized that his own right hand was deep in the pocket of his corduroys, fingering his Swiss Army knife.

"If you don't like it," Keith said, "just stay here and keep Doris company."

"Maybe you should," Howard said. "There's no reason for all of us to go. Why don't you wait here?"

"I go where you go."

"Ain't that sweet? Just the excuse Howitzer was hoping for."

"Get screwed," Angela snapped.

"Ooooo, she's got a temper."

"Knock it off, Keith," Lana warned.

"Besides," Angela said, "I'm not staying here, anyway. I'm going to the bus with the rest of you. I'm the one who finds the treasure, remember?"

"Come on, let's load up and get going." Lana finished closing her pack and hefted it into the trunk. She took Keith's pack, then Glen's, and finally Angela's. When they were all inside, she lowered the lid. Holding it down, she turned around. She bounced her rump on it, and the lock latched. "Everybody set?"

"Let's take the suitcases," Keith suggested. "They might come in handy if we find the loot."

"Couldn't hurt," Lana said.

Keith and Glen removed the two suitcases from the car's luggage rack. Glen kept one, but Keith held out the other to Howard, saying, "Make yourself useful."

As Howard took the suitcase, he saw that it was Angela's and realized he wouldn't mind carrying it.

Lana and Keith led the way across the field. Howard and Angela stayed close behind them, Glen bringing up the rear.

Howard shivered as he walked. He wished he had his coat, but was glad he'd left it with Coreen. *She needs it more than me,* he told himself. *Must be a lot colder, high up on that mountainside.*

The chilly breeze seemed to pass right through the back of his shirt. He watched the way it ruffled Lana's hair. Her hair looked silvery in the moonlight. Her gray sweatshirt was pale.

It's so damn bright out here, he thought. *If somebody looks out one of those windows . . .*

He realized that he would probably be shivering just as much if he were bundled in a coat. Shivering because of the bus.

What's it doing here?

He could see it better, now. A dozen crimson windows. Those near the front glowed slightly brighter than those toward the rear. The driver's window, like the others, was draped with red.

He wondered if it had once been a school bus. Hard to imagine that it might've ever been such an ordinary thing—full of yelling, laughing kids. It looked so forbidding. The whole field was bathed in milky moonlight, but not the bus. It had been parked at the very edge of the forest. Overhanging limbs shrouded its bulk with shadow. Except for the red of its windows, the bus looked even darker than the woods.

Is it black?

A black bus. Christ.

Somebody must live in it.

What kind of person . . . ?

Maybe it'll be empty. Empty except for Butler's loot. Wouldn't that be nice?

He wondered what the treasure would be. Money? Jewelry? It was hard to imagine finding anything of value inside that bus.

This could turn out to be a wild-goose chase.

Wild-goose chase.

How about a goose that lays golden eggs?

Fee, fi, fo, fum, I smell the blood of an Englishman.

Great. Jack and the beanstalk. That little story used to scare the hell out of him.

And here we are, three Jacks and two Jills, going for the gold.

Jack fell down and broke his crown . . .

Different Jack.

Jesus, what're we doing here?

A few strides from the side of the bus, Keith and Lana halted. They stood motionless, staring up at the windows. Listening? Howard stopped beside them. Angela took his hand. Glen's footsteps went silent.

Gazing at the covered windows, Howard held his breath and listened. He heard his own thudding heartbeat, cries of some distant birds, the wind hissing through the forest, the whisper of leaves rubbing against the roof of the bus. But no sounds at all seemed to be coming from inside.

Somebody *must* be in there, he thought.

With his hatchet, Keith gestured toward the right. He led the way. Lana followed. Angela went after Lana, and Howard stayed close to her back. He heard Glen's shaky breathing behind him.

They gathered at the rear of the bus. The windows of its emergency exit were masked with red fabric, just like all the others.

Keith looked at everyone, then turned away. Bending forward, he peered around the corner. He eased back and faced them. "The fucking *door's* open," he whispered. "The front door."

Howard went cold and crawly inside. He felt his scrotum shrivel up tight, his penis shrink as if it wanted to hide.

"Oh, man," Glen murmured.

"I don't like this at all," Keith said, his voice low and shaky.

"It'll make it easier for us," Lana whispered.

"Shit," Keith said. "Somebody's *gotta* be in there."

"I'm not quitting now," Lana said. She reached under the back of her sweatshirt and pulled out the revolver. "We'll just take it slow and easy. Any sign of trouble, we'll get the hell out of here."

Keith nodded. "Here goes nothing," he said, and stepped around the corner of the bus. Lana went after him. Angela followed her. Howard crept past the end of the bumper and saw the others just ahead. They were staying close to the side of the bus, crouching as if afraid of being seen from the windows.

These windows, like the others, were covered with red.

Beyond Keith, pale light spilled from the open front door.

When Howard crouched, his suitcase touched the ground. He lifted it higher, feeling his leg rub against it as he walked slowly behind Angela.

The forest was just to the right, some of the trees almost close enough to touch.

If anything goes wrong, he thought, we can run in there. So dark. So many trees. Plenty of good places to hide.

Just this side of the door, Keith stopped. He stood up straight and raised his left hand.

Everyone halted.

He moved into the light, turning toward the doorway, head tipped back. Then he lifted a foot onto the first stair. As he climbed out of sight, Lana entered the brightness and watched him.

After a moment, she boarded the bus.

"Must be OK," Glen whispered.

"Guess so," Howard said, suddenly feeling weak as tension drained out of him.

Keith was in. Lana was in. They'd obviously seen nothing alarming.

Angela was next to climb the stairs. At the top, she turned toward the aisle. She stared at something on her right, then faced Howard. Her lower lip was clamped between her teeth. She met his eyes. Looking worried, she lifted her gaze and peered into the darkness beyond his head.

"What?" he whispered.

She shook her head, pressed a finger to her lips for silence, then started down the aisle.

Howard swung the suitcase in front of him. He climbed onto the first stair and tried to see what was happening but a metal partition blocked his view. With the next step, he was able to see over it. Keith, Lana and Angela were standing in the aisle a short distance beyond the driver's seat, their backs to him. They were looking at something.

Something on a bench seat. Bundled in a filthy brown blanket.

Whatever it is, Howard thought, it must not be any big deal. They were just staring at it, not running away.

He climbed the rest of the way to the top.

Not as cold as outside. But almost. And the air smelled bad. Like a nasty bar, a dive. A mingling of stale smoke, sweat, alcohol, urine and a legion of other foul aromas.

Howard stepped past the driver's seat and stopped beside Angela.

Wrapped in the blanket was a woman. She was stretched out motionless on a bench that faced the aisle. The blanket covered her from neck to feet. Over her chest, it rose and fell slightly with the motions of her breathing.

Her brown hair was a tangled mess. Her face glowed bright red as if she'd spent far too long in the sun. Her lips were dry and cracked. A dark bruise smudged the left side of her jaw.

In spite of her condition, Howard could see that she was pretty.

And not very old. Probably in her early twenties.

He wondered if this was her home.

And did she live here alone?

Though he felt compelled to stare at her, he forced himself to turn away.

The bench on the other side of the aisle was heaped with clutter: grocery sacks; crushed beer cans; a hubcap heaped with ashes and dead cigarettes; packages of cookies and chips, some still unopened and others crumpled; piles of rags and dirty clothes.

"I'll check out the rest," Keith whispered.

Howard glanced at the woman. She still slept.

Keith made his way toward the rear of the bus. Some of the forward rows of seats had been removed to make room for mattresses. Three mattresses piled with blankets and clothes.

Sleeping places for three more people.

Where *are* they? Howard wondered. What if they come back and find us here?

What if they're hiding, right now, among the seats?

He watched Keith pause, standing on one of the mattresses, turning his head as he looked at the two nearby steamer trunks. The tops of the trunks were littered with junk. On one was a Coleman lantern, its twin mantels hissing, filling the bus with brilliant light.

Keith moved on. He held his hatchet high as if ready to strike. He looked from side to side, checking each row of seats.

At last, he reached the emergency exit.

Thank God, Howard thought.

Keith turned around and came back.

"Anything?" Lana whispered.

He shook his head. "We oughta have a look in the trunks. Maybe that's where . . ."

"We've gotta get out of here," Angela said. "Right now. We've gotta take her with us."

"What's the . . . ?"

"The stink of this place. The way it looks. And *her*." She suddenly crouched, slapped a hand across the mouth of the sleeping woman, and hurled the blanket away.

The woman was naked. Her skin glowed scarlet as if she'd been broiled all day by the sun. She was bruised, striped with welts, seamed with shallow cuts from a knife blade or razor. She had raw crescents of bite marks on her shoulders and breasts and thighs. Her wrists were hand-cuffed, her ankles bound together with rope.

Howard saw all this as the woman lurched awake, eyes springing open. As she bucked, trying to sit up. As Keith gasped, "Holy shit!" and Glen groaned and Lana muttered, "My God." As the woman stretched her arms down and hid her groin under crossed hands. As she settled down and lay motionless on the bench and glanced at the faces above her.

"We're here to help you," Angela said, and lifted her hand away from the woman's mouth.

"They killed Roger!" she blurted. "They killed him and they . . ."

"Charlie and the twins?" Angela asked.

"Yes! Yes! The old one's Charlie. Please, you've . . ."

"Where are they?"

"I don't know."

"Charlie?" Glen sounded confused.

"Angela's stepfather," Howard said.

"Him? My God, what's going on?"

"Where's the treasure, lady?" Keith asked.

"Forget it," Lana said. "We've got trouble. Let's get her and beat it."

Angela slipped a hand under the back of the woman's neck. As she began lifting her, Howard set down his suitcase. He stepped in close to Angela and grabbed the woman's upper arm. Glen had his knife out. Crouching, he began to saw through the ropes at her ankles.

A blast slammed Howard's eardrums.

Glen's left eye exploded. A gout of red erupted from the socket and splashed the seatback in front of him.

Howard whirled away, grabbed Angela by the shoulders and threw her to the floor. A roar thundered through the bus. Keith, facing the rear, was knocked off his feet and hurled backward. Lana aimed her revolver toward a pair of red-haired men rushing up the aisle with shotguns. From behind Howard came a series of quick, sharp cracks. Lana staggered as three slugs punched through her back. Two smacked into Howard as a shotgun blast spun Lana around. The left side of her sweatshirt was blown open. She fell to her knees, a hand jerking up and clutching the red mush where her breast used to be.

The twins stopped behind her and aimed shotguns at her head.

"No!" Howard shrieked.

More fire from behind.

Chapter Thirty-five

This was a pretty good idea, Corie thought.

She spread her coat on the ground, then pulled the sleeping bag out of its nylon sack.

Here on the broad, gentle slope beyond the end of the trail, she would be in no danger of falling. And the mountain's wall sheltered her from the wind.

She'd been reluctant to leave her perch above Chad but he'd asked her to do it and, once he'd fallen asleep, she'd decided to go along with his request. She had tucked away the sleeping bag, loaded everything she might need into one of the packs, and made her way up the narrow trail, wincing with each step though the three pairs of socks felt thick and springy under her sore feet.

Glad that she'd done it, she arranged the sleeping bag so that the coat would cushion her from waist to shoulders. She took off Doris's baggy sweatpants, rolled them up to make a pillow, slipped into the sleeping bag and pulled its zipper up.

Nice. Warm and cozy. But the ground was no softer here.

She rolled onto her belly, feeling the granite push against

her thighs and ribcage and breasts. By folding her arms under the pillow, she relieved some of the pressure on her breasts.

Not so bad, she thought. I can live with it.

She just hoped she wouldn't be tormented by those horrible, vivid hallucinations.

Think about Chad, she told herself.

Think about how nice it will be when we're down from here.

But she knew that she was only a few yards from the spot where she'd made her escape from Hubert. She lay with her right cheek against the pillow. The edge of the sleeping bag, up high over her shoulder, prevented her from seeing the place. It didn't prevent her mind, however, from reliving what had happened there.

She saw herself riding his back as he crawled, felt his slick skin sliding against her, felt his head rubbing her groin. A heavy, leaden sickness settled in her belly as she remembered caressing him.

I had to do it, she told herself. It was my only chance, and it worked.

But the price.

Stroking his cock.

I still haven't washed my hand, she realized.

It was tucked under the rolled sweatpants, inches from her face.

Maybe in the morning, I can climb down to the stream.

She pictured Hubert falling off the edge of the gorge, the way he'd looked floating face down in the quiet pool.

I can't go there.

But he's gone, she reminded herself. The current had sent him shooting downstream like driftwood. Unless his body got hung up somewhere, he probably ended up in the lake. Not even the water in the pool would be the same water that touched him. It would be new, untainted, cold and clean.

She could go there. She would.

She would be hot and sweaty by the time she reached the bottom of the gorge.

She shut her eyes and imagined herself down there. Standing at the edge of the pool, the sun bright on its swirling surface, glints and sparkles hurting her eyes. The water so clear she can see her own shadow on its rocky bottom. She takes off her damp, heavy clothes, feeling the sunlight and soft breezes, then the icy shock of the water as she steps in. It would be awful at first, the terrible cold. But soon it would feel good. Cool, soothing caresses. She would float on her back and feel the sun's heat on her chilled skin.

She was floating, the water undulating, gently lifting her, lowering her, sliding like cool satin along her back and rump and legs.

"Yes!"

A hand slapped the top of her head, clutched her hair, jerked her head up. Pain burnt her scalp. She saw Hubert squatting in front of her, tried to tell herself this was another one of those hallucinations, knew it wasn't.

Hubert was here.

Alive.

"No!" she cried out. She clawed at the hand and forearm as he pulled her. She tried to get to her knees. Her back was stopped by the sleeping bag. She sprawled forward. Instead of throwing down her hands to catch herself, she grabbed his arm. Squirming and kicking, she was dragged from the sleeping bag. Her knees pounded the ground as she scurried forward, trying to get up.

But Hubert kept backing away.

With a twist of his arm, he flung Corie onto her back. He wrenched his arm from her grip, rushed in from the side and kicked her in the ribs. Pain erupted in her chest. Her breath gushed out. She drew up her knees and struggled to suck air.

Hubert's foot shoved her knees down. He swung a leg over her. She felt his boots tight against her hips.

He towered above her and gazed down at her.

Somewhere, he'd found clothes. The boots. Pants that were glossy in the moon's bright glow. A shaggy fur coat. He looked different in clothing. Bigger. His sunglasses were gone. Specks of moonlight flickered in the shadows of his eye sockets. His hairless head gleamed like a block of ivory.

Staring up at him as she fought to catch her breath, she wondered if this was really Hubert.

Hubert should be dead.

A twin?

But she realized he hadn't been using his left arm. It hung at his side like a dead thing. Doris's first bullet must've done that to him.

But not killed him.

And the second shot had merely creased his back. It hadn't killed him. The fall hadn't killed him. The stream hadn't killed him.

Maybe nothing could kill him.

"Don' hurd me anymore," he said.

What?

"Don' hurd me and don' run away." He spoke loudly, his words slurred as if his tongue had gone sluggish. "I won' kill you if you're good. Bromise?"

"You won't hurt me?" Corie asked.

"Huh?"

In a stronger voice, she said, "Will you promise not to hurt me?"

He shook his head. "I can' hear you. I can' hear nothin." You done id, hiddin' me. Now I'm shod." He paused for a moment, then blurted, "I'm shod 'n I hurd 'n id's all causa *you!*" Bellowing with rage, he brought up his right foot.

As he stomped down at her belly, Corie hooked a hand behind his boot and jerked it forward. Instead of smashing into her, it swept past her face. She thrust it straight upward. Hubert yelped and tumbled away.

Corie scurried to her feet. She whirled around. He was on his back, growling, pushing himself up.

Run! her mind roared.

But if she fled, he would come after her. He would chase her down.

She dashed straight at him.

He was braced on his right arm, knees high and apart, poised on his heels, about to lunge up.

Corie thrust her arms straight overhead, clenched her hands and dived between his knees. Her fists struck his face. The impact folded her elbows, drove her fists back against her own head as she pounded down on top of him, slamming him to the ground.

His head thunked the granite.

But he didn't pass out.

His right arm clamped across Corie's back. His legs squeezed her thighs together.

Crushed against him, mouth tight against his coat, she couldn't breathe. But she punched his face, raked it with her fingernails, tried to find his eyes.

His arm went away.

Lifting her face, she sucked air.

Suddenly, he had her left wrist. He shoved her arm down against her side and yanked it up behind her. Squealing as muscles and tendons tore, she writhed and arched her spine and threw back her head. She saw his face below her, the heel of her right hand shoving at his brow.

The eye, she thought. Gouge the eye!

Before she could go for it, he rammed her bent arm higher. She felt—*heard*—the bone pop from its shoulder socket. Along with the surge of the pain came freedom. He still had her arm up there, but it was loose, no longer restraining her.

She drove herself downward.

Slammed her forehead into his nose.

Letting out a soft grunt, he went limp. His hand fell away from her wrist. His legs stopped squeezing her.

Corie raised her head and snapped it down again. Again.

She scooted herself a little lower. With her right hand, she tore at the collar of his coat. The top button popped away. She tugged the coat toward his shoulder until she had bared the side of his neck.

A quick shove at his chin turned his head aside.

She stared at his thick, corded neck.

Don't think about it. Just do it. He's gonna come to.

She jammed her mouth down against the warm skin and bit. Sank her teeth in. Gnawed. Ripped.

Blood shot into her mouth.

Choking on it, she jerked her head back. The gusher splashed her face. She turned her head away and it spurted into her ear.

She scurried backward quickly, pushing at his body with her right hand. When her knees met the ground between his legs, she straightened up, gritting her teeth as her left arm slid down and swung from her shoulder.

She picked up the dangling wrist and pressed it tight to her belly.

And watched Hubert.

Ready to run.

He'd lived through everything else, why not this?

Blood was no longer pumping from his neck. That should mean his heart had stopped.

Still, Corie half expected him to sit up, to come for her.

He's dead, she told herself.

Not dead enough.

She went to his side and sat down. The granite was cold through the seat of her sweatpants as she scooted in close to him. Left hand resting on her lap, right arm bracing her up from behind, she planted her feet against his hip and ribcage. And shoved. His heavy body skidded over the ground.

She scooted close again, shoved again.

Again and again, pushing him slowly ahead of her.

Pushing him past the place where he'd crawled off the trail long ago in the heat of the day, bearing her on his back.

Pushing him to the edge of the slope.

With a final thrust of her legs, she sent him over.

She sat very still, listening. She heard nothing, not even the wind. As if it had ceased its rush through the mountains just for her.

Then came a faint sound like a foot, far away, being stamped in anger.

Corie eased backward. Lying flat with her knees in the air, she gazed up at the round, white face of the moon.

Chapter Thirty-six

It was a far-off chant. Not very loud, but loud enough for Howard to realize it was Angela's voice. Chanting. "No. Please. No. Please. No. Please." And a shrill *"Nooooooooooooo"* that twisted itself into a scream.

They're hurting her, he thought. Doing awful things to her. Things like she told me about.

Charlie and the twins.

They got her.

They got us all.

At least Angela's still alive. She isn't dead like the rest of us.

Interesting you can be dead and still think.

And still hurt.

"Don't. Don't. I mean it. *Pleeeeease!*"

And still hear.

And still cry.

The crying made him shake, and each spasm sent bolts of white-hot pain ripping through his head and back and side.

Maybe I'm not dead, he thought.

Whimpering, he tried to raise his right arm. It felt like lead, but it moved. He lifted it and fingered his face and knew he was dead.

Where his face should've been, his searching hand found gore: bits and pieces of skin, hard fragments of bone, all stuck in soft wet gobs. He had no eyes, no cheeks, no nose. Only sodden mush and bits of bone.

He *felt* as if he had eyes. They felt hot and stingy and wet from crying. His lids seemed to be there. But weighted down.

He fingered away a shard of bone, dug his finger into the mush, and touched his eyelid.

This isn't my stuff!

He suddenly remembered the last he'd seen of Lana. On her knees. Shot apart. Two shotguns aimed at the back of her head.

Oh, my God.

Like an echo, Angela cried out, "Oh, my God!"

Sobbing, Howard scooped through the mess, clearing it off his eyes and forehead and cheeks and nose. He gagged a couple of times, and the spasms triggered blasts of pain.

He found no wounds on his face.

He tried to open his eyes. The lids seemed to be glued shut. With his fingertip, he carefully rubbed more gunk away. Then he got his eyes open.

Night. Trees above him.

"Noooo!" Angela again.

I've got to help her.

He pushed his elbows against the ground and nearly screamed. His left arm jerked and twitched. But that wasn't where the pain was. The pain was behind him. Back there by the shoulder blade. And lower. Lower, he felt as if his ribcage had been struck by a sledgehammer. And higher. The top of his head. And the right side of his head.

Settling down against the ground, he reached up with his right hand. The upper rim of his ear was gone. Sliced off, leaving a straight, raw edge of fire.

379

He wasn't sure he dared to explore the wound at the top of his head. He dreaded what he might find.

The first touch confirmed his fears. His heart lurched. But he soon realized that most of the glop and bits of bone were Lana's, not his.

His was a furrow. The bullet had plowed a gouge, maybe two inches long, through his hair and scalp. He assumed it hadn't penetrated his skull, but he wasn't ready to dig around and find out.

He lowered his arm to the ground.

He thought, I've got to get up and save Angela.

He wondered if he *could* get up.

Jesus, he thought. I've been shot four times.

Maybe more.

Me and Rasputin.

Takes a licking but keeps on ticking.

Me and Timex.

What about me and Angela? What are they *doing* to her?

He realized he hadn't heard her cry out in a while. Maybe they'd stopped hurting her. Maybe she'd passed out.

Maybe they'd killed her.

No!

Not Angela! Not her, too.

But they will.

Gotta stop them.

Howard shoved his right elbow against the ground, rolled toward it, and gasped "Ahhhh!" as he thrust himself up into a sitting position.

What if they heard me?

Lana was sprawled across his legs. He glimpsed the dark back of her sweatshirt and quickly looked for the bus, afraid someone might be coming to finish him off.

The bus was straight ahead, maybe thirty or forty feet away. Trees blocked much of his view, but he could see the faint red glow of several windows. And its door, still open.

Nobody coming out.

They didn't hear me, he told himself.

But he kept watching the door, feeling that his gaze somehow held the killers trapped inside—and afraid of what he would see if he looked down. Lana pinning his legs. Keith and Glen. Even with his eyes fixed on the bus's door, he could see the dark shapes of their bodies: one beneath Lana's legs; the other on Howard's right, close enough to touch.

If he just kept watching the door, he wouldn't have to look at them.

His heart jumped and he flinched and let out another small cry as he heard a crunch. A footstep. Behind him.

Another footstep.

The snap of a twig.

He dropped down flat and shut his eyes and tried to hold his breath.

More footsteps, coming slowly closer.

Then a quick intake of breath.

"Oh, God." Hushed, stricken.

"Doris?"

"Howard?"

He opened his eyes and saw her standing to his right. She looked down at him, then at the others. She pressed a hand to her mouth.

"Help me."

She crouched at his side. She put a hand on his shoulder, and looked again at the other bodies. He heard her panting for air.

"They shot us all," Howard said. "We were in the bus. They came out of nowhere."

Not out of nowhere, he thought. One must've come through the front door while the two with shotguns came in the emergency exit at the rear.

"Where's Angela?" Doris asked.

"They've still got her. I don't think she was shot, but they've got her. They're *doing* things to her. She's been screaming."

Doris nodded. "I know. I've been here a while. I came when I heard the shooting. Snuck through the trees. I had to find out what . . . I heard a sound over here."

"That was me."

"How bad are you hurt?"

"I don't know. I was hit four times. That I know of."

"Jesus. We'd better get you to a hospital."

"We can't leave Angela."

Doris was silent for a moment. Then she said, "Can you move?"

"I can sit up." He rolled toward her and thrust his elbow into the ground. Doris pulled at the nape of his neck, helping him to rise.

As he leaned forward, she scurried around behind him. Her hands gently explored his back. He jerked when she touched his wounds. "Can't see much," she muttered. "I think one got you in the shoulder blade. Another one's down lower but it's off to the side. There's a lot of blood."

"Anything gushing?"

"No. I don't think you're bleeding a lot right now. Your lungs are OK?"

"I think so. It hurts to take a deep breath, but . . ."

"We need the car keys."

Doris crawled past him. Kneeling on the other side of Glen's body, she grabbed Lana's ankles. She backed away, dragging her. Howard felt Lana's breast rub over his knee. He shuddered. He shut his eyes after glimpsing her head.

Its top half was gone.

A second later, she was off him.

When he heard a groan, he looked. The body was on top of Glen. Doris had turned it over. She reached into a pouch at the front of Lana's sweatshirt. "Got 'em," she whispered. Her hand came out clutching the car keys. "Now we can get out of here."

"We have to save Angela."

Doris stared at him.

"We can't just leave her."

"How many men are there?"

"Three."

"They all have guns?"

"Yeah."

"Do you think you can walk?"

"I don't know."

"Let's find out."

"Yeeeeah!" Howard shrieked. "Oh God, it hurts, *it hurts!*"

Head propped up against the base of a tree, he glanced at Doris. She stood a little to the right, no more than a yard beyond his feet, pressing herself against a broad trunk, peering around its side toward the bus.

He turned his eyes to the open door.

Soon, a man appeared. Up near the driver's seat. One of the twins. A revolver in one hand while he struggled to shove his other arm into the sleeve of his plaid shirt. His jeans were open. After getting his arm through the sleeve, he pulled the zipper up and hurried down the stairs.

At the bottom, the wind flung his shirt out behind him and tossed his shaggy red hair. Muttering something, he hunched his shoulders. He trotted into the trees, coming straight for the bodies.

Nobody else followed him out.

It's just like we figured, Howard thought.

For the simple, annoying chore of finishing off a survivor, only one would come.

Maybe with just a knife, in which case the plan fell apart.

But he'd brought along a revolver for the job.

He stopped, looked at the three bodies, then raised his head.

"Asswipe" was all he said.

He walked toward Howard.

"No," Howard gasped. "Please. Don't kill me."

"Fuck you." He halted at Howard's feet and raised the gun.

"Wait. There's a girl. I know where you . . ."

The man fired, but he was already stumbling backward, yanked by the hair. Howard heard the bullet chunk into the trunk above him. He saw Doris's arm reach around. Past the man's neck. It jerked back across as she tore through his throat with the Swiss Army knife.

383

Even as blood spurted and he fell back against Doris, she plunged the knife twice into his chest. He twitched and kicked, but he didn't cry out. Howard supposed that he couldn't. Not with his throat that way.

In seconds, he was stretched motionless on the ground at Doris's feet.

"Get up," she whispered to Howard.

While he struggled to stand, she rolled the man and pulled off his shirt.

She brought it to him, helped him to put it on over his own shirt, and quickly fastened the buttons.

"I don't know who this is gonna fool," he muttered.

"It doesn't have to fool anyone for long," Doris said.

She returned to the body.

She sliced into the dead man's head. There were wet ripping sounds as she peeled off the hair.

Howard wondered how she could do such a thing. But he knew that he would've done it himself with no regrets.

She brought the scalp to him. She fitted it onto his head like a wig. It was snug. It squished and hurt his wound when she pressed against it. She fingered the dead man's hair, arranging it so locks clung to Howard's brow.

"All set," she whispered.

He staggered forward, gritting his teeth against tides of pain, beginning his journey to the bus. Doris hurried ahead of him. As she picked up the knife and revolver, he lurched past her, afraid to stop. If he stopped, he might fall. If he fell, he might not be able to get up again.

There was a gap in front of him, a clear path between Keith's body and the remains of Lana's head. He made his way through it carefully, wobbling, dreading to step on his dead friends.

Doris rushed past him. Walking backward, she pressed the revolver into his right hand.

He took another lurching step, another.

Doris turned around. Arms out as if to keep her balance, she tiptoed toward the bus.

She got there very fast.

Howard watched her crouch beside the spill of light. She rested her hand on one knee, the blade of the knife pointing at the sky.

Then he watched the doorway. It seemed to bob and sway. And get bigger.

Then he was in it, raising a foot onto the first stair, thrusting himself up.

The partition was in his way.

Good, he thought. I can't see them, they can't see me.

Face forward, he climbed the next two stairs as fast as he could. He turned to the aisle.

The woman on the bench seat was covered again. She lay on her side facing the back cushion as if trying to hide.

"Hey, George, join the . . . What the *fuck*!"

The other twin. He was standing just beyond the first row of seats, facing Howard, Angela's face at his groin, his hands clutching the back of her head. From the waist up, he was clear. Howard thumbed back the hammer and fired. The bullet punched the center of his bare chest. His hands leaped from Angela's head.

As he stumbled backward and fell, the other man looked over his shoulder at Howard. His mouth hung open. His eyes bulged.

"Get up," Howard said, knowing he couldn't shoot without a risk of hitting Angela in the back or head.

He pulled out of her and let go of her hips. Angela, wrists bound to seat handles on each side of the aisle, swung down. Her knees hit the floor. She dangled there, limp, as the man got to his feet. Standing between her spread legs, he turned toward Howard.

He raised his hands.

His erection was wet and shiny.

"You're Charlie," Howard said.

"Don't shoot. I give up. No call to . . ."

The bullet crashed through his forehead. Blood spurted from the small hole. The back of his head spat out a thick gust of red. He stood rigid for a moment, eyeballs rolling upward. Then he pitched forward and landed on a mattress.

He was in the way. Howard had to step on him. When he was standing between Angela's legs, he fired over her head. He put a second slug into the twin's chest. Then he missed and hit the floor. Then he placed one alongside the nose.

Dropping the gun, he sank to his knees. He slid his hand gently down her back, feeling the slickness of her blood, the puffed ridges of welts, the cuts. The letters C C had been carved into her skin.

Charlie Carnes.

"No," she murmured. "Please. No."

"It's me," Howard said. "We've killed 'em all."

Chapter Thirty-seven

They lay side by side, propped up on their elbows. The bedroom windows were open. A warm, morning breeze was sliding softly down Corie's back. It felt very good. She took a long, lazy breath. The air smelled of grass and roses.

"I think here," Chad said, touching a fingertip to the map which was spread on the mattress under their faces. "It's a beautiful area. I was there just last summer."

"Where's Calamity?" Corie asked.

His finger moved down and sideways. "It's a good thirty miles away."

"I guess that's far enough."

"There's a whole string of lakes. They're fantastic. And I went for a whole week in that area without running into another soul."

"That sounds good to me."

"Do you think you'll have any trouble carrying a pack?"

"Do you think you'll have any trouble walking?"

"Are you really sure you want to do this?"

Corie felt a squirmy tingle deep inside. "Yeah," she said,

"I think so. I want to and I don't, you know?"

"Same here."

"But I think we should go ahead and do it. We've only got a week before the semester starts. If we put it off till next summer . . . I don't know. I might lose my nerve by then. It was so wonderful before . . . all the trouble. I want it to be that way again."

"Nothing will happen this time," Chad said.

"Promise?"

"We'll have the guns just in case, but . . ."

The ringing doorbell stopped his words.

"Great," Corie muttered. She pushed herself up, patted Chad's rear, and crawled off the bed. "Don't go anywhere," she said. "It's probably Jehovah's Witnesses or something."

"We could pretend we're not home."

The bell rang again.

"I'll open the door like this and watch the looks on their faces."

"I dare you."

Laughing softly, she walked out of the bedroom naked.

"Hey!" he called.

"A dare's a dare," she called over her shoulder. She hurried up the hallway and into the living room, grinning. Apparently, Chad had forgotten that she'd left her robe on the sofa last night. She picked it up, slipped into it, and belted it shut on her way to the front door.

Looking through the peephole, she saw Howard Clark.

She opened the door.

Angela was standing beside him on the stoop. Pressed against her side was the Ouija board. She had its plastic heart-shaped pointer in her hand.

"You two look great," Corie said. The last time she'd seen them, just after Howard's release from the hospital, they'd both seemed haggard and grim. Now, they looked healthy. They were smiling. They even matched. Except for Angela's knee socks, they were dressed the same in white short-sleeved shirts, plaid shorts and white sneakers.

"Come on in," Corie said.

They hesitated. Howard glanced at her robe and blushed. "Is this a good time?" he asked.

"Sure. It's always a good time when friends drop by." She waved them in, backing away. "I'm not overjoyed to see *that* thing again, though." She nodded toward the Ouija board.

"Well," Howard said, "it belongs to you. We got it back from Lana's parents. They didn't want it."

"Neither do I."

"We don't want it," Angela said.

"Well, you can leave it here. I'll burn the damn thing and that'll be the end of it." Taking the board and pointer from Angela, she led the way into the living room. "Sit down and make yourselves comfortable," she said. She gestured toward the sofa. "I'll tell Chad you're here. Would you like some coffee or something?"

"Oh, no thank you," Howard said, and Angela shook her head.

As they went to the sofa, Corie set the board and pointer on the lamp table. "Right back," she said.

When she reached the bedroom, she found Chad on his feet, pulling up a pair of shorts. "It's Howard and Angela."

"What's that I see you wearing? What happened to the dare?"

"What do you think I am, a bimbo?"

She waited while he put on a T-shirt. Together, they returned to the living room.

"Morning," Chad said.

As the kids greeted him, he sat down on an easy chair. Corie sank to the floor in front of him and leaned back against his legs. "They brought back the Ouija board," she explained.

"Just what we need. So, what have you two been up to?"

Howard shrugged. He looked a little nervous. Corie realized that his hair had grown long enough to hide the missing part of his ear. "A lot," he said. "We're planning to go apartment hunting today."

"When are you gonna tie the knot?" Chad asked.

They both turned bright red.

"Mom and Dad think we should wait till after graduation."

"That's probably not a bad idea," Corie said.

"How was your honeymoon?" Angela asked.

"Great."

"Painful."

"Chad."

"And awkward."

"Stop it."

Howard laughed, but he was still blushing. "Maybe you should've waited until you were both better."

"It wasn't as bad as he's making out. How are you two doing? You're looking just wonderful."

"I get a lot of headaches, but . . ." He shrugged. "No big deal."

"He's getting better all the time," Angela said. "The doctors say he'll be fine."

"What about you?"

She shrugged.

What a pair, Corie thought. Blushing and shrugging to beat the band. They were meant for each other.

"I'm OK," she finally said.

"We've both got some nice scars."

"But we're alive and we're together," Angela said. "That's what really counts. I've never been so happy. If it weren't for what happened to . . ." Her voice went husky and tears shimmered in her eyes.

"I know," Corie murmured.

Howard put an arm across Angela's shoulders and eased her close against him.

"Doris came by a couple of days ago," Chad said. "Have you seen her lately?"

"No. How is she?"

"As obnoxious as ever."

Corie laughed, and so did the kids. Angela wiped her eyes.

"Good old Doris," Howard said.

"She's planning to sign up for my Chaucer seminar,"

Corie told them. "You two'll be taking it, right?"

"It's not an eight-o'clock, is it?" Angela asked.

"Two in the afternoon. Monday, Wednesday and Friday." She sniffed and smiled. "In that case we'll be there."

"Do you have Doris's address?" Howard asked. "We want to drop by and give her something. We have one for you guys, too." He leaned forward, reached into the seat pocket of his shorts, and pulled out his wallet. "It's the main reason we came over."

"Not just to get us out of bed?"

"Chad enjoys watching people blush."

"Anyway," Howard said, and took a slip of paper out of the wallet. It looked like a check. Angela squeezed his leg. Then he got up and came across the room and handed the paper to Corie.

A check made out to Chad and Coreen Dalton. From Angela's account, and signed by her. A check in the amount of $25,000.

She frowned up at Howard. He was already on his way back to the sofa. "What's this?" she asked Angela.

"It's your share of the treasure."

"What?"

"Let's see."

She handed it up to Chad. "Twenty-five grand?" He sounded astonished. "You've gotta be kidding."

"It's actually two shares," Angela explained. "Twelve-five for each of you. We're splitting it eight ways. Doris'll get a share, and we've already sent checks to . . ." She started weeping again.

"To Lana's family," Howard said. "And Keith's and Glen's. Everybody gets . . ." He choked up. "Or their survivors."

"Where'd it come from?" Corie asked. "What is it?"

"Butler's loot," Howard said.

"I don't . . . there *wasn't* any loot. Was there?"

Angela nodded and sniffed.

"Yeah, there was," Howard said. He took a deep breath.

"It's so weird. We never had to go to the mountains for it. I mean, we had to start out, but . . ."

"It was when we left," Angela explained. "It was taking me away from Skerrit."

"Who?"

"Angela's uncle. She lived with him. In a second-story apartment."

"He didn't want me to leave."

"But we went ahead and left, anyway."

"He was awfully upset."

"I guess he tried to come after us," Howard said. "And fell. They found him the next morning at the bottom of the stairs. His neck was broken. He was dead."

"My God," Corie muttered. "How awful."

"He was old," Angela said. "And not very nice."

"His life insurance was a hundred thousand dollars," Howard explained.

Angela nodded. "And I was named beneficiary."

"You're telling us," Chad said, "that Butler's loot . . . the treasure the Ouija board promised you kids . . . was this man's life insurance?"

"That's how we figure it," Howard said. "All he had to do was fall and get killed. That must've happened just a minute or so after we drove away that night. It means the whole trip to the mountains . . . everything . . . was unnecessary."

"Mom thought it was necessary."

"Well, yeah."

"She wanted me to find her. She wanted her body brought home. And I guess she wanted revenge."

"She got it," Howard muttered.